Cuttin' Heads

Cuttin' Heads

D.A. Watson

Copyright (C) 2018 D.A. Watson
Layout design and Copyright (C) 2018 Creativia
Published 2018 by Creativia
Cover art by Cover Mint
This book is a work of fiction. Names, characters, places, and incidents are the product of the author's imagination or are used fictitiously. Any resemblance to actual events, locales, or persons, living or dead, is purely coincidental.
All rights reserved. No part of this book may be reproduced or transmitted in any form or by any means, electronic or mechanical, including photocopying, recording, or by any information storage and retrieval system, without the author's permission.

Without music, life would be a mistake.

Nietzsche

Intro

Little Walter, Jimmy Rogers, and myself, we would go around looking for bands that were playing. We called ourselves the Headhunters, cause we'd go into clubs and if we got the chance, we were gonna burn em.

Muddy Waters

1

"You know what you are, Aldo? You're a fuckin loose cannon."

Sitting in the cramped HR office - which isn't much bigger than his own cubicle - Aldo Evans grins as he imagines himself as a maverick law enforcer raising hell on the streets of Glasgow, leaving a trail of mayhem in his wake as he tracks down bad guys with much high-speed car chasing and helicopter skid-riding while wearing a devil-may-care smile.

"Is the commissioner on yer arse, Deso?" he asks Desmond Graham, his HR manager. "The mayor giving you heat?" He can't help but smile, even though he's pretty sure he's about to be fired.

"Aye, he bloody well is," Des says, clearly not seeing the funny side in all this. "The boss has had enough. Your stats are good, Aldo. Really good in fact, but you cannae just make up the rules as you go along. You've got to follow the script, mate."

"Dude, we're doing market research cold calls. It's not *Hamlet*."

"Disane matter. You've got to read *all* the questions on the survey. That's the job. I know it's a shite job, but it's a canter, and that's the deal."

Deso was a good guy. Loved his Johnny Cash, and Aldo often went for a pint with him after work and they'd shoot the shit about music. Deso had spent a while in a blues band playing keys, but chucked it when he got married. And he understood fine well what the job in Data Location was and wasn't.

"Deso, the old boy on the phone was ninety-four years old," Aldo says reasonably. "What's the point in asking if he wants a credit card? I can get more surveys done if I don't ask questions that clearly don't need to be asked."

"Disnae matter," Deso says again. "When you just skip questions, that's data fraud."

Aldo gasps in exaggerated horror. "Well shit in ma hat! Not *data fraud?* Sweet Jesus, what've I done?"

"Aldo, I'm sorry, but that's it, mate." Deso looks genuinely upset. "You were warned."

It's getting harder for Aldo to continue seeing the funny side as the reality of the situation starts to dawn on him. Sure, it was ridiculous, hilariously so, but to a point. As stupid as the whole episode was, the consequences start to announce themselves in his head like a grim shopping list of things he suddenly can't afford. Rent. Food. The wee man's child support. The grand's worth of store debt he'd just racked up less than an hour ago while on his lunch break, treating himself to a new guitar – a Gibson Les Paul Studio Pro in glorious cherry sunburst - all the while thinking how great it was to finally have a proper full time permanent job that enabled him to get store credit. The last call centre job had been a week to week contract, and for three years he'd lived poorer than a particularly impoverished church mouse, only just making rent and doing his best to keep his temperamental Epiphone six string in tune. That guitar would detune if you looked at it the wrong way.

"C'mon, Deso," he says. "You've got to be kidding. I'm fired? For *this?*"

Deso just shrugs. "Sorry, mate. Not my call. Listen, meet me in the pub when I'm finished. I know a couple of guys in other call centres..."

"You know what? Don't bother yourself," Aldo snaps, getting up and heading for the HR office door, a slow panic swelling in his guts like a black balloon.

He knows it's not Deso's fault. He knew fine well that he could get bagged for skipping survey questions, no matter how ridiculous they were, and like the standard recorded message said, all calls were recorded for training and quality purposes. Such had been his downfall. As Deso had said, he'd been pulled up for it before, and he'd been warned it was a sackable offence. Aldo figures that despite the inevitable upshot, he actually *wanted* to be fired, and who could blame him, really? Spending nine hours a day making market research cold calls for minimum wage had to be about a step above being an equine fluffer in a horse porn movie in terms of job satisfaction. Still though, as bad as the job with Data Location was, it was money in the bank at the end of the month. A laughable amount, a pittance in all honestly, but still enough to survive on.

He walks over to his tiny work cubicle, takes his ID badge from around his neck and places it on the desk next to the keyboard. He briefly considers leaving a parting message as a flashing screen saver. Something like *Fuck you and this brain numbing soul destroying low paying dignity stripping excuse for a job!* Or maybe he could drop his breeks and take a big steaming shite on the desk.

Instead, he shrugs into his battered leather jacket, picks up the padded gig bag containing his expensive and unpaid for new guitar, and heads for the door. The Les Paul Studio Pro features a weight relief chambered mahogany body, and only weighs around six pounds in total, but at that moment, it's the monetary measure of pounds Aldo feels on his shoulder; the thousand pounds he owes for the instrument, and now has no way of paying.

As he makes his way across the call centre floor toward the exit, he's aware of several of his now ex-colleagues watching him leave with mixed expressions of curiosity, sympathy and bovine disinterest. He rolls his eyes and tips a little blasé salute to no one in particular, forcing a bemused smile onto his lips, trying to be all cool and dignified.

I don't need this. I'm better than this. This is great. No more itchy, uncomfortable headset. No more stupid survey lists. No more getting called all sorts by the poor bastards on the other end of the phone for interrupting their dinner with my questions about their favoured brand of washing up liquid.

But all the while that black panic balloon is squeezing the air from his lungs. Familiar feelings of shame, embarrassment and failure boil and bubble in his guts.

You've fucked up, ya dick. Again. What you gonnae do now, eh? No job. No money. No qualifications except three Highers and an HND in Music, which is worth the grand total of hee-haw in terms of employability. What's that make it now? Fired or quit from your last three call centre jobs? Bravo, son. Bra-fuckin-vo. You da man. You're on fire. When you going to grow the fuck up?

Aldo literally doesn't know whether to laugh or cry. Crying seems more likely.

Now, on the street outside the glass-walled offices of Data Location, Aldo stands in a daze, trying to order his thoughts and come to terms with his new state of unemployment. He turns his head left and right, looking up and down a rainy Sauchiehall Street as if expecting someone to come running up, lucrative contract of employment in hand, offering him a new job right off the bat.

That doesn't happen of course, and he can only stand there in the drizzle of Glasgow city centre, a wet, jobless chump, while a bustling river of umbrella wielding humanity flows around him, heedless of his distress, going about their own business, living their own lives. He wants to grab hold of random strangers and yell at them, *Don't you know what's just happened? I'm fucked! Fucked I tells ya!*

He feels an unreasonable surge of anger and jealousy toward the uncaring passers-by, most of whom seem to be carrying plastic bags emblazoned with high-street logos. Everywhere he looks, people are sporting carrier bags from HMV, Schuh, New Look, M&S. It's like they're mocking him.

Take a swatch at all this snazzy expensive gear I just bought, ya penniless fanny! It's great being able to purchase Dr Dre Beats *headphones with my wages, it really is. Looks like it's Tesco Value beans on Tesco Value toast for dinner for you, though, Aldo, and oh yeah, you can forget about taking Dylan to that* Frozen *stage show when you see him at the weekend, like you promised him you would.*

Guilt like something rotten sticking in his throat, Aldo breathes deeply, closing his eyes, trying to slow and silence the hard knocking of his heart in his chest, which sounds all too much like an implacable debt collector resolutely pounding on his front door. A debt collector with his ex-girlfriend's face.

Right, keep the heid. Break it down into manageable chunks. Adapt and overcome. Get somewhere quiet and work it out.

He opens his eyes and sees Squinty Ginty's, the pub across the street. It's just gone two pm, and the bar should be relatively quiet now the lunchtime crowds have gone back to work. A quick check of the change in his pocket confirms he has just enough for a pint. Probably not the wisest expense given the circumstances, but fuck it. Fuck it directly in the nose. A quick swally is just the ticket to get his thoughts in order while he plans his next move.

Aldo Evans squares his shoulders and makes his way across the busy pedestrian precinct, gamely resisting the urge to flying kick one slow moving old lady blethering into an iPhone as she makes her way up the crowded street.

2

"I tell you what, son, escaping from Stalag was easier than getting out of this place. Food was better as well."

"I don't doubt it, Duncy," Ross McArthur says to the old man in the wheelchair he's pushing. "There's a few nurses in here I imagine would've been right at home on Hitler's staff."

"Aye, yer no kiddin there," Duncy Brown agrees. "Coupe of wee crackers as well though, eh? If I was a few years younger I'd be rattling them left right and centre." He lets out a lascivious Sid James-esque cackle, thumping the padded armrest of the wheelchair a couple of times with his large bony fist for emphasis. "Young lad like you must do alright in that department, working here, eh?" He cranes his head round and looks over his shoulder at Ross, waggling his busy white eyebrows suggestively, a knowing grin on his deeply wrinkled face.

Ross laughs. "Ach, mon now, Duncy. A gentleman never tells. Though I've heard the big redhead nurse in your ward's mad for it, and has a thing for older guys. Can get a hold of a couple of Viagra for you if you fancy your chances?"

Duncy cackles again "Cheeky wee bugger!" he crows, throwing a playful but hard elbow backward into Ross's midriff. "I'll fuckin Viagra ye! The amount of bullets I've taken in ma time, son, there's enough lead in ma pencil to stock a Staedtler factory."

A young dark haired nurse passing them in the corridor bursts out laughing.

"Aye, you know it, sweetheart," Duncy says, tipping her a saucy wink as she goes by. Ross rolls his eyes apologetically at the nurse. She favours him with a pretty smile in response. Claire, he thinks her name is. One of the student nurses down from Strathclyde Uni.

"Christ sake, Duncy," he says as they roll on down the corridor toward the X-Ray department. "Leave some for the rest of us, eh?"

Ross had got to know and like Sergeant Duncan Brown immensely in the two weeks he'd been in the Inverclyde Royal recovering from his knee surgery. The old boy, who'd spent much of his life as an active member of the 51st Highland Division, 1st Battalion of the Black Watch, had an endless store of anecdotes and war stories. Some that made you laugh, others that made you want to weep. Eighty-three years old, but lacking none of his mental faculties, and still possessed of a thousand yard stare that could wither an oak tree. The medals he'd shown Ross, the bullet wound scars that pocked his wiry body in alarming numbers, they were evidence of the depths of the old soldier's life. The faded military emblem tattooed on his right forearm, its blurred, barely legible Latin scrollwork reading the motto of the Black Watch. *Nemo me impune lacessit.*

They're passing by the A&E department when Ross hears the raised voice from the waiting room.

"How much longer is this gonnae take? Ah've got shit tae dae!"

He pauses for a moment, looking through the doorway into the waiting area. Pretty busy for a Tuesday afternoon. There are six people in there, spaced out among the cheap chairs, most of which are badly worn and leaking padding from tears in the seats like yellow foam hernias. At the reception window is a big guy who looks like he's stepped out of the Neds R Us summer catalogue, resplendent in sovereign rings, a hand drawn neck tattoo, and wearing an expensive tracksuit, though he doesn't look like any sort of athlete. He's glaring through the glass at Linda, the wee receptionist on the other side. She's calmly telling him it shouldn't be too much longer, but they're busier than normal today.

"Fuck sake, ah've been here for a fuckin hour awready. Ma wean needs seen tae."

Ross sees the wean. A pale, scrawny limbed specimen in dirty tracksuit bottoms and a Power Rangers t-shirt. Dark, close cropped hair and bags under his eyes. Maybe eight or nine years old, sitting by himself. His bare right foot's propped up on the low coffee table strewn with torn dog-eared copies of *Heat* and *Now* from three years ago. His ankle's badly swollen. The kid looks scared, watching on as Neck Tat loudly expounds on the failings of the NHS with much finger pointing and colourful turns of phrase.

"Hold on a second, Duncy," Ross says to his patient.

"Aye, no bother, son," Duncy replies, watching the unfolding scene closely.

Ross walks unnoticed past Neck Tat, who's still ranting at poor Linda behind the reception window, and squats down next to the skinny kid, who regards him warily.

"Alright, wee man," Ross says with a smile. "What you done to yourself here, then?" He nods at the kid's bruised, grapefruit sized ankle. The boy drops his eyes and murmurs something barely audible. "Sorry, pal? Say again?"

"Playin fitba," the kid squeaks, only slightly louder, still avoiding Ross's eyes. His small hands twitch and fidget nervously in his lap.

"Fitba, eh? Dangerous game. Looks a sore one," Ross says, now seeing the other bruises, four small, roundish marks on the left side of the kid's neck, just above the frayed collar of his t-shirt. He rises from his crouch and sits down in the empty chair on the kid's right. As he suspected, there's another single bruise on that side of his neck. Ross feels his jaw tighten. "You get injured a lot?"

The little kid glances up at Ross quickly, then goes back to studying his hands, still twisting in his lap. He doesn't answer, but the haunted look Ross sees in the brief second their eyes meet tells its own story. It's a look he's well acquainted with, one that a lot of the kids at Eastburn had. A look he'd seen in the mirror.

Ross goes to lay a hand on the wean's shoulder, but he cringes away as if expecting a fist. "It's okay, buddy," Ross says quietly, withdrawing his hand. He nods toward the tracksuited marvel still berating Linda. "That your dad?" he asks the boy. Again, the wee man looks away, then nods.

"Okay," Ross says. "I'm gonnae go and talk to him, then we'll get you sorted out, aye? Keep the chin up, wee man."

The wee man's dad still hasn't noticed Ross, involved as he now is in making his point about the waiting time by kicking the wall beneath the reception desk window. He only becomes aware of his presence when Ross steps up beside him and says, "You need to keep your voice down, pal."

He turns and glares down at Ross. He's a big bastard. About thirty. Broad across the shoulders and big in the belly, with a boxer's face and at least three inches in height on Ross.

"Or fuckin' whit?" Sheer contempt ripping right out him. There's a familiar angry deadness in the man's eyes. Another look a lot of the kids, and a few of the teachers and orderlies in Eastburn had. The hard ones. The nutters. Flat, sharkish eyes.

Ross smiles pleasantly, then turns to the receptionist behind the partition. "Linda, could you tell me this guy's name, please?"

"I certainly can, Ross. This is Mr Neil Edward Donaldson," Linda informs him.

"Excellent. His son's name?"

"Jamie Liam Donaldson."

"And their address?"

"Flat G, twenty-four Bank Street in Greenock."

"Splendid. Thanks very much, Linda." Ross turns back to the ASBO poster boy. "Now, Mr Donaldson. We'll be with you as soon as we can. As you can see, we're a bit busy for a Tuesday afternoon. So just chill out, sit down and we'll get wee Jamie sorted soon as poss, alright?"

"Listen, mate," Mr Neil Donaldson says loudly. "I don't gie a fuck how busy it is for a fuckin Tuesday. Ah cannae be sittin aboot here aw day."

"Mr Donaldson. Sit down and shut up, or I'll have to ask you to leave." That gets his attention.

"Aye? You gonnae fuckin' make me?"

"If needs be," Ross says.

He knows the punch is coming. He'd known it the second he looked into the guy's eyes, and sure enough, Donaldson's face twists, he leans back slightly and raises his fist.

The punch never comes though. As soon as the prick's arm's up, Ross's left hand clamps into the exposed armpit, his thumb planted firmly into the brachial plexus nerve. In an instant, the expression on Donaldson's face changes. He makes a strange wheezing noise and immediately collapses to his knees. Crouching and keeping his thumb pressed into the man's oxter, Ross leans in close. "This is what you call a pressure point, fannybaws," he says affably. "Now, we're walking."

Quickly stepping behind him, Ross sets his left hand with a fistful of Adidas polyester and his right on the back of the father's neck, his talented fingers deftly finding the sensitive little hollow just behind and beneath the man's right ear. He thinks of the bruises on wee Jamie's neck and presses a little harder, making Donaldson cry out in agony.

"There we go," Ross says, "Uppsy daisy." Despite the man's size, Ross coaxes him to his feet with a slight twist of the fingers working his greater auricular nerve. Donaldson emits a strangled yelping sound and stands up in a hurry. Unceremoniously frogmarching the big ned towards the waiting room exit, Ross glances back over his shoulder at Duncy Brown. The old veteran is smiling broadly and softly applauding.

"I'll just be a minute, Duncy," he says.

"Take yer time, son," Duncy replies. "I'll look after the wee yin." He gets up from the wheelchair, spry as a man a quarter his age, and goes to sit beside the scrawny kid, Jamie, who's now wearing a priceless look of awe on his face as he watches his arsehole of a father dragged about like an empty binbag.

Outside, Ross propels the other man round the corner to the rear loading area of the hospital. He looks left and right, checking there's no one around, making sure he's out of sight of the CCTV, then pushes the larger man against the wall. Donaldson starts to slide down the brick surface. Ross again takes hold of him, keeping him on his feet, this time with his right hand clamped around the man's windpipe. Donaldson's eyes widen in alarm as his air's suddenly cut off. His hands claw ineffectually at Ross's fingers.

"Now you listen to me, ya fuckin prick," Ross says. "You're gonnae to go back in there, apologise to Linda in reception, then you're gonnae sit on yer arse and shut the fuck up. Agreed? Nod if you agree."

The man nods, his face now turning a definite shade of purple. Spit hangs from his lips as he gasps and croaks for air. Ross takes just a little pressure off. Just enough so the cunt can squeeze a breath in, then brings his face closer, so close their noses are almost touching.

"And if I ever see that wean in here again with bruises in any place they shouldn't be, I swear to Christ I'll find you and I'll break your legs. I know your name. I know where you live. We clear? Nod if we're clear."

They're clear.

When they return to the casualty admission room a few minutes later, Ross finds Duncy Brown sitting next to young Jamie, who's looking up at the old soldier, enrapt as Duncy entertains him with the story of how during the 1943 invasion of Sicily, armed with only a half empty pistol, a dagger and a few well-aimed rocks, he single-handedly took out a nazi machine gun nest in the foothills of the volcano Mount Etna while there was an eruption going on. Ross had heard the story. Was a belter.

Ross stands close behind the now contrite father as he mumbles an apology to Linda before sitting down. Quietly. It might be Ross's imagination, but the kid's demeanour isn't quite so whipped anymore as his father slumps down into the plastic seat beside him, a sullen look on his face as he by turns rubs at his armpit, neck and throat.

"Right, big man," Duncy says to Jamie. "I best get on. Don't let the bastards grind you down. What's our motto?"

The boy smiles, then says shyly, "*Nemo... me... im... impune... lacessit.*"

"Excellent pronunciation," Duncy says. "And what does it mean?"

"No one attacks me with impunity," Jamie says. And Ross definitely reckons there's a bit less fear about him now. Then again, talking to Duncy Brown could make you feel like that. Duncy's also looking at Donaldson, that thousand yard stare of his in full effect.

Ross can't help but smile a little as he brings Duncy's wheelchair over and the old boy groans dramatically as he shuffles into it and gets himself seated.

"Take care, buddy," Ross says to the kid, "and just holler if you need anything, okay?" He makes a point of flicking his eyes in the father's direction on that last point. Jamie Donaldson smiles and nods, and Ross tips him a wink before turning away and wheeling Duncy out of the waiting room.

"Nicely done there, son," Duncy compliments him as they continue to roll on down the corridor to X-Ray. "You know your stuff."

"Just hope the wee man's alright. You see the marks on his neck?"

"Aye. Cruel big cunt. Well, whatever you said to him outside, looks like you've put the fear of God into him."

"Hope so."

His blood's cooled, the anger's passed, and now Ross McArthur just feels depressed. He knows putting the frighteners on the father was no guarantee of Jamie Donaldson's long term safety or happiness. At most, he'd probably given the wee guy a reprieve, and maybe, hopefully, a little heart. Likely, though, his dad would chill for a few weeks, maybe as long as a month or even a year, then continue smacking his son about, right up until the day Jamie was big enough to fight back. Ross had once shared a room with a boy who'd been very much like Jamie, and on the day *he* was big enough to fight back, he'd stabbed his father to death.

"So what you up to tonight, then?" Duncy asks. "Playing with your band?"

"Aye," Ross says. "Lookin forward to it."

And he was. Fuck aye he was. The porter gig at the hospital was alright, and paid well enough, but it could be a bastard sometimes. Getting little glimpses into the stories of those who came and went through the hospital doors, all their little every day cruelties and tragedies. It could bring a man down, and get him het up. The band cheered him up. Made him forget the anger. As satisfying as it sometimes was to temporarily cripple an oxygen thief with just the precise application of his fingers, Ross McArthur enjoyed the feel of his hands on the frets of his Fender Jazz bass infinitely more.

3

"Woah, woah, *woah*, hold up there!" Luce Figura shouts, grimacing as if tasting something foul on her tongue and holding a clenched fist in the air.

The band stops playing, their painful attempt at an AC/DC cover coming to a clumsy, faltering halt with a discordant whine of off-key feedback and an uneven drum roll. The three music students turn to their ensemble lecturer, frowning and plainly mystified as to why she would stop them in mid flow.

"What's the problem?" Gordy, the singer and guitarist asks, turning from the microphone and letting go of the Strat copy strung around his neck.

"For a start," Luce says, "*you're* way out of tune. Did you get the intonation on that plank fixed like I told you to?"

Gordy shrugs and runs his hands through his greasy shoulder-length hair, a picture of teenage nonchalance. "The tuning's not that bad. Sounds okay to me."

Luce grits her teeth. "Not that bad? How long have you been playing guitar?"

"Almost a year." Gordy smirks as if this automatically confirms him as a master of the instrument.

"Then you should've learned on the first day that there's no such thing as 'not that bad' about tuning. You're either in tune, or you're not. If you're not, you sound awful."

Gordy shrugs again, as if such trivial musical concepts as being in tune were of little importance. Luce resists the urge to throttle the spotty nineteen-year-old.

She turns to Heather, the bass player. The lanky girl with the bleached blonde dreadlocks and dressed head to toe in strategically ripped black clothing, is tapping away at her smartphone, her bass propped precariously by its neck against the amplifier behind her, a loud fart away from toppling over. Luce forces herself to count to five before speaking. "Heather?"

The girl doesn't respond, but snorts laughter at something on her phone, seemingly unaware that her lecturer's talking to her. Luce steps past Gordy to the microphone, takes a deep breath and tries again to get the girl's attention, this time aided by two hundred watts of amplification.

"*HEATHER!*"

The girl squeals at the deafening blast from the PA speakers, jumping a near foot straight into the air and dropping her mobile, much to Luce's gratification. The sound wave also causes her delicately balanced bass to go over, hitting the floor with a loud low-frequency clang, and Luce's depressed to see the girl ignore her fallen instrument, scrambling instead for her mobile which she picks up and checks carefully for damage as if the device was a newborn baby. Heather shoots Luce a murderous look, her pale, powdered face and heavily kohl darkened eyes making her look like an angry raccoon.

"Oh, I'm sorry, Heather," Luce says. "Didn't mean to startle you there. I was just going to ask why you were playing sixteenth notes in a waltz time over the top of a straight four-four back beat."

Heather looks at her as if he's speaking in tongues.

"Remember what we talked about? About the bass locking in with the drummer?"

Nope. Nothing.

Luce sighs. "The bass and the drums need to play as one," she tells Heather. Again. "The rhythm section's the backbone of the band. If you're doing one thing and the drummer's doing another, it..."

Heather's phone interrupts her with a jaunty whistle, and she goes to check it.

"Heather, I swear to Hendrix," Luce says evenly, "if you don't put that phone away right now, you're off the course. I'm not even close to kidding."

Heather scowls and reluctantly puts the mobile in her pocket. "Sorry," she mumbles, sounding anything but.

"As I was saying," Luce continues with saintly levels of patience, "if the bass and drums are doing two different things, it sounds woeful. There's no groove. No *feel*. Right?"

Heather nods, not looking at her. Luce reckons that's about as good a response as she can hope for. She then turns to Lyle, the bespectacled, whippet-thin kid in the Slipknot t-shirt sat behind the drum kit, engrossed at that moment in rooting in his nose with his pinky.

"Pick us a winner there, Lyle," Luce says.

"Eh?" Lyle responds, wiping a large bogey on his jeans.

"Nevermind. You need to tighten it up and keep it simple. This is AC/DC we're playing here, not Rush."

"Who?"

Never hit a student, never hit a student...

Luce opens her mouth to explain who Rush are, but finds that words simply fail her. At twenty-seven, she's only eight years older than the three harmonically challenged youths, but at that moment, she feels ancient.

"It doesn't matter," she says, shaking her head. "Just keep it simple, steady and tight. Hats, kick, snare, cymbal. Don't worry about throwing in four bar tom fills and triplets. You don't need them here."

"But they sound awesome!" Lyle protests, grinning broadly and waving his drumsticks in the air. "*Bubbada bubbada bubbada!* Yaaas!"

"Yes, yes they do sound awesome," Lucy agrees, "but you have to play them at the right time, in the right song, and more importantly, know *how* to play them."

Lyle looks at her like Luce's just spat on him. Clearly no one's critiqued his rhythmic ability so plainly before. Luce wonders what exactly Chris Turner - the department's other drum tutor who was Lyle's one-on-one instructor - has been doing in his lessons. "Here, let me show you," she says.

Lyle trudges out from behind the Pearl four piece and grudgingly hands his sticks to Luce, who takes his seat. "If you're going to play a triplet fill," she says, "and again, there's no triplet fills *in* this song, but if you're going to try, take it slow and easy to start with. Kick, right hand on the floor tom, left hand on the snare." She demonstrates the three stroke fill.

Thud-boom-*crack*.

Then again, slightly faster.

Thudboom*crack*.

"Got it? Kick, left, right. Kick, left, right. Once you've got it steady, gradually build up the speed. Like this..." She repeats the triplet fill, again and again, slowly increasing the tempo, faster and faster, until she settles into a perfectly metronomic galloping rhythm.

Thudboom*crack*thudboom*crack*thudboom*crack*thudboom*crack*.

As she locks in, Luce closes her eyes, and the world goes away. The students. The sour smell of teenage BO in the cramped rehearsal room. The ripped sound insulation padding on the walls. The battered amplifiers. Even Heather's knocked over bass and Gordy's out of tune guitar. It all fades. There's only her and the beat.

She gradually slows it down, the thundering trip hammer roll once more becoming three separate and distinctive strokes, and then she stops. The world comes back into focus.

Luce looks up and sees Lyle, Heather and Gordy looking at her very differently now. They're actually smiling, that light in their eyes. That *spark*. Luce feels her frustration lift, and remembers why she got into the job in the first place. For that *spark*.

"Woah," Heather says, shaking her head. "That was... woah."

"Now let's try it again from the top," Luce says, stepping out from behind the kit and handing the sticks back to Lyle. "And this time, can we try to not sound like a one man band falling down the stairs? That'd be nice."

4

"We all good?" Aldo asks into the mic, glancing at Ross and Luce in turn. Tuned up, levels set, they nod back.

"Alrighty. *Mend the Black*. When you're ready, Luce."

Behind the kit, Luce counts them in on the hihats, setting the rhythm and tempo, *one-two-three, one-two-three,* then drops into the slow waltzing beat of the intro, accompanied by Ross dropping in with his grumbling fuzzed-out bassline. Aldo hangs back for a few bars while his rhythm section lays down the groove, smiling to himself, rocking back and forth slightly on his heels with his eyes closed. Almost unconsciously, the fingers of his left hand find the frets and strings of his new guitar, falling snugly into position on the neck as Luce goes into a rolling drum fill signalling the end of the intro bars.

One-two-three, one-and-a...

Aldo joins in, strumming out digital chorus washed chords. The new guitar sounds as good as it looks. Etheral and shimmering, hitting all the sweet frequencies. *Singing.*

Though he's been stressing about it all day, the large chunk of new debt the Les Paul represents doesn't even enter his mind right now. Neither does paying the rent, or even Dylan's child support money, because what's all that compared to this? The notes, chords, riffs, fills, solos and middle eighths? Soon lost in the song, Aldo's problems about money and debt and responsibilities are illusions. Glammers.

Real truth, he knows, real *grace*, is found in moments like these. In verse and chorus.

They play, and the music feels like it washes Aldo clean. The day's worries and shame slide off him like a layer of greasy tattered skin. He doesn't care about being fired earlier. He doesn't care that he's flat broke, living in a cold, mouldy bedsit which he now can't even afford. None of it matters. It all goes away as the moody arrangement of *Mend the Black* - one of the first songs he'd ever written - flows around and through him, filling him up.

They play, and for the first time that day, for the first time since their last jam three days ago, Aldo is at peace.

An hour and five songs later, they down tools for a smoke break.

Leaving the stuffy college practice room, still redolent with the youthful BO of the day's students, they make their way through the empty corridors of the music wing toward the exit.

Outside, Ross sparks up a joint, fogging the evening air with an aromatically illicit cloud of home grown White Widow. He and Aldo had ordered the seeds from some Amsterdam based website months ago, wrecked one night in Aldo's bedsit and well into a two litre box of cheap white wine and a couple of lines of chico, courtesy of a guy in Ross's work. Until the seeds came through Ross's letterbox one day weeks later, they'd completely forgotten all about their lofty cocaine fuelled plan to get a high quality, Heisenberg from *Breaking Bad* level grow operation on the go.

Sober, they hadn't expected it to work, but with a bit of Googling and creative jury rigging of lamps, mirrors, tin foil, fans, and the commandeering of the outlet pipe from the back of an old tumble dryer, Ross had somehow constructed a half arsed, but functional enough grow space in his hallway cupboard, where there now lived a respectably bushy wee cannabis plant Ross had named Earnest, who kept him and Aldo in free weed.

Aldo's leaned back against the roughcast wall of the building, watching the cars go past on the main road, his ears ringing pleasantly, hands and fingers still buzzing with the feel of the Les Paul.

"Soundin no bad, eh?" Ross says, passing the reefer.

Aldo takes a drag, enjoying the flavour and blowing an appreciative smoke ring. "Not too shabby," he replies. And it's not too shabby at all. They're sounding good. They're tight, and the songs are there. Over the past year they've started getting some decent gigs. The Garage and King Tuts in Glasgow. Fat Sam's in Dundee, and the Wickerman festival last year. That was some weekend, Aldo remembers with a smile. The three of them wandering about in a field in Dundrennan, full of acid, music everywhere, watching the fire jugglers as the sun went down. Amazing. They'd shared the bill with Stiff Little Fingers. Not on the same stage of course. Public Alibi played in a small tent off to the side, the one for unsigned bands, but still. They were on the same poster, and that was pretty fuckin cool. There'd been a good crowd packed into that tent watching them, and they'd been getting into it, even forming a modest mosh pit of five or six guys good naturedly knocking the shite out each other.

"The gig at the 13th Note's up on the Facebook page, by the way," Luce says.

"Cool, cool," Ross says, nodding. "Should be a good one. Friday night. Ladies night." He waggles his eyebrows and does a little hip swaying dance move. "Oh yeah."

"I've said to the students in my class if they don't come to the gig, they're not passing the course," Luce adds. Aldo guesses she's joking, but with Luce, you're never quite sure, and he's known her for nearly twenty years. She took her music seriously, that was for damn sure.

"Get em telt, Luce," Ross says, still gyrating his hips, now playing a little air-bass. "Any foxy wee student rock chicks in your class coming?"

"Away you go, ya sleazy bastard. You're nearly thirty."

"Few years off that yet," Ross objects. "A couple of boys from work are coming up to the gig as well. I told them it's two for one on voddies."

"Is it?" Aldo asks.

"No idea."

"So what you going to do for work, Al?" Luce asks. He'd told them about how his day had gone when they were setting up. He thought *Loose Cannon* was a decent song title.

"Fuck knows," Aldo says, passing her the joint. "I seriously can't face another call centre."

"I'll see if there's any jobs going in here."

"Nice one."

"I'll have a wee ask about in the hospital as well, dude," Ross chips in.

"Cheers," Aldo says. "This shit needs sorted. I need funds, pronto." Earlier, in Squinty Ginty's, he'd sat down with his pint, a notepad and pen, and wrote down all his income and expenses. It made grim reading.

The banking app on his phone informed him that he had precisely forty-eight pounds and twelve pence available, which was all that was left of the three grand overdraft currently owed on the account. He'd already had a letter from the bank the week before, giving him notice that they would in fact be reducing his overdraft limit to a hundred pounds in four weeks' time. At the time, he'd called the bank and let them know everything was cool, he'd been in a new job for a few weeks and would start depositing his wages into the account within the month. The Indian lassie on the other end of the phone, who had the unlikely name of Morag, had agreed to Aldo paying off the overdraft by a hundred pounds a month. No worries, he told her. He could afford that. After all, he was a responsible adult with a full time, permanent job.

Then he got fired a week later for not asking an octogenarian if he wanted a credit card.

So, sitting in that dim lit pub, sipping sparingly at a pint he couldn't afford, the income column of Aldo's scribbled balance sheet had read forty-eight pounds and twelve pence (which was really the bank's forty-eight pounds and twelve pence) and the sad little collection of change in his pocket. Without any real hope, he'd opened the iTunes app on his phone and checked the band's account. The seven song EP they'd recorded in a cheap studio and put online a year ago had sold zero copies in the past three months, and less than a hundred since its release. No unexpected windfall from royalties, not that he'd really expected any.

Then he looked at the list of expenses in the other column of his accounting sheet, and knew he had a serious problem.

He already knew he had a lot more outgoing than incoming funds, but seeing those outgoings written down in hard black ink was a kick in the stones. The numbers, bound in inarguable mathematical laws, sneered at him from the page. Rent, food, council tax, child support, internet connection, gas and electric, mobile, payments on the eight hundred pound bank loan he'd taken out last year, the three grand overdraft, and the grand now owed at Coasters Music for his new Les Paul.

He tried to wrestle with the expenses, beat them down into smaller, more manageable digits, seeing what could be cut.

Tesco Value everything when food shopping. Lots of pasta. Other food in tins. In bulk if possible. See about getting a card meter in for the gas and leccy. Find a cheaper tariff for the mobile, or maybe even do without?

He'd have to call the bank, and then the benefits office. He'd been on the dole before, but never quite in such dire circumstances.

Dylan's child support. Christ. He still didn't even want to imagine that conversation with Ashley, but knew he'd have to do it eventually. As it was, he only got Dylan every other weekend.

Aye, and what did you do? Got fired from a job a retarded badger could've got a promotion in. Good luck seeing more of your son now, ya fuckin clown.

Sitting in the bar, his ill-afforded pint soured with guilt in his mouth and a bad case of debt dread crawling on the skin of his forearms, Aldo had decided to take the Les Paul back to the shop. It represented a thousand pounds on the expenses column. Ninety-five quid a month in payments. A debt he could really do without, and which was, after all, a luxury. Not necessary for survival. He'd only had it a couple of hours. Hadn't even taken it out the case. Surely the shop would take it back.

By the time he finished his pint, he'd talked himself into bringing it to jam, just to see what it sounded like. Just to have a shot. Just to say he'd had a Les Paul for a little while. It was the guitar he'd always wanted, ever since the day he'd seen the video for Guns n' Roses' *Garden of Eden* on MTV, sitting on the floor in the living room in the house he grew up in. He'd only been five or so at the time, but can still remember it clearly. How he'd been awestruck by the sight of the band in that wall-eyed video, all flying long hair, cigarettes, sunglasses and leather. The song. Fast and dangerous, like a machine that could mangle you if you got too close. And Slash, crazy afro flying and shredding the shit out of that bad ass riff on his black Les Paul...

That had been it for Aldo Evans. From that moment, he'd never wanted to be anything else other than a rock star, and by the end of the first hour of jam tonight, he'd known he was keeping the guitar. At least until the debt collectors came and took it.

Fuck you, expenses column.

"Who we playing with again on Friday, Al?" Ross asks him now.

"Shattered Twilight. Kinda gothy, heavy Cure type thing going on?"

"Oh fuck. *Them*? We played with them last year, mind? They're pish."

"Aye. Strawberry fields. Were you no winching the facepaint off their bass player that night, Luce?" Aldo asks.

"Ya durty mare," Ross says, nudging Luce with his elbow.

Luce blushes and punches him in the arm.

5

"Can I have a P please, Bob?"

"You should've went during the break, ya daftie," Ross tells the contestant on the TV screen, adding an obligatory *ba-boom-tish* drum fill in the air for comedic punctuation. The old ones were the best.

"What P," Bob Holness asks, "is a region of wilderness in South America, shared by Chile and Argentina?"

"That'd be Patagonia, Bob" Ross informs the immaculately groomed host.

The contestant - a bespectacled student in a horrendous yellow and purple knitted sweater – is completely baffled by the question. "Erm… Peru?" he ventures. Ross rolls his eyes.

"No, I'm afraid that's incorrect," Bob tells the geographically challenged buffoon. "I'll have to pass it over." He repeats the question to the opposing two-man blue team; a rather homely girl sporting a remarkable backcombed mountain of frizzy blonde hair and huge red hoop earrings, and a skinny guy with a day-glo pink tank top and a leonine mullet. Born in '89, Ross is always grateful he missed the questionable, often plain inexplicable fashion sense of the mid-eighties. The two-man team confer briefly, before Mullet Man confidently provides Bob with the correct answer, winning his team the princely sum of a fiver before selecting the next hexagonal segment of the game board. "I'll have a J please, Bob."

"Good call, Billy Ray," Ross says, sitting forward on his couch, hands going to his rolling board on the coffee table. Aldo and Luce are picking him up in about twenty minutes for the gig at the 13th Note. Time enough for a sneaky pre-show doob, which he rolls and enjoys as the vintage re-run of *Blockbusters* on the Challenge channel continues. After a shaky start, the hideously jumpered solo contestant in the white team manages to pull it back and makes it onto the Gold Run. Standing alone on the Hot Spot though, the pressure gets to him and he folds at the decisive moment like soggy cardboard, running out of time with only two correct answers. Crestfallen, he leaves the show with a grand total of eighty-five quid, an Oxford dictionary and *Blockbusters* branded cardigan and filofax.

Pleasantly stoned, Ross flicks over to Channel Four, and enjoys the seductively intellectual charms of Rachel Riley and Susie Dent on *Countdown* while he waits for Aldo and Luce to arrive.

His mobile rings, and Ross sees on the display it's Aldo. Crossing his small living room and looking out the window, he sees Luce's silver Nissan Micra idling at the pavement, seven floors below. The Tardis, they call her motor affectionately, on account of the number of times they'd managed to squeeze themselves, their instruments and a full backline of amps and drum kit into the small vehicle, seemingly in defiance of the laws of physics. Happily, there's no need for such logistical trickery tonight. The 13th Note has its own backline, including an old but serviceable Line 6 bass combo which he's used in other gigs.

Ross picks up his mobile and answers the call. "Alright, man," he greets Aldo. "Be down in two secs." He reaches for the TV remote. *Countdown* is just about finished, Nick Hewer about to reveal today's *crucial* conundrum. The famous thirty second jingle starts up as the letters appear.

E A R F U S I O N.

"Nefarious," Ross says out loud, and like a boxer landing a knockout punch and strutting back to his corner before his opponent has even faceplanted into the canvas, he raises a fist in triumph and switches off the TV while the two contestants are still frowning at the jumbled up letters. He grabs his gig bag from the hall and leaves the flat, cheerily whistling the *Countdown* theme as he descends the graffiti adorned, hint-of-pish smelling communal stairway.

"Evening all," he says as he climbs into the back seat of The Tardis. "How we all doing?"

"Not too shabby, dude," Aldo says from the front passenger seat, looking over his shoulder. "Good day off?"

"Aye, sweet, man. Slept in till eleven, couple hours practice, spot of lunch, few reefers and a bit of telly. Did you know Harry Houdini's real name was Erich Weiss?"

"I did not."

"You do now. How's tricks, Luce? Manage to press gang your students into coming along tonight?"

"Aye, should be a few turning up," Luce says as she fiddles with the car stereo. A moment later, The Tardis fills with the frenetic drums and low-frequency guitar fuzz of Kyuss, pressurising the small car's interior with vintage stoner rock.

"Good call," Ross says, smiling and bobbing his head in appreciation as the car pulls away from the pavement.

He loves this part, the commute to the show, almost as much as he loves playing the gig itself. The free and easy banter with Aldo and Luce, the car throbbing with music and the lengthy, often animated discussions of said music's pros and cons. He loves watching the world go by outside, the pre-show excitement buzzing in his bones. That feeling of doing what you're happiest doing. The thing you're built for. Ross was well into his teens before he found any sense of belonging or purpose in his life, and a big part of the discovery had been in picking up a dusty old bass guitar.

It didn't even matter if the gig turned out to be near empty, as was often the case. Just last month they'd driven for over three hours to a gig up in Aberdeen and played a set in front of a heaving crowd of ten, consisting of the two barstaff, the sound guy, the other band on the bill, an old man passed out blitzed in the corner, and the scabby looking mongrel at his feet, who'd watched their set with disinterest between prolonged sessions of enthusiastic ball-licking. As disheartening as it could be, for Ross McArthur even things like that weren't enough to take away the joy of playing the gig and the road trip to get there.

He's looking out the car window, the streets and schemes of Inverclyde passing by a visual mismatch to the sounds of Kyuss on the stereo, music that makes Ross think of wide open places, burning sunshine and tumbleweed, and late night generator powered parties in the Californian desert. He can almost smell the weed, sweat, beer and woodsmoke.

Inverclyde has its share of beer and weed, and weather permitting, manages the occasional bonfire, but there, any similarity to the Californian desert rock scene ends. Passing outside the car window is a tired urban landscape of industrial estates, office developments and residential streets, many of them in advanced stages of decay, with most of the windows in the tenement blocks securely glazed with steel plates. It's an area in decline, with a dwindling population. The shipbuilding disappeared from the Clyde decades ago, with only one or two yards left along the riverbanks once world renowned for maritime quality. More recently, the computer industry that had replaced the shipyards and had kept the area afloat ever since the seventies had all but vanished, too. The big IBM plant they drove past outside of town was empty now. The mile-long strand of factories and offices nestled in the hills now just a big ugly scar in the greenbelt, wide empty patches of overgrown scrub and half collapsed industrial ruins, as if the demolition teams couldn't even be arsed with it, and had just left it to nature to finish what they'd started.

Heading for the M8 which will lead them to Glasgow, the Tardis skirts the Oak Tree Mall in the town centre. Ever since what experts liked to call the 'financial downturn' of recent years, businesses that had been established in Inverclyde for decades had closed down one after the other. Their spaces in the mall now filled with cheap emporiums, card shops and pawnbrokers, many of which would themselves be closed before the next tax year. Gone were local institutions like Rhythmic, the wee record shop where Ross had bought his first Black

Sabbath vinyl and the ticket to his first concert (Dropkick Murphys at the Barras, St Patrick's Day, 2006. Carnage.) and Mungin's Tailors, where Gregor, Ross's foster father, had seen him kitted out with a suit for his first job interview after leaving school. The suit had seemed to do the trick, and he'd got the gig, had done his time on the headset circuit doing customer service in one of the offices at the now defunct IBM plant. He'd worked in the same team as Aldo, who was bagged a few weeks later after phoning in 'sick' for the eighth time in three months.

"How's the job hunt going, Al?" he asks now. It's been three days since he got bagged from the market research place. It was always going to happen. Aldo just wasn't the type to last in that type of job. Couldn't keep his brain turned off long enough. Repetitive call centre work could be serious brain damage, especially for a guy like Aldo, who was smart enough, but a creative to the core. Problem was, with no useful qualifications to speak of, and no employable skills outside of music, it was one of the few types of work Aldo could hope to get.

"Shite," Aldo says. "Been checking S1, Indeed, the Jobcentre, all the usual sites, all the usual pish. Even the customer service ads are only after Finnish and Norwegian speakers. I've sent applications out for a few bar and outbound sales jobs. Registered with the agencies. Not heard anything back yet. Anything going at your places?"

"Sorry, mate," Ross says. "Checked the vacancy board in the hospital, but bugger all."

"Nothing at the college either," Luce says. "Unless you're an HR administrator with two years' experience and a degree, or a time served electrical engineer?"

"Mmmm... nope."

"Ach, chin up," Ross goes, giving him a slap on the shoulder. "You never know, mate. This could be the gig the A&R guy from Sony shows up waving blank cheques around. Did you know Rod Stewart was discovered when a record company guy heard him singing to himself on a train station platform?"

"I did not."

"You do now."

6

"*We're Shattered Twilight, and we're here to rule the world!*" shouts the leather-clad, facepainted ghoul on the stage.

"Aye, good luck with that, Morticia," Ross says, chuckling and taking a swallow of his pint.

The first band of the night start their opener; a de-tuned dirge of a tune, all darkly ponderous guitar lines, slow and awkward tempo, the vocal melody a plaintive half whisper. The bass player, whose name Luce can't quite recall – Gaz? Garbo? - has been giving her the eye and a series of sleazy wee knowing grins since they'd arrived. Even now, on the stage - which isn't really a stage at all, just a slightly raised platform at the far end of the room - he's slowly gyrating his hips as he plays, staring straight at her in a manner she supposes he thinks is darkly seductive, but which is actually skin-crawlingly creepy. She shudders a little inside, cringing at the hazy memory of their brief liaison last year. She'd been *really* drunk.

Shattered Twilight have brought a pretty decent gaggle of Goths with them, and the area in front of the stage is crowded with about twenty slowly moshing, shoe-gazing figures, uniformly dressed in black. As promised, quite a few of Luce's students have turned up as well, and the cramped candlelit basement of the 13th Note is respectably crowded. It's a good turnout. They might even make a little cash from the gig, for a change.

They're sitting round a shoogly-legged table against the wall halfway down the room. Across from her, Aldo's surveying the crowd, nervously drumming his fingers on the tabletop. Like a lot of frontmen and women she's played with, he always gets a bit twitchy before a gig, but he seems more wound up than usual tonight. When they were putting the setlist together earlier, he was very deliberate about what songs should go where in their half hour slot, and during soundcheck he was pickier than usual about the levels, stopping their run-through several times to get the guy at the mixing desk to bring the guitar up, get more low end on the vocals, a bit less on the monitors. It's good to see him so motivated. Aldo can be hit and miss sometimes in his onstage delivery, especially if there isn't much in the way of an audience. It seems like his new circumstances are the source of his focus tonight, and while she feels for her frontman, it can only be a good thing for the band. She hasn't seen Aldo look this hungry since they started out.

Placing her rubber drum pad on the table in front of her and getting her sticks out, Luce runs through her warm up exercises, going through her rudiments. She finishes her pre-show ritual by bending and flexing the muscles and tendons in her hands, wrists and ankles. She does this before every gig and every rehearsal, religiously so, and with far more devotion then she'd ever felt as a child during the complex rituals of Mass.

A daughter of devout Catholics – devout *Italian* Catholics no less – Luce'd never really caught the Jesus bug as a kid. All the elaborate bowing and kneeling and guilt and endless Latin recitals. It wasn't that she didn't believed in God at that age. In her simple, child-like way, she did, and she certainly liked the pretty dress she'd been given for her First Communion when she was seven. She just didn't think that God would be all that fussed about all the incense and hymns and sacraments and catechisms. Why would God or Jesus or the Holy Ghost care if you ate fish on a Friday or not? And it didn't seem fair that Brian McGill, the wee boy next door that she played with sometimes, would burn in hell for all eternity just because he was a Protestant. Surely God had other things to worry about with a whole universe to look after? Karen, Luce's best friend, had never shared any of her doubts. Karen never missed Mass in her life. She actually *enjoyed* going to chapel. Kind-hearted and achingly pretty, without a malicious bone in her body, Karen never went in or out of her front door without a wee splash of holy water and a heartfelt genuflection. Her unquestioning belief in the church and the Holy Trinity had been unshakeable.

"That dude at the bar," Aldo says, interrupting Luce's memories. "I've seen him before."

Glad of the distraction, she looks over her shoulder and sees the tall guy watching the band on stage. He looks bored. Dressed all in black, with wavy dark hair falling around his shoulders, at first glance he could be taken for another Goth follower of Shattered Twilight. On closer inspection, his smart leather jacket, tailored button-down shirt and trousers and high-shined shoes set him apart. On the bar at his elbow, there's an expensive looking camera next to a whisky tumbler. He's very good looking, his long hair and fine sculpted features, thrown into sharp relief by the dim candlelight of the basement bar, giving him a sort of rock n roll Jude Law look. It's hard to gauge his age in the low light.

"Right enough," Luce says, turning back to Aldo. "I think he was at the gig in Ivory Black's last month. Maybe one of those freelance photographers. Did he speak to you after that gig? Try and sell you some pics?"

Aldo shakes his head. "Nope, which is weird, because he was definitely taking snaps of us that night."

"So what's his deal?" Ross says, raising his eyebrows. "You think maybe…"

"Aye. Could be an A&R guy."

Luce glances over her shoulder again and sees the guy looking back at her, a little smile on his face. He nods and raises his whisky glass in salute, but makes no move to approach their table. "He's definitely checking us out," Luce says, turning back to Aldo and Ross again. "We should go over and say hello."

"Aye," Aldo says, and starts to rise from his seat. At that moment however, the frontman of Shattered Twilight brings their set to a close.

"Thanks for coming out," he yells into the mic amid a prolonged rolling drum fill and a wall of muddy guitar distortion. "*Fuck you and goodnight!*" Despite the abusive sign off, the little Goth crowd in front of the stage cheer and applaud lustily, chanting *Twilight! Twilight! Twilight!*

Their half hour of glory over, Shattered Twilight unplug guitars and unscrew cymbals, and Luce feels the familiar rush of queasy nervous excitement that always precedes going on stage. Now it's their turn.

"Guess the schmoozing's going to have to wait," Aldo says, picking up his guitar. "Time to go to work."

"Let's do it," Ross says, getting to his feet.

"Listen, guys," Aldo says, "Let's do this one right. If that guy *is* A&R, we need to make an impression, aye? No fuck ups."

"No fuck ups," Luce agrees. This is good to see. Aldo means business.

* * *

"*Well*," Ross says, forty-five minutes later. His sleeveless Black Sabbath t-shirt is soaked, his big muscular arms and grinning face gleaming with sweat in the candlelight. "That went alright, eh?"

Luce can only grin in response. Her whole body's tingling with a peculiar mix of exhaustion and elation, her limbs feeling curiously weightless. Without a doubt, Public Alibi have just played their best set to date.

"Dude," Aldo says, smiling and shaking his head, his long hair hanging in his face in sweat tangled ropes. "That was fuckin sweet."

When they'd started the set, the area in front of the stage had been scarcely populated - just the handful of Luce's students that she'd strong-armed into attending, the two thirsty guys from Ross's work, and a couple of other random punters.

By the time they'd finished the last song, the standing area in front of the stage had been packed with a sweaty, jumping throng of people six or seven deep. Even the Goths who'd come to see Shattered

Twilight had been up and getting into it. Luce knew that Public Alibi could knock out a decent set, but tonight they'd delivered a peach. They were *tight*, loud, and precise.

Aldo had most definitely meant business. He hadn't just played the songs. He'd attacked them. Owned them in a way he'd never done before, playing and singing with a confidence and controlled aggression that she'd never seen. Ross too had played a blinder, never missing a note and perfectly synching his basslines with Luce's rhythms to create that hallowed, perfect groove.

As for Luce herself, she knew she'd rarely nailed it like she had tonight. From her first four-count in until the final cymbal crash half an hour later, she hadn't played a single stroke out of place. Now, drenched in sweat and trembling, the three of them sit once again round their little table, drinks in hand, basking in a jittery buzzing afterglow.

That's when Luce hears a voice behind her saying, "Pleased to meet you. My name's Gappa Bale. Easy Rollin Records. We need to talk."

7

"Song to mortals, of all things the sweetest," the man in black says. He's grinning and spreading his arms.

Looking at him, the word *magnetic* comes to Aldo's mind. The stranger who's just strolled over to their table and introduced himself as Gappa Bale instantly comes across as one of those people who exude an aura that makes you sit up and pay attention. The natural charisma and presence of a skilled politician or fire-and-brimstone breathing preacher.

"Musaeus," says Ross, smiling and pointing a finger at the man.

Bale smiles back at him. "You know your philosophy, Mr McArthur. Or Ross, if I may?"

Bale offers a long fingered hand and Ross shakes it, beaming like a wean on Christmas morning. He's got a weird accent, Aldo notices. Sort of Russian sounding, but not quite. His English is perfect, but you can tell it's not his first language.

Bale then turns to Luce. "Lucia Corrada Figura. It's a genuine pleasure to meet you. *Piachere.*"

Luce, already looking slightly befuddled at the use of her full name and the suavely delivered Italian, blushes as Bale takes her hand. Instead of shaking it, he bows and plants a little kiss on the back of her fingers, all the while looking into her eyes. Somehow, he makes the old-timey gesture look cool as fuck rather than cheesy. Luce apparently thinks so too. She's got a look in her eye like she's considering jumping the dude's bones right there.

"And of course, Alan Michael Evans," Bale says, turning to Aldo, nodding slightly to himself, as if confirming something.

Aldo reaches across the table and shakes his hand. His grip's strong, dry and warm.

Be cool. This could be the most important conversation of your life.

"Nice to meet you," Aldo says, trying for a measure of nonchalance into his voice. "Take a seat. How do you know my middle name? And Luce's?"

"I have many contacts in the local music fraternity, Alan," Bale replies as he sits down with them, "and I have been watching you three for a while. I like to know all about those who interest me. About those whom I choose to do business with. If they too are willing, of course." Bale makes three business cards appear between his fingers. Aldo takes one and reads it.

"Easy Rollin Records?" he asks, looking across the table. "Never heard of them."

"A small offshoot of a larger, better known entity," he answers in that clipped, precise tone. "We are what you might call a specialised label, only taking on a very small, very talented number of acts once in a while."

"Alright," Aldo says. "Let's talk."

"Excellent," Bale says. "Though might I suggest we discuss this matter somewhere more suited to conversation? I have a car outside if you'd care to join me."

"Uh, yeah," Aldo says, "but we've got all our gear here. Luce's kit…"

Bale turns away and motions in the air with his fingers, nodding toward the stage, and three massive guys in black t-shirts and jeans emerge from the crowd, make their way onto the stage and begin stripping down and packing up the Alibi's instruments, working with the speed and efficiency of an experienced road crew.

"Woah, what the fuck," Luce says in alarm, getting to her feet, ready to storm the stage and start swinging at the strangers putting their hands on her kit without permission.

"It's quite okay, Lucia," Bale says, laying a hand on her shoulder. "My assistants are consummate professionals. Your equipment will be well looked after while we converse. Please." He gestures towards the exit.

"Fuck it, let's go," Ross says, standing up. "I like the cut of your jib, Mr Bale."

"Please, Ross, call me Gappa."

When they make their way up the stairs and onto the street, and find another big guy in black t-shirt and jeans attending Bales motor. A long, black, sleek looking thing with a high shine on the bodywork, a Mercedes decal on the bonnet and tinted windows. Bale opens the rear door for them and they pile inside, where Aldo finds the interior to be a roomy haven of soft, cream leather seats. Next thing he knows, there's a drink in his hand, which Bale's produced from a minibar. Luce and Ross are also handed glasses, and though Bale asks none of them what they want, Aldo finds that his tumbler contains Jack Daniels and Coke. Just what he would have asked for. The car moves off, the busy city centre rolling by outside the car's tinted windows.

"I didn't send a demo to any Easy Rollin Records," he says to Bale, who's sitting across from him, a whisky tumbler in his hands.

"As I said, Alan…"

"Aldo."

"As I said, Aldo, Easy Rollin are a small, exclusive associate of a larger and more well known label. Your demo was forwarded to us by them."

"Which one?"

"A major one. You'll see which one when you read the record contract. If we offer you one."

It takes a superhuman effort from Aldo not to let out a wee excited squeal at the word 'offer' followed by 'record contract'.

"If?" Ross asks, cool as you like.

"Yes. If," Bale says, turning to him. "You played well tonight. Very well, and I think you have great potential. Nevertheless, I am not given to entering into an arrangement without being absolutely positive it will be profitable for all parties concerned."

"Well, you're obviously interested enough to get us into your car and get the drinks flowing," Aldo says, surprised at how relaxed he sounds. "So what's the deal?"

Bale smiles across at him. He does that a lot, Aldo thinks, and why not? He's got a great smile. "I would like to arrange a live show for you, supporting another act. If you perform as you did tonight, or even better, then we can discuss our enterprise further, with a view to a recording contract. Either way, we will pay you for the support slot."

"How many tickets do we need to sell?" Ross says. Aldo was about to ask the same thing. That was how you made the money.

"This will not be that kind of arrangement, Ross," Bale answers. "Easy Rollin Records value and pay you for your musicianship, not for your abilities as salespeople. As such, your remuneration will not depend on ticket sales. In point of fact, the event is already sold out. Your band will be paid a fee of three thousand pounds for the show."

Aldo can't contain a burst of laughter. "Aye, right you are, pal! Three grand for one show?"

Bale nods. "Most of those who are professionals in their chosen field spend years in education, years building their knowledge and skill, and in turn, they quite rightly command salaries worthy of such time spent and experience gained. Musicians do the same, dedicating yourselves to your art for years, decades. Practicing, buying equipment, travelling here and there. *Committing* yourselves. Yet so few musicians are able to earn an honest living from their craft. And why? Club owners, promoters and venue managers insult you with offers of petrol money, a cut of door or bar receipts, or worst of all, with *exposure*." He spits this last word in clear disgust. "Why, when you have committed so much, should you be asked to play for so little, or for nothing more than *exposure*? Would you spit in the eye of the obstetrician who has just delivered your child?"

"Fuckin a-*men*, brother," Ross says, nodding vigorously.

"Easy Rolling Records seeks to change the way in which musicians do business with promotors and labels," Bale continues, "many of whom, I am sure you know, only wish to take advantage of talent they themselves do not possess in order to line their own pockets."

It's hard not to get swept up by the passion of Bale's rhetoric. His opinions, which are clearly genuine, are exactly the same as Aldo's on the matter. He considers Bale's offer. Three grand for one show. A thousand pounds each. That amount of cash would make a serious improvement to the current state of his finances. Would pay off his guitar anyway. And talk of a record contract. They need more info, though.

"When's the gig?" he asks.

"One week from now."

"Where?"

"The Barrowland Ballroom. Main stage."

Aldo looks at him askance. "The Barras?"

"Yes."

"You're talking about The Remember May gig?"

"I am. You've heard of them, I assume?"

Aldo has. Of course he has. A very decent folk rock three piece from Glasgow, fronted by Julia Stone, a diminutive female singer guitarist with a Billie Holiday-esque voice. Recently signed to Sony Records, highly regarded by music critics, and tipped to become the next big group to come out of Scotland, they were already lined up to play the main stage at next year's T in the Park, and were the current darlings of the UK music press. They weren't exactly Aldo's bag of kittens, but Luce loved them, and actually had a ticket for the gig at the Barras next Friday. The concert, the last one of a European tour, was being billed as their triumphant homecoming show before they went into the studio again to record their second album.

"Before you answer," Bale says, "please take the evening to discuss it amongst yourselves. One rule of Easy Rollin Records is that all decisions must be very carefully considered by all concerned. If we are to attain perfection, then no detail, no nuance, not the slightest aspect or eventuality can be overlooked."

Aldo smiles. Listening to this motherfucker talk is like sinking into a soft couch with a joint, a JD and coke and some Morcheeba on the headphones. It's not just his warm and softly melodious tone of voice, or the strange accent that inflects his words, but the words themselves and the way he weaves them together. He's like Morgan Freeman. Has that kind of voice you could just sit and listen to for hours, regardless of what he's talking about. Like a warm bath for your ears.

Someone nudges Aldo in the ribs. He looks round to see Luce staring at him, a puzzled look on her face. He blinks, realising that no one's spoken for several seconds.

"Right, okay," Aldo says, rubbing at his eyes. "Call you tomorrow."

"Excellent," Bale replies. "You have my card. I thank you for your time."

Aldo feels the car roll to a stop, and sees through the tinted window that they're once again parked outside the 13th Note. One of Bale's black clad behemoths - a particularly big fucker who looks like he eats pillar boxes for breakfast - opens the car door and nods to him as Aldo steps onto the pavement, followed by Ross and Luce. The big guy closes the car door again and the window slides down with an electric hum. Bale smiles out at Aldo. "Your equipment is packed up and ready to go," he says, nodding in the direction of Luce's car further along the street, where the three big roadies from earlier are standing by Luce's beat up Micra, minding the band's gear. "My staff will assist you in loading it into your car." Bale then reaches out an arm to shake his hand. "You have much potential, Aldo," he says quietly, holding onto his hand. "You could be *great*. Tell me, what are you willing to give to music?"

"Everything," Aldo says without hesitation. "Anything. It's... all I've got."

Bale releases him. "Good," he says, nodding. "That is good. Until tomorrow then."

The car glides away from the pavement, and Aldo watches the sleek black vehicle move away up the street until it turns a corner and is gone. He stands there for a few moments, not moving, but relishing the bubbling feeling of excitement in his stomach. The rush in his veins. The prickling of his skin.

Something important has just happened.

Something big.

8

They're in Ross's flat later, a little after midnight, sitting in his living room and passing a joint around as The Decemberists play through the Youtube app on Ross's telly. As difficult as it'd been, to give each of them time to think on it by themselves, they'd agreed not to talk about Gappa Bale's offer in the car on the way home from the gig.

"Personally," Ross says, "I don't know why we didn't bite the guy's hand off right there. There grand for one gig? At the Barras. Supporting Remember May? You fuckin kiddin me? Count me in for that shit."

"I know, man," Aldo says, still a bit dazed from the experience. "Shit's unreal. I don't think I need to say I'm happy with the offer. Luce?"

They both turn to her. The band rule is that everything that they do has to be agreed on by all three of them. "I don't know," she says, prompting Aldo and Ross to exchange a look of sheer disbelief. "Oh, come *on*," she says. "This doesn't feel like some sort of scam to you two? You never heard the expression too good to be true?"

"Luce..." Aldo begins.

"No, Aldo," she interrupts. "How the fuck did he know my real name?"

In truth, Aldo'd wondered about that himself. Luce never referred to herself by her given Italian name, but he'd forgotten about it when the debonair silver tongued A&R man had started talking Barras gigs, three grand payments and possible recording contracts. Luce evidently hadn't forgotten it. She looks genuinely upset, and Aldo realises that she hadn't spoken once while they were in Bale's car earlier.

"He probably Googled you," Ross says reasonably. "It's amazing what you can find out about someone just by putting their name into a search engine. Plus, Aldo said he'd seen the guy at other gigs, and he said himself he's checked us out."

"Aye, and don't you think that's a bit weird?" Luce asks, frowning over at him as she passes the joint to Aldo on her left. "Is this guy an A&R man or a stalker?"

"He's just being professional," Ross answers. "C'mon, Luce. I know it's out of the blue, but isn't that the way it goes for any band that gets interest? Nobody expects it till it happens."

"Ross, he never once talked about the band. Did you miss that?"

Ross shrugs. "So fuck? For three grand, a sold out gig with Remember May at the Barras and a shot at a record deal, the guy could be a plumber for all I care."

"Such artistic integrity. But that's another thing," Luce insists. "Who offers that kind of money to an unsigned band, no strings attached? What does this Gappa Bale character get out of it?"

Ross waves the question away, slumping back in his chair with the joint Aldo's just passed him. "He gets a support band. His outfit, this Easy Rolling mob, are obviously minted, Luce. Their own henchmen, limos and shit? He's obviously got money to throw around willy-nilly. Plus, he gets to be the guy that signed Public Alibi." He grins at her through a cloud of pungent smoke.

"Sorry, but I just don't buy it," Luce says. "Aside from him not even mentioning our tunes, or telling us who the supposed larger entity Easy Rollin's supposedly a part of, you didn't feel there was something... *off* about the guy?" She looks round at Aldo, who's staring back at her.

"Off?" he says, quietly. Then louder. "*Off*? Are you fuckin kiddin me on, Luce?"

"Hold on, Al," Ross starts, always alert to trouble a-brewing. Which it did fairly often when you had Aldo and Luce together for any length of time.

Aldo says, "All we've been talking about for the past three years is getting signed, Luce, and the first sniff we get and you think there's something *off* about it? Tell me, what was so *off* about the A&R man offering us three grand for an already sold out gig supporting the biggest band in Scotland?"

"Look, Al, I know this is important to you..." she says, looking uncomfortable.

"No, Luce, you've no fuckin idea," Aldo says. "This is it for me. I've got fuck all. *Nothing*. And no prospects of anything better. Think of all those gigs we've played in shitty wee bars with no cunt paying attention. Every pish stained club and dancehall we've set foot in over the last few years, making fuck all money. And now, when we're finally making progress, you're saying it's too good to be true? Aye it's important to me, Luce." He pauses a beat, then adds "and it should be important to you as well."

"Fuck off with that pish, Al," Luce returns, pissed off now. She's up from her seat, levelling a finger at him while Ross sits in his armchair, smoking and watching them with bemusement. He'd tried and failed to intervene. Best just to let them get on with it. Luce and Aldo loved a good band argument.

"Don't you dare tell me this isn't important to me," Lucy says. "I want a contract as much as you do, you know that, but you can't tell me there's not something dodgy about this. You're not that daft, Al."

"Bullshit," Aldo says, but finds he can't quite meet her eyes. In truth, until Luce pointed it out, he *hadn't* noticed that Gappa Bale had failed to discuss the band's sound. How had he missed that?

"Well, far as I can see, he's telling the truth about the gig anyway," Ross says, holding up his mobile. "Just checked the Barras website. The Remember May gig's sold out, support act to be confirmed."

Luce still looks unconvinced. "Google his name, and also Easy Rolling Records."

Ross taps the names into his phone, but after a few moments looks up and shakes his head. "Nothing."

"See?" Luce says, turning again to Aldo. "Don't you think that's a bit weird?"

Aldo just shakes his head. "He said they were a specialised label that don't advertise. If he was a conman, what's with the luxury car and the team of security? The guy's obviously a high roller, so why would he try and screw us? We're not rich, we're sure as shit not famous. We've got fuck all to get scammed *out* of."

Aldo feels the anger coiling up inside him, ready to bite. Can she not see this is the opportunity he – no, *they* - they've been waiting on for so long? This is it. This is their shot. He knows it, even if Luce doesn't. "Luce," he says quietly, getting to his feet so he's not looking up at her. "A thousand bucks keeps a roof over my head for a couple of months. It means I can feed myself. It means I can pay Dylan's child support."

"*If* you get that grand. If any of us do."

"Look, for fuck's sake just tell me," he almost shouts. "Are you saying no to this gig?"

"What if I am?" Luce returns, meeting his eyes, daring him.

Then I'll find another fuckin drummer, Aldo almost says, but doesn't. It occurs to him that the entire future of the band potentially hinges on the next few moments. If Luce says no, then by their own rules, they can't do the gig. But Aldo *wants* this gig. He wants this gig very badly indeed.

Ross, as he so often does when Aldo and Luce butt heads and it goes too far, moves to defuse the volatile situation. "Woah, hold up there, troops," he says, breaking the brittle silence and standing up, holding his arms out in an appeal for peace. "Let's just cool the jets for a moment, eh?" He looks at Luce. "Aye, I agree it's weird he hasn't told us what he thinks of the band, and that we know next to nothing about him or his label. Thing is though, Luce, the guy's not asked us for anything, he's not asked us for any dough, and like Aldo's saying, we've *got* fuck all anyway. We've literally got nothing to lose, so if we say yes and then we find out he's full of shite and the Barras gig doesn't happen, then we're no worse off than we are right now."

"And what if he changes his mind at the last moment," Luce asks stubbornly, "decides it's pay to play and asks us for money for doing the show?"

"Then we tell him to get straight to fuck. And I'll personally deck the bastard. How's that sound?"

Luce stares at him a moment longer, then relents and nods. The tension in the air abates a little.

"So we cool then?" Ross asks, turning from Aldo to Luce. "Let's say yes to the man, but *only* after he's told us a bit more about why he wants us and what Easy Rollin Records are about. We also tell him in no uncertain terms that the moment he starts acting the dick, we're gone. Aye? Sound like a plan?"

"Aye," Aldo says, still staring at Luce.

"I'll think about it," Luce says. "Let you know tomorrow." Then she finally breaks the staring contest with Aldo, shrugs into her jacket, and goes to leave. She hesitates by the door and turns back to them. "I just want it on record, though," she says, "that I think there's something wrong with this. Alright?"

"Duly noted," Ross says. Aldo just bobs his head slightly, not looking at her, eyes fixed on some point in space beyond the wall.

Luce regards the two of them a moment longer, looking troubled. "Good gig tonight, lads," she says, as if to herself. Then she's gone, and as the door to Ross's flat closes, Aldo shakes his head, as if sloughing off the fog of a daydream. He turns to Ross and smiles, rolling his eyes.

"Fuckin drummers, man," he says.

9

She's walking through a chapel. The one she used to attend as a child. St Michael's. Same raggedy red carpet down the aisle beneath her feet. Same intricately carved wooden pulpit pews. The same imposing crucifix on the wall with its thoroughly miserable looking Christ, and the same tiny confessional booth on the floor to the left of the dais, dark wood panels, brass fixings, looking like an upright coffin.

There are no walls to the left or right, only deep banks of vaguely shifting darkness where votive candle flames flicker like a yellow starfield. The air's heavy, cloying with the sweet smell of incense, and a voice, old as Death and dry as moldering bones, ghosts around the shadowy room, insidious, reverberant, as if spoken in a stone cathedral rather than the little chapel of Luce's childhood. That voice reads something from the book of Job. A verse that had frightened her as a child.

...*Now a thing was secretly brought to me, and mine ear received a little thereof...*

The door of the casket-like confessional slowly creaks open, and Karen emerges. She glides across the floor and stands naked in front of the dais, beckoning to Luce, blood spilling from her eyes, nose and mouth in red ribbons as her lips move, mouthing the litany in that ancient, spectral voice.

...*In thoughts from the visions of the night, when deep sleep falleth on men...*

The priest, old Father Lafferty, hatchet nosed and eyes like cigarette burns, stands beside Karen, also naked. A massive erection juts up between his spindly legs as he grins a rictus grin crammed with too many teeth.

...Fear came upon me, and trembling, which made all my bones to shake...

Karen turns from Luce and looks up at Father Lafferty with beatific devotion before kneeling in front of him and reaching for his cock.

Luce looks away, up at the big crucifix on the wall. The despondent figure of Christ has been replaced by the bass player from Shattered Twilight. She still can't remember his name, but he's grinning down at her, his lips twisted in a suggestive leer. His side's split open, revealing a ropy bulge of dripping viscera, his nailed hands and feet and thorn-torn forehead bloody with stigmata, running black in the candlelight.

...Then a spirit passed before my face, the hair of my flesh stood up...

The deep space blackness to her left and right recedes, slowly revealing crumbling grey brick walls adorned with water-stained posters from past Public Alibi gigs. Fat Sam's in Dundee. The Tunnels in Aberdeen. King Tuts in Glasgow. Studio 24 in Edinburgh. Last year's Wickerman Festival. The flyers hang feebly on the wall, barely clinging on.

...It stood still, but I could not discern the form thereof...

Luce becomes aware of music. The tune sounds almost familiar, a song she knows but can't quite place. Then she recognizes a snatch of melody from *Stone Me*, one of the band's early songs, played at a drastically reduced tempo, slow and muddy.

With the random suddenness of dreams, a dead eyed congregation are abruptly filling the pews around her, moaning along to the funereal dirge en masse, and there, up on the dais beneath the crucifix, are the band. Her band. Aldo, Ross, and herself, appearing like animated waxworks with low batteries, only their arms moving sluggishly on their instruments. Glassy eyed, waxy faced, staring ahead out over the heads of the muttering dead choir below.

...An image was before mine eyes, there was silence...

The congregation - who Luce now sees includes her parents, old schoolmates, work colleagues, ex bandmates, friends and lovers and long dead family members - groan along with the band, their lifeless faces turned up to the crucifix, where the Shattered Twilight bass player has now been replaced by another figure, one dressed all in black, long haired and handsome, smiling placidly out over the congregation below.

The music slows further, like a record on a turntable being forced down under a ragged fingernail, until it's a tonally malevolent, mumbling nonsense sound.

...And I heard a voice, saying...

The people crowded into the pews turn as one and fix Luce with hollow eye sockets, and she realises they're dead, every one of them. They begin to shuffle towards her, corpulent skin and flesh falling from their bones, and she retreats, backing toward the exit, except she finds herself somehow turned around, forced towards the pulpit as the ghoulish churchgoers surge down the aisle toward her, their skeletal clawed hands reaching for her. She struggles and bucks in panic as they seize her and begin binding her face and limbs with lengths of mouldering fabric that smell of the grave.

Then strong hands grip her by the shoulders from behind. Hands that feel wooden, tipped with carved meathook claws. A strangely accented voice, velvety as coffin lining, whispers in her ear.

...Shall mortal man be more just than God?

Luce screams into the suffocating cloth covering her face, desperately thrashing against the death shrouds knotted around her by the rotting congregation.

But then she remembers, and Luce fights to control the fear, clamping down on it and forcing herself through sheer will to stop shrieking and kicking. Immediately she feels her bonds loosen, and notices for the first time that through the material covering her face, she can make out a floral pattern on the weave of the fabric, blurry and indistinct.

The breath shudders out of her in a long sigh. She removes the duvet from her face, untangling her sweaty limbs from the bedclothes.

In the jittery aftermath of the nightmare, the first she's suffered in many years, Luce sits on the edge of her bed, head in hands. Through her still trembling fingers, she sees the digital alarm clock on the bedside cabinet. 6:58am. Her alarm's set to go off in two minutes. Now that the pounding of her heart's quieted, she can hear the birds outside her window chirping and twittering the morning chorus.

Shaking the last lingering fingers of dread from her bones, Luce pushes herself from the bed and stumbles to the bathroom.

Half an hour later, showered and breakfasted, fortified with a no-nonsense sized injection of espresso in her veins, Luce's still pensive as she leaves her small one-bedroom flat and drives to the rented studio where she gives private drum lessons on weekends to supplement her income from the college. A vague sense of disquiet, a hangover from her troubled sleep, distracts her and lingers all morning, making it difficult to concentrate fully on her students' lessons. But more than anything, she's troubled by the confrontation with Aldo in Ross's flat the previous night.

She'd told him the truth when she said she wanted a record deal. That'd always been their goal. The difference between her and Aldo, however, was that it wasn't the *only* goal in Luce's life. While she'd always been hopefully optimistic, she remained realistic about the facts of being in a band and the odds of making a living from it.

Aldo on the other hand, *believed.* As far as he was concerned, it'd always been a foregone conclusion that one day the band would get signed. Predestined, she'd heard him say once, only half-jokingly. Luce knew that by suggesting the offer Bale had given them was horseshit, she was pissing directly on Aldo's campfire, and maybe putting her own place in the band at risk. Moody and stubborn as he was on occasion, Aldo was a good guy at heart, but not to the extent, Luce now suspects, that he'd have any qualms about replacing her if he felt his dreams of rock stardom were in danger of being scuppered.

She just couldn't shake the vague feeling that there was something wrong with the whole thing. Aldo and Ross evidently had no problem with Bale's offer, but she was a firm believer in the credo that if something was too good to be true…

She'd gone straight to the shower last night when she'd arrived home, gripped by a strong urge to cleanse herself, and she'd stood under the hot pounding water for a full half hour. That'd been weird enough, but even more perplexing was the simultaneous surge of desire she'd felt. With an image of Bale's deep dark eyes fixed in her mind, her hand had lingered a while when soaping between her thighs, and then lingered a while longer. When she came, the force of it had bucked her body, every muscle contracting and the strength of her orgasm convulsively arching her spine so she rapped the back of her head against the tiles of the wetwall. She'd barely felt it, and had stumbled from the shower breathless and confused, trembling all over, every inch of her skin prickling, and still feeling a certain yearning…

"Luce? *Luce!*"

She jerks her head up. "Huh?"

"How was that?" Colin, her student asks, looking over at her expectantly from behind the drum kit. Luce hadn't even been listening.

"Oh yeah," she says, nodding. "Better. Much better." She glances at her watch, relieved to see that the one-on-one lesson with Colin was just about finished. "Good work. Keep working on your rudiments, though, okay? I'll see you again next week."

Colin nods and smiles and starts packing up his cymbals and sticks. "Are you alright, Luce?" he asks, looking over at her. "You've been pretty quiet today."

He was a good kid, wee Colin. Unusually thoughtful for a seventeen-year-old. Small for his age, he was the kind of skinny, slightly awkward and bespectacled wee guy that set bullies' victim sonars pinging. He could drum like a maniac though, and had a natural feel for jazz rhythms. With practice, Luce could see him up at the conservatoire in Glasgow in a year or two.

"Just tired after last night," she says. "Thanks again for coming along to the gig, by the way."

"You guys were awesome," Colin says, bobbing his head enthusiastically, causing his thick black rimmed glasses to slide down his nose.

"Yeah, it was a good show," Luce says, looking away into the corner. "Really good."

"No shit," Colin says, shouldering his cymbal bag. "No word from any labels about you guys getting a deal? You're really good. Best band I've seen in ages."

Luce opens her mouth, but doesn't know what to say, and then the door to the studio opens and Chris Turner, the college's other percussion tutor walks in carrying a sheaf of drum notation. Chris also uses the small studio on weekends, his sessions following Luce's at the same time every Saturday.

"Howdy doo, Lucy Lou?" he says with his customary sleaze, smiling in that wholly annoying way he had, as if he were privy to some secret joke that everyone else in the world were the butt of. He lets his eyes linger a quarter note too long on her chest, and Luce feels the need for another shower. The guy's a grade A bellend. A heavy set, bald-yet-ponytailed man in his fifties who wore Rainbow t-shirts two sizes smaller than he should. Chris Turner had drummed for some forgotten craprock band back in the eighties, and would never tire of telling you about his illustrious career as a session musician. Davie Graham, the college's full time guitar tutor, had once told Luce that in truth, Turner was a bit of a 'Walter Mitty'. Turner knew Dougie Vipond, and had filled in for him with Deacon Blue at a few rehearsals when Dougie was on holiday, and he'd once jammed with a very drunk Geezer Butler in a bar in Soho. Far as Davie knew, and Davie Graham *actually* knew a lot of people in the business, that was about as far as Chris Turner's career as a session musician went.

"You done in here?" Turner says. "You know I've got the room booked?"

Luce nods to Colin, who smiles as he leaves the studio. "I know," she says to Turner. "Same as every Saturday." As if it wasn't enough that the guy was a lecherous self-important balloon, he had a rare talent for stating the obvious.

"Heard you had a wee gig last night," he says, his thin smile condescension given form. "13th Note, eh?"

"Aye," Luce says, shrugging into her jacket, in no mood for his particular brand of shite. Especially not today.

"Aye, I remember gigging in there years ago," Chris says, all misty-eyed reminiscence. "Me and my band Woodfang played with Primal Scream in there, back before they got signed. Me and Bobby Gillespie, we were good mates, always out our tits on eccies. Ah, good times."

"Hmmm," Luce enthuses, shouldering her kit bag and turning for the door, thinking what a completely stupid name Woodfang was for a band.

"How about your group?" Turner asks, and Luce can hear the patronising smirk in his voice. "Your wee trio not having any luck getting a deal yet?"

Everything was 'wee' with this cunt, and it made Luce want to gouge his eyes out with a splintered drumstick.

"Ach, I guess yous just aren't there yet, eh? Right enough, you'd think you'd get at least *some* interest with a fine wee bit of eye candy like yourself sitting there behind the band, playing away at your drums."

Luce stops in the act of turning the doorhandle and goes very still.

She knows the word 'bristling', but until that moment, she's never quite experienced it. Now though, at Chris Turner's last comment – which righteously pisses her off on *multiple* levels – she feels a very cold and very calm rage crystallise inside her.

She turns back to Turner, who's adjusting cymbal stands at the kit, tutting and shaking his head, as if wondering what talentless know nothing monkey's been screwing around with his setup.

"Ex*cuse* me?" Luce asks.

Turner must hear something in her voice, because he looks up at her with an expression you might wear when realising you've just said something very stupid to a very dangerous individual.

"Just saying," he says after a nervous moment, waving a hand. "I mean, your wee band's not exactly setting the world on fire, is it? You though, you've got the looks…"

"We're playing with Remember May on Friday night," Luce informs him. Because they are. Fuckin *right* they are. "Could be getting signed as well," she adds.

The words just come out of her before she even thinks, but she doesn't regret saying them. Suddenly, all her doubts and suspicions about Gappa Bale's offer are gone.

Maybe it's the look of disbelief on Turner's face, but all Luce knows at that moment is that she *wants* that gig now. She *wants* that deal. It's like Aldo said. It's all they ever talked about. All they ever dreamed about. And *fuck* every Chris Turner in the world who ever told her that she couldn't or that she shouldn't or that she was too loud and that she should put down her drumsticks and come back to Jesus…

She walks slowly across the studio and stands very close to Chris. Close enough to kiss. She can smell the stale BO and cigarette smoke ingrained into the fabric of his Rainbow t-shirt. He takes a step back, nearly falling on his arse as his heel catches a cymbal stand.

"Aye," Luce says softly, looking up at him as she advances. "An A&R guy was at our wee gig last night. Loved our wee band, and offered us the support gig at the Barras on Friday. Getting three grand for it. Took us out in his limo, laying on the drinks. He's talking about an album deal. Aye, things are looking up for our *wee* band."

She loves the way Chris Turner's mouth keeps opening and closing, as if he's trying out various responses which don't quite convey his thoughts on the matter.

"That's.… good," he settles for, looking down fearfully at Luce. She takes a step closer, forcing Turner to back up another step till his back's against the wall.

"Aye, it's *very* good." Lucy agrees. "And if you ever stare at my tits or condescend me again, Chris," she says, her voice like a scalpel, "I'll fuckin drag you round this studio by that stupid wee ponytail of yours and then shove a cymbal stand up your arse. Alright?" She glares at him for a few more moments, delighting at the clear bald terror on the fat bullshitting walloper's face.

Then Luce turns and calmly leaves the studio, texting Aldo as she goes.

Verse

Rock has always been the Devil's music. I believe rock and roll is dangerous. I feel we're only heralding something even darker than ourselves.

David Bowie
Rolling Stone Magazine, Feb. 12, 1976

1

Aldo'd hardly slept last night. Catching some zees had been the furthest thing from his mind, and he'd been tied up in knots, worrying about Luce's reaction to Bale's offer. And what sleep he'd managed to get had been fractured, punctuated with strange dreams that he couldn't remember but knew were anything but pleasant. He'd woken with a lurch around 6am, sweating and gagging, as if he'd been about to spew all over his duvet. It'd passed after a few seconds, but he'd been left with a strong compulsion to shower immediately. He'd felt soiled somehow. As if he'd shat the bed or something.

Now, he's half asleep on his sofabed, exhausted, but forcing himself to stay awake because he's got Dylan today. On the tv, Dylan's *Frozen* dvd's playing. Aldo reckons you can say what you like about the film, but that *Let it Go* is a fuckin good song. Dylan's not even watching Elsa cutting about in her ice castle. He's playing in the hall, bumping around and talking to himself in that nonsensical way exclusive to four-year-olds and their imaginations. Aldo occasionally hears what appears to be someone making liberal use of Sellotape. He should really be in the hall *with* the wee man, playing along with him. He only gets him every second Saturday, but he's just so *tired*. He could just close his eyes for a minute…

The opening bars of *Debaser* snaps Aldo's eyes open again and he reaches for his mobile on the coffee table, rubbing his eyes and blinking himself awake. It's a text message from Luce.

If he genuinely likes the band and what we're about, I'm in.

Aldo grins as he reads the text, then quickly taps out a reply.

Sweet. Going to phone him now. Let you know. He sends the text, then considers a moment before composing a second message. *Thanks Luce. Sorry I was a dick last night.*

Getting up from the couch, he crosses the living room area of his bedsit and takes Gappa Bale's business card from a bookshelf crammed with guitar tablature books, takes a deep breath, trying to still the nervous flutter in his guts, and starts punching in the number embossed on the expensive looking piece of card. As soon as he does, Dylan comes charging into the room in a high state of four-year-old excitement and starts tugging on Aldo's t-shirt as he jumps up and down on the spot.

"Daddy! Daddy! I'm making a web! Come and see!" The wee man's wearing the Abbey Road t-shirt Luce got him for his birthday a few months ago. Dylan loves it, and finds the sight of Paul McCartney's bare feet enduringly hilarious. Aldo notices he has a spent roll of packing tape in one hand as he stands there, looking up at him and smiling proudly, his blonde hair a static frizzed mop and his big green eyes, his mother's eyes, shining.

"A web?" Aldo asks him, one eyebrow raised in suspicion. "What you talking about, dude?"

"Yeah! A web! I'm a spider, and I'm going to catch all the flies and eat them up. Yum yum yum! Deeeelicious!"

Aldo lets himself be dragged from the living room by his son, and finds the narrow hallway festooned in brown packing tape, the entire roll strung in sticky brown strands around the handles of the front door, the storage cupboard and bathroom. The tape's stuck to the walls, wrapped around Aldo's guitar case, the radiator, the small chest of drawers and the upright vacuum cleaner. He recalls Ashley telling him this morning while dropping Dylan off that the wee man's most recent obsession is with creepy crawlies. Two weeks ago it had been space rockets. *Bookaboo* the fortnight before. *Bookaboo* was pretty good. A wee dog puppet that was a rock star drummer, and every episode refused to go on stage unless a celebrity read him a story. Meat Loaf had been on the show.

"Well, that's a fine looking web," Aldo compliments his son, nodding in approval at the reams of packing tape making the hall impassable. "I'm sure you'll catch lots of flies." Even so, the sight of his guitar case tangled in gluey tape troubles Aldo a little, but before he can tell Dylan that he shouldn't touch Daddy's guitar because it might break, the wee man announces again that he's a big scary spider, and "you be the fly, Daddy!"

Aldo obligingly blunders forward, puts his arms among the streams of packing tape crisscrossing the hall, and starts making panicky buzzing noises. "Help!" he cries in mock insectile distress. "I'm stuck! Oh no! A scary spider!"

Dylan laughs and starts jumping on the spot again, clapping his hands. "C'mere you, tasty fly!" he shouts, then sets about biting Aldo's thigh, giggling and slobbering with adorable arachnid hunger. Aldo continues to yell for help, then frees his arms, ripping out a few hairs as he does, and goes on the attack.

"Ha! I'm free! Right you, pesky spider. I'm gonna munch *you*!" He scoops Dylan up and chomps at his ribs. Dylan shrieks and kicks and laughs, and for a few moments, there's nothing else for Aldo. No band concerns, no money worries. He just immerses himself for the moment. The sound of Dylan's laughter. The warm wriggling feel of him in Aldo's arms. The smell of him. He missed it.

"Okay, dude," Aldo says, putting Dylan down. "Daddy's got to make a quick phone call, okay?"

"No!" Dylan loudly objects. "Do the belly munch again!" He reaches his arms out to be picked up, still jumping up and down.

"Not right now, wee man," Aldo says. "You just play with your web for a wee moment and I'll be right back, okay? I'll just be a moment."

"But, Daddy, I want a *belly muuuuuunch*," Dylan insists, his bottom lip wobbling, his mood instantly plummeting from the heights of joy to the depths of misery. His face screws up, eyes suddenly brimming with ready-to-spill tears. A sure harbinger of an impending meltdown.

"No, Dylan," Aldo says a little more firmly, trying to nip the situation in the bud before the wee man gets going. "I have to make a phone call. It's very important, okay?" He turns away to go back into the living room, as if *that* were an effective way of ending a debate with a vexed four-year-old.

Sure enough, as soon as Aldo picks up the phone to call Gappa Bale, Dylan starts bawling. With a sigh, Aldo returns to the hall, where the wee man's standing with his arms by his sides, hands knotted into angry little fists and his scrunched-up face bright red and awash with tears.

"Dylan, come on, wee man," Aldo says. "I have to speak to a man on the phone, just for a wee minute."

Dylan's having none of it. "*No, Daddyyyyyyyyy!*" he wails, inconsolable. "*You have to stay and play with meeeeeee!*" A portrait in childhood misery, a long glistening rope of saliva spills over Dylan's quivering bottom lip and bungees down to the level of his knees where it swings back and forth.

Aldo feels the instinctive urge to go to him, pick him up. Hug him and wipe the tears and drool away, tell him it's okay, wee man, Daddy's here, I'll play with you forever. Wants to say he'll do all the things his own dad never did with him. And he will. But right now there's a gig with Remember May to sort out, and the possibility of a recording contract. He *really* needs to make that phone call.

"I'll be back in a minute," he says, then Aldo turns away from his son, goes back into the living room and closes the door behind him, leaving the wee man crying in the hall, calling out for him.

"*Daddyyyyyyyy! Daddyyyyyyyyyyy!*"

Telling himself that he can't give in to tantrums, that he has to be firm, Aldo ignores his howling offspring and dials the number on Bale's business card. It's picked up after two rings.

"Easy Rollin Records," a husky female voice answers, all accented and sexy. "How can I help you?" Aldo has a vivid image in his mind of some dusky skinned beauty on the other end of the line, a woman wearing some exotic, heady perfume. "Hello?" the breathy voice asks again, and Aldo realises he hasn't spoken.

"Uh, yeah," he manages. "My name's Alan Evans..."

"Ah yes. Aldo," the receptionist says, her voice a purr. "Mr Bale's expecting your call. I'll put you right through. Please hold."

Dylan's still screaming out in the hallway, his temper tantrum in full flow.

"Dylan, *be quiet!*" Aldo shouts through the door. Dylan takes no heed, and goes right on bawling.

The sexy, unseen receptionist's smoky tones are replaced by the hold music, which Aldo is pleasantly surprised to recognise as the crackling starkness of Robert Johnson singing *Love in Vain*, a song recorded almost a century ago. It's one of his favourites. A track that never fails to trace an icy blue finger down his spine and set his scalp a-prickling with pleasure. He considers how strange it is that many of the symptoms of fear are the same as those brought on by listening to a really good tune.

There's a click on the line, and Johnson's sublime slide guitar playing's cut off by Gappa Bale's voice. "Good afternoon, Aldo," he says. "It is good to hear from you. How are you today?"

"Alright, Mr Bale. I'm..."

"Gappa."

"Sorry. Gappa. Aye, I'm fine. Sorry about the noise in the background. Got the wee man round the flat today. He's a bit grumpy."

"Dylan. Your son. Four is a good age. Such chaos."

"You're not wrong there," Aldo agrees, smiling. Had he told him about Dylan?

"I have several children myself," Bale says. "They can be... a handful, yes?"

Aldo chuckles. "Aye, he's just decorated the hall with a roll of packing tape. He's building a spiderwe..."

"But we must cherish them," Bale interrupts. "They have to come first, yes? For they grow, and are gone, so quickly. You cannot imagine."

Out in the hall, Dylan's still loudly sobbing and calling for him.

"Absolutely," Aldo agrees into the phone, plugging one ear with a finger. "Anyway, we talked about your offer, and it sounds good, but we've got a few questions if you don't mind?"

"Of course," Bale says, "but young Dylan sounds very upset. Perhaps you should tend to him?"

"Nah, it's fine, he's just having a tantrum."

"Are you sure? I don't mind waiting while you calm him. Or you can call me back?"

"It's okay, he's in a mood. He'll stop in a minute."

"If you're sure?"

"Absolutely. Love him to bits, but he's just being a wee shit, as I'm sure you know they can."

"Very well," Bale says. "But before you ask your questions, which I'm happy to answer, I feel I should apologise to you. It occurs to me that we did not discuss your band's music when we spoke last night. This was unforgivably remiss of me, and I am truly sorry."

"No, no, not at all, but that's one of the things I wanted to ask you about."

"Sometimes one gets so overwhelmed with work that the glaring basics are overlooked, but if I may, allow me to salvage some professional respectability, and allay any fears you may have that you are dealing with some scatterbrained fool or hoodwinking charlatan."

"Erm... okay," Aldo says.

"First of all," Bale begins, "I must tell you that I have been in the music business for a long time. Almost longer than I can remember, and I can scarcely recall coming across a group of musicians quite so suited to Easy Rollin Records."

"That's nice of you to..."

"You three are young, vibrant and *very* talented. There is a raw energy to Pub ic Alibi that I find most appealing. I hope you do not think I am merely blowing smoke up your... ego?"

Aldo laughs. This guy's a regular *card*. "No, not at all..."

"In terms of your sound," Bale continues, "how can I put this?" There's silence on the line for a few beats. Then, "I hear the attitude and aggression of the Sex Pistols, but more refined. More technical prowess. I hear the power and groove of say... Monster Magnet, yet with more commercial accessibility. I detect shades of Nirvana in your hooks and dynamics, but without the clichéd anguish of the tortured artist. In the *drive* of some tracks, the instrumental sections and variety of riffs, I hear echoes of Karma to Burn. There is a classical influence in some of the modes used, which brings Iron Maiden to my mind, and a clear love of the blues in many of your guitar solos. Your lyrics have depth and meaning, and yet they are simple and heartfelt. Poetic without pretension, akin to someone like Kimya Dawson. It truly is a beguiling and unique mixture of influences and styles. Your group *shines*, Aldo Evans. *That* is what interests me."

Aldo knows he's grinning like a loon, but can't help it. He's always hated being asked the obvious question of what kind of music the band played. Could only ever answer in the vaguest of terms. Bit of this, bit of that. Sort of stonery, bluesy punk rock thing with a metal slash classical edge. He could never really define or articulate what he thought of as the band's sound. But Gappa Bale could. Gappa Bale fuckin *got* it.

"Well, thanks very much..." Aldo begins.

"And I can understand that you may be suspicious of what I have offered you," Bale interrupts again. Aldo hates when people talk over him, but he finds he doesn't mind so much when Gappa Bale does it. There's a politeness, a charming authority to him that makes you feel you should just shut up and listen because he knows what he's talking about. "After all," Bale continues, "it must seem too good to be true when someone offers you the kind of opportunity I have. I imagine anyone would be *doubly* wary of my intentions in light of the fact that I failed to tell them what intrigued me, musically speaking, about their group."

"Well, as you mention it, Luce..."

"And so, that said, I thought it might allay any doubts you may have if someone other than myself could reassure you that what I offer is no con. I have the booking manager for the Barrowlands Ballroom on the other line if you'd like to speak with her?"

"Um.. okay..."

"One moment."

Then Mr Johnson's back on the line, bewailing the blue and red lights on the train as it pulls away from the station, carrying off his beloved Willie Mae. The blue light for his blues. The red light for his mind, and all his love in vain. *Fuck*, it's a good tune.

"Hi! Is that Aldo?" a remarkably cheery female voice breaks in, a stark contrast to Johnson's tortured lament.

"Er, yeah, speaking."

"Hi, Aldo! So *lovely* to speak to you! My name's Rosemary Daniels. I'm the booking manager for the Barras."

"Hi, Rosemary."

"So Mr Bale's spoke to you about Friday night? The Remember May gig?"

"He did."

"And?"

"Well, we're still thinking about it, me and the other guys in the band."

"You're *thinking* about it?" Rosemary Daniels asks, as if Aldo's just told her he was thinking about cashing in a winning Euromillions ticket. "Well don't think too long. I need a support band like last week, and this could be a huge opportunity for you. If you don't mind, can I ask why you're *thinking* about it instead of biting my hand off?"

Aldo suddenly feels very foolish. "I... guess it just seemed a bit out of the blue, y'know?" he says, almost apologetically. "This guy Bale just appears from nowhere and offers us a gig supporting a band like that, talking about paying us three grand. We... *some* of us, thought it was just too good to be true."

"Och, don't worry about that," Rosemary Daniels assures him. "That's just how Mr Bale operates. Likes to play the mysterious benevolent stranger, you know? Take it from me, he's no scam artist. There's plenty of arseholes in this business, Aldo, but Gappa Bale's not one of them. I've worked with him many times before. You have my word you can trust him."

"So he's cool then? We don't need to sell any tickets, and we get three grand for the show?"

"Absolutely. The gig's already a sell-out. Remember May are about to break big time, and there's going to be a shit load of press and music biz types at the concert. I don't want to sound rude, Aldo, but you'd be an idiot to pass up an opportunity like this."

"Sounds like it," Aldo says.

"Well, I really hope to see you on Friday night. Mr Bale let me hear your demo and I've been playing it in my car constantly ever since. I'd really *love* to have you guys here."

She hangs up before Aldo can reply, and Bale is back on the line.

"Hello again, Aldo," he says. "I hope Rosemary was able to reassure you of my honourable intentions."

"Aye, she seemed nice."

"Oh she is. A *very* nice lady. So do we have an accord?"

Aldo grins. *Fuckin bet your arse, Mr Bale.* "I think we do."

"Excellent," Bale says. "Be at the stage door of the Barrowlands Ballroom at 5pm sharp this Friday. Rosemary will meet you there and I will join you later. If you perform as I know you can, we'll talk further, about a formal recording contract."

"Okay, thanks very much, Mr Bale, I really mean…"

"Gappa," he says, and hangs up before Aldo can say another word.

He puts his phone in his pocket and just stands there for a moment. He feels dizzy. Slightly drunk. After all the reassuring words, praise and promises from Bale and Rosemary Daniels, he's now aware of how quiet the flat is, and he realises that at some point during the phone call, Dylan's stopped crying. Aldo crosses the living room and opens the door to the hall.

Dylan's lying on the floor on his belly, his face turned away from Aldo. Sulking, as he often does after a tantrum. His spiderweb's wrecked, and the wean's covered in lengths of sticky brown packing tape, tangled all around his limbs and body, as if Dylan had destroyed it in a fit of kid-rage and then went for a wee nap, exhausted from wreaking such destruction.

"Come on, wee man," Aldo says with a smile as he bends down to pick Dylan up. "Are you being a grumpy sausage?" He gives him a tickle in the ribs, but Dylan doesn't respond.

It's only when he lifts Dylan up that Aldo feels the limpness of his body, notices the strand of packing tape wound tight around his son's throat, and sees the horrible deep crimson colour of his face.

Fear like he's never known slams through Aldo like a car crash, instantly tripling his heartbeat, stealing the warmth from his blood and squeezing the breath from his lungs in a wordless moan. For a moment, he can't think. Can't move.

But then his muscles unlock and his fingers fly to the tape round Dylan's neck, fumbling at the tight wound gluey brown strands, trying to loosen them, but it's no good they're wound too tight and his fingers can't get purchase and oh fuck oh no no oh fuck no Dylan's making this horrible dry hissing croaking noise and his legs start kicking then Aldo's in the kitchen yanking a drawer clean out of the cabinet and groping on the floor amongst the spilled contents for a knife a knife a knife *where's all the fuckin knives?* and then he finds one and he's back in the hall trying to get the knife between the tape and Dylan's neck and the wee man's squirming on the floor, his face starting to go dark purple and Aldo's trying to hold him still as he gets the knife under the tape, scraping the boy's neck with the blade and he starts sawing and sawing and sawing and please Jesus fuck no no please don't…

The tape snaps and Dylan's back arches up off the floor as he pulls in a huge gulp of air and goes into a prolonged coughing fit. Aldo's got him in his lap, holding him close. "That's it, wee man, you're okay, you're okay," he babbles, the panic not quite subsided yet. "Just breathe, breathe, Jesus Christ…"

Aldo's heart's still crashing in his chest, one hundred proof dread pumping round his body as Dylan's breath slowly returns to normal and his face drains of that horrible purple colour. His eyes open – you can see where the blood vessels have haemorrhaged in the whites - and he looks up at Aldo for a moment, then starts crying.

On severely wobbly legs, Aldo carries him into the living room and sits on the couch with him in his lap, tears of relief tracking down his face. "It's okay, wee man, it's okay," he whispers, his voice breaking as he strokes Dylan's hair and back. "It's alright. You're fine. It was just a wee accident."

Christ that was close. If the phone call with Gappa Bale had gone on just ten seconds longer...

If you hadn't made the phone call in the first place, or you'd been paying attention to your son, maybe Dylan wouldn't have almost died just now, ya selfish fuckin prick.

"No," Dylan whimpers against his chest, his little hands grabbing fistfuls of Aldo's Guns n Roses t-shirt. "*Wasn't* an accident." Dylan mumbles something else Aldo can't make out. He can feel his little body trembling against his own.

"What'd you say, pal?"

Dylan looks up at him, and Aldo sees that his son is terrified. "Someone *pushed* me," he whispers, then buries his face in Aldo's neck, clinging to him for dear life and crying his wee heart out.

Ashley arrives to pick Dylan up a few hours later. She looks tired and hassled from her day's shift in the kitchen at Club Velvet where she works as a commis chef, but still pretty as ever. There's a pleasant smell of steak and onions coming off her, and Aldo's stomach growls as she steps into the hall.

Dylan's on her like a shot. Charging out the living room and wrapping himself around her legs. Ashley immediately shoots a questioning look at Aldo before bending down to pick the wee man up. Dylan sniffles into his mother's neck, his face turned away from Aldo. "I want to go home," he says quietly.

"Sweetie, what happened?" She looks down at him in her arms and sees the big red scrape on his neck. And the bruising. "What happened?" she repeats, turning to Aldo, her voice only a few degrees above freezing as she gently strokes Dylan's hair.

"It's okay," Aldo says. "We had a wee accident with a spiderweb, didn't we, dude?"

"I *told* you, Daddy," Dylan insists, his face still turned away. "It wasn't an accident."

Aldo sighs. The wee man's not letting go on that one. Trying to make his voice sound casual, as if was just a wee domestic mishap, he says, "He made a spiderweb in the hall out of a roll of packing tape, covered the place in it, and we were playing in it. I was on the phone for a minute, and he got some of the tape wound round his neck..." Aldo raises his hands in a calming gesture as he sees Ashley's eyes widen. "It's okay, he's fine. I had to use a knife to cut it off him..."

"Dylan," Ashley says, not taking her eyes off Aldo. "Go and wait in the car, sweetie." She puts the wee man down, turns round and unlocks the wee Micra parked at the kerb behind her with a press of the key fob.

"Okay, wee man," Aldo says, holding his arms out for Dylan. "Come and give me hugs. Time to go home." He hates this part. Every second Saturday he gets to be a dad for a few hours, and then the wee man goes away again. He's asked Ashley about getting more time with him, but she's not budging. Not until Aldo can hold down a job. That's the deal.

Show me six straight months' wage slips, Aldo, and six months of you not cancelling the time you already get with Dylan because you've got a gig or a band practice. Do that, then we'll talk about it.

Ashley puts the wee man down and Aldo crouches down to his level, arms out for his goodbye hug and kiss. Dylan just looks at him, and Aldo's heart fractures a little at the look of mistrust he sees on the wee man's face.

"Come on, wee man," Aldo says softly. "You know Daddy needs his hugs."

"Say bye to Daddy," Ashley prompts him, but still Dylan doesn't move. He just stands there, one hand still clutching Ashley's coat, his eyes flicking nervously between the ground and Aldo, who remains crouched, his arms still held out.

Reluctantly, he steps forward and Aldo holds Dylan a little tighter, a little longer than usual. He plants a big kiss on his cheek. Jesus, he'd never been so scared in his life. Seeing the wee man like that, lying on the floor breathless and kicking and his face that horrible purple colour…

And who's fault was it?

"Bye, Daddy," Dylan murmurs, then frees himself of Aldo's arms and walks down the path to the pavement and climbs into Ashley's car. Ashley pushes her key fob and locks the doors again. Then she turns to Aldo.

"Right, what the fuck happened here?"

Here we go, Aldo thinks.

"Like I said, we were playing. He was the spider and I was the fly, but then I was the spider and I was munching him…"

"How did he get packing tape tied round his neck?"

"I dunno, Ash. I was on the phone…"

"And you weren't watching him? How long were you on the fuckin phone for?"

"I dunno… just a minute or…" or how long had it been, really? Five minutes? Ten?

"Or what? And what happened?"

"I found him. In the hall," That guilt comes back and squeezes Aldo's throat, making it hard to talk. "He… he was having trouble breathing…"

"What the fuck do you mean *trouble*?" Ashley says, her voice nudging the master volume up to 7. "Could he breathe?"

Aldo can't look at her.

"Aldo, could he *breathe*?"

He manages to look at her. Her lips are pressed into a thin white line. High spots of colour on her cheeks, the rest of her face pale with fury.

Aldo shakes his head.

She slaps him. Hard.

Aldo takes it.

"You fuckin stupid *bastard*," Ashley hisses.

She slaps him again. *Dish!* Right in the mouth.

"I'm sorry," Aldo says, blood on his lip and watery-eyed. "I'm so, so sorry, Ashley. But I got him free. He's okay, and I honestly have no idea how the tape could've got wound round his neck like that..."

She takes another swing at him, but Aldo manages to half duck, half block it with a forearm this time. Ashley takes a step forward, getting right up in his business. Aldo takes an involuntary stumble back, half tripping over his own doorstep.

"He's four years old, Al," she says, her voice low and deadly. "If you knew the first thing about being a parent it's that weans will find a million ways to hurt themselves if you *don't watch them.*" She physically punctuates the italics on her last three words with hard pokes to Aldo's chest.

"Well I don't get much fuckin practice only getting him once every fortnight, do I?" Aldo protests, trying to fend off her finger. He knows it's a lame argument, but he's tired of getting slapped and poked, and wants a fight.

"Oh well, round and round we go," Ashley returns, also eager for a verbal scrap. Aldo can see it in those green eyes of hers. In the menacing twist of those lips. Lips he used to worship. "You can see Dylan as much as you want as soon you get your act together. You know the deal. Six months. Six months work, no cancellations and no fuck ups. It's not a lot to ask. How's your job hunt going by the way?"

Aldo's having trouble thinking of a good comeback. But then he remembers. "We might be getting signed," he says. "The band."

Ashley looks at him as if he's just wiped his arse on her curtains.

"I'm serious, Ash. Signed. With a real label."

"Get yourself to fuck, Aldo," Luce says sceptically.

"I mean it. We're supporting Remember May on Friday night. At the Barras."

She's still pissed. Righteously so, but Aldo can see that that's got her attention. Whatever she could say about Aldo - and she could say a lot - he'd never lied to her. Ever. And responsible working mother she now may be, but just five years ago, Ashley McColgan had partied just as hearty as anyone, and had been very much into the band scene. She'd played keyboards in a few groups herself, and sang backing vocals with a pitch perfect sweetness that would shame a songbird. Point was, she knew what the Barras gig meant. She knew how big a deal getting signed was.

"Are you for real?" she asks suspiciously. "What do you mean *might be* getting signed?"

"The guy, Gappa, he says if we play well at the Barras, which we're getting three grand for by the way, then we can start talking about an album deal."

Ashley doesn't say anything, but there's the slightest softening of the I'm-about-to-chew-your-balls-off expression.

"A formal recording contract is how he put it on the phone," Aldo goes on, "and I was speaking to the booking manager at the Barras, and she's promised us the three grand up front for the gig. And the guy, Ashley, the guy who gave us the gig? Cool as fuck. Minted by the looks of it. Took us out in his limo after he watched the 13th Note show last night, laying on the drinks and talking contracts." He's ranting, and knows he's ranting, but fuck it. Ranting feels good right now. "He loves the band, Ashley. He really does. He *gets* it, know what I mean? He talked for a good bit on the phone about the Alibi and our sound and what we're trying to do. You know?"

That miniscule, momentary break Aldo'd thought he'd seen in Ashley's anger is gone. As if it never was.

"That all sounds like more than a minute or so," she says quietly. "That's what you were talking about on the phone? The band? For who knows how long, while Dylan was lying in the hall suffocating?"

Shame rises in Aldo's throat again like vomit.

Way to go, Aldo, ya utter fanny.

"Of course it was, Aldo," Ashley says, all weariness and regret. She doesn't say anything else. Just shakes her head, then she turns and walks the ten feet to her car, gets in and drives away. Not so much as a glance back at him.

Aldo stands in his hall doorway, watching the car move away up the street, turn right at the junction by the corner shop, then disappear.

He stands there for a while longer, feeling gutted, just letting the chilly autumn air and drizzle blow against him, dampening his thin Guns n Roses t-shirt.

2

Luce parks The Tardis on East Campbell Street, and she and Ross get out and grab their gear from the boot. They walk down the road onto Gallowgate, and just stand for a moment, looking across the busy main road at the iconic marquee of the Barrowland Ballroom, forty feet of neon yellow lettering against a backdrop of glowing blue and white shooting stars.

"Did he say he was meeting us outside?" Ross asks, staring at the marquee.

"Didn't say," Luce replies. "Just said he'd get us here." Aldo had broken tradition, choosing not to join the two of them for the drive to the gig. He'd sent Luce a text that morning, saying he was going to get there early to get a feel for the place, and would meet them when they arrived.

"Fuckin Barras, man," Ross says, still looking up at the neon marquee, nodding slightly and smiling.

"Fuckin Barras," Luce agrees, checking up and down the Gallowgate for any sign of their frontman, who's nowhere to be seen.

They've had rehearsals every night for the past week, and Aldo'd been focussed as you like, but quiet, not speaking much except to shout out the tunes or to call a halt when he felt something wasn't right or tight enough. He was all business, not even stopping for a smoke break. Distant and sullen he might have been, but by fuck he was on good form. They'd all upped their game, in fact. Ross had noticed it, too They were playing with a tightness, confidence and swagger they'd never quite reached before.

"Well?" Ross asks now, gesturing across the street.

"Let's," Luce concurs, shrugging her cymbal bag up on her shoulder.

They wait for a break in the busy five pm traffic on the Gallowgate, then cross the road and head for the stage door round the side of the building, which opens before they reach it. Standing there is a short, pleasantly plump woman with dyed pink hair, a NOFX tank top, leather mini skirt, a lot of tattoos and what looks like a few kilograms of chrome facial piercings.

"Luce! Ross!" she cries delightedly, as if being reunited with two long lost friends, holding her tattooed arms wide as if in expectation of a big group hug. "I'm Rosemary Daniels, the booking manager. It's so *awesome* to meet you both!" She does a funny little jump in the doorway, clapping her hands together like a six-year-old who's just heard the ice cream van arrive in her street.

"Erm, likewise," Luce says politely, bemused by the enthusiastic welcome. "Is Aldo here? Our singer?"

"Oh, yes, yes," Rosemary says, ushering them through the door and onto a narrow flight of stone stairs ascending from the stage door, which she closes behind them. "He's been here since early this afternoon."

"Getting a feel for the place," Luce says, half to herself as she goes up the stairs.

"How about the esteemed Mr Bale?" Ross asks as they go through a door at the top of the stairs and emerge into a corridor. "Is Gappa in the house?"

"Indeed he is, Ross," Rosemary says, stepping beside him and linking her arm through his. She smiles up at him. "He's been here all day. He's with Aldo right now. My, but you're a big one aren't you?"

"So legend says," Ross replies with a wink.

Rosemary shrieks a sudden peal of laughter that echoes and reverberates around the brick corridor and swats him on the shoulder. "Oh, you're a *rouge*, you are!"

She leads them through another door, turns left into an adjoining corridor and stops at another door halfway along on the right hand side. This one has a piece of paper tacked to it, with Public Alibi printed on it in bold red lettering. Luce and Ross exchange a look and a smile. Their own dressing room!

Rosemary knocks on the door and Luce hears a voice answer from inside. The booking manager grins at them over her shoulder and opens the door.

Aldo's there, reclining on a beat up but comfy looking red leather couch, a drink in his hand. He smiles up at them, toasting their arrival with his glass. "Alright, troops!" he says cheerily, all traces of the sullen intensity of the last week gone from his face. Is he drunk? Luce wonders. There's a peculiar light in his eyes, and he seems *too* relaxed somehow. But no, he can't be drunk. He wouldn't do that. Not for this show.

Gappa Bale, who's sitting on a matching couch across from Aldo, smiles over his shoulder then gets to his feet and comes across to greet them. "Good evening, my friends," he says in that suave, hard-to-place accent.

As before, he's dressed all in black. Black leather jacket over a black shirt, tight fitting black jeans and black, highly polished expensive looking shoes. His hair hangs to his shoulders in a luxurious tumble of ebony waves and curls, and Luce wonders what it would be like to drop her drum bags and run her hands through it. When he takes her hand and plants that gentlemanly little peck on the back of it, there's a slight flutter of disquiet as his lips brush her skin, but she doesn't mind so much. Gappa Bale's been on her mind quite a bit over the past week. It was only natural, she supposed, considering what he was doing for the band. And she couldn't deny that he was a fine looking man.

Gappa lets go of her hand and turns away, shaking heartily with Ross, who claps him on the shoulder companionably and thanks him for the gig.

"No, thank you," Bale says, "all of you, for making yourselves available on such short notice. I have a feeling this will be a special evening. Can you not feel it?" His eyes linger on Luce's and he nods knowingly. So unusual, his eyes. Direct, knowing, a deep dark blue that seems to swim and shift hypnotically around pupils black and deep as space.

Rosemary sidles up to Bale and lays a hand on his shoulder, fingering the leather of his jacket. "*I* can feel it," she says, looking at him with canine devotion.

Luce feels an unexpected pang of jealousy, but manages a half smile, then turns away, dumps her jacket and drum gear on another red leather couch against the wall and goes over to the fridge in the corner of the room where Ross is already examining the contents and nodding in appreciation. Cold beers and bottles of water fill the shelves, with plates of sandwiches, cold meats, salads, dips and breadsticks arranged on a long trestle table at the back of the room.

"I'm liking this level of hospitality, Rosemary," Ross says, taking a beer from the fridge.

"You're very welcome," Rosemary replies with her customary chirpiness, leaving Bale's side, yet letting her fingers linger a moment on his shoulder as she moves away, as if reluctant to break contact. "And before I forget, here's your hard earned." She takes three brown envelopes from her purse. "One thousand pounds each, and of course, my heart-felt thanks, though it's just the cash that's in the envelopes." She giggles girlishly as she passes them out, and smiles a friendly smile as she comes to Luce, but then tightens her grip on the envelope for a half second when Luce tries to take it from her hand. Rosemary's smile slips and then she's just baring her teeth, and there's an unmistakable warning flash in her eyes.

Mine. Stay away, bitch.

Then she lets go of the envelope and moves on to Ross, all smiles again. Luce's thrown for a moment, startled a little by the abrupt switch in Rosemary's manner. Then she feels a momentary urge to run up behind her, grab a couple of fistfuls of that stupid pink hair and drag her down to the deck and start booting into her head, cheeky wee fat cunt, who did she think she was?

Luce gives herself a shake. Where did *that* come from?

"Lucia," Bale says. "Are you all right?" He's smiling at her.

"Don't call me that. It's Luce. I'm fine."

"Of course you are," Bale agrees.

Luce notices everyone looking at her strangely, but the weird moment's broken when there's a knock at the door, and a heavily bearded guy with long blonde hair and glasses sticks his head into the dressing room. "Okay if we come in and say howdy?" he asks.

"Alright, Marcus," Rosemary says, grinning and waving him in. "Good to see you, honey. Come on in and meet your support band."

The beardy guy smiles and enters, followed by a thin, loose limbed drink of water in a Stone Island jacket and a mod haircut, then a pretty, elfin looking girl carrying a guitar case and wearing a red and black Paisley pattern shirt. Luce feels a little buzz of excitement as Remember May, the night's headline act, come in and Rosemary introduces everyone.

"Nice to meet you," the pixie-esque girl with the guitar says to Luce with a shy smile as they shake hands. Luce's a little star-struck. Over the past year or so while Remember May had been growing their reputation, Julia Stone had become one of Luce's favourite singer songwriters. On more than one occasion she'd been moved to chills and tears by the diminutive singer's blues roughened voice, poetic lyrics and folksy arrangements. "Thanks for stepping in for this gig," Julia says. "I heard your demo. You guys are really good. I love your drumming."

"Thanks," Luce says, having to repress a giggle. *Julia Stone loves my drumming!* "What happened with the original support band? Can't believe someone would pass up a gig with you."

Julia shrugs. "All we were told was that they'd backed out. Don't know anything else. Pain in the arse, but still, their loss is your gain, eh?"

"Hell yeah," Luce laughs. "It's going well for you guys, eh?"

Julia shakes her head, a look of bemusement on her face. "It's crazy. Ever since the cover story in NME it's been non stop. Been out on tour round the UK and Europe for most of the last year and this one, and we're going into the studio again next month. Then there's the video shoots, the publicity events, the interviews. The record company's already booked a full on world tour for next year. Hard to get your head around it. It's mental."

"Fuck, it sounds amazing," Luce says, thinking *That could be us.*

"Damn straight it is," the skinny mod-looking guy says, coming over and offering his hand. "Jim McElland, at your service."

"Luce Figura," Luce says, shaking with Remember May's drummer. "Nice to meet you."

"Fuckin love your demo, by the way. That one tune *Mend the Black*? Don't often hear waltz rhythms these days."

"We try to keep 'em guessing," Luce says with a smile. "And as they say, three's the magic number."

They look round at the sound of laughter and see Ross and the long haired bearded guy, Marcus Tatum, Remember May's bass player, are engaged in a game of Rock Scissors Paper.

"What's going on?" she asks, going over to stand beside Aldo, who turns to her, a big grin on his face and a light in his eyes that she hasn't seen in weeks.

"They're playing for the right to date Rachel Riley when they're famous," Aldo says. "Turns out they're both *Countdown* geeks."

"Oh, for fuck's sake," Luce says, though she can't help laughing. "That's just sad. And quite possibly offensive."

"Ah-haaaa!" Ross crows in victory as his stone defeats Marcus' scissors. He does a little hip-swaying jig and sings a few bars of *The Girl is Mine* while Marcus shakes his head wistfully. As fine a bass player as Ross is, he has a terrible singing voice, and his short rendition of the Jackson / McCartney duet is offensive to Luce's ears.

"I hate to interrupt, guys," Rosemary says, smiling as she comes over to them, "but it's soundcheck time. You ready?"

"Born for it," Aldo says.

"Let's do it," Ross agrees, then bumps fists with Marcus. "Better luck next time, brother."

"You best treat her right," Marcus says, pointing at him and bugging his eyes crazily behind his thick glasses. Ross laughs and promises that he will.

Luce retrieves her snare, cymbal and stick bags from the couch and takes a deep breath, trying to still the jitters running the length of her legs. As they leave the dressing room she looks back and sees Bale staring at her, that strange little smile, somewhere between seductive and mocking, still playing around his lips, and those dark basilisk eyes fixed intently on hers.

3

Daddy! Do the belly munch again!

The low murmur of the waiting crowd. Laughter. Whistles. Clapping. The buzz of some two thousand people jammed into a single room. The PA system plays *Riders on the Storm*.

No, Daddy! You have to stay and play with meeeeeee...

Aldo has his eyes closed. His fingers drum nervously on his knees. His heart thumps so hard he can feel it in his earlobes. He's sitting on an old Marshall cabinet backstage, in the wings to the left of the stage. Ray Manzarek's bass notes thrum up from the floor, through the cab and vibrate along his spine.

What are you willing to give to your music?

"Everything," Aldo whispers to himself.

"That is good to hear," a familiar voice says, and Aldo flinches. His eyes snap open, and Bale's standing there. He's not looking at Aldo, but gazing out over the crowd in front of the stage.

"What?" Aldo says, his voice a croak.

Bale turns and smiles at him. "It is good to hear. The sound of the crowd. Does it not thrill you?"

Aldo, who for a second there had thought that Bale read his mind, goes and stands beside him. The hall's packed out. A sea of bodies jostles and heaves, filling the famous sprung dancefloor from the barriers in front of the stage all the way back to the raised disabled platform at the back of the room. The atmosphere's warm and close with the heat of the crowd, thick with the smell of sweat, beer and anticipation.

"I'm scared," Aldo says. And he is. He often got a little nervous before a show, but he's never suffered from real stage fright. Had always felt most at home when playing a gig, whether in front of a crowd of five or fifty. Now though, he's shaking from the toenails up.

"Excellent," Bale says, still staring out at the crowd, a strange expression on his face. Aldo thinks of a lion watching a herd of gazelle. "Fear sharpens the senses," Bale says. "It brings the world into focus. No man is more alive than when he is afraid." Then he turns to Aldo and lays a hand on his shoulder, that weird hungry look instantly replaced by a benign smile. "I want you afraid, Aldo," he says. "If you were not afraid right now, it would mean that you did not care. If you did not care, I would have no use of you."

Aldo frowns and opens his mouth to reply, but then a meaty hand suddenly slaps him on the back, and Ross is there, grinning like a fool, bass in hand. He's in his cut off jeans and lucky Black Sabbath vest, his Greenock Morton sweatbands on his wrists. Luce stands behind him, peering out at the crowd, a look of intense concentration on her face as she *tap-tap-taps* her sticks against her thighs.

The stage lights go down, and a half-hearted cheer rises up through the crowd. On the big backdrop screen at the back of the stage, the band's name is projected. Public Alibi, writ in black Impact font letters six feet tall on a blood red background.

"Holy shit!" Ross says, pointing and laughing. He jumps up and down on the spot like a sprinter warming up.

Bale turns to Aldo and puts both hands on his shoulders. He peers deeply into Aldo's eyes. "Show them," he says. "Show *me*."

A young stage hand comes up and hands Aldo his guitar, freshly polished, brand new strings tuned, ready-stretched and gleaming, and he slings it round his neck. He lays his hands on the fretboard, and just like that, the fear is gone.

He feels armed.

He turns to Ross and Luce, excitement now bubbling like a chemical reaction. "You know what this means, right?" he says, raising his voice to be heard above the increasing volume of the crowd, who're now chanting and clapping in rhythmic impatience.

"Means we can't fuck it up!" Ross laughs.

"This is where it pays off," Aldo says. "All those unpaid gigs in scabby pish-stained pubs with nobody watching. Every fuckin callus and blister we've had and every minute we've jammed. This is where it's got us."

He grabs Ross and Luce by the backs of their necks and draws them into a fierce three way band hug.

"And every arsehole promoter that tried to rip us off. Everyone that said we were pish. Every cunt that said we needed to grow up. *Fuck. Them. All.* I love you guys."

He releases his bandmates, turns, and walks out onto the stage.

4

A-LI-BI!
   A-LI-BI!

Aldo sits in the dressing room again, staring into space, his ears whining with tinnitus. His whole body's soaked in sweat and quivering.

A-LI-BI!
   A-LI-BI!

They finished their set five minutes ago, but the sound of the crowd chanting the band's name still pulses through the building. Aldo can feel the vibration through the thin soles of his Converse All Stars. He can see the crowd in the way the beer in the bottle between his feet trembles behind the brown glass.

AL-I-BI!
   AL-I-BI!

He can't remember much about the set itself. It's all just a riotous, jumbled haze of sound and multi-coloured lights in his mind. He looks down at his shaking hands, staring at them in dumb astonishment. Though he can't recall specifics, he knows that he's just played the best set of his life. He couldn't have sung a bum note if he'd tried, and it was as if his hands and his guitar had taken on a life of their own, leaving him a mere bystander.

The gig they had played at the 13th Note last Friday had been good. The best they'd played up until that point. Tonight had been on another level. Aldo'd never imagined the band could sound like that.

And the *crowd*. He remembers looking out over the audience during the middle eight of *Blowhole* and seeing them going ballistic, what seemed like every punter from the front of the hall to the back, jumping up and down in a mass pogo session.

Across the room, Ross and Luce are hugging and laughing. Aldo looks over at them and feels a slow smile stretch his lips.

We fuckin nailed it.

There's a knock at the door, and a moment later Gappa Bale enters the dressing room, Rosemary on his heels. Both of them grinning hugely.

"Holy *shit*!" Rosemary squeals in delight, clapping her hands in that little girl way she has. "Did I really just see that? You guys were amazing. Just *amazing*! They're going mental out there. I'm so *proud* of you!" She hurries over and embraces Luce and Ross, enfolding them in her big tattooed arms.

Bale says nothing, only stands there in front of Aldo with his arms out to the side in a gesture that at the same time says 'hug me' and 'what did I tell you?' But right now, it's words Aldo wants to hear. Very specific words. He gets to his feet and meets the other man's eyes. "So?"

Bale opens his mouth, but then there's another knock at the door and Remember May come into the dressing room. The three of them look like kids who've just unwrapped their birthday presents to find geology textbooks.

Julia Stone's looking straight at Aldo. "Good set," she says, but the compliment comes out in a flat monotone, genuine as a mouldy chocolate coin.

"Thanks," Aldo says as Luce and Ross come over. "It was… a lot of fun."

Marcus is looking at Ross and shaking his head. "Dude," he says. "That was…"

"What the fuck was *that*?" Jim, the drummer, says, stepping forward, spreading his arms as if demanding an explanation.

"Woah, easy there, Jim," Rosemary soothes, laying a hand on the drummer's arm.

He shrugs Rosemary's hand off, levelling a finger at Aldo. "Listen mate, I don't know who the fuck yous think you are, but that… that wisnae cool."

"What's your problem?" Luce asks, taking a step toward.

"It's cool, Luce," Aldo says, standing and facing the angry mod. "What's your problem?"

Julia Stone speaks up. "It's just that this gig was a big one for us. We've been out on tour for so long, and it was supposed to be special, you know? Like a way to thank the fans that were there from the start."

"And?" Aldo prompts. He knows what she wants to say, but he knows that *she* knows how lame it'll sound to actually say it.

"And yous've fucked it up for us," Jim says through gritted teeth. He points through the wall. "Just fuckin *listen* to them. They're still going! Yous are the *support* band!"

A-LI-BI!

A-LI-BI!

"Listen, Jim," Aldo says, trying to keep the smile from his face. "This was a big gig for us as well. We've got a lot riding on this show, and I'm sorry if we stole your thunder." Then he stops himself, frowning. He looks to the side and sees Gappa Bale, standing against the wall by the door, seemingly oblivious to the confrontation as he examines his fingernails.

Aldo looks back at Remember May's drummer, sweeps his eyes over Julia and Marcus, and a surge of contempt rises in his throat. "In fact, no. *Fuck* that," he says to the three of them. "I'm not sorry. The day I apologise for playing a good show's the day I chuck music. You expect us to hold back because you think this gig's your personal arse kissing convention? Catch a grip of yourself, mate."

"Dude," Marcus says, "all we're saying is you didn't need to get the crowd so wound up. How are we supposed to follow that?"

Aldo laughs, shaking his head. "That's no our problem, Marcus. Yous are the ones with a deal with a major label. Go out and fuckin earn it."

From the corner of his eye, Aldo sees the sudden livid twist of Jim McElland's face. He hears Rosemary gasp, but before he can move, Ross is in front of him, seizing Jim's hand before it can even form a fist and bending his wrist backward. He forces the drummer backwards across the room, slamming him against the wall. Julia lets out a squeal of fright while Marcus watches in astonishment, eyes wide behind his thick lenses.

"Nope," Ross says icily, shaking his head as he holds the struggling drummer in place, one hand still on his awkwardly bent wrist, the other with a fistful of Jim's Fred Perry polo shirt. "Nope, nope, nope."

Joined by Luce, Aldo hurries over and lays a careful hand on Ross's chest. "Easy, big man," he says. Ross has got the deadlamps on, fixed on a suddenly chalky Jim, and there's a few tense seconds when Aldo half expects to see the skinny drummer get a serious doing, but Ross slowly releases him and steps away, never taking his eyes off him. Jim slides to the floor, and him bandmates rush over to him.

"What the *fuck*?" Julia Stone demands angrily, turning to Ross, her pretty face all running mascara and high pink spots on her cheeks. "You could've broken his wrist! As if you haven't fucked up this gig enough!"

"If I wanted his wrist broken, it'd be broken," Ross points out.

"I think the three of you need to get the fuck out of our dressing room," Aldo says. "What do you say, Rosemary?"

Rosemary Daniels is standing to the side, anxiously wringing her hands. "Aye," she says shakily. "Aye, I think that's best. Come on, guys." She goes to the dressing room door and holds it open. Remember May trudge out in sullen silence, Jim McElland gingerly rotating his wrist and giving Ross a black look over his shoulder as he leaves. Ross smiles and tips him a friendly salute as Rosemary shepherds her headline act safely from the room.

"Have a good show," Luce calls sweetly as the dressing room door swings closed. She turns to Aldo and Ross. "Fuckin arseholes." Then the three of them burst out laughing.

"Well, that was certainly exciting," a voice says behind them. Aldo turns and Bale's there. He'd forgotten the man was even in the room. He moves towards them like a stalking cat, then suddenly claps his hands together, once, with a crack like a gunshot.

"Let's talk," he says, grinning that perfect, toothy grin.

5

There's a crowd waiting for them when they exit the stage door.

The punters, Luce reckons at least three hundred or so of them, have swamped the pavement and the main road outside the Barras, bringing the late traffic on the Gallowgate to a standstill. The moment Bale opens the stage door, she winces in the sudden storm of camera phone flashes and the roar of voices and whistles as the crowd let loose a great cheer and surge forward, yelling and chanting.

AL-I-BI! AL-I-BI!

They're only held back by the crowd control barriers and the team of black clad bruisers manning them, big grim eyed lumps who Luce recognises as Bale's guys from the 13th Note gig. The punters nearest the band reach out their hands, begging to touch and be touched. Dumbstruck, and not a little unnerved by the unexpected reception, Luce stands there bewildered, looking out over the crowd, her heart pounding. There's a lot of guys in amongst the press of bodies looking directly at her, blowing kisses, holding their arms out to her, and all the while the camera phones *flash-flash-flash-flash.*

"Holy crap," Ross says beside her, staring at the press of jostling bodies with a bemused smile. He gives a little wave, and the crowd respond, cheering even louder. And beside him, Aldo, who looks to be in his element, is laughing as he waves and applauds the crowd. They're going fuckin bonkers, and Luce hears a stony scrape of metal on stone as the barriers separating them from the mob are pushed back by the weight of the throng. The security guys at the barrier have to link arms like riot police to hold back the human tide pressing up against them.

Bale steps forward, nodding in approval. He snaps his fingers and one of the security team hands him a megaphone, then he holds his arms up in the air for calm, and the crowd eventually settles down.

"Thank you all very much," he says, his amplified voice cracking out over the crowd. "Thank you for being part of this very special night. We will be holding an after show party later this evening, and you are all invited."

The crowd erupts again at the announcement, and Bale lets them go for several seconds before raising the megaphone to his lips again. "Tickets for the party are available from the box office here. Once again, thank you all for coming, and one more time, raise your voices for *PUBLIC ALIBI!*"

The crowd roar their acclaim, and the chant goes up again, each syllable punctuated by hundreds of fists punching the air.

A-LI-BI!

A-LI-BI!

Then Bale's leading them away from the stage door, hustling them along the pavement past the crowd pressed against the barriers. Luce high fives a few of them as she passes, laughing and smiling, caught up in the fevered excitement of the mob. Then someone seizes her wrist as she passes. Luce catches a glimpse of him, a lanky young man with cropped hair and mad eyes. He pulls Luce toward him and she finds herself enveloped by the crowd. Suddenly there's hands all over her, patting, hugging, caressing, touching her hair and face and body, thrusting mobiles in her face, snapping pictures. She tries to laugh it off at first, even managing to smile for a few selfies and thanking the crowd, but when she tries to pull away they won't let her go. As she struggles against the mob's greedy, clutching hands, fear rises up in her. But there's too many, and she's going "please, don't, please, no, let me go, let me *go*," but the hands grab at her, demanding and aggressive, clutching at her clothing and body. The sense of suffocation and claustrophobia's all too familiar, and Luce's suddenly right back in the dead congregation in the chapel. She feels a scream build as her fear quickly escalates towards panic. The hands continue to clutch and paw, one sliding into her top, groping at her breasts, then she hears the fabric ripping and the bottom drops out of her stomach as she feels herself being lifted up and over the barrier...

"*Let. Her. Go.*"

The words cut through the raucous bedlam of the crowd like a sword. Instantly, Luce feels the crowd release her, and she falls back to the pavement, scrambling to her feet and stumbling away, safely out of the mob's reach. She looks round and Gappa Bale's standing before the crowd. The mob quickly back away from him as if faced by a squad of eager, baton wielding riot cops, then Bale's putting his jacket and a protective arm around her, supporting her and helping her along the pavement into his waiting car, where Ross and Aldo are already sitting in the back, drinks in hand, toasting their success and completely oblivious to what's just happened.

Then Ross sees Luce's face and her ripped top as she climbs in with them. "Woah, Luce! What happened?"

It's Bale who answers him. "A few of the fans got a little... over excited," he says. "It is quite alright, however. No harm done."

"Fuck, Luce, you okay?" Aldo asks her. She just nods, covering her ripped top with Bale's jacket, still too shaky, too scared, to speak. That feeling of utter helplessness as the fevered arms of the crowd had hoisted her over the barricade, she'd never felt anything like it, and never wanted to again. They could have torn her apart, and there would have been absolutely nothing she could have done about it.

"Call it an occupational hazard," Bale says as the car moves off. "One that you may have to get used to. You especially, Lucia."

"Don't call me that," Luce mutters, looking out the tinted car window as they speed away through the streets of Glasgow's east end. "It's Luce."

"Of course," Bale continues without missing a beat, his voice soft, lulling. "Your talent, and your beauty, gives rise to great passions in those who would follow you. To some, at moments of excitement, the baser instincts can come to the fore, and the borders of adoration can easily blur into violent realms of possession."

Luce feels her heart gradually slowing, her breath coming a little easier. Bale's voice, so smooth and easy on the ear, calms her.

"Artists like you, like all of you, are special because you remain in touch with that state of grace that all humans are born with, but most lose with the passing of years. That state of grace, that light that shines from you, it inspires others, who feel it in the goosebumps that rise on their skin when they hear a piece of music. The dilation of their pupils when they see a painting that touches their soul. The quickening of their hearts when they read a book and feel that the author is speaking directly to them. For those with a *darkness* in their true self, that feeling of having discovered something special in another human can all too easily distort into something... unsavoury. You have heard the term 'kill your idols' I am sure. As they say, it is a fine line between love and hate, and tonight, some two thousand people fell in love with all three of you."

"Yes," Luce says, still nodding slowly. It all made so much sense. She could listen to this guy talk for ever. His voice, his smile, his kind eyes were making the memory of the terrible, crushing feeling of helplessness fade. And he'd saved her from the crowd.

"Well, there wasn't much love in the room from the headliners," Aldo says. "I don't think we'll be supporting Remember May again."

"No, you will not," Bale agrees. "That same sensitivity so common in the artistic soul has many facets, and for some, such creativity goes hand in hoof with a deep desire for acclaim. To be held up to the light. Tonight, you stole that light from Remember May. You outshone them, and for that, they resent you."

"Boo-fuckin-hoo," Ross says. "I'm all broken up inside."

Bale grins over at him. "Are you familiar with the term 'cutting heads'?" he asks.

"It's a blues thing, right?" Ross says. "Like a showdown?"

"Correct. In the early days of the blues and rock and roll, when a musician or band upstaged another, it was said that they 'cut the heads' of the lesser talent. That, my friends, is what you did tonight."

"Cuttin heads," Aldo says thoughtfully, nodding to himself. "Good album title."

"Yes," Bale agrees, his big toothy smile expanding. "Yes, it most certainly is."

6

Julia Stone, Marcus Tatum and Jim McElland trudge despondently off the tour bus idling in front of the Glasgow Hilton, then watch silently as the doors hiss closed and the big coach pulls away into the night.

Julia has tears in her eyes, and the guitar case in her hand feels like it's full of broken bricks. She turns to her two bandmates, but Marcus is staring fixedly at the ground, and Jim's already walking away, angrily pushing through the doors into the hotel lobby. "Jim..." she calls after him, wanting to say something.

"I need a fuckin drink," he snaps without looking back at her.

"C'mon, Jules," Marcus says softly, putting a hand on her shoulder. "A drink's probably a good idea."

Julia wipes her eyes. "Aye," she mumbles, and follows her bass player into the hotel.

She doesn't understand. Tonight was supposed to be special. The climax of the tour, and everything had been in place to make it magical. After years of struggling through crappy gigs, desperate poverty, dodgy managers, unscrupulous promoters and endless rehearsals, they'd made it. Coming off the back of a very well received tour and debut record, the Barras sold out, the contract with Sony signed and an album's worth of new material written and ready for the studio. Everything had been going so *well*.

Then... tonight.

Shortly after the ugly episode in Public Alibi's dressing room, which Julia now felt ashamed about, they'd gone on stage to the sound of half-hearted applause from a half-empty room. She learned later from their manager that a large portion of the crowd had gathered outside the building to greet Public Alibi as they were leaving the building, and had then fucked off to their after-party.

Remember May's big homecoming show had gone rapidly downhill from there.

Her confidence badly dented, Julia had struggled through their set. Her guitar, which had never let her down before, kept going out of tune. Her vocals were off. She fluffed lyrics. Forgot chord progressions she'd played a thousand times before. And it seemed the sudden and complete loss of her mojo was infectious, because she heard mistakes creeping into Marcus and Jim's performance as well. Missed notes. An unsteady tempo. Her normally dependable rhythm section badly out of synch with each other. To cap it all off, the sound on stage – which had sounded incredible for Public Alibi - had been all over the place. Her mic randomly whined feedback. The monitors kept cutting out. And worst of all, her pedal board had decided this was a perfect night to start acting the cunt, for no reason changing tones and effects midway through songs.

She'd been close to tears on stage when she saw more of the already sparse audience heading for the exits. When the dwindling few that remained had started to boo and throw stuff onto the stage, Julia had felt something *crack* deep inside her. When some disgruntled punter's Adidas Samba struck her on the forehead, that same something – which Julia thought was probably her heart – shattered and fell in a thousand pieces. It'd been a mercy when the power on stage failed altogether, and they'd been forced to abandon the show, walking off the stage to the sound of jeers and ridicule.

Afterwards, sitting in their dressing room and deeply depressed, Julia had heard the crowd on the street outside, chanting for the support band. Then Remember May's manager, accompanied by an unsmiling executive from Sony, had come barging in and tore strips off them.

Ranting about how this was going to come out in the press, and Julia knew he was right. As much as the music rags adored you when you were on the up and up, they adored nothing better than tearing you down again given half the chance. The Sony man - some slimy wee prick who looked like he was barely out of high school and who'd probably never been in a band in his life - had said little, but had made vague references to 'renegotiating' their contract. He hinted, using deeply accented legalese, that a record deal was by no means iron clad, especially when the ink on it was barely dry. The more he used the word 'renegotiate' the more Julia Stone had heard 'cancel'.

They catch up with Jim in the Hilton's polished marble reception area, deserted at this hour but for the pretty female receptionist, who smiles and wishes them a pleasant night as they pass by. Julia suppresses an urge to start screaming at her, but reins it in, thinking she's made enough of an arse of herself for one night.

She's completely embarrassed by the way they'd acted toward the guys in Public Alibi. She'd contact them and apologise tomorrow. They'd seemed nice, and by *fuck*, could they play. Julia can't remember ever having seen a live performance like that in her life. It'd been... mesmerising. Genuinely frightening in its intensity and the level of musicianship. Small wonder she, Jim and Marcus had felt threatened, but still, it was no excuse.

They stop in front of the elevator doors and Jim jabs the call button. "I swear to fuck, I'm going to drink the bar dry," he mutters.

"Aye," Marcus agrees glumly as the lift arrives with a soft chime and they step inside. "Sony's reserved it and they're picking up the tab. Might as well get what we can out of them while we've still got a contract."

Julia reaches for the lift's touchscreen control panel and presses the icon for the Sky Bar on the twentieth floor. As the lift starts to ascend, she wants to tell Jim and Marcus that it'll be alright. That they'll get a lawyer if the label try to cancel their deal. She wants to say it's just a glitch. A bump in the road. But the words disintegrate on her tongue. Tonight's complete clusterfuck of a show felt very much like fate telling them in no uncertain terms that their fifteen minutes of fame are well and truly up. Fair enough, it happens to just about every band, she tries to reason. Except *their* implosion had literally come out of nowhere, and this what she can't understand.

She's thinking about the future, feeling dread seep through her bones at the thought of going back to work at the nursery where she'd been a childminder, when there's a loud metallic grinding noise from above, and the lift shudders to a halt.

"Oh, perfect," Marcus says, pinching the bridge of his nose. "Just fuckin *grand*!"

Jim starts slapping angrily at the lift's control panel. "C'mon, ya cunt…"

The elevator doesn't respond, and when Julia lifts the phone on the wall marked Assistance, there's nothing. No dial tone, not even static.

Then the overhead light flickers and dies, immersing them in near perfect blackness. The only light comes the glowing red numerals above the lift's doors, which shows they've stopped on the thirteenth floor.

Acutely aware that they're now in a metal box suspended over a thirteen storey drop, Julia's heart quickens. Beside her, Jim continues cursing and slapping fruitlessly at the dead control panel.

"It's alright," Julia says, trying to keep the tremor from her voice and trying not to think about the dark elevator shaft yawning beneath them. "This is the Hilton. They must have a whole team of guys to sort this kind of thing. Someone'll get this moving in a minute." She tries the Assistance phone again, but it's just lifeless plastic in her hand.

A huge rending crash suddenly slams through the pitch black elevator, causing the three of them cry out a discordant three part harmony of fright. Then, from above, comes a frantic scrabbling scraping sound. Julia's skin seems to freeze over. For some reason, she has a vivid mental image of something like a huge black rat in the darkness of the elevator shaft, clawing and gnawing at the roof, trying to get in.

"Ohhhhh, Jesus," Marcus moans in the darkness. "What the fuck is that?"

Julia can hear Jim on her left, still angrily trying to punch life into the unresponsive control panel as his voice rises in jagged spikes. "C'mon, c'mon, *c'mon...*"

"It's okay, it's okay," Julia says, her voice breathless and shaky. "It's... it's just the engineer, it's just the engineer guy..."

But she doesn't believe that for a second, because she's aware of how cold it's suddenly become in the lift, aware of the strange, sick pressure building in her head. The blackness around her feels like it's closing in, squeezing her...

Julia finds herself whispering rapid Hail Marys, which she hasn't done in years, because that maddening scraping and scratching and *chewing* is getting louder, more frantic, and she's absolutely sure it's the sound of something trying to gnaw its way into the elevator to *get* them, and she's so scared she plugs her ears with her fingers and fixes her eyes on the only light available which is the number thirteen glowing in red above the elevator doors... but... hotels don't *have* a thirteenth floor, do they?

Julia has the oddest sense of *expansion,* as if the elevator's abruptly winked out of existence and time and space have warped out of true, and she feels certain that she's not in a broken down elevator the Hilton anymore, that she's in some lightless alien place where there are no rules and no reason, and in this blackness, which feels as vast and empty as the spaces between stars, she can hear Marcus shrieking hysterically, and Jim's angry curses have turned to wordless, gulping sobs of terror. And she knows they're not in the elevator anymore, because her bandmates shrieks sound far far away.

Then Julia starts screaming herself, because that frenzied gnawing sound's stopped and given way to the hideous rasping breath of a beast which she feels on the back of her neck, and there's the hot stink of carrion enveloping her, and she knows, knows with more surety than she's ever known anything in her whole life, that something's right *there* in the black with them, some nameless, ancient presence that's cold and evil and pitiless and very *very* hungry.

Chorus

There were a lot of weird things that happened within Sabbath that we couldn't explain. It might have been the drugs, but I don't think so.

Tony Iommi

1

Alan Michael Evans wakes up and finds himself in a world of hurt.

First thing he's aware of is the headache. His eyes still closed, he can actually see it, pulsing in time with his laboured heartbeat in sick red strobes across the backs of his eyelids. The pain squeezes his temples, threatening to squirt brain matter from his ears. If only it would. Anything to relieve the pressure.

As his senses slowly come alive in reluctant, frightened stages, he feels the gurgling sickness in his guts, which ache with the pain of strained muscles, presumably pulled in the action of an almighty spew. That makes sense, because he can still recognise stale vomit amid the foul concoction of tastes in his mouth, alongside the memory of a thousand cigs and a bath of Jack n Coke. When he breathes in, the inhaled cocktail of death on his tongue makes him gag. When he breathes out again, he winces, feeling the scorched rawness of his nostrils. He has a hazy memory of himself and Ross getting in amongst a power of chicco at some point last night. Chicco served by a smiling stunner with long black hair, a short black dress and centrefold legs, the cocaine nostril-ready, served with a slim silver tube, chopped and drawn into generously chubby lines and arranged on an oval mirror with a wooden frame carved in the shape of a lizard. One of the few details he has of the after-party.

He opens his eyes, very slowly, with bomb-disposal caution, and sees an ants-eye view of the living/sleeping area of his bedsit. From his prone position on the floor, one cheek pressed into the jaggy fibres of the cheap beige carpet, he can see the scuffed legs of the coffee table, the bottom half of the small tv cabinet with the wonky drawer in the corner across the room, and a shamefully unhoovered section of the floor beneath the sofabed, which he'd evidently failed to navigate himself into whenever it was he'd got home. Among the dustballs and hair, he sees one of Dylan's toys. A yellow plastic Minion figure in dungarees and goggles that yells 'banana!' when shaken. He remembers Dylan's smile when he found the toy in his Happy Meal box during one of their Saturdays together a month or two ago.

He pushes himself into a sitting position, unsurprised to find that he's still fully clothed, and sits holding his precariously fragile skull together for a moment, his hair hanging in his face, waiting for the room and his guts to stop spinning. When they do, Aldo drags himself to his feet, stumbles into the bathroom, bouncing like a pinball off walls and doorframes as she goes, and throws up into the toilet.

A few minutes later, feeling only marginally better, he shuffles into the cupboard sized kitchenette area and fills an unwashed mug with water from the tap. Holding onto the chipped formica counter for dear life, he sips the tepid, iron-tanged tapwater carefully, mindful of his perilously sensitive stomach. Unwilling to move his head too much, he gropes blindly in the crooked wall-mounted kitchen cupboard to his right and finds a few paracetamol capsules, which he swallows with another mugful of council brand water. Then, moving with slow and careful movements, he manages to make a cup of coffee. Black, and loaded with enough sugar to frighten Willy Wonka.

Slumped on the sofabed in the living area, Aldo sits with his eyes closed, head waltzing, skin ill-fitting and his hair sore, trying to piece together his fractured recollections of events after their gig at the Barras. It's not easy. His head feels like a ripped bin bag full of glass shards.

He remembers the big crowd in the street going mental, then being in Gappa Bale's car with Ross, Luce and Bale himself. They'd been laughing and talking, drinking from the big motor's seemingly bottomless minibar and buzzed up to fuck with adrenaline. He remembers

Luce being quiet at first - that's right, some bams in the crowd had got a bit grabby with her – but she'd loosened up after a few drinks and a joint of Ross's home grown.

He'd had a bit to drink in the car, but remembers they'd driven for what seemed like ages, eventually stopping outside a big three-storey house in the country somewhere outside the city. There'd been a crowd of punters waiting for them there too, not as big as the one outside the Barras, but still a fair number, and Aldo remembers the three of them being escorted inside by more of Bale's big black-clad security guys, high fiving the cheering mob flanking the path to the big house as they went inside.

Then it all got a bit hazy.

It must've been some nightclub they were in, because he remembers big high-ceilinged, low-lit rooms full of multi-coloured lights, strobes, dry ice, people and really loud music. A lot of really good music, including their own demo, which he now recalls hearing being played several times, and with each play, there'd been people cheering and dancing. He remembers a lot of smiling folks coming up to him, hugging him, shaking his hand, patting his back, saying how amazing the band were. Handing him drinks. Someone had given him a pill... Then he was sitting with Ross and the leggy black-haired beauty doing lines of coke off that snake framed mirror. Then...

Aldo's eyes open and a smile spreads across his face as he remembers something else about the girl in the black dress. His dick remembers it too, and he feels a warm swelling down below as he recalls the feel of her tongue in his mouth, then how she'd slid off the couch and knelt in front of him, her hands hungrily undoing his jeans, and then her head bobbing up and down in his lap...

Holy shit!

Then, sometime uncertain amount of time later, he half remembers being with Ross and Luce in another room, a quieter room. Circular, its curved walls covered floor to ceiling in bookshelves. Gappa Bale had been there, sitting at a desk with documents on it...

Aldo lurches up from the sofabed as if from an ejector seat and stands there, gulping air, trying to remember more about that one fragment, but it dances away from his mind.

Oh fuck, oh shit, oh Jesus H Christ on a pogo stick, did we sign?

He can't remember.

A sudden loud burst of guitar riffage makes Aldo let out an involuntary yelp. Then he recognises the opening lick to Monster Magnet's *Slut Machine* and realises it's his mobile ringing. In a state of high excitement bordering on panic, he slaps clumsily at his pockets, but his phone's not there, and he starts stumbling around the room, bumping into things like he's still blitzed, throwing cushions hither and yon and scattering music magazines as he hunts for his elusive mobile. He manages to stop ransacking the bedsit long enough to pause and take a few deep breaths, his frantic mind belatedly realising he should just follow the noise of the ringing phone instead of trashing his crumby abode. He tracks the badass swinging, compound timed riff into the hall and then into the kitchen, looking around in bewilderment till he zeroes in on the toaster.

What the fuck is my phone doing in the toaster?

Apparently, reasoning like only the cataclysmically wasted can, he put it there for safekeeping last night, and when he manages to pry it out, Aldo sees Luce's contact picture on the screen, showing her sat behind her kit sneering a Johnny Rotten sneer and holding her sticks behind her head like antennae.

"Luce! Did we sign?" he blurts into the mobile. "Did we sign last night?"

"Well hello to you too. Dude, I'm feelin *rough*."

"Luce, c'mon. Did we sign with Easy Rollin last night?"

"I was about to ask you. I don't remember much after we got to the party. Are you at home?"

"Aye, but fuck knows how. Woke up on the living room floor still in all my gear. Where are you?"

"In the house. Don't remember getting back either."

"Have you spoke to Ross?"

"Nope. Just woke up. Dude, I'm feeling *so* bad. Have you checked your phone?"

"Ehhh, no. Was in the toaster."

"Uh? You were in your toaster?"

"What? No. My phone was."

"Ah. Right. That makes... slightly more sense. Anyway, check it. There's nothing on mine, but see if you've got any missed calls or messages or anything. What time is it anyway?"

Aldo hadn't even looked at his watch since waking on the floor. He does so now. "Fuck. Nearly half two."

"Oh, bollocks. Was supposed to go to my mum and dad's house for lunch this afternoon."

"You'll be popular."

"Aye. Anyway. Check your phone. Think I'll go hurl."

"Way ahead of you. Speak to you later."

Aldo ends the call and hesitates as he regards his mobile with a certain amount of dread. There might be something on there that helps him fill in the blanks from last night. Something that confirms they're now a signed act with a recording contract. A picture, or post on the band's Facebook page.

Then again there could well be something - possibly several somethings - hideously embarrassing and regretful. Wouldn't be the first time he's found cringeworthy evidence of forgotten drunken shenanigans on the mobile. With a trembling finger, he checks his notifications.

Nothing. No missed calls or text messages. Thankfully no ill-advised texts or phone calls to Ashley either, which he's done in the past, with nothing good coming of it. He breathes a sigh of relief, thankful that he's at least not made an arse of himself whilst wellied.

When he checks the band's Facebook page, however, he lets out a short coughing bark of combined laughter and shock. The band's page notifies him they almost three thousand new likes and several messages posted on the timeline from the new followers saying how great the gig was and how awesome the band are. They've also been tagged in countless photos and videos from last night. Trembling now, Aldo brings up his phone's Youtube app and types the band's name in the search bar.

Holy crap. We've gone viral.

At least a hundred videos of the Barras gig, the titles proclaiming PUBLIC ALIBI – BARRAS - BEST GIG EVER, and AMAZING NEW BAND and NEW FAVOURITE BAND, and YOU. MUST. HEAR. THIS.

His heart slamming now, Aldo stumbles in a daze the five steps it takes him to travel from the kitchen to the living room, and slumps down on the couch again. He flicks though the Youtube videos. The sound quality on them isn't great, the pictures are shaky and go in and out of focus, but he has a strange, almost out of body experience as he watches the clips of himself, Ross and Luce on the Barras main stage. He'd known at the time that they'd played a good set, a *damn* good set, but seeing it now is... unnerving.

Is that really us?

His phone rings again, number withheld, and Aldo hits the green icon to accept the call.

"Hell*ugh*?" he squeaks. He clears his throat and tries again. "Hello?"

"Good morning, Aldo," Gappa Bale says. "How are you feeling?"

"Mr Bale..."

"Gappa."

"Right, aye, Gappa. I'm... Christ I don't know. Feeling pretty rough. Was just checking the band's Facebook page, we've got..."

"Two thousand, seven hundred and forty-six new likes. Each and every one well deserved. I was just calling to make sure you were okay. You were... rather the worse for wear when you left the after party. Totally understandable, of course."

"Mr Ba... Gappa, what happened last night? I don't remember much after arriving at the party. Don't even know how I got home. Did we... I mean... are we..."

"One of my staff drove you home. I will send you an email now that may dispel some of the rest of your confusion. We will speak later. Drink some more water. We have much to do. Goodbye."

He hangs up, and Aldo can only stare at his phone, his brittle mind fizzing with a million questions and his muscles quivering with nervous energy. Then a polite beep informs him he's received a new email. He opens it.

The sender is displayed as Easy Rollin Records. The message is short, and has a picture attachment.

Congratulations. We begin recording sessions tomorrow, and will be ensconced in the studio for a minimum of two weeks. Pack what you need. A car will pick you up at nine pm this evening.
Warmest,
Gappa Bale.

P.S. Check your bank account.

Aldo opens the attached photo, and sees himself leaning over the big dark wood desk in that circular room he only partially remembers from last night. He's smiling, and has tears on his cheeks as he signs his name at the bottom of a text heavy document. In the background, Luce and Ross are hugging, and Gappa Bale is holding a bottle of champagne and three glasses.

Unable to breathe, not sure if he's about to pass out or throw up, or both, Aldo then taps the icon for his mobile baking app.

There's a deposit in the amount of £27,000, received at 12:03 that morning, courtesy of Easy Rollin Records.

2

In the admin wing of the Inverclyde Royal Hospital, Ross McArthur closes the door to the HR office behind him and stands for a moment in the corridor outside, leaning against the wall, his eyes closed.

He's still feeling the effects of last night's indulgences, but the phone call from Aldo earlier and the conversation, such as it was, that followed, had gone a long way to making him feel better. The news that you've signed a record deal and suddenly have a bank account twenty-seven grand to the better can do that, and a fuckload more effectively than two paracetamol, a bottle of Irn Bru and a crispy bacon and totty scone roll.

Roused by his mobile ringing, he'd woken up fully clothed, for some reason lying in his bathtub, a pillow under his head and his bass in his arms. In a state of profound confusion and generally feeling like a burst ball, he'd answered the phone to the sound of Aldo alternating between weeping and pishing himself laughing.

It'd taken Ross a while to get any sense out of his mate.

Now, having just handed in his letter of resignation, Ross makes his way from the hospital admin wing to the porter's station to say cheerio to the lads in there. Big Russell, the head porter who'd been Ross's immediate boss for the last five years, says he's sorry to see him go, but of course understands his decision and wishes him well. *Shag a groupie for me*, he says. Ross says he'll do his best.

He stops by the staff canteen to make his farewells to the ladies in there. Wee Mags, the five-foot-two grey-haired harridan who runs the canteen with an iron fist, smiles a rare smile and hugs him tightly before resuming character and sternly ordering Ross to make sure he eats right and stays away from drugs. He says he'll do his best.

At the A&E desk, he bids adieu to the lassies in reception. Linda squeals in excitement at his news and insists on him signing an autograph, before becoming dewy-eyed and saying she'll miss him. *Who'll deal with all the bams?* she asks. Ross promises that once he's made his first million, he'll hire ruthless professionals to track down and severely punish any upstart that comes into casualty and starts shit in his absence.

He goes round a few more wards and departments, stopping at nurses' stations and doctors' offices to say goodbye to those he's worked with. Everyone wishes him all the best, hugging him and shaking his hand, and asks him not to forget them when he's a big time rock star. He says he'll do his best.

He was happy enough in the porter job, and knows he'll miss the place. Ferrying patients around the hospital, chatting away to them, doing what he can to help keep their chins up, and of course dealing with the odd disruptive patient, was a nice enough way to earn a living. He'd never call himself a champion of the downtrodden or anything so dramatic, but the job let him help those who needed it, at least in some small way. Ross McArthur believes in paying your debts and doing whatever you can to make the world a slightly less ugly place. He'd known ugliness from a young age, and it'd been a constant companion for much of his youth. Only three years old at the time, he didn't remember the car crash that had killed his parents. He'd been in his child seat in the back, pulled from the wreckage without a scratch. The M8 Miracle, the media had called it. He'd gone to the library and found the story in the newspaper archives when he was a teenager.

The first real stability of his life hadn't happened till he was taken in by Gregor Picken when he was thirteen, and it was that stability, that kindness, that he tried to repay in some small way every day he worked at the hospital. Aye, he'd miss the job a bit, but against twenty-seven grand in the bank and the freedom to be a full time musician…

With one more stop to make before going home and packing for the studio, Ross takes the lift up to H ward to say goodbye to Duncy Brown, but in his room, he finds the old soldier's bed occupied by an elderly lady in a pink flannel dressing gown reading a *Hello* magazine.

Back out in the corridor, he goes over to the nurses' station and finds Raj Luthra, Duncy's doctor. Raj is brand new. Plays five-a-sides on a Sunday night with Ross and a few of the other boys from the hospital. Got some left foot on him. The young Indian consultant's sat in an office chair behind the counter, tapping a pen thoughtfully against his teeth and frowning at something on a computer monitor.

"Alright there, Raj," Ross greets him.

"Ross! How are you?" Raj says looking up. "Working today?"

"Not this soldier. Came in to hand in my notice."

"Really? You're leaving us?"

"Aye, fraid so. The band just got signed to a record company. We're going into the studio tonight to record an album. It's madness." No matter how many times he's told people that this morning, it still sounds unreal.

Raj smiles and stands up to shake his hand. "That's brilliant, mate. Congratulations. We'll be a man down at fives, though. Inconsiderate of you."

"Sorry, Raj. It's the minstrel's life for me. I'm sure you'll get someone better for fives."

"Well, it wouldn't be hard. You're shite at football."

Ross laughs. He can't argue though. Playing fives was always more about the fitness than the skill for him, and he really was pretty terrible.

"I was looking for Duncan Brown to say cheerio before I left. Has he been discharged?"

Raj's broad smile falters and he makes a small, pained expression. "Mr Brown was moved down to the ICU. He suffered a heart attack last night." He shakes his head. "I'm afraid he doesn't have long left."

His senses and reactions dulled by his hangover, that takes a second or two to kick in, but when it does, the happy dazed bubble Ross has been floating around in all afternoon abruptly pops. "A heart attack." he repeats stupidly, feeling like he's just been sucker punched. "But he was... he was..."

He was what? Too tough to have a coronary? To vital and full of life? Duncy Brown was ninety-three years old, and had cheated death more times in his life than any man had a right to.

"I'm sorry," Raj says. "I know you were friendly with him. He liked you, too."

"Aye," Ross says, unable to meet Raj's eyes, his voice strained by his tightening throat and the empty plunging feeling in his stomach. "Can I see him?"

Raj nods. "I'll phone down and let them know you're coming."

"Thanks, mate," Ross says, turning away from the desk. "I'll see you later, Raj. All the best."

"And to you, Ross."

Brittle-legged, he walks out of H ward to the lifts and presses the call button.

Get a grip.

It's not the first time a patient he'd got to know had checked out. Working in a hospital, it was part of the job. In the past five years, hearing about the passing of other patients he'd got to know a little had saddened him, course it had, but he'd always understood and accepted that Death had a residence in every hospital in the world.

With Duncy, it's different. Ross is wounded by the news. Maybe because the old battle-scarred soldier had only been in for a routine operation and was otherwise in rude health. Maybe because despite his age, he'd seemed fuckin indestructible, especially when you heard about the things he'd seen and done in his life.

And that was it, wasn't it? He'd got to *know* Duncy. Had gone out of his way to visit the old boy every day he was working.

He should've known better.

He quickly clamps his mind shut on the thought. He's not going there. Not again.

The lift doors open on the floor for the ICU ward, and Ross makes his way over to the nurses' station. Lorrie Murray, the senior staff nurse, looks up as he approaches and offers a smile. In her fifties, the matronly Lorrie had an open, friendly face and compassionate eyes, the dyed bright copper of her meticulously permed hair a cheery counterpoint to the gloomy atmosphere of the ICU.

"He's in room three, Ross," she says quietly. "He's asleep just now, but you can go in and sit with him for a while if you want."

"Thanks, Lorrie."

He walks down the corridor past other rooms, his trainers squeaking on the vinyl floor, disturbing the hush of the ward. He passes a room on his right and sees through the partially open door a young woman sitting by a bedside. Silent tears on her cheeks as she holds the hand of the grey-haired man lying there, eyes closed, his face sunken and sallow around the life support mask covering the lower half of his face.

The cold sinking feeling that's been in Ross's guts since hearing about Duncy has seeped into his legs now, like he's walking on brittle stilts of rotten wood as he approaches room three. He imagines just turning and walking away. He's only getting closer. He could forget about Duncy, turn, and just *walk away*.

Ross opens the door to Duncy's room.

He stands at the foot of the bed for a moment, looking down on the old man lying there, the slight rise and fall of his chest the only indication that Ross isn't looking at a corpse.

For a moment, he tries to convince himself there's been a mistake, because that's not Duncy. It can't be. Not this broken, frail looking thing on the bed, all jutting bones and yellow parchment skin. This withered, near skeletal patient simply bears no resemblance to the aged but vital soldier with the dirty jokes, the Sid James cackle, the thousand-yard stare and the razor sharp mind full of piss and vinegar and war stories.

But there's the tattoo on his right forearm. The motto of the Black Watch. *Nemo me impune lacessit.* No one attacks me with impunity.

The coronary had, though. Had attacked with vicious impunity, and seems to have stripped the very flesh from Duncy. The husk-like form on the bed before Ross looks more like an advanced stage cancer patient. Emaciated and brittle. Again, he thinks there must have been a mistake somewhere, because heart attacks don't do *this* to a person. Not that he'd ever seen.

Ross sits down in the plastic chair next to the bed. He can see the whites of Duncy's eyes beneath half lowered lids, as if even the tiny ocular muscles had been robbed of the strength to close properly. His mouth is a dry black hole, hanging open, slack-jawed. His breath stuttering and erratic. Cheyne Stokes they call it. The name they gave to the failing respiration of a dying human. That horrible wheezing uncertainty. As if every breath could be the last.

It's a sound Ross knows. Three days Gregor had breathed like that.

Ross asks himself what he's doing here.

He thumbs salt water from the corners of his eyes and lets out a long shuddering breath. "How you doin, big yin?" he asks quietly. "I just came by to say cheerio. Just handed in my notice. The band… we got signed last night."

Duncy d esn't answer. He just lies there.

Unable to bear the grim silence of the room, broken only by Duncy's irregular breathing, Ross rambles on, just to fill the void. Just to deny the reality of what's happening in some small, pointless way.

"That guy I was telling you about, Gappa Bale, he signed us up to his label and gave us twenty-seven grand a piece as an advance. Can you believe that, Duncy? Took us out to this big mad country house in the middle of nowhere after the gig at the Barras. Mind how I was telling you about the Barras gig? Jesus, I wish you could have seen it. It was unreal."

Duncy doesn't answer. Just lies there. Gasping his last.

"Don't even remember much of the after party," Ross murmurs, staring off into the corner of the dim lit single room. "Fuckin woke up in the bathtub at home this afternoon, still in my gear and hugging my bass. Didn't even know we'd got signed till Aldo phoned me and woke me up. I'd like to have remembered it, you know? Signing the contract. We were so blitzed, though."

Duncy doesn't answer. Just lies there. Dying.

Ross tells himself to just face it. Duncy's for the off, but he decides he'll just sit here with him anyway. He glances at his watch. He's got an hour before the car picks him up at his flat to go to the studio. He should really be leaving the hospital about now if he's to get back in time. But it's not right. Duncy's got no one else. Someone should be here with him when he goes. But how long was that going to take? Was he going to risk not going to the studio just so he could sit here and watch Duncy die? But would Duncy have wanted him to do that? Or would he have told Ross to stop greetin like a wee lassie, get his arse in gear and get up the road?

Ross wipes his eyes again and leans in closer, laying a hand on Duncy's wasted forearm, the radius and ulna like two sticks beneath a cold sheet of tracing paper. "I wish I'd known you longer, Duncy, but I'm glad I knew you as long as I did." He stands up and brings his right hand to his hairline. "At ease, big man," he says. "I'll see you around."

His heart like a painfully clenched fist in his chest, Ross turns for the door.

"Moon... shadow."

Duncy's voice is barely a whisper.

Ross returns to his seat at the bedside and leans forward, taking Duncy's hand. "What'd you say, mate?"

Duncy doesn't answer.

"Moonshadow?" Ross prompts. "The Cat Stevens tune?" Surely that's not what he said?

"Wasn't... wasn't a cat he had," Duncy murmurs after a long moment. "Dugs. Big black... hounds." His eyes open, but he doesn't look at Ross. Just stares up at the ceiling.

"Is that right?" says Ross, wanting to keep Duncy talking. Keep him awake. Awake and alive. "Cat Stevens had dugs? Oh, the irony. I love that tune, though. *Moonshadow.*"

"Naw... naw, son," Duncy mutters, "there's nae love... no in him."

"Was he not a mad hippy?"

Duncy's head rolls slowly back and forth on the pillow. His breathing's a little more urgent. "That bastard... fuckin evil... bastard..."

Ross now suspects Duncy's not talking about Cat Stevens. "Who, Duncy?"

Now he turns his head towards Ross, and Ross goes cold. It's that thousand-yard stare of his. But more. A million miles. A hard million miles of bad road with corpses stacked in the embankments. "*Mertz*," Duncy hisses, his big bony hand like a pale tarantula suddenly clutching Ross's forearm. "The... *rapportfuhrer*... block nine... Stalaag..."

The concentration camp. The one where Duncy'd been held during the winter of 1944 before escaping.

"It's alright, Duncy," Ross says gently. "Just relax. Don't think about that."

Duncy goes back to staring at the ceiling, his eyes now fever bright with memory, an expression of deepest sorrow twisting across his wizened face. "The poor... those poor weans... he... he set the dugs on them... in the pits..."

"Shhhh. It's okay, Duncy."

"...made us watch... oh Christ... he's... he's no..."

"It's okay, big yin."

"...naw...naw... I saw him... saw him in the moonlight... one night... standin ootside the block..." Duncy turns his head on the pillow suddenly and stares at Ross. His bony hand clutches his sleeve urgently. "His moonshadow, son... wis... wisnae... wisnae a *man*."

It's just his failing mind. Malfunctioning synapses firing, conjuring random memories. The horrors of Stalaag, real and imagined, becoming twisted and confused. All the same, Ross feels a very real chill at Duncy's words and the torment in his eyes.

Then it seems the air just goes out of the old man, leaving him in a prolonged rattling sigh, and his death grip on Ross's arm relaxes. His head sinks back into the pillow and his eyes close again. "You've... you've a good soul, son," he whispers, so faintly Ross has to lean in close to hear him. "Don't... don't give..." His voice fails. His chest hitches once. Twice.

"Duncy?"

But Duncy Brown's at ease.

3

Cymbals, snare and stick bag. Check.

Clothes. Check.

Toiletries. Check.

Tablet and USB stick. Check.

Phone. Check.

Chargers for tablet and phone. Check.

Notation paper, writing pad and pens. One black, one blue, one red. Check.

Purse. Check.

In her flat, Luce sits on the couch and thoughtfully taps a pen against her front teeth as she looks at her packing checklist. Surely there's something she's forgotten? It would be a lot easier if she knew where they were going and for exactly how long, but the email Aldo'd received from Bale and then forwarded on to her had been vague at best. Two weeks in the studio at least. Pack what you need. Car arriving at nine pm sharp.

Organised and meticulous as she is, the lack of details bothers Luce, plus it doesn't help that she hasn't fully recovered from last night.

There must be something she's forgotten. There *must* be.

But there's not. She knows there's not, and Luce sighs, tossing the writing pad and pen onto the coffee table. Her means of procrastination finally exhausted, she picks up the phone and dials her parents' number, steeling herself for the conversation to come. Calling Luke

Carson, her boss and head of the music department at the college, had been easy. Just about all of the music faculty were or had been touring musicians and session players at some point, and lecturers quitting to go on the road or into the studio with a band was a common occurrence. Luke had simply congratulated her, wished her all the best, and said her job would be waiting for her if she needed it again.

Breaking the news about the record deal to her parents would be a more difficult conversation. She'd called them that afternoon, apologising for missing lunch and saying she wasn't feeling well, but hadn't said anything else. After speaking to Aldo again and finding out about the contract, the advance, and going into the studio, her head had been all over the place, simultaneously brutalised by her hangover and buzzing with excitement. She'd needed time to settle herself and get her mind at least partially straight before telling her folks. Now, with her watch showing the time as 8:45pm and the car picking her up in fifteen minutes, she can't put it off any longer.

After a few rings, it's her dad who picks up. "Hello?"

"Papa. *Sono io*," Luce says, switching to Italian, as tradition demanded for any family conversation.

"Lucia," her dad says. "are you feeling better?"

"Yeah, still feeling a little rough, but I'm okay. I've… I've got some pretty big news."

"Big news? Tell me. No, hold on. Let me put the phone on loudspeaker so your mother can hear."

Fuck. She'd hoped to make this as quick and painless as possible. There's a click on the line. "Itria! Lucia's on the phone! She says she has big news."

"What news?" her mum says in the background, raising her voice above the applause and rapid fire chatter of an Italian game show on her parents' TV. "Salvo, turn the volume down! Hello, Lucia. What is this news?"

"Hi, Mamma. Okay," Luce takes a deep breath. "You know my band?"

"Yes?" her mum says carefully, and Luce can just see her rolling her eyes in that infuriating way she does. "You have left it?" Itria asks, and at the hopeful note in her mum's voice Luce grips the phone a little tighter, gritting her teeth. This was why she never discussed the band with her parents. Not with her mum anyway.

"No, Mamma," she says evenly. "We signed a contract with a record company last night."

There's a few seconds of perfect silence. Then, "I don't understand. What do you mean?"

"I mean we signed a contract to make a record. We're going into the studio tonight."

"But what about your job?"

Here goes.

"I resigned, Mamma. The record company..."

"*You resigned?*" her mother repeats, clearly baffled. "What do you mean you resigned? How could you... how could you do something so *foolish*, Lucia?"

"Mamma..."

"How will you live? Did you even think about that?"

"The record company already paid me twenty-seven thousand pounds as an advance," Lucy explains patiently. "That's a lot more than I make at the college in a year. Then there'll be royalty payments, money from touring..."

"It's not about money, Lucia," Itria interrupts, even though *she'd* brought the subject up. Her voice is taking on a jagged edge which sounds like desperation. "This music business, it's no good for you. It never was."

"Itria, *calma*..." Luce hears her dad say, his voice weary, but Itria Figura will *not* calm down.

"No, Salvo! Our daughter is throwing her life away on a child's dream..."

"Mamma, *silencio!*" Luce shouts into the phone, her patience for her mother's disapproval run dry.

"No, I will *not* be quiet, Lucia, and do not talk to me that way. I am your mother." Luce hears her taking several deep breaths before going on, her voice calmer now. "When you took the music course at university, we supported you, even though we thought it a waste of time. When you didn't want to work in the restaurant, and took the job at the college instead, we supported you, even though we knew it was no real career. And now this." Her mother sighs heavily. "Always you use your music to avoid dealing with…"

"Dealing with what, Mamma?" Luce asks, her voice taking on a cold edge.

"You know what I mean," she says softly, her voice now regretful. "You turned away from God after…"

"No, Mamma. Don't.

"But it's the truth!"

"No."

"You were a different person. You…"

"No, Mamma. I don't want to talk about that."

"…would not speak. You locked yourself in your room for days…"

"Mamma, *please*…"

"…playing your drums, and we let you do it, if that's what you thought you needed to help you…"

"Mamma…" Luce tastes salt water on her lips, and realises she's crying.

"…but only Christ can help you, Lucia. This music business, it will only cause you pain." She's pleading now. "Please, listen to me. I'm only trying to protect you, because I love you more than anything in the world. No good will come of this. They'll use you like a whore and throw you aside. But God will *always* be there…"

"*God can go and take a flying fuck to himself!*" Luce yells into the phone, her voice choked and bitter. "Where the fuck was *God* when Karen…" Rage clogs her mouth like a glob of black bile and she can say no more.

On the phone, her mum is at last silent, shocked speechless at Luce's language and blasphemy, and in the empty quiet, in her mind Luce sees a pretty thirteen-year-old girl lying on the raggedy red aisle carpet of St Michael's, her body half in and half out of the confessional booth.

On the other end of the line, there's the hard flat sound of the living room door slamming in her parent's house, then a click on the line as the speakerphone's disengaged. "Ah, Lucia." Her dad.

"Papa, I'm sorry," Luce says, wiping her eyes, "but she just... she's..."

"I know, *mi amore*. I know. But she cares for you and only wants what's best. We both do."

"This *is* what's best for me, don't you understand?"

Her dad's silent for a few moments, then he sighs deeply. "You're a grown woman, Lucia, and you know your own mind. You're also as stubborn as a mule. You get that from your grandmother. You know, when Etna destroyed our village, your uncle Corrado and I had to drag her from our house? Even with the lava coming into our back garden she refused to leave. Stubborn as a mule."

Luce smiles and manages a wet, snottery laugh. Her dad had told her the story many times. The destruction of Pollina, the tiny village on the slopes of Mount Etna where he'd grown up, had been the event that saw him move to Scotland as a young man with a single suitcase, his new bride in tow, and a dream of building a restaurant.

Her dad sighs again. "Tell me truthfully, Lucia. Are you happy? Do you truly believe this is a good thing for you?"

"Yes, Papa. I do."

"Hmm. I can't say I approve. I always saw you taking over the restaurant one day. Running the business when we're gone and passing it on to your children."

"I know, Papa. But it's not me. The band, making a record... *That's* my dream. Just like the restaurant was yours."

"Ah, wicked child. You're turning my own philosophy against me." Her dad's quiet for a moment. "Promise me you'll be safe, and promise me that the moment you are not enjoying what you're doing, you'll come home."

"I promise."

"I hope so. I don't want to see you on the news like those poor souls last night."

Luce frowns. "What do you mean?"

"Have you not seen the papers today? Have you not watched television?"

"No, I've been busy all day getting ready for the studio." Between getting the call from Aldo telling her about their deal, digesting the news, calling the college to resign, packing for the studio and fretting about speaking to her folks, Luce's mind had been occupied all day. She hadn't turned on the TV, looked at a newspaper, or even turned on her laptop. Martians could have landed in Glasgow Green and she wouldn't have known about it.

"At the Hilton in Glasgow last night," her dad says. "A band who were staying at the hotel were killed. Murdered. You haven't heard?"

"No," Luce says, a little twist tightening her stomach. "What happened? What band?"

"Ah, a terrible thing," her dad says. "There were three of them, like your group. What was their name? I can't remember... Ah, yes. Remember May. That's it. A terrible thing, Lucia. Truly terrible. It was a crazy fan, the police think. You really haven't heard about it? Lucia? Are you there?"

"Erm... no," Luce hears herself say. "I mean yes, but no, I hadn't heard."

"Lucia? Are you alright?"

"I'm... I'm fine, papa."

Julia. Marcus. Jim.

"I've got to... I've got to go."

"What's wrong, *mi amore?*" her dad asks. "Did you know this band?"

Because she never discussed the band with her parents, she hadn't told them anything about Gappa Bale, or about playing at the Barras with Remember May last night. Now certainly wasn't the time, though.

"I'm okay," Luce says. "Just still not feeling so great. I... I need to go, Papa. Tell Mamma I'm sorry, okay? I'll call you later."

"*Va bene,*" her dad says. "Be safe. I love you."

"I love you too. Ciao, Papa."

"Ciao."

Her dad hangs up and Luce puts the phone on her coffee table. She sits very still on the couch for a minute, trying to process what her dad's just told her. Then she picks her mobile up again and hits the Google icon. A soft beep prompts her to speak.

"Remember May Hilton," she says in a shaky voice.

A moment later, the voice activated search engine fills the phone's screen with a list of news items. Luce taps the link at the top of the page and reads the story on the BBC news website, her eyes widening as they move over the text. Certain words stick out, flashing in her head in flickering red neon as bright as the Barra's marquee, lodging in her brain like fishhooks.

Remember May. Rising stars of the Scottish music scene. Disastrous gig at the Barrowlands Ballroom. Booed off stage. Last seen in Glasgow Hilton. Found dead in an elevator. Mysterious circumstances. Murdered.

Decapitated.

There are pictures. The interior of an elevator car messily decorated with dripping red, running in streaks down the mirrored walls and pooling on the floor. Three bodies, arranged side by side, pixelated from their chests up to spare the viewer the visual details. She recognises the Paisley patterned shirt Julia Stone had been wearing at the gig last night, and the blood splattered guitar case lying next to her. Luce's eyes flick back to the article.

Decapitated.

When a car horn loudly sounds outside her flat, Luce almost screams.

4

After phoning Luce and Ross and filling in the blanks in their memories about the after party - babbling mostly, punctuated with frequent bursts of laughter - Aldo just sinks down on his ratty sofa bed and sits gazing into space for a while, letting it all sink in.

Signed.
Twenty-seven grand in the bank.
Off to the studio to record an album in a few hours.

In a distracted way, he knows there's a shit-ton of things to think about, a big old pile of details to organise and sort out, but with his head buzzing like a happy hornets' nest and his heart pumping exhilaration with every hard, joyous slam, he can't focus his mind on any one thing for more than a few seconds. So he just sits there with his eyes closed, letting it all wash over him, surrendering to the intense flood of emotion, alternatively laughing and weeping in happiness.

The triumphant feeling of achievement, like he'd just completed a thousand back-to-back marathons and crossed the finish line in his slippers and smoking a cigar to the rapturous applause of an adoring crowd. The overwhelming sensation of being suddenly unburdened of all the problems that've weighed him down for so long, the relief in putting down that big sack of worries is so strong he feels almost weightless, liable to float right off the sofa bed and breakdance on the bedsit's peeling, nicotine stained ceiling.

And he's not too big to feel a hefty undercurrent of swaggering, *get-it-right-fuckin-up-ye* vindication swirling in the river of emotions flowing through him.

It's too much, and so he sits there, head back, eyes closed and arms spread out along the back of the sofa, opening himself to it, accepting it all. And he laughs, hoots, cries, trembles, punches the air and shouts out his delight in a mad-happy delirium, as careless of his raving as a man in a padded cell. He wonders what the neighbours might be thinking about all the noise, and the thought makes him laugh even harder. He laughs until it turns to crying again, then laughs some more.

After a while, when he feels he can think straight again, he gets up, wipes his eyes, brews up another cup of coffee and sits down on the couch with a pad and paper to once again sort out his personal finances. He grins, remembering the last time he'd done this, sitting in Squinty McGinty's with a pint of lager he couldn't afford while anxiety and guilt twisted his stomach. Counting his beans is a lot more fun this time, and Aldo spends the next hour on the phone and his laptop transferring funds, shooting down his financial woes like an old west gunslinger.

The grand owed for the new guitar. *Pew!* Gone.

The outstanding rent and council tax payments. *Pew!* Gone.

The overdue gas and electric bill. *Pew!* Gone.

His overdraft and bank loan. *Pew-pew-pew!* Gone.

And with every debt he crosses off, the colour of his money goes from the bloated swollen red of Past Due notices to the trim healthy black of credit balances.

Finances sorted, Aldo then logs into his email account and takes great delight in unsubscribing from the various job website alerts he'd signed up to, deleting each message in his inbox informing him of customer service, market research and janitorial vacancies.

He also opens and reads the email from Gappa Bale, over and over again. He wants to print it out and frame it, and quite possibly make sweet love to it.

Then he calls Ashley.

"Are you working at all today?" he asks when she picks up.

"No, I'm off," his ex says. She sounds tired. "I'm just heading out the door, though. Taking Dylan down to Funworld."

Aldo remembers some good times in Funworld, the local soft play centre. You never got tired of bouncy castles, giant slides and rope swings, even when you were in your twenties. "Can you hang on for half an hour?" he asks. "I need to speak to you about something. Okay if I come over?"

"I'm literally heading out the door, Al. I just put Dylan's coat on."

"Please, Ash? It's important."

She sighs, but agrees.

A swift shower, a vigorous tooth-brushing and another couple of paracetamol later, Aldo's heading out the door. As he waits at the unsheltered bus stop next to the corner shop at the end of his street, standing there under mottled grey skies in the wind and drizzle but glowing inside, he thinks about buying a car, and loves the fact that he can even entertain such a thought. Just yesterday he couldn't have afforded a second hand bicycle.

When his bus comes along, he boards and gets off ten minutes later at the depo in the town centre, then walks up past the college into the west end. Ashley and Dylan stay in a small, but nice enough flat out here. It's a quieter part of town. Not so many neds. Nice, well-kept gardens and big sandstone tenement flats on tidy, tree-lined streets, not far from the flat where the three of them had lived when they'd been a family.

They'd been happy living here. When they found out she was pregnant, Aldo and Ashley, with a little help from Ashley's dad, had scraped enough money together for a deposit on a rental flat, and thrown themselves into family life with the usual potent mixture of panic and joy experienced by first time parents. When Dylan was born, awestruck by every little thing about him, every tiny development his new son showed, Aldo had never been happier or more content with his life. For the first time since he was a teenager, days went by without him even thinking about music or picking up the guitar. He'd almost come to tears the day Dylan discovered his own feet and set about enthusiastically exploring them with his gums. And when he'd started walking, Aldo'd taken a few days off work from the call centre where he'd been working at the time. He hadn't been there long enough to qualify for holidays, so he'd called in sick, just so he could stay at home, watching in amazement as Dylan tottered unsteadily around their tiny flat, supporting himself on the walls and furniture like a drooling miniature drunk.

Unfortunately, the management at the call centre hadn't shared his fatherly enchantment at the wee man's early attempts at perambulation. Some grassing arsehole in Aldo's team had shown the team manager the videos which in a moment of paternal stupidity, he'd put up on Facebook. One of those videos had featured Aldo himself, smiling and laughing, and clearly *not* bedridden by a mysterious stomach bug as he'd claimed on the sickline, and he'd been summarily fired.

The happy family life he, Ashley and Dylan were enjoying had gone downhill pretty fuckin rapidly from that point.

At Ashley's place, when Aldo rings the doorbell, she opens the door and just stands there, a frosty look on her face, evidently still pissed off with him. "What is it, Al?"

Dressed in jeans and a simple black top, her hair a pleasing tumble of blonde shoulder length curls, she looks good, but weary. Her carefully applied make up doesn't quite hide the tiredness of her eyes.

"Nice to see you too," Aldo replies. "Can we go inside?"

Ashley opens her mouth to reply, but then Dylan comes charging up the hall behind her. "Daddy!" he yells delightedly, dodging round Ashley's legs and throwing himself at Aldo. He grins and picks the wee man up, tickling him under the arms to make him giggle then hugging him tightly, feeling the familiar warm rush of simple, unconditional love as Dylan's arms go round his neck. "Are you coming to Funworld with us, Daddy?" Dylan asks, bouncing in his arms with excitement and tugging on Aldo's jacket, his big green eyes shining at the prospect of a day spent with Mummy *and* Daddy together. It breaks Aldo's heart a little.

"Sorry, wee man, I can't today," he says. "I've got to go somewhere to play my guitar."

"Can I come?" Dylan asks hopefully. The wee man looks pale, and feels a bit light in Aldo's arms, as if he's lost weight, and the scratch on his neck from the kitchen knife's still there. Faded, but still there.

"I'd love you to come, dude," Aldo says, "but I'll be away for a wee while. You have to stay here and look after Mummy, okay?" Dylan looks disappointed, but nods dutifully.

"Al," Ashley says impatiently. "What do you want? Did you just come here to tell Dylan all the things you can't do with him?"

That stings, and Aldo bites back the urge to have a go at Ashley for that sally, which was a definite low blow. Instead, he kisses Dylan's head and puts him down again. "Okay, go and put your coat on for Funworld, wee man. I need to talk to Mummy for a second okay?"

"Okay!" Dylan replies cheerily and charges away down the hall again, any disappointment at not going with his dad on some mysterious guitar-based adventure instantly forgotten when reminded of the waiting ball pits, mini Dodgems, inflatables and climbing nets.

Aldo turns to Ashley. "We're signed," he says. "We did it."

Ashley doesn't say anything for a moment. Just sort of tilts her head to the side and frowns, the way she always does when she suspects someone's shovelling bullshit in her ear. "Signed?" she says with a heavy dose of scepticism.

Fuck, it sounds even better when someone else says it, Aldo thinks. He just grins and chuckles, and has to make an effort not to jump up and down like an excited four-year-old about to go to Funworld. "Signed," he repeats, nodding his head. "We're going into the studio tonight."

"That's..." Ashley begins, half a smile threatening to break on her face. Then she lowers her eyes and shakes her head. "That's great, Al," she says. "I'm happy for you. Really."

"Really?" Aldo says, deflating a bit at her lukewarm reaction. "Aye, you look like you're fit to burst."

"How long will you be in the studio for?"

"I don't know. At least two weeks."

"At *least*? So you're not taking Dylan next weekend then?"

Aldo hadn't even thought of that, and a momentary flicker of guilt goes through him. "Well, no, I can't," he says, the guilt quickly giving way to irritation. "Ash, we're recording an *album*." He holds his hands out as if presenting her with something plainly obvious.

"And I'm happy for you. What then? You'll be going on tour I take it?"

"Maybe. Fuck, I don't know. We've not talked about that yet, but… yeah, probably."

"Great. So you'll not be seeing Dylan for, what? A few months? A year?"

"Ashley," Aldo says softly, his irritation swelling. "You know what this means to me. To the band. What do you want me to do? Say no thanks, no recording contract for me, I'm taking the wean to the cinema next week?"

"I want you to be a *father*, Al," Ashley says in an angry whisper. "Dylan needs you."

"Ashley, we blew the biggest band in the country off the stage last night. When we left the Barras there was a crowd outside waiting for us, hundreds of them blocking the road, going mental and chanting for us. Have you not heard?"

"*No, I haven't fuckin heard,*" Ashley hisses. "I've been up since five this morning with Dylan. He's hardly slept for the last week, and he has nightmares when he does. He's not eating properly and can't stand to be alone, even for a minute. Ever since last weekend he keeps saying the spider's going to get him."

Aldo's annoyance fades and he looks at his shoes, the nauseous self-loathing at what had nearly happened to Dylan resurfacing in his craw like undigested food.

"He keeps saying someone pushed him," Ashley goes on, and Aldo looks up at her again, hearing the note of real concern in her voice.

No, not concern. *Fear.*

"Ashley, he had a close call," Aldo says, "and I'm so, so sorry about it. But no one pushed him. There was no one else in the flat but me and him, and I was in the living room. It was an accident."

"I know," Ashley says, "But he's... he's not been himself since it happened. I'm worried."

"He'll be fine," Aldo assures her, not assured of that at all, but not knowing what else to say. "He just had a scare."

And just like that, the mum rage is back in Ashley's eyes. "Aye, it's easy to brush off for you, isn't it? You're not the one getting woken up every night with him screaming, are you? You're not the one that has to leave work and go and pick him up from nursery because he won't stop crying. Three times this week, Aldo. *Three fuckin times!* And all because you were on the phone and weren't watching him..."

Aldo's had enough. He feels bad about the incident and he's sorry Dylan's not over it yet, but he's apologised and beat himself up for it plenty. There's only so many times he can say he's sorry.

And besides, he's got other things on his mind right now. Important things. Ashley, who evidently doesn't give a shit about his success, ranting on about a few nightmares, trying to make him feel like a prick, guilt tripping him and bursting his nut with this domestic crap is shit he doesn't have time for right now.

He glances at his watch. He still has to get back to the flat and pack for the studio.

"Ashley," he says. "Enough. I'm sorry, I really am, but I've got to go. Tell Dylan I'll see him when I get back." He turns to leave.

"Aye, just fuck off to the studio to make your record, Al," Ashley calls after him. "Go on and be a rock star. Just leave me to deal with real life. As usual."

Aldo turns back. She's standing in the doorway, tears on her face, glaring at him. Dylan's reappeared at her side. He's holding on to Ashley's leg, looking out at Aldo with unshed tears shimmering in his eyes, achingly cute in his Fireman Sam jacket and Angry Birds hat. So small and vulnerable it hurts to look at him.

"Don't go, Daddy," he says. "Please?"

A bitter bubble of sadness and longing swells in Aldo's throat, and for a moment he imagines going back up the path, taking them both in his arms and going inside with them. Inside, out of the cold and wind and drizzle, where they can just sit on the couch watching cartoons on the Disney channel. Like they used to.

But the car's coming to pick him up to go to the studio in a few hours.

"I'll see you soon, wee man," he says, his voice thick, half-choked. Then he looks at Ashley. "Check your bank account," he says. "There's ten grand in it. From the advance I got."

Then he turns and walks away.

Back at home, Aldo packs for the studio. Not much to pack, in all honestly. A rucksack with a few changes of clothes. His guitar, leads, picks and pedal board, of course. Notepad and pen. Wallet, keys, smokes and phone in his jacket. With twenty minutes till the car arrives, he sits on the sofa bed and flicks channels on TV, his insides wound tight, chain smoking as he impatiently watches the time display on his phone approach nine pm.

As if synchronised with special forces accuracy, on the stroke of nine, a car horn announces itself outside the bedsit. Aldo goes to the window, and parked outside in the rainy dark of the evening is Gappa Bale's big black limo with the high shine and tinted windows, the streetlamps above casting orange sodium highlights on the sleek bodywork. The driver emerges and makes his way towards Aldo's building. Feeling like a ten-year-old about to go to Disneyland, Aldo quickly shrugs into this leather jacket and practically skips into his hallway to meet him at the door.

Unlike the black clad behemoths Aldo's previously seen under Gappa Bale's employ, the man at his door, dressed in a sombre black suit and tie, white shirt and a peaked driver's cap, is an elderly gentleman of around sixty, thin and tired looking with a heavily lined face and white hair showing beneath the brim of his hat. He stands there on Aldo's doorstep wearing a hangdog expression. "Mr Evans," he says, his dry, English accented voice every bit as weary as he looks. "I'm John. I'm here to take you to the studio. Are you ready to go?"

"Umm, aye," Aldo replies, though he wonders if his driver's ready. John looks like he's been driving that car non-stop for about forty years, and is in dire need of a good kip. Aldo has a vision of the old dude crashing out at the wheel and wrecking the car before they're out of the housing estate. "No offence, chief, but you look shattered. Sure you're okay to drive?"

The driver makes an attempt at a reassuring smile that barely makes it past his thin lips, and goes nowhere near his bloodshot, rheumy eyes. "Yes, I'm perfectly capable," he says. "You have bags?"

Aldo regards him an uncertain moment longer, but John just stares back at him, waiting and expressionless. Aldo shrugs. "Aye, two secs," he says, then goes back into the living room to turn off the lights before leaving. Back in the hall, the elderly driver's come in and is gathering up Aldo's guitar case, backpack and pedal board bag.

"It's okay, mate," Aldo says hurriedly, reaching for the bags, "I'll get the gear." The last thing he wants is his driver having a heart attack in his hallway, but with a quickness and surety surprising for his age and stooped figure, John's already slung the pedal bag's strap over his shoulder, has the heavy guitar case and backpack in his hands, and is making his way out the door and back to the car. With no option but to follow, Aldo leaves the flat and locks the door behind him before hurrying after the old chauffeur. John swiftly stows Aldo's gear in the boot of the car then opens the rear door for him. "Cheers, John," Aldo says as he climbs in. John nods, but doesn't reply, then closes the door behind him.

The roomy leather-scented interior of the car's pleasantly warm after the chill of the rainy September night outside, and Aldo sinks back gratefully into the soft luxury of the heated seats, stretching his legs out and giving a contented sigh. The tinted partition window between him and the front of the car slides open with an electronic hum, and John looks back over his shoulder.

"Feel free to make yourself a drink, Mr Evans," he says, as on a panel on Aldo's right, a little door slides opens, revealing the now familiar fully stocked and refrigerated mini-bar. Soft chillout music then fills the air as the mellow drum beat and lazy slide guitar of The Beta Band's *Dry the Rain* floats from concealed speakers. Aldo smiles.

"I could get used to this, John" he says, reaching into the mini-bar and pouring himself a Jack n Coke. Hair of the dog that mauled you and all that. "So where's the studio, anyway?"

"North," John replies vaguely. Then the tinted partition between them slides closed again, ending the conversation.

Obviously not the chatty cabby type, Aldo thinks as he settles back into his seat, sipping his drink, enjoying the ambient beats and the soft, leather-scented warmth of the swish vehicle.

With near silent power, the car moves off, rolling smoothly away from the pavement, velvet wheels on a silken road, and Aldo's mind drifts as he watches the run-down estate pass by, all overgrown hedges and weed-choked communal lawns littered with broken patio furniture and rusty bikes. He regards the cracked and litter strewn pavements, the tired looking council tenements with steel plate covered windows, their walls encased in broken stone chip cladding decorated with gang graffiti courtesy of the local young team. Though he's only separated from it all by inches, encapsulated in the warm, lavish cocoon of the luxury motor, Aldo feels a world away from the cold, rain washed urban deprivation outside.

Maybe I'll never come back here, he thinks, feeling a weird mingling of melancholy and relief, and thinking how strange it was that a person could feel so much like an outsider, so out of place, in a town where they'd lived their whole life. And how stranger still it was that there was a subtle sadness in the thought of leaving it.

Right there, along that overgrown pathway between the public park and his old primary school, is where he was robbed at syringe-point a few years ago by a dead-eyed junkie who took his mobile and the change in his pocket. And there, in the shadows behind the now derelict computer component factory, is where he and Ross had once shared a carry out of four Tennents Supers and a bottle of Electric White cider when they were fifteen. Aldo smiles as he remembers how they'd gleefully guzzled the rocket-fuel strength bevvy, pretending to like the taste, all adolescent machismo and hormonally charged rebellion, before they'd both whiteyed and spewed all over the place, Aldo befouling his beloved Smashing Pumpkins hoodie in the process.

The car pulls up outside Ross's place a few minutes later, and through the tinted window, Aldo sees his bass player standing waiting with his bags in the vandalised bus shelter outside the high rise. John gets out and helps Ross load his stuff into the car.

"Curer?" Aldo asks, holding out a cold Bud from the min bar as Ross joins him in the back, but then he sees the look on his mate's face. Clearly far from his usual affable self, and a million miles from being as happy and excited as Aldo would expect given their circumstances, Ross looks thoroughly dejected as he climbs in and sits down.

"Alright," he mumbles, not even looking at Aldo as he takes the beer.

"Dude, what's up? You okay?"

Ross doesn't say anything for a moment. Just shakes his head, still avoiding eye contact, his gaze fixed on the label of the beer bottle in his hand, which he's picking at nervously. "The old boy at the hospital I was telling you about," he says quietly as the car pulls away from the pavement. "Duncy?"

Aldo nods. "The old soldier." Ross had talked fondly about Duncy Brown a few times over the past few weeks, his liking and admiration for the veteran evident in the way he'd regaled Aldo and Luce with some of his war stories and feats of derring-do. Aldo winces as he realises what's probably happened. "Ah shit, man. Did he…"

"Aye," Ross says, his voice a near whisper, his usually lively blue eyes dull. He takes a deep swallow of beer before continuing. "Had a heart attack last night. He was still hanging on in the ICU when I went to see him earlier. He woke up and spoke to me a wee bit, but then… he died. Right there in front of me, man. He just… he just went."

"Fuck. I'm sorry, mate," Aldo says, his good mood and excitement suddenly turning to dust to see Ross as he is at that moment. Though he was a gregarious all-round good guy, friendly to everyone he met and always ready with a handshake, a smile and some wise-ass patter, Aldo knew Ross was wary about getting attached to people, and that aside from himself and Luce, he had no other close friends. It was sad, but it was understandable. You didn't have to be Inspector Morse to figure out Ross had endured a rough time in Eastburn and the succession of foster homes he'd lived in as a kid, but he never went into details. Which was fair enough. Everybody had their own personal shit that was exclusively theirs to deal with in their own way. Bad memories and experiences resulting in paper cuts to the soul, little wounds that never quite healed, the kind that even a loved one couldn't help with. Luce was the same. You didn't talk to Luce about religion. Again, she never gave details, but theological discussion was a subject that was understood to be off the table as far as his drummer was concerned.

"Want to talk about it?" Aldo asks Ross now.

Ross just shakes his head. "Nah, man. Shit happens, right?"

Aldo nods. "All too often, mate. Just got to roll with the punches."

Ross lets out a long sigh and wipes at his eyes with a thick forearm. "On to happier thoughts," he says, forcing a smile. "Dude. We're fuckin signed."

"Signed, sealed, delivered," Aldo agrees, lifting his glass. Ross knocks his Bud against it. "Just wish I could remember it. How fuckin wrecked were *we* last night?"

Ross gives a half-hearted chuckle and shakes his head. "Mate, that was some wild shit. I'm still feelin shady."

"Hell yeah. Do you remember much?"

"Not a lot. I remember driving way out into the country, arriving at the place and going inside. After that? Just a blur. Bits and pieces. We were on the marching powder, weren't we? And did someone give us pills?"

"Aye, think so. Do you remember the round room? Where we actually signed the contract?"

Ross thinks for a moment. "Sort of. I mind being in a room with you, Luce and Gappa, but that's it."

Aldo gives a sly grin and a waggle of the eyebrows. "How about the lassie in the wee black dress? The one that brought us the charlie."

Ross's eyes widen. "Oh shit! She started blowin you right there in front of me, didn't she?" He bursts out laughing.

"Hope *she's* at the studio," Aldo says, laughing along.

"Aye, and she brings some pals."

Their lewd cackling tails off as they feel the car slowing again, and through the car window Aldo sees they're outside Luce's place.

When John opens the door to reveal her standing on the pavement outside the car, Aldo sees that she's also not in as good a mood as he'd expect. Unlike Ross had, though, Luce doesn't just look sad. She looks downright nervous, and makes no move to get into the car. Even more alarming, Aldo realises, she doesn't have her bags with her. "I need to talk to you both," she says, her voice tight.

Aldo exchanges a quick look with Ross, who shrugs. He looks back at Luce. "Sure. Come on in."

"Out here."

Aldo frowns, but gets out of the car into the drizzle, followed by Ross. "What's up?"

Luce walks away a few steps, apparently so John, who's still standing holding the door, can't hear what she wants to say. When they're at what she apparently deems a safe distance for privacy, she turns to them. "Have you heard?"

"About the bird?" Ross asks. "Everybody knows that the bird is the word." But Luce's obviously in no mood for jokes, and shoots him a dark look.

"Not now, Ross. Have you heard about Remember May?"

"That they're prima donna dicks? Sure," Aldo says.

"They're prima donna *dead* dicks," Luce replies. "You've not seen the news today?"

Aldo and Ross stand there, shivering in the wet and chilly night air, wisecracks all used up as Luce fills them in on what happened to last night's headliners.

"Well," Ross says after a few seconds of uneasy silence. "That's... nasty."

Behind them, John the driver gives a polite *hurry-the-fuck-up* cough.

"Nasty indeed," Aldo agrees. "But can we talk about it in the car? Fuckin freezing out here."

Luce doesn't move.

"What?" Aldo asks impatiently, spreading his arms for an explanation. Then he starts to get a bad feeling about where this is going. "Luce, c'mon tae fuck. Tell me you're not thinking about backing out."

Luce doesn't reply. She doesn't move either. Just stands there, looking down at the pavement, her hands nervously tap-tap-tapping on her thighs.

John coughs again.

"*Luce?*" Aldo says through a jaw clamped shut.

"You remember what Bale said last night after the Barras?" she says in a quiet voice, still studying the pavement.

"I don't remember much at all about last night."

She looks up at him. "About... cutting heads?"

For a moment, Aldo's genuinely lost for words, and stands there gaping in disbelief. "Are you serious?" he says carefully. "What? You think... you think Bale's somehow *involved* in... get the fuck out of here with that pish, Luce!"

"No," she replies uncertainly. "I just... I don't know..."

"No, you *don't* know," Aldo agrees. "You don't know because what you're saying is fuckin mental." He pauses to get his voice under control. "Let me tell what I know. I know we've each got a twenty-seven grand advance in the bank. I know we've got a signed record contract. I know there's a car right *there* waiting to take us to a studio to record an album."

John coughs again.

"*Hold the fuck on!*" Ross turns and shouts at him. John doesn't reply, but Aldo sees him making a point of looking at his watch.

Aldo looks back at Luce. "And I know I'm too cold, too tired and too hungover to be having this conversation with you. That's brutal and, alright, pretty fuckin weird what happened to Remember May, but it's got nothing to do with us, or Gappa, or Easy Rollin Records." He stops to take a deep, calming breath. "C'mon, Luce," he says, gentler now. "This is it, mate. We're signed, we're minted, and we've got an album to record. Don't freak out on us now. We need you."

"I know, Luce," Ross says, putting a hand on her shoulder. "If anybody slayed Remember May, it was us. Slayed them right off the fuckin stage. Obviously horrendous, them being dead and everything, and I'm sorry to hear it, even if they were dicks, but… shit happens. You need to… you need to just roll with the punches."

Luce doesn't say anything for a long, long, *long* moment, and Aldo's on the verge of losing his shit completely when she says, "Alright. Let me get my bags." Then she turns without another word and goes back inside, closely followed by John.

"Fuckin' drummers, man," Aldo says, shaking his head and making throttling motions in the air as he and Ross walk back to the car.

5

As Queens of the Stone Age might have said, the fun machine had taken a shit and died.

In his head, Ross had imagined the journey to the studio, wherever it was, would be a gas. The three of them laughing and joking, congratulating each other on their success and enjoying a party atmosphere punctuated with the fleshy slap of many a high five and the constant crystal clink of champagne flute toasts.

Of course, that had been before his good mood had taken a kicking in the Inverclyde Royal ICU ward that afternoon. And before Luce had told them about what had happened to Remember May last night, not to mention her wavering on the cusp of backing out of the whole shebang.

As it is, with the car rolling smoothly along the M8, rather than the three of them pishing glitter, the feeling in the back of the big motor's subdued. Aldo, as a good band leader should, makes a few attempts to lighten things up, asking what he and Luce are planning to do with their advance money, trying to start a discussion about the songs they want to put on the record. He offers drinks from the mini-bar and makes jokes about how blootered they'd been the night before, but his attempts to force a good feeling into the road trip don't catch on, and they soon lapse into silence. Too much heavy shit going on, Ross supposes, and they're all still rough as fuck from the night before.

Ross feels bad about it. They *should* be happy. They *should* be partying, but his heart's just not in it. Earlier, when he'd been talking to Aldo about last night, he'd managed a few chuckles and thought maybe he could shake off the bad thoughts born from being witness to Duncy Brown's strange last moments.

Well, scratch that. The brief respite from the sadness he felt over the old soldier's death hadn't lasted, and the things he'd said with his parting breaths keep going round and round in Ross's head.

And then there was what Luce had told them about Remember May. Ross remembers going toe to toe with their drummer, Jim, last night. The old red mist had descended, and he'd been perilously close to knocking the fresh fuck out of the skinny mod cunt that had tried to take a swing at Aldo. He was dead now, that skinny mod cunt. Ross had looked up the story on his phone. The three of them. Dead in a lift, their height dramatically reduced. It wasn't on the official news sites, but the talk on the various social media channels had it that the band's management team were being questioned. It was also being whispered online that the severed heads of Julia Stone, Marcus Tatum and Jim McElland hadn't been recovered.

Now, with the car speeding across the Erskine Bridge and the River Clyde a black meandering ribbon far below, this magical mystery tour's proving to be a lot less fun than the cheery Beatles song would suggest. Up until now, Ross had kind of liked the whole mysterious stranger vibe of Gappa Bale and the way he did business. But now, rather than being intrigued by the fact that they don't know where they're going, Ross feels decidedly uneasy.

But it's just The Fear getting to him, he decides. Still feeling ropey from last night. The nervy aftermath of all the pills, chico and bevvy making him jumpy as fuck. Add in a triple murder and the death of a friend, and it was no wonder he was feeling a bit shady.

Looking out the car window at the undulating black snake of the Clyde winding west, its banks etched in points of orange streetlights, Ross's thoughts are of a decidedly gloomy hue. On the car stereo, the last verse of the last track of Nirvana's *Unplugged in New York* is playing. Cobain's chilling smoke-scorched voice jumping up that sudden octave, hollering Ledbelly blues with raw, goosebump-inducing intensity as he demands *where did you sleep last night?*

In the bath, Kurt old chap, Ross thinks, and then has to repress a little shudder as he recalls the song's line about a mysterious decapitation.

Ah, *The Fear*! Ugly cousin of the hangover, because your body can never feel so bad that completely unreasonable paranoia and self-mind-fuckery is out of place. All to be expected after an epic pints, pills and powders session, of course. Expectation doesn't make it any less unpleasant, though.

They come off the bridge and merge onto the A82, passing the little riverside towns of Old Kilpatrick, Bowling, Milton and Dumbarton, all lifeless and still in the cold, rainy autumn night. Outside the car, the only movement comes from dead leaves tossed through the air and blown along the pavements. Near skeletal trees shiver and sway by the roadside while occasional gusts of hard wind-driven rain slap and spit at the car's windows, and Ross thinks of Duncy Brown standing at a window in a Nazi concentration camp almost seventy years ago, seeing the moonshadow of something inhuman.

The streetlights and towns peter out and are left behind as the car turns north into the night, toward Loch Lomond, the Trossachs and the highlands beyond. Heartsick, exhausted, and generally feeling like a mouldy sack of rusty spanners, the smooth roll of the car and the music on the stereo – a mournful slide guitar bleeding the sublime misery of Ry Cooder's *Feelin' Bad Blues* – lulls him and covers him like a warm black blanket.

Ross's eyes grow heavy, and he feels himself slipping away even as troubled thoughts continue to caper in his head. Screaming children and hounds with hungry jaws. Death and decapitation. Grim pictures randomly ricocheting around his heavy, aching skull like shotgun pellets in confined space of a blood-splattered elevator car.

He's jolted from sleep some unknown time later, waking up with a lurch as the lulling motion of the car is rudely interrupted by a sudden bump and the sound of tires crunching on an unpaved road beneath them. Across from him, Ross sees Aldo and Luce, who'd also crashed out, coming to and looking around, disorientated.

"What time is it, man?" Aldo mumbles, yawning as he runs his hands through his hair.

Ross rubs his eyes then checks his watch. "Just gone one," he says, surprised to find that he's been asleep for over three hours. He doesn't feel particularly rested, and has the impression that he'd only closed his eyes for a few seconds. He's bursting for a pish, though.

"Where are we?" Luce asks, looking around at them. "Have we arrived?"

Looking out the window at his side, there's nothing to see. Outside the car is perfect blackness.

"Fuck knows. Feels like we're on a dirt track or something," Ross says. He twists round and knocks on the little tinted window behind him, which immediately slides open. "We there, mate?" he asks the driver.

John looks briefly over his shoulder at Ross and replies in a robotic monotone. "Yes. We'll be arriving in just a minute."

Through the windshield in the wash of the car's headlights, it looks like they're driving along a forester's road cut through deep woods. Ross can make out a rutted dirt track with a line of weeds up the centre. The road's crowded at the sides with heavy tangled undergrowth and tight ranks of pine trunks. Then the partition window slides closed again, blocking his view.

"Sleep well?" Aldo asks, massaging his shoulder muscles and wincing as he rotates his head left and right to relieve a crick in his neck.

"Not really. Conked out just after Dumbarton, I think," Ross says. "Still feel knackered, though. How you feeling, Luce?"

"Buggered," Luce mutters, hunching forward with her face in her hands. She looks up and Ross can see her face is pale and tight, her eyes bloodshot. "I need a proper sleep. At least twelve hours in a comfy bed."

"I hear that," he agrees as the car continues to bump and jostle along the trail with the occasional harsh scrape of rocks grinding against the undercarriage.

"What the fuck, man?" Aldo says, struggling to stay in his seat as the car hits a large pot hole. "We going off road here or what?"

Then the rough terrain suddenly smoothes out, the banging and scraping from under the car becoming the homely crunch of a pebbled driveway. Looking through the window on his left, Ross sees a weak light bleeding into the darkness, revealing a vague impression of the dense woods by the roadside. Then the trees start to thin out, and as the car crests a slight rise, he sees the building ahead, nestled at the bottom of a winding slope.

"Looks like this is the place," Aldo says, leaning forward with his head next to Ross's as the car draws closer and slows.

Lit by bollard lamps in front, it's a single-storey Georgian style structure with white walls, constructed in a U-shape. Ross counts four panelled windows in the centre section and two on the inward facing sides of each adjacent wing. The car parks in the pebbled courtyard space in the middle, coming to a halt in front of a large black-painted wooden door flanked by ornately carved stone pillars. And there, standing by the entrance, smiling his familiar knowing smile, dressed in tight black jeans and silk shirt, his long hair tied back in a tight, oiled ponytail, is Gappa Bale. He steps forward to greet them, his arms held out as if for a big old welcome hug as John comes round and opens the rear door, letting in a sudden cold wind that rushes into the car's warm interior, instantly sheathing Ross's bare forearms with goosebumps.

"Welcome, friends," Bale says, shaking hands with Ross as he steps out onto the courtyard and stands in the freezing night air. He notices that Bale doesn't shiver, despite only wearing that thin silk shirt.

"Alright, Mr Bale," Aldo greets him with a weary smile as he emerges from the car behind Ross and shakes Bale's hand. "Where are we?" he asks, looking around at the surrounding forested hills, the trees

Cuttin' Heads

half-lit in the outer limits of the light cast by the bollard lamps in the courtyard.

"This is Easy Rollin headquarters," Gappa tells him proudly, turning and making a grand gesture at the humble building behind him. "The heart of our operation, and site of our custom built recording studio. This is where the magic happens."

"But where *are* we?" Luce asks as she joins them, more than a hint of tired annoyance in her voice, and making no move to shake Bale's offered hand. Ross has known Luce long enough to know that she's not a morning person, so is understandably prickly waking up at one in the morning after three hours sleep in a car. And of course, the mood she was in earlier...

Bale never misses a beat. "Deep in the northern wilds, my dear," he replies smoothly, turning his offered-but-ignored hand into another sweeping gesture towards the darkened woods behind them. "Seventeen miles from Inverness to be precise. Please, come inside before you catch your deaths." Then he's ushering them towards the black painted door. "John," he says curtly over his shoulder as he leads Aldo away, one arm around his shoulders. "Bring their bags."

The aged driver, who's standing by the car with his usual robotic expression, nods silently and moves to the rear of the car to start unloading their gear and luggage.

Ross follows Bale, Aldo and Luce towards the door, but something makes him hesitate on the threshold, and he looks back at the car.

The old driver - who Ross could swear he's seen somewhere before - is standing by the open boot of the black car, grey and motionless as a stone carving, staring at him. He's about twenty feet away, so Ross can't be sure, but for a moment, it looks like there's the slightest waver on John's usual impenetrable poker-face. The tiniest crack in that expressionless wrinkled façade. Something that Ross somehow feels in his nutsack more than he sees with his eyes.

And what he feels is a warning.

What he sees in John's old, old eyes, is pity.

Verse II

If you don't deal with your demons, they'll deal with you. And it's gonna hurt.

Nikki Sixx

1

Swimming up from a deep black and dreamless sleep, Luce wakes to a deep chill in the air.

She opens her eyes and sits up in bed, rubbing her forearms, feeling the cold on the tip of her nose and earlobes. She looks about the room, which she only vaguely remembers being shown into by Gappa Bale last night after they'd arrived. After John had brought her bags in, exhausted and feeling like stir-fried shit, she'd barely made it into her pjs before climbing into bed and faceplanting into her pillow.

Looking around now, it's quite a big room. Bare white-painted walls, and a decidedly funky carpet that looks like a remnant from the late seventies with its floral pattern design woven in faded creams, oranges and browns. Her double bed's tucked in the corner across from the door. Next to the door are a large wardrobe and dressing table, both as dated and kitsch as the disco'era throwback carpet. Above the dressing table, weak sunlight filters through a panelled window dressed in yellowing lace curtains.

Luce reaches over and picks up her watch from the bedside cabinet. It's seven am. On the dot. Swinging her legs out from under the thin duvet and shivering in the chilly air, she gets dressed in a hurry.

Once clothed, she leaves her room, finding herself in a corridor about thirty feet long, with doors on her left and windows looking out onto the courtyard on her right. In contrast to the dated, and rather scabby state of her room, a luxuriant blood red carpet lies underfoot in the hallway, woven a lush thickness Luce can feel beneath the soles of her Converse All-Stars. Above is a polished oak panelled ceiling with recessed lighting. The walls are painted a sunny scorched orange tone, and hung with large black and white art prints of iconic bands and musicians in legendary concerts. The Ramones at CBGB. The Stones at Hyde Park. Hendrix at Monterey. Jim Morrison, letting loose a demented scream on stage at the Hollywood Bowl.

The coldness in the air, brisk enough that Luce half expects to see her breath crystallise in front of her face, is out of place with the warm-hued décor around her. The colours should lend a welcoming, cosy feel, but the atmosphere's strangely… dead. There's no sound. Not the slightest whisper. No ticking of a clock, creak of a settling timber, the squeak of a floorboard or even the moan and whistle of the wind, which she can see moving through the swaying boughs of the forest outside. Luce has the peculiar feeling that there's no one else here, no one else within a thousand miles, that she's standing in a long abandoned building that's been inhabited by nothing but ghosts for a long, long while. Troubled by the queer thought, she moves along the corridor, nervous now, her pulse quickening with a sudden swell of anxiety and the unreasonable yet undeniable feeling that she's alone in this strange and cold place.

But after a few more steps she catches the scent of fried food and coffee on the cold air, and from an opening on the left just a few steps away, come the muted sounds of clinking tableware and the low murmur of voices. A moment later, Luce's standing in a large open doorway leading into a spacious dining room, where Aldo and Ross sit at a huge mahogany table, the two of them getting wired into plates stacked high with eggs, mushrooms, bacon, black pudding and sausages. Ross, his mouth full, sees her standing there and tips her a quick salute with his fork.

"Morning, sunshine," Aldo says round a bite of toast. "Grab yourself a seat and get some brekkie." When he speaks, Luce notices the deadened quality of the sound, and raps her knuckles on the wall at her side, noting the lifeless, dampened quality of the sound. There's no reverb. None at all.

When a hand suddenly comes down on her shoulder from behind, Luce just about shits herself. She whirls round, hands raised in front of her, and sees Gappa Bale standing over her.

"I am sorry, Lucia," he says. "I didn't mean to startle you."

Luce struggles to get her breath and heart rate under control for a moment. Dressed in his usual tight black jeans and black silk shirt, Bale's hair's down this morning, hanging around his shoulders in sculpted waves so black they're edged with blue where the light hits them. Again, there's that thrumming undercurrent of horniness. Luce feels her blood flowing a bit quicker, diverting itself to her cheeks, breasts and groin, and for a dangerous moment there's something in her saying *do it just do it he's so fuckin hot* and she wants to bury her hands in those coal black tresses, lock her fingers behind his neck and pull him down in a deep *deep* kiss that'll just go on and on and...

"It's Luce," she says, taking a step back, hoping the frost she puts in her voice covers her embarrassment.

"Of course," Bale says, making a quaint little half bow of contrition. "Apologies."

"This place is soundproofed?" she asks, trying to keep her voice neutral as she sits in one of the high backed, beautifully carved mahogany chairs at the table and begins filling her plate from the heated metal serving trays. "Like, all of it? Not just the studio?"

"Correct," Bale smiles. "You could stand right here and scream your throat to bloody ribbons and someone standing outside that window would hear not a whisper. This entire structure is in effect an advanced anechoic chamber." Bale walks through the doorway into the dining room. Luce sees he's carrying a brown leather folder at his side. "As I said before. Custom built. This is a recording studio like no other, I assure you. I want to get *all* of your music. Every sound you make. Every breath you take."

"You'll be watching us?" Aldo asks, pointing at Bale and raising an eyebrow.

"Every move you make," Bale confirms with a wry chuckle. "I do so love The Police." He and Aldo do a little fist bump, and Luce can't tell if their wee exchange is funny or cringeworthy.

The anaesthetised sound of everything here - their flat voices, the dull clink and scrape of cutlery on plates - is bothering her. The muffled quality of every noise would take some getting used to, and hadn't she read somewhere that people can get a bit loopy staying in acoustically sealed environments for any length of time? She's not convinced by Bale's talk of custom construction. Why would you soundproof an entire building instead of just the studio, wherever it was? Unless he wants to record in different parts of the house. Like Zep did on *When the Levee Breaks*, Bonham laying down that legendary drum track with his kit set up at the bottom of a staircase in Headley Grange. That could be cool, except with the universal soundproofing, there was no booming reverb to be had here, and no staircase.

"So what's the plan of attack?" Ross asks through a mouthful of bacon as he tops up his coffee cup from a large cafetiere on the table.

"Making sweet music, Ross," Bale says, taking a seat at the head of the table, placing the leather folder at his elbow and pouring himself a coffee. He adds five sugars, Luce notices. You'd never had thought it from the pristine condition of his teeth, even and pearly-perfect in that inviting, completely seductive smile of his.

"But first," he says, "I feel there is something we should all discuss as a small matter of urgency." He opens the leather folder on the table beside him and withdraws three thick brown A4 envelopes. "Here are your contracts," Bale says, handing them out. "From speaking with you yesterday morning, Aldo, it has become apparent to me that your recollections of exactly what transpired between us following your performance at the Barrowlands may be slightly... uncertain?"

That didn't sound good, and Luce frowns suspiciously. "Isn't there some sort of legal rule about signing contracts while under the influence?"

Bale gives a little shrug. "Do not trouble yourself. You have not been scammed while insensible. You are a legally signed band with a recording contract with Easy Rollin Records for one album, and have been paid a monetary advance against future royalties. Everything is above board and legal, and you are free to have any lawyer of your choosing scrutinise the contract at any time you please. In fact, I personally recommend that all our acts have their own legal representation."

"Okay..." Aldo says, opening his own envelope, a smile on his face.

Bale returns his smile. "You can see your signatures and seals at the bottom of the last page."

Seals? Luce opens her envelope and withdraws the thick sheaf of papers. At the top, centre aligned and written in a decorative old-fashioned calligraphy style in big black letters are the words 'Artist recording contract', with the band's name, her full name, and Easy Rollin Records printed underneath. Below that are several lines of dense text almost too small to read. She flicks to the back and sees a scrawl of black ink at the bottom, recognising it as her own signature.

The dark red fingerprint next to it comes as a bit of a surprise.

"What's this?" she says, feeling a peculiar clench in her throat as she stares at the rust coloured imprint. "Is that..."

"Your blood, and your fingerprint. Yes," Bale says with a nod.

"Our *blood?*" Ross repeats, frowning across the table at Bale and then looking quickly to Aldo, who's also staring down at his contract, an astonished expression on his face.

"Yes indeed," Bale says, and gives a dry little chuckle. "You really do not remember much at all, do you?"

Luce looks down at the page again.

Hold the fuckin phone just a moment. Our blood?

"This should refresh your memory," Bale says airily, then takes a small remote control from his shirt pocket and presses a button. In the corner of the room, the doors of a large cabinet slide open, revealing a big flat screen TV. Bale presses another button and it flickers to life.

And there they are, captured on film, the three of them and Bale in the round room with its curving bookcase-filled walls and the big desk in the centre. The point of view is from a position on the ceiling behind the desk, caught with a wide angle lens that covers the entire room.

Not some grainy and silent security video this, though. This is full HD with stereo sound, and Luce cringes as she sees herself on screen, standing in the centre of the room, doing The Twist with drunken abandon as the sound of Chubby Checker's famous dance hit plays in the background. Aldo stands talking with Bale by the desk, a drink in one hand, gesticulating wildly with the other, and a bleary smile of happiness on his face. Ross is standing over at the wall, holding onto the bookcase to keep himself upright, a beer bottle raised in salute, eyes closed and singing lustily along with Chubby in that God awful voice of his.

"I record all my signing appointments," Bale says, smiling at the screen. "For legal purposes. All with your full consent of course."

Proving that this is no secret recording Luce's watching as on the screen, she sees herself dance/stagger across the round room toward the camera, hooting and clapping her hands. Then she looks up at the lens and waves. "*Waaaaaaay!*" her image cheers. "We're on the telly! Ciao, Mamma! Ciao, Papa!" Aldo and Ross stumble over and join her, laughing like idiots, pogo-ing up and down, chanting *Al-i-bi! Al-i-bi!* and toasting the camera. Then Luce lifts her top up, exposing her breasts. "*Wooooooooo!* Set them puppies free!" she declares, before covering up again, giving the camera the finger, jiving back across the room, tripping over her own feet and piling to the floor where she lies on her back, cackling like a witch on meth.

"Oh my God," Luce says, burying her hands in her face, completely mortified. Across the table, Aldo and Ross are pishing themselves laughing.

"It goes on more or less like this for some time," Bale says, pressing a button on the remote again to fast forward the video.

Her face burning with embarrassment, Luce can only watch through a gap in her fingers as she sees the three of them dancing and capering round the office. At one point, Ross takes his top off and starts doing star jumps while Aldo runs an unsteady lap of the round room with a plastic wastepaper bin on his head, before tripping over his own feet and throwing up in it. Luce and Ross, cheering and roaring with drunk idiot laughter, dive on top of him in a pile-on, and all the while, Bale remains leaning against his desk, arms folded, watching them with a bemused expression.

"Ah, here we are," Bale says, and the video resumes normal speed. They're all gathered round the desk now, and Luce watches them signing their contracts.

"As a little tradition," Bale says on the screen as he shakes their hands, "I like to make these occasions special." He moves behind his desk, opens a drawer, takes out something too small to see then holds it up in his fingers before them. "Music is in your blood, yes?" he asks them. "What better way to seal our deal than to imprint it with your very essence?"

At the breakfast table, Luce looks across at Bale and sees he's looking back at her, a sewing needle held up in his fingers.

On screen, Ross says, "Ha! I like your style, Mr Bale," and holds out his finger. They all do, and Luce watches Bale give each of them a quick prick on the tip of their right index fingers. They each push a bloody fingerprint onto their contracts next to their signatures. Then they're all hugging and laughing and crying and staggering around the room in a clumsy huddle, bouncing off the bookshelves.

The screen goes dark.

"I assume you have heard about Remember May," Bale says before anyone else can speak.

Luce's embarrassment at the state the three of them is suddenly gone, and she glances across the table at Ross and Aldo. Ross is staring down at the empty plate on the table before him, his face blank as he scrutinises a toast crust. Aldo meets her eyes, and a slight tilt of the head conveys his unspoken message. *Don't start.*

"Aye," Luce says quietly, still looking at Aldo. "It's…"

"Horrific," Bale puts in. "Senseless. Mindless brutality."

Luce turns to him. *Jesus Christ, is he smiling?*

"Such a shame," Bale continues. "Their light has gone out. Their moment of grace. Their fabled fifteen minutes. Ended with savagery incomprehensible."

No one speaks, but Luce feels like she's swallowed a tray of ice cubes as she remembers the photos she'd seen online, digital images of a blood-splattered elevator and the red blur of the three half-pixelated, headless bodies inside it.

"But not a waste," Bale says into the uneasy silence. "Their energy. Their *mojo*. It goes on. It endures, and inspires others. For that is music. That is the soul of it. Infinite and everlasting. Yes?"

"Yes," Aldo repeats tonelessly, nodding and looking at Bale with something like awe.

As disturbed as she is by the triple murder and the thoroughly inappropriate smile on Bale's face, Luce has to admit that he's right. It's just what she'd always believed about music. Music went on. Rock stars died, but their songs didn't. And the music changed form and evolved, from simple sound waves emitting from a speaker or set of headphones, into kinetic energy generated by a kid's arm swinging a stick at a cymbal, and from there into sweat and skinned knuckles and tears and memories and broken bloodstained drumsticks. The music ignited that spark, that spark she loved seeing take flame in her students. That spark that could make you feel strong and alive when you were weak and scared, and it drew the pain out of you when your mind wouldn't stop remembering a little blonde girl lying on a chapel floor…

"So do not be sad to see your fellow troubadours go into the sweet by and by," Bale continues, his voice soft now, full of velvet empathy. "Instead, rejoice and use their energy. From death comes life. And here, in this place, we are going to give life to something very special. Something amazing. Something that people will remember for a *very* long time."

"We gave you our *blood*," Ross mutters after a second of silence, still concentrating on that crust of toast on his plate.

"Yes. Yes you did, Ross. A noble gesture of your commitment to our enterprise, and I do admit to having a penchant for the dramatic. A fondness for the symbolic." Bale looks at the three of them in turn, then when no one says anything, he stands up and rubs his long fingered hands together eagerly. "Shall we begin?"

2

Bale leads them out of the dining room into the main corridor then turns left, opening another door further along the passage and ushering them inside.

Aldo looks around the large lounge area in which they find themselves. Along the wall on his left are four thick wooden shelves that run the length of the room, filled floor to ceiling with vinyl records. A space in the middle of the shelves gives room for a high end Bang and Olufsen turntable and amplifier, and Aldo sees speakers discreetly mounted high up on the walls in the corners. At the far end of the record wall, a large entertainment cabinet nestles in the corner, featuring what looks like a fifty inch TV, a Blu Ray player, an Xbox One games console and a selection of movies and games. The centre of the lounge is taken up with a huge L shaped sofa upholstered in cream corduroy fabric and positioned around a big circular glass coffee table. On the far wall opposite the doorway is a large bay window with a peach of a view, a wide lawn that slopes down to the forest below, with mountains in the far distance rising up beyond the trees. Beneath the window, there's a waist high, fully stocked drinks cabinet.

To Aldo's right there's a door to an adjoining room, which Bale informs them is the kitchen, and further along the wall, in the far corner next to the bay window, a second door. Bale goes to it and produces a key from his back pocket, unlocking and opening the door to reveal a flight of descending stairs that run down into inky blackness. He flicks a light switch on the wall, revealing a narrow passage of rough stone walls, apparently tunnelled out of the bedrock beneath the house. He starts down the steps, Aldo, Luce and Ross in tow. At the bottom, they turn right and arrive at another door, which Bale unlocks with a second key.

"Here we are," he says, pushing open the door and sweeping an arm into the room beyond like an estate agent proudly displaying a show home.

It's a large, low-ceilinged space about thirty feet long, with a hardwood floor, walls adorned with acoustic panels and strategically placed sound baffles. In the near corners to Aldo's left and right are windows, the one on the right looking into the enclosed vocal booth, the one on the left to the studio control room.

A drum kit sits on what looks like a Persian rug at the far end of the room. Same model of Tama kit as Luce's own, only this one looks brand new, the steel rims of the kit's midnight blue shells and the hammered bronze cymbals and hi-hats lustrous and glowing under the recessed ceiling lights.

"Wow," Luce says softly, walking straight over to the setup and taking a seat on the drum stool. There's a holster full of drumsticks hanging ready on the mic stand next to her, and she takes out a pair, but doesn't start playing. "Just my size. Vic Firth 7A," she says, holding them up. Aldo watches as she just sits there, softly touching each drum with a stick, running her hands over the skins, rims, stands, cymbals and shells, a contemplative look on her face. Then she plays a few bars of a jazz beat, her sticks dancing around the drumheads and cymbals in quick rhythmic flurries. She stops and looks over at them. "Perfect," she says. "I don't even need to adjust any of this for my height. The stool, all the stands, the angles of the toms, even the tones are set up exactly as I like them." She looks at Bale. "How?"

"You will remember my staff packing up your equipment after your performance at the 13th Note?" Bale asks. "They took the details of your setup so your kit would be ready for you when you arrived."

"But we hadn't agreed anything with you then," Ross points out. "We'd only just met you."

Bale turns to him. "Ah, but I *knew*, Ross," he says, clapping him on the shoulder. "I have always known you three were special. Does your own setup meet with your expectations?"

He gestures to a beast of a Trace Elliot bass stack on the left wall. A hulking rectangular bulk, standing there damn near six foot tall. A pair of big four speaker cabinets, all shiny black metal mesh and hardened plastic, placed one on top of the other, the pair of cabinets crowned by an amplifier head with an illuminated bank of knobs, switches and diodes glowing green and red. Ross's effects pedals are already laid out on the floor in front of the stack, connected and ready to go, nestling between three wedge-shaped floor monitors. His bass itself sits in a guitar stand to the side, the tobacco burst finish of the body freshly polished, new stings shining.

Ross walks over to the setup and examines it before nodding appreciatively. "Aye," he says, smiling broadly. "I think this'll do just fine."

Aldo's gear's set up on the other side of the room directly across from Ross's, and he feels a tingle as he walks over and lays his hand on his own amp stack. Like Ross's, it's made up of two massive four speaker cabinets, topped with a hundred watt tube amp head, the bank of controls cast in Marshall's iconic gold and black, the power switch glowing Terminator red. Aldo glances over the array of knobs and buttons, running his fingertips softly across them. Getting the feel. Saying hello. Four channels – clean, crunch and two overdrives, each with their own independent EQ knobs for bass, middle and treble, already set to the values he uses on his own, much smaller Marshall Valvestate combo amp. Just standing next to the stack, Aldo feels the contained power of it resonating through his flesh and bones. A warm, valve-driven subsonic hum.

Nice. Very nice indeed.

On the floor in front of the stack, next to a microphone in its stand and a bank of monitors, his own multi-FX board is plugged in next to the footswitch for the amp, and his Les Paul, newly polished, oiled and strung, sits in a guitar stand to the side. The light glints off the strings and pickups, winking at him as if in anticipation of impending good times.

"Why don't you all warm up?" Bale says. "Play a few songs and get a sense of the space and tone of the room. Afterwards, we can discuss any specific production approach you would like to take."

"Sounds good," Aldo agrees, slinging his guitar strap over his head and plugging the input cable into his guitar. The fingers of his left hand automatically fall into an E chord on the strings, the fingers of his right going to his jeans pocket and taking a plectrum. He looks over at Ross. He's just standing there, staring at his amp stack with his hands in his pockets, rocking back and forth on his heels. Luce's sitting behind her kit, looking back at him, an unreadable expression on her face.

It's the blood thing, Aldo knows. He'd seen their reactions at seeing themselves on video, blitzed and sealing their contracts with a pinprick and a drop of claret. Weird, no doubt, but when he thought about it, Aldo found that he thought it was actually pretty cool. Symbolic. Like Bale said, a gesture of commitment. Shit, the three of them had done dafter things while drunk anyway.

Like having unprotected sex with a girl in the toilets after a gig at the Cathouse five years ago?

As much as he loved Dylan, that had been pretty fucking daft. Compared to that decision, a drop of blood on a recording contract was no biggie as far as Aldo was concerned. To be honest, if someone had asked, Aldo would gladly have sacrificed a toe or two for a recording contract and almost thirty grand in his bank account. No bother at all. A wee drop of blood was hee-haw in comparison.

"Well?" Aldo says, eyebrows raised and holding his hands out. Luce keeps staring back at him for a moment, then nods, once, and picks up her sticks. Aldo turns to Ross. "Roscoe?"

Ross makes no move to pick up his bass. Instead, he looks over Bale. "Who's John?" he asks. "The driver."

His smile never falters. "As you say, he's the driver. He's also looks after this place, and acts as my personal assistant."

"But who *is* he?" Ross repeats. "He looks familiar, and is he not a bit old to be a roadie?"

"John is a consummate professional," Bale replies, and is that a hint of impatience in his voice? "Strong as an ox despite his age, and he has been in my employ for many years. Is there a problem?"

Ross doesn't reply. Just purses his lips and nods slightly. "Nope," he says eventually. "No problem. Just thought I'd seen him somewhere before." Then he picks up his bass and turns to Aldo. "Let's dance."

Aldo grins, strums out a chord and turns to the amp stack, rolling up the master volume knob and filling the room with a swelling, squeaky-clean toned E major, the punch of the Marshall amp stretching his smile further as the sound wave washes over him.

Holy *fuck*, it sounds good.

Ross picks out a floorboard-shuddering low E note, perfectly in tune with Aldo, then plays a few runs in the same key, the bass frequencies like the humming of giant under the bedrock below them. His notes begin to take form, becoming a grooving lick, something Aldo's not heard him play before. He likes it, and nods over to Ross. "Keep that going, man," he says into the microphone. His voice comes clearly from the PA and the monitor speakers on the floor in front of him. The level perfectly set, with just the right amount of reverb.

Aldo hears the metallic *tss-tss-tss* of hi-hats finding time as Luce zeroes in on the tempo and rhythm of Ross's bass notes. Aldo looks over at her just as her sticks come down, and her kit begins to speak. A percussive language of precise pops, snaps, thuds, hisses and soft splashy crashes, nailing the beat neatly into place with Ross's bassline. That was the thing Aldo loved about his rhythm section. Ross and Luce laid a foundation better than any bass and drum combo Aldo'd ever played with.

Aldo strums the E chord again, then hears Luce approach the end of a bar with a intricate drum fill. Ross hears it too, and scales up from a low E note, getting louder, building… building…

Aldo comes in on the new bar, his tattered Nike coming down on the footswitch, going to the Overdrive One channel, and just letting his fingers do their thing.

The riff comes from nowhere, as all the best ones do. It's not so much that Aldo's playing it, more like he's just helping it happen, acting like a conduit, or like a midwife at a birth. This riff's a good one. A distorted, swaggering, swinging blues-tinged stomper. Hard, but sexy. Like getting punched in the mouth by an angry, but beautiful stripper.

Ross lets that big fat E note ring out on the bass while Aldo establishes the riff with a couple of repetitions, taking the idea and making it a *thing*. Then after another complimentary flourish on the drums from Luce, Ross joins in with Aldo on the next bar, perfectly replicating the newborn riff on his bass, giving it a low-down dirty depth and don't-fuck-with-me authority. Luce puts the cherry on the cake, settling into a distinctive, unexpected beat, cool and right in the pocket, perfectly embellishing the new riff.

And suddenly, out of nowhere, out of the *neverwhere*, Aldo knows Public Alibi have a new song. Potentially a fuckin cracker, too. He laughs out loud, and sees Ross and Luce smiling and nodding. They know it too. They can feel the new song in the air, as real and tangible as if a friendly stranger had just walked into the room and introduced themselves.

Aldo sees Bale standing behind the glass in the control room, leaning over the mixing desk and looking out at them, his head bobbing in time with the music, grinning like he's just unearthed a diamond. Aldo hadn't been aware of him leaving the room.

"You getting this down, Gappa?" Aldo asks into the mic, still playing. The riff just doing it by itself now. Behind the glass, Bale nods and gives him a thumbs up.

That makes Aldo happy, and from his happiness comes a guitar solo. As a new bar begins with another percussive flurry from Luce, he stomps on the footswitch again, the Marshall amp sliding smoothly into Overdrive Two like a sports car finding another gear, and Aldo's

Cuttin' Heads

Les Paul Custom starts to cry, his fingers conjuring electric sadness, cutting the air with soulful blue notes.

3

On the big, comfy-as-fuck couch in the lounge four hours later, Ross hits the settings icon on his mobile, trying to find a network.

Not a sausage.

"Any of you got a signal on your phone?"

Luce and Aldo check their mobiles but nope, nothing. "Was the same this morning," Aldo says. He picks up the Xbox controller again and un-pauses his game of *Call of Duty: Advanced Warfare*, going back to running amok in a futuristic junkyard with a grenade launcher and a rocket pack.

"No wifi either," Luce says, looking over from where she's flicking through the shelves of records. She selects one and holds the black and red sleeve in her hands for a few moments, then carefully slides the LP out and places it gently on the Bang and Olufsen turntable. Moments later, the soothing sounds of Grand Funk Railroad come rolling out from the swanky wall-mounted speakers. *Sin's a Good Man's Brother,* deep and warm and deliciously crackly as only vinyl can sound.

After the morning studio session, the three of them having a lunch of bacon rolls in the lounge, Ross had turned the huge telly on to find no satellite signal. No Sky box, no freeview, nothing. The massive screen, now showing Aldo's COD soldier picking off enemies from a watchtower with a sniper rifle - camping bastard that he was - was apparently good for games and Blu Rays only. There wasn't even an old TV aerial cable anywhere.

"No outside distractions," says a voice behind him, and Ross turns in his seat as Bale comes through the door leading down to the studio. "Think of this place as a musical immersion chamber. You are here to create. No television, no internet, no radio, no mobile signal."

"You've at least got a landline?" Ross asks, a mite uneasy with the idea of being rendered incommunicado.

"Of course," Bale answers pointedly. "For emergencies and business only."

Ross frowns at the curt tone of Bale's voice. "Fair enough. Was just asking."

"Indeed," Bale says, holding his gaze for a moment.

Ross doesn't like the way Bale's looking at him. The unmistakable *don't-fuck-with-me* look of the seasoned hardman. The dead eyes, capable of simultaneously issuing a warning and a challenge. Never one to back down from a confrontation, Ross doesn't look away. He's good at reading eyes, gauging reactions and emotions, but it's weird looking into this cunt's peepers. There's just… nothing there. Like, *nothing*.

Bale breaks their wee staring contest and resumes his usual easy smile. "So how do you all feel this morning went?"

Aldo pauses the game again, freezing the screen as a computer generated baddie's head explodes in a high definition cloud of blood and brains. "Well," he answers with a grin. "Mighty well."

And it had, Ross thinks. The sound in the studio, clear and perfectly balanced, had been so sweet on the ears that they'd just jammed and jammed almost non-stop all morning, the mojo in full flow, playing out their skins. And that unspoken musical communion between them, the language of form and dynamics, where they'd all instinctively known when the changes were coming up and reacted to them, complimenting each other, knowing the song without knowing it, conducting the music between the three of them with subtle hand gestures and nods of the head.

Strangely, they hadn't played a single note of their usual set. Instead, in the four hours they'd spent underground in the studio, they'd got the bones of three brand new songs down. Aldo could write a cracking tune when he put his mind to it, but he'd never been that prolific. In the five years the band had been together, they'd amassed a back catalogue of just thirteen finished tracks. Now they'd battered out three in the space of a single morning.

"There is magic here," Bale says, gesturing around the room. "I think you will find that the isolation is a great enabler of creativity. Here, free from the influence of the outside world, you can concentrate fully on our undertaking. As Zeppelin did at Bron-Yr-Aur while recording their third album. Soak up the atmosphere. *Drown* yourself in music."

"What about the police?"

Ross looks up at Luce, who's still standing by the wall of vinyl. She's facing Bale, her arms crossed in front of her, her face set. "Won't the police want to speak to us about what happened with Remember May?"

"Whatever for?" Bale asks casually, unruffled at the sudden change in subject.

"Well, we had that argument with them in the dressing room," Luce says. "It came pretty close to kicking off."

Good point, Luce, Ross thinks, looking at Bale for an answer.

"The good men and women of the constabulary have already talked to Rosemary at the Barrowlands," Bale says. "If they wish to speak to any of you, they have my number. In any case, I'm sure they already know you were in my company all evening after the Barrowlands, witnessed by many at the after show celebrations, far from the scene of the crime, yes?"

Luce nods, but looks far from convinced. Neither is Ross, to be honest. He's seen enough cop shows on TV to know that the first thing they always ask is if the deceased had any enemies. Though he wouldn't classify himself, Aldo and Luce as 'enemies', of Remember May, they hadn't exactly parted on the best of terms, and he can't imagine why the police wouldn't be interested in at least speaking to them.

Ah well, nothing he could do about it with no lines of communication. The ball was, as Bale said, in the coppers' court if they wanted to have a chat.

"But onto happier thoughts," Bale says. "We should discuss your release show."

"Our what now?" Ross asks.

"Yes, indeed. We discussed it at some length the night you signed your contracts," Bale explains, looking round at the three of them, his eyebrows raised as if waiting for them to remember. When it's clear no one has a scooby what he's talking about, he lets out a little laugh and rolls his eyes. "My, my. You *were* deep in your cups."

Well, there's no denying that. Ross has an uneasy moment as he wonders again just what kind of shenanigans he might have signed up for while blitzed. Signed up for and sealed with his bloody fingerprint, no less, *and just what the fuck was that all about?*

"So what's the dealio?" he asks.

"The dealio, Ross, is that Public Alibi will play a headline show at Glasgow Green, once the album is recorded," Bale says. "Coinciding with the release, it will be your grand arrival on the big stage. An announcement of your talent to the world. Fifty thousand people, including a large contingent from the media, will bear witness to what we have created here. It will be, I'm sure, a truly singular event. A rock show for the ages. But it must happen soon. While you are in the spotlight."

"Woah, slow down there, Mr Bale," Aldo says, smiling, but unsure. "It was a good show at the Barras. Seemed to get a great reaction on Facebook and Youtube, but are we not still a bit, well… unknown for what you're talking about?"

As if on cue, the door to the lounge opens and in comes John, dressed in his usual sombre back suit, his weathered face impassive as he wordlessly hands Bale a bunch of newspapers and magazines then shuffles out the door again.

Bale tosses the papers down on the big glass coffee table. "You underestimate your power, Aldo," he says. "There was already a sizeable media presence at the Barrowlands, there to document Remember May's triumphant homecoming. What they saw instead was an unknown band blowing one of the biggest acts in the UK off the stage. The unfortunate demise of the headliners following their own, apparently very poor, showing, has only added to your exposure." He lets out a sudden, hard bark of laughter. Ross flinches a little at the sound of it, and feels a little ill. "Public Alibi are already part of music folklore," he goes on. "I spoke to Rosemary this morning, and she has told me that a lot of people have asked about your band. *Who are they? Where are they now?* They want interviews, stories for their magazines and websites and television shows."

"Wait, *what*?" Luce says. "Television shows?"

"Mmmm. Just last night Rosemary spoke to someone from the BBC who wanted to interview you all. Your performance turned a lot of heads, made a lot of influential people sit up and take notice. So, imagine the fanfares," Bale says softly, now looking into the middle distance as if gazing on some grand vision, "when we announce that the band they all want to know about is playing a special showcase concert to launch their debut album. Believe me, my friends. When I say this will be a rock show for the ages, I mean exactly that." He gestures at the papers and mags on the table. "Read for yourself. The pages concerning you are marked."

Ross leans forward and picks up a copy of the Sunday Herald while Aldo snags a copy of the Mail and Luce takes a Mojo.

The now familiar photograph of the bloody lift containing the pixelated corpses of Remember May takes up most of the front page of the Herald in Ross's hands, blown up to bloody broadsheet proportions under the headline *HORROR AT THE HILTON*. Ross feels the bacon rolls he devoured for lunch take a queasy turn in his guts, and quickly flicks to the page marked with a yellow post-it note, where he finds the music section, and a review of the Barras gig. Presumably out of respect for the dead, the journalist only touches briefly on the headliner's apparently woeful performance, and instead spends most of the article raving about *the previously unknown support band, a dynamic* three piece named Public Alibi, who came out of nowhere, and took the roof off the Barras with a storming, virtuoso performance, completely upstaging the main act.

Ross finds his hands are shaking.

"Holy shit," Aldo says quietly as he looks down at the paper in his hands. "The best, most exciting live act this cynical journalist has seen in years," he reads. "With just one show and the circumstances surrounding it, Public Alibi have carved an indelible mark on the face of a tired industry where there are no more heroes anymore."

"Listen to this," Luce says, reading from her copy of Mojo. "Bootleg footage of Public Alibi's extraordinary support set at the Glasgow Barrowlands on Friday night has since gone viral, with clips already viewed on Youtube millions of times. The previously unheard of trio's Facebook page currently has almost half a million followers, the number continuing to grow by the hour. Ticket vendors and venues have been inundated with calls and emails from the band's new legions of fans, demanding to know when their next show is."

Luce drops the magazine on the table and slumps down on the couch next to Ross, staring into space, her hands doing that nervous little drum roll on her thighs. "This is mental," she murmurs, shaking her head slightly. "I don't believe it."

"Fuckin believe it, Luce," Aldo says, grinning over at her, slapping the newspaper in his hands. "It's right there, babes. They *want* us. We're huge!"

Ross feels strangely numb, like he wants to get up and dance a jig around the room, but at the same time, he's scared that if he does, he'll wake up back in his one bedroom flat in the dodgy end of Inverclyde. And though he knows it was a good show, the best they'd ever played, he suspects that a lot of the sudden attention is due to what happened to Remember May.

Saying that, though. They'd rocked the absolute *shit* out of the Barras.

Bale just stands there, hands in his pockets and smiling down on them. "So, you see," he says. "We have work to do. I have instructed

Rosemary to let the press know that you are currently ensconced in a secret location recording an album, and that news of a special live event will follow shortly." He turns and walks over to the door leading down to the studio. He opens it and stands there, one arm held invitingly into the dark stairway. "Shall we get back to it?"

4

Space and time were two commodities Aldo Evans has never had much of. He'd always *made* as much space and time as possible in his life for music, but there'd never been quite enough. The real world had always been there to distract him, eating up hours, most of them working in one miserable job or another, or worrying about not *having* a miserable job. Worrying about paying bills. So much time wasted, when he could've been playing music and writing songs.

Not so much of a problem these days. Now he has all the space and time he wants, and the weird thing is, now that he has them, neither seem that important.

Time for instance. Cut off, with no TV, phone or internet to draw his attention and mark its passing, it becomes strangely fluid. Hours and days lose their structure. There are no clocks anywhere in Easy Rollin HQ. No calendars either. Bale tells them this is quite intentional. There's the time display on Aldo's phone, he supposes, but with no mobile signal out here in the arse end of the highlands, it's remained neglected in Aldo's jacket pocket since he arrived. He doesn't wear a wristwatch, and even if he did, he doubts he'd make use of it, because regular units of time don't matter here.

Bale never says anything about taking any time off, and no one else mentions it either. No one *wants* time off, because there's nowhere they'd rather be and nothing they'd rather do. They're in the groove and don't want to leave it. Aldo, Ross and Luce eat when they get hungry and sleep when they get tired. The rest of the time, it's like Bale says. A musical immersion chamber, and they're happily drowning themselves. Just like he said they should.

There *is* no time. Only the cycle. Eat breakfast. Into the studio. Eat lunch. Into the studio. Eat dinner. Into the studio. Maybe chill for an hour or two at night with a movie, some tunes or some Xbox, then sleep. Except sometimes Aldo *can't* sleep, his brain refusing to shut down, or he wakes suddenly in the middle of the night, a new riff, a melody or a lyric line repeating in his head, the urge to pick up his guitar or pen like an urgent need to piss.

Then it's the cycle again.

A hazy number of days pass like this. After the third, Aldo stops counting. Units of time that aren't measured in bars don't matter. Not here. Not now.

In terms of space, again, it's something Aldo *used* to think about. All he knows of the space outside Easy Rollin Manor is that there's lots of it. Empty space, filled with nothing but mountains and forest, seen only when they go outside into the courtyard for a smoke. Aldo's universe shrinks to the space inside the walls of the whitewashed U shaped building, and the new centre of that universe is the underground studio below. In that long, wood-floored and acoustically optimised room, standing in front of his Marshall stack with a guitar in his hands and a mic in front of him, Aldo Evans feels more at peace, more *right*, than at any point in his life. It's as if he's been on a long, almost thirty year journey to get here, and has finally come home and put his feet up in front of a cosy log fire.

He occasionally thinks about other things. Dylan. Ashley. Remember May. Their apparent fame back home and the upcoming showcase gig at the Green. But it's mostly just background noise. Aldo's thoughts are concerned with riffs, verses and choruses. Bridges and middle eights. Intros and outros. Drum breaks, bass lines and solos. Every time he goes down the stairs from the lounge into the studio. Every time he picks up his Les Paul and switches on the stack, the power light warming up to that glaring red glow, Aldo Evans dives deep and finds his own personal corner of heaven. He finds gold.

And it just keeps on coming.

So, they play. They play well. Loose but tight. Free but regimented. The concepts of space and time blur, losing cohesion and meaning. But fuck it all. It's all about the music.

Gappa Bale, the man who's made it all possible, is there with them. Hovering on the edges, barely seen outside of the studio, most of the time just a shadow glimpsed through the window to the control room where he lurks, without being prompted making minute adjustments to the room's sounds and levels as needed. Recording every note they play. Now and again his voice comes through the monitors, chipping in an occasional idea. *Maybe slow that down just a hair. Perhaps play that riff a few more times before the change? How about going to the half time there? Why don't you try the chorus effect on that progression?* He never intrudes, though.

And by fuck, the guy can play.

A few days ago, two, three maybe, Luce comes up with this mental drum beat. A real bone rattler somewhere between hardcore punk and jazz. Quick, aggressive, complex, and right in your face. Aldo feels the need for speed, and starts riffing away, hard, fast and nasty. Ross picks it up and fills it out, and bingo bango let's get mangled, there's another new song. They agree it needs something odd and spooky sounding for the half time section. Ross suggests violins. *Weird* violins. Bale says there's one upstairs somewhere, and comes into the live room a few minutes later with an old battered looking fiddle, the finish on the instrument's body faded and worn away completely in some places from long years of use. Bale says he can play a bit, and offers his services, just to see how Ross's idea sounds. Always open to jamming with anyone willing to have a go, Aldo invites him to have a lash at it.

Bale goes into the control room, flicks some switches, then comes back out and sets himself up with a mic and an acoustic pickup linking the violin to a multi effect unit. They start the song again, and Bale plays not a single note. He stands there with his eyes closed, the violin in his left hand, the bow in his right. He doesn't move a muscle. Not until the half time. Then he comes to life, and lays down a violin solo that'd melt the faces of all the angels in Heaven.

Musically, Aldo knows he's no slouch, and right now he's in the best form of his life, but Gappa Bale's on another level. Several levels. He's First Violin of the Vienna Philharmonic on meth. Impossibly fast one moment, shredding out notes like a minigun, then breaking your heart with sweet soulful strains the next. Then he's freaking you out. He uses the pedal on the board as a pitch shifter, bending his notes to produce eerie wails, and when he adds a hefty pinch of delay, a little flange and a dash of fuzz... holy shit. The *noises* he makes. Aldo's pretty good at making his guitar gently weep, but Bale makes that old violin scream like a gang rape victim.

They finish the song with a big crescendo, building tension, pushing the tempo faster and faster then eventually just going batshit freetime, making as much demented high-gain noise as loudly as possible and thrashing their hands raw on their instruments. Key and time become irrelevant, and Aldo's hoarse, desperate screams and the multiple voices of Bale's shrieking shuddering violin howl above the storm like souls begging for mercy. No orchestral Phil Spector wall of sound, this. This is a violent, black ocean of fifty foot soundwaves. A scorched continent of atonal noise.

They eventually finish, sweating and panting and the tinnitus loud and proud in their ears. Aldo's broken three strings and is bleeding from his right hand where he's thrashed his fingertips raw, smearing blood and bits of torn skin on his guitar's scratchplate. Luce's missing a stick, the other one's broken, and her snare skin's burst.

Bale looks well pleased, and says it might make a good track to close the album with.

Aldo agrees.

5

Bless me, Father, for I have sinned. It's been fourteen years since my last confession.

A long time, the half-seen priest beyond the partition says. *What sins have you committed in the last fourteen years, my child?*

I've dishonoured my mother and father. I've used foul language. I've been vain and self absorbed. I've used drugs and drank alcohol to excess. I've had lustful thoughts, and intercourse outside of marriage. I've lied. I've had hateful feelings towards one of my colleagues, and threatened them with violence.

Luce's greasy hands wring themselves in her lap. Her satin Confirmation dress, an uncomfortable lacy thing glowing pristine white in the cramped gloom of the confessional, makes soft whispery sounds as she fidgets and squirms. Shame flushes her cheeks and traces little circles of self-disgust in her stomach. She is a *bad* girl.

Is there anything else? the priest asks after a few seconds of heavy silence.

Yes, Luce whispers. *I've taken the Lord's name in vain. I've blasphemed. I've... turned away from Christ, cursed His name, and worshipped false idols.*

Tears track down her cheeks. She is *such* a bad girl.

Wicked child, the priest mutters.

I'm sorry, Luce squeaks. *Please, forgive me.*

There is no forgiveness here, the priest tells her, his voice dropping abruptly to a husky snarl. *Not for you, you little cunt.*

Please...

The priest just laughs at her.

Her tears come harder, spilling down her cheeks, tasting of burnt iron as they drip from her lips and splash crimson specks on the perfect snowy white of her Confirmation gown.

Then the blood suddenly bursts from her ears, her nose, her mouth. Her face feels like it's melting, pouring in red torrents down her body and splashing on the floor of the confessional, which begins to fill. The gathering blood rises over her patent white leather shoes, creeps above the snowy white cotton of her frilly ankle socks and up her legs. The walls of the booth close in, creaking and cracking with the sound of breaking bones as the blood rises quicker, pooling over her lap and up around her chest while the priest laughs and curses her in a ragged, bestial voice that sounds like nothing human. Outside the confessional is a clanging racket of bells playing a discordant series of chimes, and even as the blood rises and the priest howls laughter, her trained ears identify the bells' notes as clearly as her eyes identify letters on a page. There's a low G, another G an octave above, and there in the middle, unexpected and eerie, a C sharp. A specific arrangement of notes the church would have hanged you for playing just a few centuries before. The tritone. The diminished fifth. *Diabolus in musica.* Luce's been studying music long enough to know the devil's interval when she hears it, and her scream lasts only a moment before the blood rises over her chin and floods her mouth and now she can't breathe she's drowning and thrashing...

...and sitting up in bed.

Her chest unlocks like shattering ice, and Luce collapses back onto the mattress, her breath coming in ragged gasps. She lies there, staring into the deep shadows of the room, heart slamming and her body tense, as if ready to bolt at any moment. The nightmare, like dreams good and bad often do, is already fading from her memory, leaving her with vague notions of being in St Michael's again.

It's cold in her room. Freezing. Luce checks her watch. Almost three am. She slides out from beneath her sweaty bedclothes, shivering as she pads across the room to the window. It's closed tight, and she feels no stray current of air as she passes her hand round the frame. It's just an old, cold building with an old, shitty heating system. Outside in the courtyard, wind and rain lash the night. At the edge of the light cast by the bollard lamps she can see the boughs of the pine trees of the surrounding forest thrashing in the storm.

Wide awake and shaky from her nightmare, the first she's had since after the 13th Note gig, Luce knows there's no chance of getting back to sleep right now. She crosses the chilly room to the dresser and quickly pulls on an old but warm and comfortable hoodie bearing the University of Glasgow crest, then grabs her Kindle and leaves the room. As long as she's awake, she may as well get some reading done and warm herself in front of the big open fire in the library.

Bale had briefly shown it to them when giving a quick guided tour of the house's interior after they'd wrapped the studio session on the first day. Easy Rollin Manor, as they'd taken to calling it, wasn't that big a building, and the tour hadn't taken long. There was an old but large en-suite bathroom adjoining Luce's Room, a smaller bathroom at the opposite wing of the building where Aldo and Ross had their rooms, and the kitchen, dining room, lounge and library along the main corridor. Bale said his own quarters were downstairs off the studio, and told them John, the rarely seen driver / assistant, had a small residence in the rear grounds of the property.

In the main passage outside her room, Luce opens the first door on her left. The library's a large, yet cosy room, mostly crammed floor to ceiling with loaded bookshelves. Luce hadn't had time to properly browse when Bale was giving his tour, but at a glance she'd seen that there were books of fiction and poetry mixed in with encyclopedias and atlases, biographies and reference books alongside magazines. No alphabetisation, no arrangement by type or genre, all just chaotically shoved together in no discernible order. The neat freak and book lover in Luce disapproved, but she had to admit there was a certain shabby charm to it. That charm was also markedly added to by the one wall dedicated to Bale's collection of instruments. Basses, guitars, bits of drum kits and sticks, and even an old Wurlitzer keyboard.

The only light in the room comes from the open fireplace to Luce's left, where an inviting blaze is crackling away in the big rough stone hearth, filling the room with warmth and the inviting smell of roasting pinewood, casting a cosy orange glow over the wooden floor and the large black leather couch in front of it.

Bale's there, facing away from her so she can only see the back of his head and part of the left side of his face. He's not reading. He's not doing anything. Just sitting there, and he doesn't look round when Luce enters.

She stands there for a moment, just looking at the back of his head. Since they'd been here working on the album, her unease around Bale has diminished considerably, and it wasn't just his mysterious charisma and his looks, though there was no denying he was a a fine looking man. Since they'd been in the studio, though, he'd proven himself an absolute joy to work with. He had an instinctive feel for music, for the band itself, where they wanted to go and what they wanted to do. He called a halt when he felt something wasn't right and he'd been bang on the money. Not criticising, but making suggestions that invariably enhanced whatever they were playing.

And no instrumental novice himself, Bale had almost become like a fourth member of the band. Ever since providing that frankly disturbing violin part that sounded like a pod of Orcas being slaughtered, he'd chipped in a few other bits and pieces. Not much, just subtle little things that coloured the song. A shake of maracas here, a subtle acoustic guitar track there, and a piano track on a deep and heavy blues dirge Aldo'd come up with, using a bottleneck slide and a Slayer guitar tone. Bale's weighty barrelhouse piano chords, low down on the keyboard and played sparingly, gave the song sudden moments of dark, startling depth. Like slipping into a bath at midnight and finding no bottom to the tub.

"Good morning, Lucia," Bale says without looking round.

She walks round the couch and stands to the side of the fireplace, its crackling warmth immediately chasing the chill from her bones. Bale doesn't look up at her. Doesn't give her one of his customary smiles. He just continues staring into the flames as if entranced, his face expressionless, reflected fire dancing in his dark, dark eyes. He has an open bottle of single malt in his lap which he raises to his lips, taking a healthy swallow.

"How'd you know it was me?" Luce asks.

"You have trouble sleeping sometimes," he replies, still not taking his eyes off the fire.

Luce frowns. She had a lot of nightmares as a child, and they'd recently started coming back. But how did he know that?

"I too occasionally find rest elusive," he says. "In the dark, it can be difficult to control one's thoughts." He takes another drink and then holds the bottle out toward Luce, still not looking at her, still with that unsettling blankness on his perfectly formed features.

Luce steps forward and accepts the whisky, reading the label. Thirty year old Glenfiddich. She's no expert, but she knows it must cost a fair whack, and Bale's necking it straight from the bottle like cheap cider. This change from his usual manner – totally in control, cultured in the strangest, most laid back way, and of course that dangerous smile – it's all making her distinctly uneasy. Right now he looks almost... vulnerable. Something she wouldn't previously have thought possible. Not of him.

"This looks like a very nice wee tipple," she says. "Expensive. Shouldn't we be using glasses?"

Bale just shrugs. "It does the same either way," he says. "It brings oblivion."

She can't argue with that. Luce takes a sip, intensely aware that her lips are touching the same surface that Bale's had only moments before. She sits down on the couch beside him. "Are you okay?"

He says nothing. The only sound in the room is the soft crackle and occasional pop of a pine knot in the fire.

Luce studies him in profile. The way the firelight brings out his high cheekbones, the deep darkness of his eyes, the contrasting black of his fine, arched eyebrows and that beautiful long wavy hair against his pale skin. She finds herself inching a little closer. Wants to reach out and touch him. Bring him comfort. He's obviously troubled about something. Hurting.

"What are you reading?" he asks.

Luce doesn't even wonder how he knows that she's holding her Kindle, as engrossed as he obviously is in the fire. Has he even blinked?

"*The Death of Grass*," she says. She takes another sip of the malt and offers him the bottle. "Have you read it?"

Bale takes the bottle, but doesn't drink. Just lets it rest in his lap. "An excellent book. Such an incisive commentary on the human condition. Strip away a man's comforts, take him down to the bare bones of existence, and what are you left with?" He looks at Luce for the first time since she entered the room. Up close, it's not some cheesy romantic notion of drowning she feels as she looks into Bale's eyes. It's an odd, not entirely unpleasant *emptying* sensation, as if some ineffable part of her is being extracted and drawn towards the dark drain of Bale's pupils.

"It never ceases to amaze me, how easily the descent into savagery comes to man," he says softly. "It is so simply done."

"That's a pretty cynical view," Luce says. "They're just trying to survive, trying to make it to the farm in the valley and protect their families."

Bale smiles. But it's not a pleasant smile. "Do not be naïve, Lucia. Look at the character Pirrie. A perfect psychopath in waiting, his true nature exposed by mere circumstance. Even John, your mild-mannered engineer. Scratch any man's skin hard enough, and there is a willing killer hidden below."

"Woah, no spoilers," Luce says. "I'm not that far into it yet. They've only just got out of London."

Bale turns back to the fire, that smile that was more like a sneer disappearing. "You will see, Lucia," he says, then takes another long swallow of whisky.

"Why do you do that?" Luce asks. "I've told you I don't know how many times not to call me Lucia." Saying that though, she finds that she doesn't mind it so much anymore. She's kind of got used to it.

Bale hands her back the bottle. "It is your *name*," he says. "And it is a beautiful name. To say and to hear."

"Well, thanks." She lifts the bottle to her mouth, taking another swallow. A slightly bigger one this time. She feels colour rushing to her cheeks, colour that has little to do with the high quality single malt.

"If I may ask," Bale says, "why do you mind so much? Why does your own name cause you discomfort?"

Luce raises her eyebrows. "Discomfort? I wouldn't say that. It's just... I don't know. Everyone calls me Luce. Only my folks call me Lucia. When anyone else says it, it sounds sort of patronising."

"You have issues with your parents?"

Luce takes another swallow. "Well. With my mum, mostly."

"Why?"

"She's... difficult to deal with. She's never been on board with me being a musician. And she's religious. Old school religious. Italian Catholic old school religious."

Bale smiles. A real one this time. "And you are not?"

Luce takes another sip of whisky, never taking her eyes from Bale's. "I did my time," she says evasively, handing the bottle back. There's not much left in it, and Bale returns the cap and puts the near empty bottle on the floor. How much has she just drank? And why has she just told him all that?

A warm, pleasant tingle spreads over Luce's skin. A slight numbing of the fingertips. Her tongue feels thick and half anesthetised.

"But no longer?" Bale says. As if by accident, his hand moves on the couch, his fingers brushing over hers. They stay there. Luce makes no move to pull away.

"No," she says, shaking her head slightly and feeling the room wobble a little around her. "No longer." That spreading blush on her skin, so warm and welcoming, flows downward.

"You have issues with your heritage? Your culture? Your *God*?" Bale whispers. His hand slides over Luce's onto her wrist, curling round with serpentine silkiness and gently brushing his fingertips at the point where her pulse beats beneath the skin.

"Yes," Luce says, also whispering. Looking into Bale's eyes, she feels that peculiar draining sensation again, stronger now. She wonders, in a very distracted, unimportant way, why she's telling him this. She never talks about this stuff, not even with Aldo or Ross. But her doubts are easily squashed and silenced because she knows she can trust Gappa Bale, she can trust him to beyond the stars and back.

"What did He do? Your loving God?" Bale murmurs, moving an inch closer on the couch. His left hand slides up her arm, brushing her hair before resting lightly on the soft skin of Luce's neck, just below her jaw. "*Tell me.*"

His fingers, those long, smooth, graceful fingers, again find her pulse, and brush over it with feather light strokes. Luce shudders and closes her eyes. "My... friend," she hears herself say, her voice no more than a needy whimper. "When I was a little kid... She... died..."

She feels Bale's other hand on her thigh, raking his fingernails up along the fabric of her pyjama bottoms with maddening slowness, leaving little furrows of pleasure in their wake. Some part of her that still has a shred of sense puts her hand on top of his, halting its ascent, but it's a weak, half-hearted attempt at best, and when Bale's hand moves again, sliding higher and dropping inwards, Luce's resistance crumbles, and instead of stopping it, her hand guides his towards the junction of her thighs.

"What happened?" Bale whispers, leaning close, his voice directly in her ear now as he slowly rolls his wrist, applying a sly, teasing pressure between her legs. Luce feels it like a warm wave that radiates up from her clit and out through her entire body, and she gasps, her hips rising up off the couch.

"*Che e successo, mi amore?*" Bale asks again, his breath and lips brushing her ear.

"Brain haemorrhage," Luce moans, helpless, the hot, bubbling tension inside her ruling her body and mind and desperate for release. "She... Karen had... an aneurysm... while she was... in chapel... confessing... oh... oh... *fuck... please...*"

"*Cosi crudele*," Bale sympathises, leaning in to kiss her, his hand slipping under the waistband of her PJs. "*So cruel.*"

6

Aldo's sitting up on the bed in his room, his back against the headboard, headphones on and eyes closed.

As usual, the quality of the recording's top notch, fresh from the studio and perfectly balanced, courtesy of Mr Gappa Bale and his mixing board sorcery.

The track playing at this moment, which they recorded just a few hours ago, is a beast. A sludgy, doom-mongering slice of riffage, way down in the dungeons of a dropped C tuning. With the basic instrumental idea down, now Aldo has to give it language. Try to come up with a vocal, something real, something honest, but dress it up some. Fit words around a beat and a give them a melodic hook that sticks in the brain. Make it just lyrical enough to be cool, but not so much that it's pretentious. Make it relatable. Don't be cheesy though, or unoriginal. Simple, but weird, that's the ticket.

But not *too* weird.

Aldo has a pen in his hand and a writing pad on his lap. His lyric book. He's had it for eighteen years, and the scuffed brown leather cover of the notebook and the dog-eared pages show it. He stares down at the dreaded blank page. All that taunting, impatient whiteness with no words written on it.

He'd never been a prolific lyricist, which explained the fact he'd had the same notebook for eighteen years without filling it. Most of the time, lyric writing's a daunting ordeal for Aldo Michael Evans. It's a frightening prospect, to bare yourself in that way.

But of course, that was before all these amazing things happened. Just as the riffs have been flowing as if they're on tap, Aldo's notebook's been seeing a lot more ink recently, getting well scribbled in, the lyrics just pouring out of him. Like everything else, here it's all just so natural. And with everything that's happened lately, good and bad, he's certainly not in want of subject matter.

Want. That rhymes with haunt.

The track on the headphones is all low, slow and doomy. Like *Ironman* on Mogadon, and it needs a dark lyric. Something real. Something honest.

He pauses the playback and his pen moves on the page, scratching out a few words.

Got everything I wanted, but this house is cold and haunted

Aldo squints down at what he's just written, tapping the Sharpie against the page. Not bad. Not amazing, but the syllables fit the rhythm and the melody he has in his head.

What else rhymes with haunt? Daunt? Flaunt?

Not great words for rhyming purposes. Sounds a bit forced. Haunt is probably too strong a word anyway. It conjures thoughts of footsteps in an empty corridor in the dead of night. Spectral apparitions and the ghostly wailing of the lost dead. This house, though there *is* a permanent chill in the air, isn't like that. It's not Scooby Doo haunted.

But still.

Aldo Michael Evans is loving it here, make no mistake, friends and comrades. Literally living his dream. As wrapped up in it all as he is, though, he can't deny that there's a fuckin weird vibe about the place in Easy Rollin Manor. He's focussed, giving the music his all, but he's not daft.

The music for a start, and the way they've come on, performance wise, in the space of a couple of weeks. They'd always been a tidy enough act. Aldo's never been into playing sloppy shows, and Luce flat out refused to play anything live until thoroughly convinced the song was gig ready. But ever since that show in the 13th Note, it's like they've been on rock steroids.

And the music just kept coming. They all knew exactly what they were doing, though all the songs were brand new. There was the normal communicating mid-song changes with nods and hand gestures, but everybody was instinctively understanding the *feel* of the song, knowing what the others were doing and anticipating what they were going to do next. Aldo'd heard stories of it before. Ginger Baker talked about how Cream sometimes would find themselves all playing the same phrases out of nowhere, feeling as if there was something playing the instrument for you. Playing *through* you. Through everyone in the band. Baker had said it frightened him sometimes.

The band's near psychic connection, and their sudden acceleration of skill? Sure, they'd done nothing *but* jam for...

How long is it now? A fortnight? Longer?

...days on end, and playing that often inevitably sharpened you up.
But still.

Aldo'd been genuinely unsettled by one or two moments that seemed to go... beyond normal. When he'd felt like he was just standing back against the studio wall, watching himself, a sweaty grimacing avatar screaming into a microphone, demented.

Ah, but then there were the sweet moments when the three of them were just pulling awesomeness out of the air like they were catching butterflies, and feeling that sensation when the music's all around you and coming through you and your friends... It was something beyond rational. It was Heaven. It was Nirvana.

But still.

There are other wee niggly weird things that Aldo's noticed since he's been here.

These wee niggles are in the perfect sound-proofed silence of the place whenever there's a lull in the noise level. An unsettling calm. So still you could expect to see a fly frozen in mid air, as if God had pressed pause on his cosmic remote control. It's a quiet that amplifies your thoughts, which can make them take strange paths if allowed to wander.

And these wee niggles are in the way the land outside the building sometimes seems vaguely threatening when they go out for a smoke break. As if Nature here was watching them with a brooding consciousness. And the whole space and time thing, which had been the subject of another severely weird tune he'd come up with. Although he had plenty of both and was glad of it, he'd begun to notice just how oddly malleable space and time were in this place. It was hard to judge them. The end of a room or corridor sometimes didn't seem to be quite where your eye thought it was, as if the lines and angles of the walls, ceilings and floors were ever so slightly skewed to create subtle optical illusions of scale and distance. And hours regularly flew by when it seemed only minutes had passed. Right enough, time flies when you're having fun and all that, and Public Alibi were having all the fun they could handle.

And as for the land seeming threatening, he reasoned, it's October in the Scottish highlands, and winter doesn't fuck about up here. The wind and rain had barely let up since they arrived, and it'd been snowing earlier when they went out for a smoke after finishing the evening session. Now, looking down at the near blank page of the pad on his lap, kind of like a blank snowfield itself, with just that one line written at the top, Aldo decides another nicotine injection's well in order.

He puts the writing pad and pen on the little bedside cabinet next to him and swings his legs off the bed, sitting up and rubbing his gritty, tired eyes. He runs his hands through his hair. It hangs down around his shoulders, greasy and lank. Aldo remembers having a shower at some point in the last few days, but he's not been keeping track, and isn't sure exactly how long ago that was. Plus, washing and changing clothes just didn't seem to matter all that much. An experimental sniff under his armpit confirms that he's getting a bit ripe, though, and Aldo resolves to go for another shower in the morning.

Crossing the room, he shrugs into his leather jacket hanging on the wardrobe door and takes a fresh packet of cigs from one of the three cartons that had been sitting there on the dresser waiting for him when they'd arrived at Easy Rollin Manor. They were the same brand he usually smoked. Just one of several cool touches courtesy of Gappa Bale.

The main corridor outside his room's cold, empty, and lit only by the dimmed recessed lights in the oak-panelled ceiling. Hendrix, The Ramones, Morrison and Jagger look down from the burnt-orange painted walls, and he salutes them as he walks by.

The cold seizes him the moment he steps outside into the night. Closing the heavy storm doors behind him, Aldo turns his back to the bitter highland wind and hunches over, cupping his cig and lighter in his hands to light up, which he manages only after several failed attempts. Cigarette lit and flooding his system with sweet nausea, Aldo shivers and blows out a plume of smoke as he surveys his surroundings.

Where the gravelled courtyard ends, it gives way to snow-covered moorland which ends in the thick forest which blankets the hills rising up behind the building. Turning his collar up against the chill, Aldo walks across the courtyard, past the Balemobile - as Ross has taken to calling the big black motor - and out of the light cast by the bollard lamps. His feet crunching on the snow, cold seeping through the thin material of his trainers, he goes a short distance before stopping. Then he turns his eyes skyward.

As he's done on several occasions since being here, Aldo looks up at the starscape above, revealed in all its fearsome glimmering vastness in the dark beyond the illuminated courtyard. He feels the familiar mixture of wonder and nervousness that he always gets when contemplating the immensity of the night sky. On stage, when he's doing his thing and the gig's going well, Aldo Evans sometimes feels ten feet tall, but standing here out in the hills, looking up at the yawning infinity above him, he feels less than microbial. It's an awareness of size and space that's humbling, and a little frightening.

But he keeps looking up, smoking his cig, following the path of satellites and watching a shooting star leave a long white burn mark across the firmament.

Aldo stays there till he feels a scorch on his lips, having smoked his cig right down to the filter without knowing it. He winces and flicks the glowing butt aside, then turns and walks back through the snow toward the building, thinking that *firmament* is a pretty cool word. Not the easiest to slip into a lyric right enough, and it rhymes with fuck all.

He's just a few steps from the lights of the courtyard when he feels something tugging at the back of his jacket.

Aldo lets out a cry and whirls round, tripping on an unseen rock hidden under the snow. He lands on his arse, winded with fright, whipping his head side to side.

There's nothing there. The expanse of snow covered ground between him and the surrounding forest is empty.

But then he hears a sound, seeming to come from the darkness of the woods in front of him, carried on the icy still night air. It's a sound that usually makes him smile. A sound that he usually loves. Now though, a bleak chill sheathes Aldo's skin from scalp to toenails, and it's got nothing to do with him sitting in the snow, because he's thinking of standing on Ashley's doorstep not so long ago, with Dylan in his arms, tickling him and making him giggle, and the wee man tugging on his jacket, asking him if he's coming to Funworld.

Once again, Dylan's giggle comes from the darkness between the trees.

"*Daaaaaaaaaddy,*" his son calls out, his wee voice followed by the sound of rustling branches and quick running feet in the snow.

What the fuck? What the fuck?

"*Daaaaaaaddy,*" Dylan's voice calls out again from the black woods. "*Come and play with me! I want a belly munch!*"

Unseen in the dark, the wee man starts to sing, his high childish voice wavering and off-key. It's a song Aldo recognises from *Frozen*. *Do You Want to Build a Snowman?* has never sounded creepier.

Aldo pushes himself to his feet and stands there, trembling. "Dylan?" he calls out, his voice cracking half way though. This wasn't possible. How could Dylan be here? He hadn't told Ashley where he was going. He hadn't even known himself. Had *Gappa* brought Dylan up here? As a surprise?

Dylan laughs again. *"Come on, Daddy! Come and find me! Let's play hide and seek!"*

Bale must *have brought him up here,* he tells himself, desperately groping for an explanation.

So why didn't he bring him inside earlier?

It's a surprise. I always go outside for a smoke.

Right, very good, ya bumper. Bale brought your four-year-old son all the way up from Inverclyde, then left him outside in the woods and the snow for fuck knows how long, all so he could surprise you when you eventually went out for a cig.

Right.

So where are his footprints?

Aldo looks down at the snow between him and the forest. The only footprints visible are his own, ending at the spot where he'd been standing, smoking and stargazing. And that can't be, because he'd felt a small hand tugging insistently on his jacket in that way Dylan always does when he wants attention. His surprise visit theory falls apart, and Aldo feels that bleak chill on his skin sinking bone deep.

He looks, fearfully now, back up at the dark ranks of trees in front of him.

If that's not Dylan, and it can't be, then...

Now there's not a sound. Not even the wind in the pines.

Cabin fever. That's it, he thinks. *The isolation's making me nuts. Too long locked away from the real world. Too much change too fast. Dylan, or... something else, is absolutely* not *out there in the forest.*

Trembling, he turns and walks back towards the brightly lit courtyard, making an effort not to run.

"Please, Daddy, don't go back inside," Dylan calls out behind him, his voice small, scared.

Aldo freezes, his scalp and ballsack crawling. But hearing the note of distress in his son's voice, Aldo can't help but turn around again. He looks back at the woods, and the air leaves his lungs like he's just been kicked in the chest with a steel toe-capped boot.

Dylan's standing there, solid and undeniably real, wearing his Fireman Sam jacket and Angry Birds hat. Close enough for Aldo to see the ruddiness of his cheeks and his breath condensing in the cold night air. He beckons to Aldo with one mittened hand, a pleading, frightened expression on his face, then he turns and vanishes into the shadows between the trees again.

Knowing fine well that none of this is possible, but parental instinct overriding reason, Aldo runs after him, floundering through the knee-deep snow and tripping over hidden rocks. "Dylan! Wait!"

The forest swallows him, and then Aldo's blundering through darkness that only deepens as he goes, colliding with barely-seen tree trunks, branches lashing his face. Acting on sheer reflex, his mind, useless in such circumstances, has taken a back seat, and he stumbles on, sightless, heart hammering in his chest, unthinking but for the single frantic notion that he has to find the wee man because he can't be running about in these dark woods because he might fall and hurt himself and what the *fuck* is he doing out here in the first place it doesn't make any *sense*...

A sound, somewhere behind Aldo, halts him, and he stands there in the pitch black pine-scented void, listening.

The dry rustle of disturbed foliage. A soft footfall in the underbrush.

Aldo turns in a circle, trying to track the sound of movement, though he can see absolutely nothing in the inky gloom and may as well be blindfolded. "Dylan?"

Slowly waving his hands before him like a kid playing blind man's bluff, trying to feel his way in the black, Aldo moves slowly forward. The fingertips of his left hand brush the rough, sap-sticky bark of a tree truck. "Dylan? Where are you, wee man?"

Nothing.

Unnerved and disoriented by the absolute lack of light, Aldo turns his head up for a glimpse of the night sky between the treetops, but there's nothing there. Just more well-bottom blackness.

The ground under his trainers feels different too, he realises. Harder, less giving than the soft, loamy ground of woodland. Feels more like bare rock. With the blackness in every direction and the feel of uneven stone under his feet, Aldo suddenly has the distinctly unpleasant impression that he's standing in a cave.

Trying not to think about the fact that he can no longer smell the earthy pine scent of the trees, he takes another step forward.

"Dylan?"

Oh fuck. Even the sound's changed. His voice is flat and dead. No sense of space at all. Like he's in a soundproofed room.

"Daaaaaaaaady."

Aldo's blood instantly turns to thick slush as the voice – not Dylan's voice – slithers out of the black directly behind him. A hoarse, scaly whisper, dry and mocking and hungry.

Aldo makes a nonsense sound of sheer terror, and runs.

A second later, the stony ground below his feet disappears, and then he's falling, a scream ripping free from his throat as he plummets down and down and down and down...

... and Aldo gulps in a huge mouthful of air like a drowning man breaking the surface. A massive muscle spasm snaps through his body, and his head raps painfully against the wooden headboard of the bed.

The notepad on his lap falls to the floor.

He sits up, hyperventilating and looking around wildly, trying to comprehend where he is, then recognises his room in Easy Rollin Manor. Shaking, he looks down and sees a pen in his hand. In the early morning light streaming through the single window, he can see his jacket still hanging on the hook behind the bedroom door.

His heart gradually slowing, Aldo leans over the side of the bed and retrieves his lyric book from the floor. He opens it to the last used page. At the top is the scrawl of his own handwriting.

Got everything I wanted, but this house is cold and haunted.

The rest of the page is filled with lyrics, crammed together in spidery black letters that are barely legible, and scratched into the page so hard the paper's ripped in places. Strange, hopeless and dark words, about being cold and afraid and alone.

But... they're good. Really good. Weird and scary, but *saying* something and telling a story. A story about chasing what you love and then falling forever in blackness through the stars and beyond with *no hope no love no light no re-demp-tion.*

There's accent marks and a few amateurish lines of musical score scrawled on the paper, a vocal melody with the lyrics written below. The last line simply reads:

Down and down and down and down.

7

Ross sits beside Bale at the recording desk in the control room, looking out the Perspex window into the live room. Luce's there at the kit, headphones playing a guide track, putting down her drums for the first of the eleven new tracks they've written. A whole album's worth. The writing phase is done. Time to put it down for real.

She's on her fifth take, and getting visibly frustrated. Which is weird.

Not weird that she's getting frustrated. Luce always got pissed off with herself on the rare occasions she fluffs her beats. What's weird is the fact she's screwing up so much in the first place, especially seeing as since being here, she's been absolutely on fire. They all have.

Now, it seems Luce's lost whatever groove they'd found themselves in. She's distracted. Not playing with her usual precision and power. Even as Ross has the thought, she misses the change from the first verse into the chorus on the track they're putting down. Ross sees her squeeze her eyes close, seething with herself. Then she lets out an emphatic *"FUCK!"* and launches her sticks across the live room.

Beside him in the control room, Bale taps the spacebar on keyboard in front of him, stopping the playback. "*Calma*, Lucia," he says in a soothing tone, leaning towards the in-built mic on the mixing desk. "You are tensing up. You need to relax."

In the live room, Luce nods and takes another set of sticks from the holster beside her. She takes a deep breath and adjusts her headphones slightly. "Alright, sorry guys. Let's go again."

That's another weird thing, Ross thinks, and there's been a few over the course of the last week or so. Luce no longer seems to mind Bale using her given name, or addressing her in Italian now and again. Maybe she's just got used to it, but her general attitude towards Bale's become noticeably friendlier, especially in the last few days, when he'd caught the way Bale and Luce looked and smiled at each other.

It was no big deal if they *were* pumping. The only band rule in that regard was that there were no horizontal mambos going on within the group itself. But, fair fucks to her if there was something going on between her and Bale. Ross could hardly blame her. He was a good looking dude, minted, a music lover, and suave as you like. As if the Milk Tray man had a day job as a record producer.

It was just a bit of a three-sixty for Luce, who up until last week had been very cool towards Bale, her initial suspicion about the guy and his intentions verging on being outright hostile. It wasn't lost on Ross that her sudden loss of concentration coincided with the reversal of her attitude towards Bale, which gave weight to his suspicion that their producer / engineer / promoter / manager was now slipping her a length.

"*Va bene*," Bale says into the desk mic. "From the top then. Just relax and let yourself glide into it. Do not think. Just play. Here we go."

He starts the playback again and Aldo's intro riff for the song, pre-recorded during the live sessions last week, fills the control room. A funky, shuffling lick effected with a wah-wah pedal. Luce nods along with the cue, eyes closed, brow furrowed in concentration, then comes in with a rolling flurry of toms before settling into the beat.

Ross leans back in his chair and folds his arms, staring out at Luce and nodding along. She's getting it down, keeping it steady, but still… there's something lacking. None of her usual *oomph*.

In the low light of the control room, Bale's face is lit with the shifting colours thrown by the blinking lights and diodes of the wall of effect racks, the flashing LEDs on the desk channels, and the backwash from the two computer monitors which show the lines of digital soundwaves produced by the recording software.

"How is Aldo progressing with his lyrics?" Bale asks, turning to Ross. It's the first time he's spoken to him that morning, though the two of them had been alone in the control booth for almost an hour. As friendly as he'd been toward Luce the past few days, Ross had noticed that Bale was a tad less affable with him, ever since that first day in the studio when Ross had asked about John.

"Honestly couldn't tell you," Ross says. "He's not the co-writing sort. Keeps the lyrics to himself until he thinks they're ready. He's been writing though." Aldo's lyric notebook has been getting a lot of attention recently. At least, it has any time Ross has seen him in the past few days outside of the studio, which was really only during mealtimes. The rest of the time, Aldo's barely left his room. Even at the dining table, he's there scribbling away, humming melodies to himself, silently mouthing the words, headphones on and plugged into an MP3 player where he has the live recordings playing. He's upstairs somewhere right now, immersed in his creative hot streak.

"Good," Bale says, nodding and turning back to the desk. He sighs and stabs at the spacebar on the keyboard again, halting the playback, then speaks into the desk mic again. "Lucia. You are dragging."

Behind the kit, Luce's shaking her head, jaw set and lips tight. "Sorry," she mutters. "I don't know what's..."

"Once again," Bale says, and starts the track from the beginning. Aldo's intro riff plays. Luce nods along, visibly tense, then comes in with the tom roll. Bale stops the playback again before she plays another bar. "No. You are off. Again."

C'mon, Luce, Ross thinks.

Bale restarts the playback. He lets it go almost to the first chorus this time before stopping it. In the live room, Luce drops her sticks and slumps forward, head in hands. "Fuck *SAAAAAAAKE!*" she screams into her snare drum.

"Do you want to take a few minutes?" Bale asks.

"No," Luce says, rolling her shoulders and giving herself a shake before picking up her sticks again.

"Do you want to try another song?"

"No."

"Do you want me to put the click track on to keep you in time?"

Ross grimaces. *Careful there, Gappa. Luce Figura doesn't do click tracks.*

"No," Luce says, looking into the booth, a dangerous edge to her voice.

"Do you want me to use a drum machine instead?"

Ross looks over at him, alarmed at the suggestion and his sixth sense for brewing trouble setting off klaxons on his head.

Luce doesn't respond for a moment, and Ross could swear that he feels the temperature in the studio drop a few degrees at the look in her eye. "No," she says, perilously quiet. "I can do this."

"Are you sure?" Bale asks doubtfully.

Ross unconsciously leans back in his chair, as if someone's just produced a lit stick of dynamite in the studio.

"I'm. Sure." Luce makes the two carefully spaced words a threat.

"I only ask because so far this morning, you are playing with all the skill and passion of a retarded two-year-old."

Ross closes his eyes.

Oh, crap.

He suddenly has a strong urge to be elsewhere. He opens one eye and sees Luce glaring into the control booth, sitting very still, her face blanched white but for spots of high colour on her cheeks. He knows that some record producers use this technique to get their artists on track. Goading them into a performance, calling their ability into question until the player in question goes *oh yeah, arsehole?* And plays an angry blinder.

A vexed drummer was a dangerous entity, though. What Bale's doing is the equivalent of poking an angry rattlesnake with a stick.

"I mean, really," Bale continues, "I would like to get the drums for at least *one* song recorded today, but it appears you have other more important things on your mind. What is it, Lucia? Hmmmm? Are you thinking of your parents? Is that it? Are you upset that you cannot make them proud? That you are a disappointment to them?"

The fuck?

"Woah, easy there, Gappa," Ross says. "That's out of order." Winding her up to get a recording done is one thing, but that's a step too far.

Bale ignores him. "Or perhaps you are thinking of me," he says, lowering his voice. "You are distracted by thoughts of you and I the other night in the library, yes? The feel of my hands on you. My fingers inside you. The taste of my cock."

Ross is half aware that his mouth's gaping open. Even though what he already suspected has been confirmed, he can't believe Bale's just said that.

In the live room, Luce looks for a moment like Bale's just slapped her in the mouth. Then her face darkens like a thunderhead. "You total fuckin *prick*," she snarls, then launches her sticks again, this time at the control booth window where they clatter off the Perspex.

"Oh, well, look at that," Bale crows, clapping his hands. "There *is* some fire in you after all. Perhaps if you showed some of the same passion you displayed the other night, the same eagerness to please, we might actually get something *done* this morning."

"Gappa, come on, man," Ross says. "What the fuck are you doing?" Bale doesn't even look at him.

In the studio, Luce stands up from the kit, kicks over her drum stool and reaches for the headphones, evidently about to cast them aside, storm the control booth and lay waste. Ross starts to get up from his seat, to go to try and diffuse the situation.

"Sit. Down."

Luce freezes absolutely still. So does Ross.

He hadn't shouted or screamed, but those two words had been spoken with a permafrost coldness. Bale's voice was a blade. For the first time in several years, Ross feels a little quiver of real fear spiralling up his spine and along the nape of his neck.

There's a moment of perfect silence in which no one moves, then Bale speaks again, switching back to his usual voice – all exotic, soothing warm tones like soft leather and cigar smoke. "Sit down, Lucia, and try it again."

Luce, an expression on her face somewhere between anger, embarrassment and fear, rights her drum stool, sits down behind the kit, and takes a third set of sticks from the holster at her side.

"Here we go, then," Bale says pleasantly. "From the top." He hits the spacebar on the keyboard, restarting the guide track again.

Some four minutes later – four minutes in which Luce gives a flawless and powerful drumming performance – Bale stops the playback.

Behind the kit, Luce is glaring into the control booth, her eyes conveying a clear *fuck you*. Bale had played a dangerous game calling down the thunder like that, but you couldn't argue with the results.

He leans back in his big leather chair, then turns and grins at Ross. His teeth look too big, and again Ross feels that little tickle of dread, a fear which he hasn't felt since his last day in Eastburn Children's Institute.

"Better," he says to Ross, his big teeth like white marble gravestones. "Much better."

Later, Ross knocks on Aldo's door.

There's no answer, so he knocks again.

Nothing.

The door doesn't have a lock, so Ross opens it a few inches, and calls inside. "Al? You here?" He pokes his head round the door. The room's dark, with the heavy tattered velvet curtains drawn over the window. "Al, you asleep?"

Nothing.

Ross steps inside, opening the door behind him to let in more light from the hall. In the dimness, he can see Aldo's bed in the far corner across the room.

Aldo's lying on the bed naked, and for an awkward moment, Ross thinks he's perchance walked in on his mate having a fly wank, and goes to duck discreetly back through the door. But then he sees the headphones. And the writing pad. Then Aldo starts singing. Shouting really. Just two words. *Smother* and *mother*. Then Ross recognises the melody, and between Aldo's yelling, can just hear the music playing on the headphones, even from across the room. Aldo must have them up at full burn. It's one of the new tunes they'd been jamming for the past week or ten days or however the fuck long they'd been here.

Deciding to postpone his invitation to Aldo to join him for a smoke, Ross decides to leave his friend to whatever freaky lyricist writing ritual he's engaged in, backs out of the room and closes the door.

Ross shakes his head as he walks along the corridor to the main door.

Writing in the dark. In a purposefully blacked-out room. Naked. How could Aldo even see what he was writing?

A few minutes later, Ross is standing outside the building under the awning next to the front door, sheltering from the snow which has been falling on and off for the past few days. He's shivering, taking deep, calming drags of a cigarette, and thinking of another day in the snow, years earlier.

Awright, Roadkill.

Ross unconsciously grits his teeth as he hears the voice in his head. *His* voice. Jimmy Weir's voice.

After the car wreck that had killed his folks, with no family members apparently able or willing to take on the sudden life-altering responsibility of a newly orphaned toddler, Ross had become your classic ward of the state. His memories of his early years in and out of the Eastburn Children's Institute were patchy. He didn't remember much about the strange grown-ups from those times, who were just half-recalled, anonymous phantoms. Big indistinct shadows, cold and distant, and sometimes scary. He has scattered recollections of random things from those years. A wooden toy bus that had a chipped paint and a wheel missing. A dark-haired woman with sad eyes and clothes that smelled of cigarettes and lavender. A giant bald man with a beard, a hooked nose and a loud, angry voice. Crying in a tub of tepid bathwater. The needling burn of shampoo suds stinging his eyes. And in another place, a man with a soft, almost girlish voice and breath that smelled of onions, a draughty bedroom with peeling, clown-patterned wallpaper, and windows that rattled and shrieked when it was windy. Even as an adult, sometimes these faint memories would wake him in the still black silences between three and four am, sweating, and for a few seconds feeling acutely threatened by the pools of darkness in his bedroom.

He tosses the cig end into the little iron bucket by the door that serves as an ashtray and stands looking out over the snowy covered courtyard, shivering.

There's nothing to fear but fear itself.

What a load of shite that saying was. There was always spiders. But that was just it. He *was* ratted. Genuinely rattled for the first time since his last day in Eastburn. And it was all to do with Gappa Bale, and that look he'd had on his face down in the studio. The flick knife quick change in character. The things he'd said. The way he'd said them. Like he just loved sticking the boot in.

Just like Jimmy Weir.

Ross is just about to turn round, go back inside out of the cold and wipe his brain of all thought with a few levels of mindless *Call Of Duty* mayhem, when something round the back of the building screams, and he goes very still.

It's a fuckin horrible, arsehole-puckering noise. Carried clear and easy on the icy air. A sort of torn, high-pitched agonised howl that goes on for two, maybe three seconds, then ends with a low bleating grunt that sounds hideously human. There's nothing for a few seconds, and Ross realises he's holding his breath. He finds himself being very careful to exhale quietly.

Then again, from round the back, a sound like ripping canvas. A few more guttural grunts, followed by muttering. A man's voice. Can't make out what he's saying, but he definitely sounds good and pissed off about something. Aldo, Luce and Bale are all inside, so it can only be the rarely seen John. Ross has been meaning to have a word with John.

Though the noises coming from round the back of the building set Ross's teeth on edge and prickle his forearms with goosebumps, he squares his shoulders, tells himself not to be a pussy, and follows the gravel path to his right that leads round the side of the building to the rear grounds, where those noises are coming from.

At the side of the building as he passes by the windows of Luce's room, ahead of him the immense rear grounds of Easy Rollin Manor spread out. A huge green about the size of a couple of football pitches, blanketed with snow. Beyond, stretching to the horizon in all directions, nothing but wintry forest and mountains under a leaden sky.

Ross turns to the right at the back of the building, and just about falls arse over tit at what he sees.

It's John. The old dude's standing there, half turned away from Ross, stripped to the waist, his wiry torso and arms and ... aye, his face, covered in blood. He's holding a big meat cleaver in one hand. In front of him, hung on an upright wooden rack, is a skinned and half-butchered body.

Ross instinctively recoils at the sight, and as he staggers back, sees the corpse's head lying on the ground by the rack.

Sees the antlers.

Just a deer.

But holy fuck, just for a moment there, he'd been sure that was...

The carcass, all shiny red exposed flesh, is so badly mutilated it could be anything. It's just a vaguely four-limbed mess of blood, flesh and splintered bone, all hacked and chopped to fuck, shot through with veins and pale ribbons of fat. A heap of glistening innards, some of the guts still half attached to the mangled deer, lie on the snow in front of the skinning rack, steaming in the cold. Ross is enveloped in the heady ripe smell of raw meat and freshly spilled blood.

John snaps his head round and glares at him, his thin old man lips skinning back from his teeth like a wolf protecting its kill, a disturbing image made worse by the fact that there's blood smeared around the old guy's mouth. He stands there, breathing hard from his exertion through clenched teeth.

Christ on a bike, has he been eating the carcass?

For a bad moment, Ross firmly believes the elderly gent's about to come at him, swinging that cleaver and hungry jaws agape, but the snarl vanishes from John's face as if it had never been, and he just stands there, instantly adopting his usual robotic character. It was creepy before, that expressionless stoicism. It's even freakier when he's standing there in just his trousers, splattered waist to hairline in dead Bambi. For fuck's sake, his feet are even bare.

"What?" John asks quietly, his face and voice conveying all the emotion of a brick wall, as if he'd been disturbed while ironing a shirt instead of... whatever the fuck he's doing. He's still holding the cleaver down by his side. For an old guy, there's a wiry definition to his bare torso, the ropy cords of muscle in his arms, chest and stomach highlighted in fresh dripping red.

"Just..." Ross's voice comes out in a squeak, and he clears his throat. "Just wondering what all the noise was. You... doing a bit of food prep there, John?"

John just stares at him for a few seconds, then turns back to his gory work with a dismissive grunt. He raises the cleaver and starts whacking away at the deer's carcass again. An experienced roadie and driver he may be, but he's no master butcher. There's no finesse or care to his wild chopping. It's more like he's taking out a world of anger on poor Bambi than trying to cut some venison fillets from the beast's flanks.

Maybe he's making mince instead of steaks, Ross thinks, and has to clamp a hand over his mouth to stop an involuntary bray of laughter at the idea. Nothing about this is funny. That horrible scream he'd heard, the blood around John's mouth...

Ross just stands and watches him for a moment as John hacks at the dead deer with messy abandon, sending little bits of raw meat, bone chips and splatters of blood into the air. He's so engrossed in his work he doesn't spare Ross another glance.

"Where do I know you from, John?" Ross tries. "I *do* know you."

John doesn't reply, but he pauses in his resolute hacking for a moment, stepping back from the riven carcass and studying it for a moment like an artist critiquing his own work. Then he shakes his head, as if not satisfied with how his project is turning out, or maybe he's denying that Ross knows him. Either way, a moment later, the cleaver comes up once more and he goes back to work, attacking the deer with renewed violence. Ross sighs. He knows this old guy. He knows he does. But John's giving him nothing.

"Nice talking to you, mate," Ross says and turns to leave Bale's manservant to his bloody work.

"Get away."

Ross quickly turns back, but John's still attacking the deer's carcass with grim determination, as if he'd never said a word.

"You say something, John?" It hadn't been much more than a grunt in between the thick meaty smacks of cleaver on raw flesh. "John?"

But John's done talking, it seems. He doesn't even look at Ross. He just keeps on chopping, and chopping, and chopping.

Ross turns away and begins making his way back round to the front of the building, his legs ever so slightly unsteady, and the gamey stench of fresh blood, raw meat and exposed innards high and ripe in the cold mountain air. He feels like it's been sewn into the lining of his clothes, absorbed into the fleshy lining of his nostrils and throat. The smell of rubbish bins out the back of a butcher's shop.

In the courtyard again, he decides another smoke's in good order and lights up a second cig, wishing with all his heart that he'd thought to bring some of his home grown with him on this shindig. He'd forgotten, though. Right enough, he hadn't been in the clearest state of mind while packing for the studio following Duncy Brown's death.

His death, and the things he'd said on his way out.

Trying to shake off the gloomy, and decidedly unsettling thoughts vying for attention in his brain...

what the fuck was that scream why was there blood round John's mouth why were his feet bare

...Ross tries to think of something funny. He knows avoidance is a form of cowardice, but right now there's just too much weird shit going through his head and he needs to take a step back, enjoy his smoke and find a happy place for a bit.

As he often does when the black thoughts raise their ugly depressive heads, he thinks of his favourite movie. *Wayne's World.* Garth in the diner with *Foxy Lady* on the jukey. Stacey piling into that parked car on her bike. The immortal *Bohemian Rhapsody* scene. Scenes that never failed to raise a smile, even when only replayed in memory.

But the scene that pops into his head now is the one with Ed O'Neil as Glen, the deranged and possibly homicidal owner of Mikitas, holding court in the doughnut shop and telling his customers that if you stab a man in the dead of winter, steam will rise from the wound. He'd always liked that scene, except now, it doesn't seem so funny. Too close.

Ross realises there'd been a lot of steam in the air during that bloody little scene round the back of the building a moment ago. He'd seen his own breath billowing in the air in front of him, and there'd been plenty of steam rising from the butchered carcass and the pile of guts on the snow.

He hadn't noticed it at the time, distracted as he was at the gory sight, but Ross realises now that the only thing *not* emitting steam into the freezing air, had been John. He'd been going at it like a man possessed, chopping...

eating?

...the dead deer to pulp. That wolfish look on his face when Ross found him, teeth bared and panting like a marathon runner. But no steam.

Ross takes another deep draw of his cig, and sees how it trembles in his fingers. That tremble's got fuck all to do with the temperature.

Get away.

Chorus II

After silence, that which comes nearest to expressing the inexpressible is music.

Aldous Huxley

1

Luce's bent over, breathing hard. The sweat that covers every inch of her skin drips from her hair and face, shaken loose by the rhythmic impacts pounding through her body.

"Harder," a rasping voice whispers in her ear. "Faster."

She grits her teeth. Goes harder. Goes faster. Her breath scrapes in her throat, desperate and strained with effort as exhilaration and exhaustion throb in her muscles.

"Come on," the voice urges. "Keep going. Harder."

Luce's gasps turn into grunts, animalistic and primal. She goes harder.

"Do not slow down. Do not stop. You *will not* fucking stop," the voice commands.

She's building to a climax. Wants to scream with the exulting joy of it all. The world goes away. All is white. All is feeling and sound and the rhythmic pounding.

Karen peeks out from the half closed door of an intricately carved wooden confessional booth, her eyes leaking thin red streamers before she vanishes into the darkness as if snatched by something hungry.

"Come on, bitch. *Harder. Faster.*"

The dead church-goers from her dream, led by a naked a engorged Father Lafferty, surround her, urging her on. Mouldering arms and meathook hands reach for her, pawing at her skin, whispering and gibbering approval.

Luce cries out, her arms and legs flailing and shaking in a helpless St Vitus dance. An explosion in her head, radiating out through her body in rolling waves and fleshy spasms. Luce's world, her mind, her *self*, disintegrates, and she hears someone scream. She can't tell if its herself, or if it's ripped from the throat of a thirteen-year-old girl with blonde hair and unflinching faith in Jesus who drank His blood and ate His body and died too young, lying in the door of a confessional, a spreading puddle of blood flickering with reflected votive candlelight as it pools around her head, a darker shade of crimson on a raggedy red carpet.

Rage flares like a chemical reaction. There's a series of loud crashes, bangs, thumps and cracks. Pain flashes through her, mixing with the black fury and the glorious ecstasy of release, enhancing the feeling, taking it higher, up and away over the world and all that creeps and crawls upon it, the sensation becoming something elemental, beyond understanding, beyond heaven.

Luce slumps to the floor, spent and gasping.

Then, in the fade, a dislocated stillness. Golden light fills her head, and Luce feels like she's floating free from her broken, exhausted body, leaving it behind as if she were an exorcised spirit.

In her ears, slow applause. And the voice again. *His* voice.

"Remarkable," Gappa Bale says. "Truly remarkable."

Lying on the floor of the studio amid the overturned pieces of her comprehensively trashed drum kit, Luce opens her eyes. Her arms are so tired she can barely take the headphones off her head. She staggers to her feet and leans shaking against the wall, trying to get her breath back. Her limbs buzz and tingle as if filled with scuttling insects. "I'm done," she gasps.

"Yes, you are," Bale says. She looks up and sees him standing there amid the wreckage of her kit, grinning at her. He hands her a bottle of water and a fresh towel, then makes a dusting motion with his hands. "All. Done."

Luce takes the water and towel with gratitude, and feels a surge of shame at just how grateful she is to Bale after what he'd said to her earlier. But the water is sweet and cool in her throat, the towel luxuriantly soft and fresh, clearly woven by angels.

She's never played like that. Never. That last track - the fucked up crazy one with Bale's violin part and the cataclysmic crescendo - she feels like it nearly did her in. Her head's still spinning, her shoulders and wrists feel like they've been rubberised, and she reckons there's a good chance she could black out at any given moment.

Thirteen songs. Thirteen songs nailed in... how long? She feels like she's been sitting at the kit for an eternity, but it could only have been an hour or... maybe two? Ever since Bale had got her going that morning, saying the things he'd said.

Well, it's done now. She starts sliding down the wall, empty in mind, body and soul. But Bale steps forward and steadies her. Even as she leans on him, glad of his strength, taking in the smell of him and the steady feel of his supporting arm, part of her's thinking that he's a fucking prick for goading her like he had. But all the same, she couldn't deny the results. She knows she'd been having a nightmare session that morning until he wound her up.

And he'd been right. She *had* been thinking of what had happened between them, hadn't been able to *stop* thinking about it, and really, who could blame her. The sex had been... worlds failed her. Epic? No. Galactic? Timeless? Spiritual? All and none of the above, your honour.

Even so, there's still a glowing ember of anger in Luce at what he'd said to her, even if it *had* resulted in her recording thirteen tracks of the best drums she'd ever put down in her life. All in one take. And now he's there holding her up, all warm and strong, looking down at her with that maddening little secret smile. Luce finds it in herself to stand on her own and steps away from him.

"What the fuck was that about earlier?" she asks, not quite getting the amount of anger in her voice she's shooting for. She just sounds tired. Plaintive.

"I am sorry, Lucia," Bale says, and to his credit, he does look suitably apologetic. "But drastic measures were called for. When a musician as talented as yourself is performing to such an unworthy standard, I find it effective to use… shock tactics, shall we say?"

"You humiliated me. And that stuff about my parents, you don't think it was too much?" She hears the weakness in her voice. The whine. She hates it, but can't help it.

"It worked, did it not? Your performance today has been magnificent, with all the fire and passion I have come to expect of you. My sweet Lucia. I will not say I am sorry, for what we have captured is something very *very* special, but for hurting you, know that while I deemed it necessary, I myself, am truly wounded."

And there it is. That slight broadening of his smile, just enough to reveal a few more of those perfect, perfect teeth, and that glimmer in his eyes, like a sliver of light in the black abyss of an ocean trench. He takes a step towards her, slow and cool and confident. He reaches for her, and Luce steps into his arms, the last of her anger dissolving, and rests her head on his chest. She's so tired, and he's so warm and comforting and solid and *real.* His hands drop to her waist as his mouth finds her's. His tongue, that amazing, acrobatically cunning tongue of his, flicks between her lips, lizard quick, lighting her up, and Luce responds, moaning into his mouth and pressing herself against him. She's about half a second away from whipping her top off when Bale breaks away and walks back across the studio to the control room.

"Go and get Ross," he says, not even looking back over his shoulder, his voice suddenly icy. "I want to start on the bass tracks."

Luce can only stand there, confused and hurt and aching for him, a plea on her lips. She hears herself murmur *please*, and doesn't give shit one about the pathetic begging tone in her voice, like a dog pining for its master. Then he's gone, closing the door to the control booth behind him, leaving Luce standing alone in the studio.

But she has to go and get Ross, like Gappa told her to. So she walks, stiff-legged from the studio, not entirely of her own volition, her head fogged with a confused blur of conflicting thoughts and emotions, clomps robotically up the stairs and pushes through into the lounge. As the door behind her closes, through a grey haze she sees Ross sitting on the couch, playing the Xbox. She stumbles into the room, the world around her spinning.

"Luce, you okay?" Ross says as he looks up, then hurries across the lounge and takes her by the shoulders. "Jesus, what's wrong?"

At the look of shock on Ross's face, Luce feels a distant flicker of panic. "Bale," she hears herself murmur, but her voice seems to come from someone else, someone speaking from the end of a long metallic tunnel. "He... he wants you downstairs."

"Luce? Luce, c'mon what's wrong?" Genuine fear in Ross's voice. That's scary. Ross isn't afraid of anything.

"I'm fine," she mutters, her voice a little closer, but still all weird and tinny and watery in her own head. "Just... just let me sit down a minute."

Then she's vaguely aware of Ross walking her over to the couch and sitting her down while the world around her reels and spins, flashing strange colours and tracers like she's tripping out her nut while on the waltzers at the carnival.

"Christ, Luce, you're chalk white," she hears Ross saying. "Stay here a minute."

"No, please... stay," Luce moans. Or thinks she does. It may have been just a wordless groan. Then she's just sort of floating in a weird cloudy nothingness, aware that she's breathing too fast, stomach flipping, and feeling a cold fever ripple over every millimetre of her skin.

"Here, drink this," she hears Ross say. A hand goes behind her neck, helping her lift her head. There's a cool glass at her lips, then sweet tepid liquid in her mouth. Sugared water. Good old Ross. She takes a few sips, then lies down and closes her eyes, concentrating on taking deep breaths. After a minute, she's able to open her eyes and look around without feeling like she's on the deck of a storm tossed ship.

"Better?" Ross asks.

Luce nods slowly and takes another long draught of the sugar water before trying to speak. "Sorry," she mumbles, one hand pressed to her clammy forehead. "I don't know... don't know what happened." She shakes her head. Thinking back over the last few minutes, how she'd felt, how she'd acted towards Bale, the simpering canine devotion and neediness...

Shame twists her guts and she feels like she could throw up. That wasn't her. No way. Bale had... got into her head somehow. Like he was some malicious hypnotist, toying with her thoughts, manipulating her emotions and actions. He'd been doing it ever since the other night, ever since they'd...

She looks up at Ross, who's sitting beside her on the couch, watching her anxiously. "I fucked him," she says.

Ross just shrugs. "Can't really blame you for that, sister. He's a suave motherfucker. Probably not the best move you ever made, though, and..." He hesitates.

"What?"

"I'm guessing I'm not the only one getting some bad vibes off Mr Bale?" Ross suggests.

Luce manages to sit up, though she's still shaking. "Just now, down in the studio, Jesus, I was ready to shag him again, even after what he said to me this morning. You know me, Ross, right? That's not me. It's just fucking *not*. What the hell's wrong with me? For a few minutes, it was like..." this time Luce hesitates, before finishing quietly, "like I wasn't even there. Like someone else was driving."

Ross frowns, looking fixedly at the floor. "Nothing wrong with you, Luce," he says. "But there's sure as shitfire something wrong with *that* dude. He..." Again, Ross shakes his head, as if deciding against saying whatever he was about to say.

"He scares you, doesn't he?" Luce asks.

Ross glances at her quickly, opens his mouth as of to deny it, but then looks away again and nods after a few seconds. "Aye."

Luce lays a hand on his shoulder. She can feel how tense he is, the tightly coiled, tension. "It's alright, Ross," she says. "There's nothing wrong with being scared."

"Mmm. So they say," Ross replies doubtfully, still not meeting her eyes.

"You've seen something, or felt something, too?"

Please, please let him say he's feeling the same way I am and this isn't all just in my head.

Ross nods slowly, looking into the middle distance. He doesn't speak again for a few beats, but then he tells her about what he'd seen earlier, out the back of the building. About John. The deer.

"I know that guy, Luce," he says. "John. I *know* I do." Ross lets out a long breath and runs his hands over his close-cropped hair. "We need to tell Al."

"Have you seen him today?"

"More of him than I wanted to."

Ross tells Luce about walking in on Aldo's *au natural* singing and songwriting session. He forces a smile. "Make sure you knock before you go into his room. Or close your eyes. It wasn't pretty."

"Noted," Luce says, unsure whether she feels bemused or unsettled by the image of Aldo lying in the buff in an unlit room, headphones on and yelling into the darkness while writing lyrics he can't see. She gets up from the couch, still a bit weak in the knees. "Let's go."

"You go," Ross says, also getting to his feet. "You said Bale wants me downstairs. I think it's time I had a talk with him. Man to man, like."

"Not by yourself. We'll come down with you."

"It's cool, Luce. Go and get Aldo and I'll see you down there. I want a little alone time of my own with Mr Bale." Again, there's that tightening of his features, which he tries to cover with a devil may care smile.

Luce reaches out and takes his hand. "There's something way weird going on here. You know that, don't you? You don't have to go. Like I said, there's nothing wrong with being scared."

Ross squeezes her hand and his smile falters just a little. "That's just it, Luce. That's exactly why I *do* have to go."

Luce abruptly feels like crying at the rare glimpse into the hidden depths of Ross McArthur. Level headed and chilled as he is on the surface, there's a lot more to him. He could be every bit as stubborn as she was, and would absolutely *not* be moved from a course of action once he decided it was the right thing to do, especially if his own character was called into question, or he perceived that it was. Like he constantly had to prove something to himself.

Before she can say another word, he lets go of her hand, and goes to the door leading down to the studio. He looks back over his shoulder, winks at her, then goes down the stairs.

Distinctly uneasy at the thought of Ross alone with Bale, Luce walks quickly from the lounge and follows the corridor to Aldo's room at the far end.

She's just raising her fist to knock on his door when it opens in her face, and Aldo just about jumps out of his trainers, letting out a comical little yelp of fright as he stumbles back into the room, hands raised in front of him as if Luce'd come at him with a blade.

"*Fuckin hell, Luce!*" he gasps, a hand on his chest. "You nearly gave me a fuckin coronary!"

Luce raises an eyebrow. "Bit jumpy there, Al?"

Aldo lets out a long shaky breath and runs his hands through his matted, greasy hair. He looks a wreck. Dark patchy stubble covers his jaw, cheeks and neck, there's a few ripe looking zits on his face, and he's notably thin in the body and features, to the point of being haggard. He looks like he hasn't slept for a week, his bloodshot eyes sunken in hollows ringed with deep purple bags.

"You're not looking your best, Al," Luce informs him kindly as she steps into the dim lit room, wrinkling her nose at the close, fusty air mingled with the sour smell of BO. The room's in just as bad shape as Aldo. Curtains drawn over the windows. His guitar lying on the unmade bed next to a set of headphones and a writing pad, every inch of the visible page filled with Aldo's cramped handwriting. The floor's strewn with his bedding, unwashed clothes and dirty plates, most containing half-eaten meals spotted blue and black with fuzzy mould.

"Fuck sake, dude," Luce scolds, looking around in distaste at the mess. "Could do with a bit of maid service in here."

Aldo shrugs. "Been on a bit of a roll, getting some words down. What day is it?"

"It's..." Luce realises she's not sure. "Wednesday? No, Thursday. I think."

Aldo shrugs again, like it like it doesn't matter anyway. "How's recording going. Drums done?"

Luce nods, tight-lipped. "Drums are done. Al, we need to talk."

"So talk," Aldo says, stepping past her into the corridor. "I'm going for a smoke. I really want to smoke. Coming with?"

Luce, now noticing the weird twitchiness around Aldo's sunken eyes and the jingle jangle junky-like quality of his movements, has no choice but to follow him as he walks quickly down the corridor to the main door and goes outside. The cold's teeth sink into Luce like a sharkbite the moment she steps across the threshold into the courtyard, her thin, sweat-soaked top all the protection of wet tissue. She's about to tell Aldo she's going to go and grab her jacket, but he's already walking away across the courtyard, past the Balemobile and stepping off the path onto the moor, heading toward the forest.

"Al! Where you going?" she calls after him, but he doesn't so much as glance back at her. "*Al!*"

Off he goes, and again, Luce's forced to follow, shivering and cursing under her breath all the way. She winces as she steps onto the moor and a foot of snow covers her legs almost to the knees, the deadening cold quickly numbing her feet.

"Dude, what the *hell?*" she calls after Aldo.

He stops a short distance from the wall of dark pines in front of them, lights a cigarette, and then just stands there, looking into the woods.

Luce comes up behind him, her arms wrapped around herself in a futile effort to keep the leeching chill at bay. She fights back the urge to complain about her discomfort, though, as she sees the look on Aldo's face, or rather, the lack thereof.

It's like he's left the building, leaving an empty shell behind. He's so still, apart from his eyes, which are still doing that freaky twitching thing, the nerves in the eyelids tick-tick-ticking and his pupils flicking rapidly left and right as he stands there, as if he's searching for something elusive in the trees.

"Al?"

Nothing. She might as well be back inside for all the response she gets. Luce hits him a cuff on the shoulder. "*Hey!* You want to tune the fuck in?"

Aldo flinches, then looks over at Luce like he's never seen her before. "What?"

"What's wrong with you, Al? You look like a zombie. You're barely here. And why the actual fuck are we standing in knee deep snow looking at the trees?"

He gives her this funny look, like she's the one acting like a mental case. Then he leans over and whispers in her ear, as if afraid of being overheard. "He was *here*."

Luce has no idea what he's talking about, but all the same, at the haunted conviction in his voice, her guts twist. "Who?" she asks, and wonders why she, too, is whispering.

"Dylan."

"Dylan was here?"

"In the trees."

"Fuck off. When?"

"I don't know. A few nights ago. Or maybe last night. Time's... different here. Have you not noticed?"

Luce chooses to ignore that observation. "How could Dylan be here, Al?"

"He threw snowballs at me. Wanted to build a snowman. I chased him through the forest." Luce's skin crawls at the breathless wheeze of laughter that Aldo lets out, ending in a series of deep hacking coughs. She takes a deep calming breath, trying to think. Trying *not* to think the one thought that keeps repeating in her head. That Aldo's losing it.

"It was so dark, Luce," he says, turning back to the wall of trees rising up before them, his voice far away and his eyes even further. "So dark in the woods. Just... black. The stars went away. There was no sound. Just... nothing."

"Al…"

"And I could hear the wee man. He was… he was screaming. Oh, Christ, Luce, I think something was chasing him. He sounded so scared…"

"Al…"

"Then… then I wasn't in the forest anymore. It was like… a cave or… There was something in there. Grabbed at me. I fell."

"Al, please. You need to listen to me."

"Down and down and down and down…"

Luce punches him on the shoulder this time, and Aldo turns to her, blinks a few times and shakes his head. He still looks a bit unsure about where he is.

"Sorry," he mumbles. "I guess it was a dream or something. I think. Anyway, what did you want to talk about?"

"Can I tell you as we go back inside?" Luce says through chattering teeth. "Could cut glass with my nipples here."

Aldo flicks his unsmoked cig away, nods and they start walking back towards Easy Rollin Manor. Luce notices that he keeps looking back over his shoulder at the woods as they go.

"Aldo, there's clearly something screwed up about this place," she says. "About Bale."

Aldo sighs. "You still talking about that? I thought you were cool with Gappa now?"

"I was."

"So what's changed?"

"I hooked up with him the other night."

Aldo stops walking and turns to her. "Woah, hold the phone. You *shagged* him?"

Luce feels an automatic stab of annoyance at the disapproving tone and the look he gives her, even though she herself now badly regrets what happened. "Aye, I shagged him," she retorts. "Rode him like Seabiscuit. Did the wild thing."

"Fuck sake, Luce." Aldo starts walking again. "So what? You had a wee falling out with him now? You *know* this kind of shit screws everything up."

"Al, it's not like that."

"So what's it like then?" he asks as they cross the courtyard. "Tell me. What happened?"

"This morning... he was giving me pelters in the studio when I was trying to get the drums down..."

"And?" he asks. "Was he right?" They pause outside the main door, facing each other.

Luce grits her teeth. "Aye. He was right. I was playing like shit, but you had to be there. The things he said... and then later on..."

Aldo shakes his head, says something under his breath that sounds suspiciously like *fuckin drummers*, and reaches for the door handle.

Luce grabs his wrist.

"Al, to tell you the truth, if I wasn't in danger of hypothermia right now, I wouldn't go back in there. Not if you paid me."

"In case you didn't notice, Luce, he *has* paid you. Paid you very well." He shrugs off her hand and pushes through the door, leaving Luce in the courtyard.

She stays where she is for a moment. She really doesn't want to go back inside, but this shit needs sorted. A particularly hard gust of freezing wind flays her face with sleet, and she stands there, indecisive and miserable. She turns and looks over the surrounding hills and forest, wind-whipped and darkening in the day's failing light. She imagines standing out here as night falls and the temperature plummets further, and her reluctance is finally killed off. She steps over the threshold again and pulls the doors closed behind her.

She catches up with Aldo at the entrance to the lounge and grabs his arm again. "Dude, I'm not fuckin around here," she says. "There's..."

Aldo rounds on her and Luce takes an alarmed step back from him, thinking for a moment he's going to take a swing at her. "*You're not fuckin around?*" he snaps. "Really, Luce? You're shagging the guy who gave us a record deal, and now you're annoyed because he pulled you up for having a shite session. Tell me what I'm missing here."

"I'm not shagging him – not anymore - and I'm not annoyed, Aldo," Luce replies carefully. "I'm frightened."

He scowls at her. "Frightened?"

"It's not just the things he said to me. It's the things I said to *him*. Things I've never told anyone. Not even you or Ross. It's like he was… in my head, breaking me down. Then he used those things against me, and he was loving it, Al."

Aldo just gives her a condescending raise of the eyebrows, and Luce feels the urge to slap those eyebrows right off his coupon. But at the same time, she hears how vague and lame her explanation sounds.

"You had to *be* there," she says again. "Even Ross is freaked out. And you're acting plenty freaky yourself, in case *you* hadn't noticed."

Aldo's eyes slide away from her and he shakes his head again. "Bullshit," he says, but you'd have to be dense not to hear the lack of conviction in his voice.

"Bullshit? Come on, Al. How much more weirdness do you need before you admit there's something seriously fucked up about this place and everything that's happened?"

"Luce…"

"No, I mean it, Aldo. Enough's enough. You can't pretend this shit isn't happening. You can't ignore everything that's gone down since we met that sleekit bastard…"

The tirade dries up in Luce's mouth at the sight of the slow smile spreading on Aldo's lips. She finds herself taking another step back.

"Ignore it?" he repeats quietly. "Luce, I'm fuckin *loving* it. It's like Bale says. There's magic here. *Real* magic. You feel it too, don't pretend you don't, and you like it just as much as me."

He takes a step closer.

"There's the link. How *strong* it is here. The three of us have been practically psychic with each other when we're jamming recently. Don't try and tell me the way we're playing, the way we've been playing ever since we met that 'sleekit bastard', isn't the best you've ever felt in your life."

Luce opens her mouth to call bullshit on that, but the words die in her throat as she realises Aldo's absolutely right. Nothing, not her family, any boyfriend, her job, or any drink or drug had ever made her feel as right and complete as music. It wasn't just what she did. It was who she was. Who *they* were. And the music had never been as good as it'd been over the past few weeks.

Aldo starts making angry bullet points in the air with a stabbing finger as he lists their recent fortunes. "A gig at the Barras. Crowds going mental for us. A recording contract. Big advances. An album on the way. A release gig in front of fifty thousand fans at Glasgow Green." He stops and looks at Luce again, shaking his head in wonder. "What the fuck have you got to bitch about? We're living the dream here, Luce." He drops his voice and leans close. "Not just mine. Yours and Ross's as well. It's what we always wanted from day one. Now we're playing and writing better than we've ever done before, and we're doing it full time. I'll take a bit of strangeness with that no bother if that's the price. Christ sake Luce, I can write in the *dark* here."

"Yeah," Luce says softly. "I heard about that."

"I swear to God," he says, his voice abruptly dropping to a reverent whisper. That weird twitchiness around his eyes is back. "The magic. It's real here. When the lights are out and I've got the headphones on, I get my gear off, and... and I can *feel* the music. Actually physically fuckin *feel* it, washing over me. Running over my skin like rain. Though my head. My pulse syncs in with it. I'm part of it. *In* it. And I see things, Luce. And then, it's... holy shit it's like I'm just fucking *gone*, you know? I can't feel anything anymore and I'm just floating in a sea of noise, the guitars and the bass and the drums all just *pummelling* me, right? And then the words, they just come out of nowhere, blowing right through me down my arm and into the pen. And when I come back and put the lights on, there they are. The words. Good ones. Dark as fuck some of them, but good..."

Luce interrupts him. "And you don't think there's something a bit wrong with that?"

"Wrong?" Aldo looks disgusted with her, then that leering grin's back on his face. "Lucia, my dear, it's never been so *right*."

"Don't you fuckin call me that," Luce says, her own voice taking on an edge as anger flickers to life in her again. "Don't try and sound like *him*."

"Who? Your fuck buddy?"

"Fuck you."

"No, fuck *you*, Luce. This is my nirvana, you understand that? This is my heaven. This is fuckin Graceland. And you're busting my nut with all this negative shite because you've had a fight with your boyfriend? You've got a fuckin cheek, you know that? Oh Bale's shady. Bale's at it. I don't trust him. He's up to something. Then two minutes later you've got a red carpet hanging out your fanny for him, putting the whole thing at risk so you can suck his cock."

"You can take your face for a shite with that pish, Aldo," Luce comes back, raising her voice and taking a step forward herself. "You've been sucking his cock since the moment we met the prick. What is it? Are you jealous because I shagged him before you did?"

"Get yourself to fuck, Luce," comes Aldo's snappy retort. "All this time you've been acting like you're not really going along with it all, but if I've been ignoring weird shit, it's no more than you have. Three grand for a show out of nowhere doesn't happen, you said, but you still went along with it." Aldo's eyes are blazing now, spittle flecks his lips and unshaved chin. He takes a step closer. "Those dead Remember May pricks you were so concerned about. You still got in the fuckin car and came here when we picked you up. Contracts we can't remember signing, sealed with our blood, but you're still *here*, aren't you?"

Another step, and Luce finds herself backed into a corner. Aldo grabs her wrist. Hard.

"You think I missed all that? I'm not a fuckin idiot, Luce. *Don't call me a fuckin idiot!*" he yells, now red in the face. "I don't care. Not about a bit of weirdness, not about the contracts, and certainly not about three dead cunts that couldn't handle getting their *heads cut.*"

Aldo slams a fist into the wall by Luce's head on the last two words, making her flinch. His face is all twisted, bared teeth and mad pitbull eyes.

"*You fuckin get me?*" he rants, his voice rising to a near shriek. "*I. Don't. Care.* Bale can be as freaky as he wants. I'm fuckin *in.*"

He's so close up by now that Luce can feel his spit on her cheek. Though she's trembling inside, horrified at the look on Aldo's face and the things he's saying, she sees things clearly now, and knows what she has to do. She slowly wipes saliva off her face and clears her throat.

"Then I'm out," she says quietly. "Fuck this. I'm going home."

Aldo's face clears for a moment and he blinks, takes a step back. "What? You can't go home."

"Watch me."

"But… but you still need to do your backing vocals."

"Use the rehearsal recordings. Sing them yourself. Get your bum chum Bale to do them. Use an auto-tuner. *I* don't care. I'm done."

"Is there a problem?"

Luce looks over Aldo's shoulder, and there he is. Standing at the top of the staircase leading down to the studio, his arms crossed, leaning casually against the door frame, the corners of his lips turned up ever so slightly.

His lips…

Luce has to bite her tongue and dig her nails into her palms in an attempt to dislodge the sudden memory of Bale kneeling between her thighs in front of the open fire the other night…

"I want… I want to leave," she says, hating the tremble and sudden lack of belief in her voice. "The drums are done. You don't need me here. I don't need to be here."

"Sweet Lucia," Bale says, gliding like smoke across the lounge towards her and cupping her cheek in one hand. Luce shivers in repulsion and desire. She wants his hand off her, right now. But then she'd surely die if he took away his touch.

"You are only half correct. No, I do not need you here. But you..." His hand slides down from her cheek, trails a deliciously feathery touch across her neck and brushes the side of her breast before taking her numb fingers in his. "You *do* need to be here. Do you not?"

Luce feels her head moving and realises she's nodding like a novelty dog in the rear window of a car. She can't look away from Bale's eyes, those black hole eyes that she suspects she could quite literally drown in, sucked down and down and down into crushing black nothingness.

"In any case," Bale says softly, lifting her hand to his mouth and planting a little kiss on her fingers. She feels the briefest flick of his tongue as he tastes her skin, a quick touch that feels like a delicious electric shock, "there *is* no leaving here."

He drops her hand and motions at the window, and Luce looks over and sees the blurry white curtain of the blizzard outside. "John has informed me that the roads are already impassable," Bale says, then turns to Aldo, dismissing Luce as if she's simply ceased to exist. And it *hurts*.

"Aldo, my good friend and maestro. How are your lyrics coming along?"

"Very well, Mr Bale," Aldo says, also doing an impression of a nodding dog, beaming in the light of Bale's attention. "*Very* well."

Luce wants to slap him. Maybe go for his eyes. Dig them out with her nails.

"Excellent," Bale says. "Ross is about to begin the bass recordings." He crosses the room towards the stairs again, opens the door and stands there ushering them down into the darkness below. "We are just getting started."

2

Down in the control room, Aldo and Luce sit in big padded leather office chairs. Bale's at the desk in front of them, his hands dancing across dials, buttons, sliders and knobs, his long fingers quick and graceful as a concert pianist's.

Through the Perspex window looking into the live room, Aldo can see Ross standing there, headphones on, head down, just noodling away on his bass, playing little runs and riffs as he warms up and Bale finds the right tone and texture. Ross hasn't looked up since they arrived. Beside Aldo, Luce is doing his head in with her fidgeting. Drumming her hands on the arm rests of her chair, constantly changing her sitting position, squirming in her seat and casting frequent nervous glances over at Bale. Aldo has the impression she's about a blink away from bolting from the room.

He can't believe she's shagged Gappa! The rules were clear. Set in stone from the day the band formed. No fucking around with fellow band members. Simple.

Okay, maybe Bale wasn't an actual full time member of the band, but with everything he'd done for them, and the few sessions he'd played on the record, he was the next best thing. And she had to go jumping his bones and then having a hissy fit when he pulled her up for playing pish. Talking about wanting to leave. Like a wean. It's my ball and I'm going home.

Then I'm out.

Aldo'd felt a momentary panic when she'd said that upstairs, but you know what? Fuck it. Fuck *her*. If she wanted out, she could do one. With all the apparent buzz back home about the band, there'd be drummers queuing up to take her place if she couldn't handle it.

But still. She really would *have gone, too. She had that look.*

Aldo's known Luce for twenty years. Since primary school. She'd never had a boyfriend of any note. Never been in love, she'd told Aldo a few years back, drunk one night after a gig in a half-empty pub in Kilmarnock. She wasn't sad about it. Never really had time or the inclination to make an effort at a serious relationship, devoting the majority of her days to studying and practicing and teaching and jamming and gigging. Which was why she was so good.

Aldo knows in the roots of his heart that Luce loves the band as much as he does. Well, maybe not *that* much, but she loved it more than she ever loved any guy, which was why this whole thing about her being upset because Bale criticised her drumming made zero sense. That just wasn't Luce.

So why was she so freaked out?

That'd be the freakiness.

Fair point. Well, as he'd said - perhaps a little over zealously- upstairs, as far as he was concerned, Aldo wasn't overly concerned with certain clearly weird shit that'd been happening lately. Hey ho, on we go. Evidently, Luce was having a harder time adapting to their new, admittedly strange, circumstances. She was all over the place. Even after everything she'd just told Aldo, the moment Bale had stepped into the lounge upstairs, she'd been a different person, all simpering and unsure, and now she can't sit still, sitting there in her chair fidgeting like she's got midges in her knickers.

At the desk, Bale's long-fingered hand moves on a slider, and the thick warm honey of Ross's bass swells from the big monitor speakers on the wall, filling the control booth. Aldo feels the chair seat vibrate under him. The fine hairs on his arms and neck stand up like punters at a gig getting to their feet when the band starts to play.

In the live room, Ross - who still hasn't looked up from the floor - lets a long rumbling E note go, takes a deep breath, then starts giving it the bass intro to Sabbath's *NIB*, thickening the air in the control room with big doomy blues notes, low down and dirty as the worn-out sole of a tramp's shoe.

Bale chuckles softly and nods along. "Nice," he says into the desk mic. "Very nice indeed, Ross. Are you ready?"

Ross finally raises his head and looks in at them, and Aldo sees his face.

Eyes half closed. Mouth half open. A goofy grin. The general air of bleary, not-quite-sure-what's-going-on happiness particular to chronic stoners.

Ross is wasted. Like, *seriously* wasted. Stoned out his chicken.

"Alright there, Al." Ross greets him. He points a finger in at Luce. "Luce Lou, how'd you do?" Luce visibly flinches, and a strange expression that looks a lot like terror crosses her face.

"Tell you what, boys and girls," Ross says with a big bleary smile as he continues to play fuzzy homage to Geezer Butler. "Got me a front row seat for funkytown today."

Aldo can't help but smile. Strangely, he'd not even been thinking about weed since they'd been here, and as Ross hadn't said anything, he'd just assumed he hadn't brought any of his home grown. He must've been keeping a joint for when he went to record the bass. Good on him. Aldo himself got a bit clumsy on the guitar after a smoke, imaginative, but clumsy, but give Ross McArthur a reefer before he jams, and it's like he's ingesting the very concept of groove.

Aldo looks over and sees that even Luce's smiling now, nodding along to Ross's solo and tapping out an accompanying beat with her hands on the arms of her chair. She looks a little wasted herself in fact. Her eyes like triple-glazed windows.

Aldo leans forward toward the desk mic and presses the talk button. "Fuck shit up, man," he encourages Ross. "Lay that foundation!"

"No," Bale says, in a low voice that for some reason makes Aldo think of a coffin lid slamming closed. Or possibly open. "Do not lay the foundation, Ross. *Fuck* the foundation. *Rape* it."

He cues up the first track, and a rolling, crashing avalanche of Luce's drums comes pounding out of the speakers. And by fuck, does it sound good. Whatever Bale had said to Luce to get her to play like that, it'd worked a treat.

Ross looks in at Aldo, and just for a second, just for the briefest, quickest breath of a second, they lock eyes, and Aldo has another strange notion. For a heartbeat, he has the definite feeling that Ross is screaming behind that stoned smile.

But then he lowers his head again and goes to work. And works it to the *bone*.

Aldo leans back in his chair, closes his eyes, and just lets the sound wash over him, the drums and first bass track on what he now has absolutely no doubt will be a record that people will talk about for a very *very* long year.

Some indeterminate amount of time later, Bale says, "Done," and Aldo wakes as if from a drum and bass fever dream. He opens his eyes, looks through the plastic window and sees Ross in the live room. He's a sweat-soaked, bleeding mess, swaying on his feet. His eyes again meet Aldo's for a moment, and the undisguised fear he sees there makes him squirm in his chair.

With visibly shaking arms, Ross lifts his bass off and drops it to the floor, sending a dischordant low frequency *claaaaang* blowing through the control booth like a thick wind. Then Ross staggers, trips over the floor monitors, takes a couple of drunken steps across the studio and collapses in a heap.

Huh. Look at that, Aldo thinks, bemused.

Beside him, Luce makes a weird noise in her throat. Like she's choking on something. Then she says, "Ross," more of a moan than a word, and she's up out her chair, stumbling over for the door.

Aldo blinks, shakes his head as if to clear it of fog, and goes after Luce into the live room. His breath catches in his chest as he sees

Ross's eyes are open, and there's a trickle of blood running out of one nostril, painting a vivid crimson line against the ghostly pale shade of his skin. For a bad moment, he thinks Ross is dead. But then he starts shaking and twitching, his eyes rolled back in his skull. His arms and legs give sudden violent spasms, as if he's being tasered.

Luce's crouched over him, trying to hold him still. She looks up at Aldo. "Grab a stick."

Aldo's got no idea what she's talking about, and stares back at her, his mind a complete blank.

"*Grab a fuckin drumstick!*" she shouts, hitting him a swat on the arm. "For his mouth!"

"Right, right," Aldo says, catching up, and grabs a drumstick from the floor, noticing for the first time that Luce's kit has been trashed. Broken sticks, the toms, cymbals, and stands are strewn about the floor, as if kicked over. Weird. Luce *never* trashed her kit. She loved drumkits like other girls loved kittens.

She snatches the stick from his hand and manages to get it between Ross's teeth. Aldo kneels down beside her.

"C'mon, Ross, you're alright," Luce's saying, sounding a lot calmer than Aldo feels. When Aldo lays his hands on Ross, the way his friend's muscles are rapidly expanding and contracting under his skin makes him think of a sack of live rats. He manages to grab Ross's flailing right arm, takes his hand, and winces as Ross's thick fingers close painfully over his own.

"Easy, big man," Aldo says, doing his best to sound like he's not freaking out big style. "Watch the fingers, eh? Still got to do my guitar parts." He tries to force a laugh, but it sounds more like a whine, and tears are springing up in his eyes as Ross's big bass-strengthened hand squeezes his.

"*Call a fuckin ambulance!*" Luce yells over her shoulder, and Aldo turns and Bale's standing there, leaning on the wall looking down at them, a thoroughly bored expression on his face. Ross is making low grunting, growling sounds in the back of his throat, his big square teeth gnawing furrows in Luce's 7A Vic Firth stick, drooling slevers around the splintering maple.

"I think I already told you, Lucia," Bale says, condescending as fuck. "The roads are quite impassable."

"Get a helicopter then." Luce angrily suggests. "Call a fuckin snowplough. *Just get help, ya prick!*"

Bale just rolls his eyes, turns away and slowly walks back to the control room, all the time in the world.

Mercifully, Ross's crushing grip on Aldo's hand slackens off a bit and the muscle spasms die down. He's still pale, and though his hand's ice cold, Aldo can see beads of sweat on his forehead and the dampness of the hairs on his arms. The tremors finally pass, and Ross's eyelids flutter a few times before opening all the way.

Then Ross sits up and looks about, ignoring Aldo and Luce, not as if he doesn't know where he is, but as if he knows fine well where he is, doesn't like it one bit, and is expecting to be jumped at any moment. He wipes the blood off his face with the back of his hand and looks at the red smear, frowning as if confused to see his own blood outside of his body.

"Christ, man, you okay?" Aldo asks, putting a steadying hand on Ross's shoulder. "What happened?"

"Ross? You with us?" Luce says, smiling. There are tears in her eyes.

Ross looks from Aldo to Luce then back again, shrugs off their hands, then abruptly lurches to his feet and storms across the live room in the direction of the control booth.

Aldo has a very bad feeling about this.

"Woah, woah, chill, Roscoe, take it easy, dude," he says, getting up and stumbling after him, sure that his bass player's about to go postal. Ross reaches for the control room door, hesitates, then goes instead to the door leading out to the stairs. Aldo follows him, relieved Ross hadn't kicked the control booth door in and delivered a sound pasting to the man within.

But why would he ever do that? Aldo wonders, and decides not to answer his own question.

Ross takes the stairs two at a time, clearly on a mission of some variety. Aldo climbs after him, breathing hard with all the exertion and excitement. He feels so weak. When was the last time he ate?

"Dude!" he gasps. "Slow down! Where you going?" He hears Luce behind him, shouting something at Bale as she too exits the studio. He doesn't quite catch exactly what she says, but it's certainly not a compliment. At the top of the stairs, Ross is through the door and into the lounge. As Aldo reaches the top of the steps, a whine of feedback in his ears, hanging onto the doorframe for dear life and pretty sure he's about to pass out, he sees Ross on the other side of the room. For who knows what reason, he's running a finger along the spines of the vinyl records that fill the shelves stretching the length of the wall.

"Dude," Aldo says, reeling and slumping down onto the big L shaped couch. "What are you... wha you doin?" His mouth feels like it's stuffed with a dirty sock.

The whine of feedback in his ears is getting louder, escalating fom a whine to a distorted howl and Aldo winces, gripping his skull. Now Luce's in the room, standing behind Ross, saying something to him, and Ross is holding a record sleeve out to her, pointing at the album cover and saying something, but Aldo can't hear anything but the discordant, horribly atonal howl in his head, and now through half-closed eyes he sees Luce standing over him, shaking him by the shoulder, shouting something at him but he can't hear anything but the fuckin awful grinding shriek that feels like if it goes on for too much longer it's going to pulp his brains like soft warm spuds under a potato masher and *Jesus Christ it's really starting to hurt now...*

Aldo grits teeth which feel like they're twisting loose in the gums, ready to explode like bloody popcorn kernels. He squeezes his eyes closed, feeling a scream build in his throat as the pain intensifies.

Then there's a cool hand pressed to his forehead, soothing and fresh, and the pain quickly fades and the awful scratching screeching howling in his head recedes, replaced by a soft, melodious voice, pleasant on the ear as an angels' choir.

"It is your time now," the voice says, and he opens his eyes. Sees Gappa Bale standing there, one hand on Aldo's forehead like he's checking his temperature, the other hand holding his Les Paul. Strangely, only Bale and the guitar are in focus. Behind him, it's like the room's filled with a thick shifting fog, and Aldo can just about make out two other figures, Ross and Luce presumably, obscured in the haze. He feels his head move on his neck in a slow nod, and he's aware of his body standing up, taking the guitar from Bale's offering hand and following the tall dark man from the room, through the door and down the stairs. Behind him, he hears other voices, calling to him, but they're muffled and indistinct. Unimportant. Annoying really. The tiny whine of insects.

Without really knowing, or caring, how he got there, Aldo finds himself standing in the live room, his guitar round his neck, hands on the strings, headphones on. There's a microphone in front of him, perfectly set to his height, and beside him, the Marshall stack emits waves of power that he feels rippling on his skin like static electricity. The weird fog filling his head lifts and dissipates, and he's as clear-minded as he's ever been. A feeling of purpose, of destiny, of being in exactly the right place at exactly the right time, thrums through him like a perfectly played chord, and all is right in the world. He knows, absolutely fuckin *knows* it, that this is right, this is good, this is where he's meant to be and this is what he's always been meant to do. Standing here, he feels like he's just placed the final piece of a million piece jigsaw. One that's taken twenty-seven years to complete.

"Are you ready?" a voice asks in his headphones.

Aldo looks across the live room at the Perspex window into the control room and sees Gappa looking back out at him. He thinks Ross and Luce might have been in there with him, but they're nowhere to be seen. Then Aldo recalls there'd been some sort of hassle earlier, hadn't there? Something Luce was bent out of shape about, and something had happened with Ross as well.

Ah well, fuck them, Aldo thinks. He's sure it isn't anything to worry about. He has to get his game face on. No time to be worrying about whatever piddly pish his rhythm section's moaning about.

"I'm ready," Aldo says to Bale through the mic, and he feels a great swell of gratitude and love for this strange man who's so completely turned his life around and made every dream he ever had come true. "Thank you for this, Mr Bale. Really," he says, and isn't a bit embarrassed to hear his voice tightening up with emotion and feel the sting of tears at the corners of his eyes.

"No, thank *you*, Alan Michael Evans. Let us make history." He makes a little finger gun gesture at Aldo and grins a wolf's grin.

Then music fills Aldo's head as the playback starts and he closes his eyes, giving himself to the perfectly recorded drums and bass, bright, tight and right. He surrenders to it, and when he hears the sweet clang of a guitar joining the mix like a splash of new and vivid colour, he realises he's already playing along.

3

Where you goin, Roadkill?

Jimmy Weir was a hollow-eyed psychopath from Govanhill in Glasgow, not yet thirteen. He arrived in Eastburn Childreen's Institute when Ross was ten years old.

Way bigger than he had any right to be, bigger even that some of the fifteen-year-olds, it was whispered Weir had been transferred from another children's home after an incident that involved a craft knife and a teacher that'd lost several pints of blood. Still a few years shy of qualifying for a stay in Polmont, the young offender's institute in Glasgow, Weir had somehow landed in Eastburn, and had quickly established himself as the number one headcase on his first day by comprehensively knocking fuck out of Shug Owen, who'd until that point been the resident number one hardman.

Geez yer fuckin dessert, Roadkill ya wee prick.

Ross never knew why Weir took an interest in him, or how he'd found out how Ross's parents had died. Not that it really mattered. From the day he stalked onto the Eastburn playground, Ross had had a target painted on his back, and was henceforth known to Jimmy Weir as 'Roadkill'. Three long years of hell had followed.

The fuck you lookin at, Roadkill?

Survival in a juvenile jungle like Eastburn *depended* on knowing how to handle yourself, and from a young age, Ross had been schooled in the art of the square go. He'd been targeted by wide-boys looking to up their credentials many times in the past, but even if he came off the worst at the end of a fight, he'd always land a few decent digs of his own before he went down. Most of the bullies and serial bams tended to prey on the weak and timid, not troubling themselves with anyone who'd have the temerity to actually fight back. That was too much like effort for most, and it became known among the resident echelon of hard cases that if you had a go at wee Roscoe McArthur, you might come out on top, but you'd probably go to bed with at least a black eye. Because of that, he was mostly left alone.

Think you can fight, do ye, Roadkill? I've had harder shites than you, ya wee orphan cunt!

Possessed with an unslakeable thirst for physical cruelty and no novice in the subtleties of verbal malice, Jimmy Weir was a nutter of a different colour. He *thrived* on combat. Blossomed on meanness. Every day there was a poisonous barbed comment about Ross's folks, and at least once a week, he would be on the receiving end of a sound doing.

He always tried to fight back, but Weir was a machine. Too big and strong, and apparently armour-plated. Despite his best efforts, Ross never once managed to draw a drop of blood from his tormentor. Had never managed to raise a bruise or draw so much as a grunt of pain from his thin, sneering lips. As much as it had sickened him to do so, Ross once tried to play submissive, refusing to fight back, hoping that Weir would lose interest and get bored. Not the case. That had just made things worse, and after a particularly severe bleaching, Ross had been left in a bloody, concussed heap, his nose resembling a crushed tomato, both eyes reduced to swollen slits and his left arm broken in two places. Weir had left him alone until the cast was off, and Ross could only assume that this was due to some warped sense of principle. Knocking seven shades of shite out of a one-armed victim was apparently distasteful to Jimmy Weir, in breach of some psycho code of honour, and Ross had enjoyed a brief hiatus from having his arse handed to him. But the very day the doctor had cut the cast away and proclaimed Ross's arm healed, Weir had resumed his campaign. Fuck sake, he'd even come up and with what seemed like genuine concern in his voice, asked Ross how his arm was, before butting him square in the coupon and breaking his nose. Again.

And so that was his life for three years. Three years of looking over his shoulder for Jimmy Weir, living in perpetual anticipation of getting his cunt kicked in. Three years that only came to an end the day he left Eastburn for the last time.

It'd been snowing that day. He'd been sitting on a bench in the playground, reading an old Dean Koontz paperback, *Watchers*, which he loved and had read many times before. He'd not been able to get into the adventures of Einstein and The Outsider that day, though, because he knew he was off to another foster parent later that afternoon. The first in almost four years.

Then a shadow had fallen over him.

What you reading there, Roadkill, ya wee fuckin spunkrag? How to Scrape your Maw n Da aff the Pavement?

The familiar dread that Jimmy Weir's nasal, mocking voice always inspired had flooded his veins as if mainlined. But when Weir tried to snatch the book from his hands, another voice, kind of like his own, but deeper and more assured, had spoken up in Ross's head.

No more, it said.

Before Weir could say another word, Ross sprung to his feet, and turning the thick paperback in his hand, rammed it spine first into the bigger boy's throat. Weir made a very odd gasping-gulping noise and staggered back, his eyes rolling in his head.

Ross, a pleasantly detached calm in his head, had followed him, hooked a foot behind Weir's retreating ankles and tripped him. Then, with a circle of other Eastburn children crowding round in a baying, bloodthirsty circle, Ross had straddled Weir's chest, pinning his arms with his knees, and gone to town.

By the time he finished, his copy of *Watchers* had been an illegible fistful of sodden red paper, dripping crimson on the snow.

He'd left Eastburn for the last time later that afternoon, and had never felt scared again.

Later that same day, Ross is standing in his new room, in his new house, with his new rent-a-parent.

He hasn't said more than ten words since this new guy, Gregor Picken, came to pick him up that afternoon. No point getting close. He knows it won't last long. Sooner or later, probably sooner, this guy'll either turn out to be another in the long line of arseholes, or he'll figure out that the adoption grant from the council just isn't worth the hassle of caring for him.

He seems alright so far, though. He's a big guy. Straight backed and solid shouldered, with a nose that's obviously been broken more than once. But he's got kind eyes, an easy smile and a relaxed manner. Seemed like he got the message Ross didn't want to get chatty in the car, and he hadn't tried to force a conversation while they were driving down from the 'Burn, apparently fine with making the trip down the M8 in silence.

As far as foster homes go, this one's better than any he'd been sent to before. A decent-sized three bedroom semi in a quiet cul de sac in what looks like a not bad area of Inverclyde. Neat garden outside. Clean, warm and well-kept indoors. Deep blue carpet and plain white walls. Smells like coffee and furniture polish. Lots of pictures on the walls, among them several black and white photos of a rather plain, but happy looking woman with dark wavy hair. Other than in the framed photos, though, she's nowhere to be seen. In another picture, a younger Gregor Picken stands at attention in a military uniform, a red beret on his head and medals on his chest.

His bedroom. A single pine bed under a window that looks down the hill onto the River Clyde. A plain wooden wardrobe and matching chest of drawers with a small TV on top. There's a bookcase on one wall, and Ross wanders over, tilting his head slightly to the side to read the titles, finding it's a pretty random collection of hardbacks and paperbacks of varying size, shelved in no apparent order. There's a bunch of novels, mostly adventure, mystery and horror titles by Jack Higgins, Wilbur Smith, Stephen King, Robert McCammon and interestingly, a few by Dean R Koontz. In amongst the novels, there's a number of reference books and non-fiction. *The Encyclopaedia of Jazz and Blues. Ripley's Believe it or Not 1997. Self Defence Made Simple. The Art of War. The Guinness Book of Records 2001. Krav Maga: The Illustrated Guide.*

Looking around the room, the only other things that stand out are the big hi-fi in the corner, and the big four string guitar propped against the wall beside it. The hi-fi's a hulking silver plastic and pine wood finish thing with a record player, radio controls and double tape decks that looks like it was state of the art sometime in the early-to-mid-eighties. No CD player. It's got a baffling array of buttons, switches, dials and sliders, with a built-in storage space at the bottom filled with records. The guitar, a bass, is a big red and white beast of a thing, standing next to a small mesh fronted box about the size of a footstool with a row of four dials along the top. Ross thinks it must be an amplifier, but he doesn't know much about that kind of stuff.

"Do you like music?" Gregor asks, nodding over to the bass and stereo.

Ross just shrugs in reply, then dumps his rucksack containing his clothes and a few books on the bed. He walks over to the bass and plucks the thickest of the four strings with his thumb. A low metallic twang comes off the thing, all deep and dusty, and Ross places his hand on the back of the long segmented part of the guitar, feeling the vibration in his fingers, rippling all the way along his arm to the shoulder.

Cool.

Unexpected, he feels a smile pulling at the corners of his lips, and a little alarmed and his reaction, quickly straightens his face again, turning away from the bass and looking out the window.

"I got that bass when I was about your age," Gregor says behind him, coming over and standing beside Ross at the window. He doesn't look at Ross. Just stands there gazing down over the river and the hills beyond. "Played about with it now and again but I never really had the patience or talent fot it. Always thought it looked cool though, so I kept it more as an ornament."

Ross makes a non-committal noise in his throat, like he's already bored half to death by the story of Gregor Picken's failed music career. He really wants to go over and pluck that big fat string again, though. Wants to hear that moody note again and feel that weird trembling ripple in his arm. Can't do that though. Fuck no. Don't get close. Keep the walls firmly up. Stay cool. Stay distant.

"My wife, she was pretty musical," Gregor says, still staring out the window. "Played piano. The records there are hers."

"Where is she?" Ross asks before he can think better of it.

"Dead," Gregor says, just stating a plain fact. "She had a weak heart."

"Oh."

There's a few moments of awkward silence. Ross feels like he should say something. Sorry, maybe. But why should he be sorry? He never knew this guy's wife. He wasn't the one that gave her a dodgy ticker. He never even knew she existed until a few seconds ago. So why does he feel like a prick for not saying something?

"Listen, Ross," Gregor says, turning from the window and looking down at him. "This is as weird for me as it is for you. I've never fostered before, alright? And me and Gaynor never had kids."

"Why?" Ross asks, and again wonders why he cares.

"It wasn't just her heart that was weak. She never kept in the best of health. She just… wasn't strong enough to carry a baby, but she always wanted to be a mother. She had a lot of love in her."

Again, Ross wants to say something, but what? Sorry your wife was born buckled inside?

"We always wanted to adopt," Gregor goes on, "but her health…" he shrugs. "The adoption people won't even look at you if there's any medical problems."

"So what?" Ross asks. "You're doing this for her?" Giving in to the strange urge he feels, he goes over to the bass again and plucks a different string, hearing the different, higher pitched note it gives off. He runs his hand along the long bit of the bass, the neck, he thinks it's called. He fingers idly at the big metal things sticking out the side of the part at the top, turning them and studying the way the strings are attached, wound around the four metal pegs.

"In a way," Gregor says behind him. "But I wanted to foster just as much as Gaynor did."

Ross turns to him. "And now you can?"

"Aye. Now I can."

"Good for you. I'm sure your wife would be happy." Ross winces inside as soon as he says it. He hadn't meant it to come out the dickish way it did, as if he was taking the piss.

Gregor Picken just looks at him for a moment, then: "Twelve foster homes in ten years, right?" Ross feels his jaw tighten at the mention of his adoption record. He doesn't reply. "None of them lasting more than a few months," Gregor goes on. "You ran away from three of them, the first time when you were six, the last when you were ten. The woman in that case told the people at Eastburn you tried to stab her husband with a kitchen knife. Want to tell me what happened?"

Ross just stares at him, the familiar cocktail of fear and hate starting to bubble in his guts and at the base of his spine, and in his mind he hears the squeak of bedroom floorboards in the night. The rattle of a loose window pane, the rasp of heavy breathing and the stink of onions. The feel of a big calloused hand on his belly, trying to force its way inside his pyjamas...

Gregor takes a step toward him, and though Ross instinctively starts to back away, he holds his ground, his hands automatically balling themselves into fists. He won't be afraid. Not anymore. Not after this afternoon. Not after Jimmy Weir.

"You've got a reputation as a scrapper," Gregor says. "Violent outbursts. Withdrawn. Uncommunicative. I get it. You've had to look after yourself since you were three years old. I don't pretend to know what you've been through, Ross, and I won't say I understand you, because I don't know you, but I swear to you right now; I won't ever hurt you. Ever. I'm no quitter either. I'm not going to send you back to Eastburn unless you want to go."

Ross just stands there. He seems like an alright guy, this one, and he finds himself wanting to believe him. But that was nothing new. He'd thought a lot of cunts were alright at first, and had wanted to believe all the others who told him he was welcome in their homes and that he'd be looked after. All the others who promised they'd never hurt him or send him back to the 'Burn.

Don't fall for it. Not again.

Gregor Picken leans down slightly, seems to study Ross head to toe for a moment, then steps back, frowning. "Your stance is all wrong, by the way," he says. "You're right-handed, right? You should have your left foot forward a bit. Plus, you're flat footed. You need to be on the balls of your feet to generate enough power to land a decent punch. And don't clench your fist too early. Your hand moves faster when it's relaxed."

Thrown off by the sudden change in subject, Ross isn't quite sure how to respond to that, but he does unclench his fists. "What are you, a kung fu master?" he asks with uncertain sarcasm, thinking of some of the titles in the bookcase on the wall. What the hell was Krav Maga anyway?

Gregor Picken says nothing. He smiles and walks past Ross to the hi-fi, crouches down and flicks through the albums in the storage compartment. After a moment he selects a particularly worn-looking record, all tattered round the edges, with a black and white photograph on the front, showing a good looking guy with slicked back hair, standing alone in the middle of a dusty road, wearing a black suit and holding a beat up guitar. He's staring sullenly at the camera, a cigarette dangling from his bottom lip. He looks simultaneously bored out of his mind and cool as fuck.

Gregor pushes a button on the hi-fi and there's a low click and a subsonic hum from the speakers. He flicks a switch, adjusts a few dials and takes the vinyl from the sleeve with something like reverence, before placing it on the turntable. After a few seconds of scratchy rumbling silence, a sudden burst of loud, high tempo shuffling music comes leaping from the speakers, and Ross can't help but jump a little at the abrupt noise in the room.

It sounds mental. At the same time chaotic and organised, like it's played according to some underlying rules that Ross can hear but not understand. There's no singing, just a constant barrage of pounding drums that seem to be all over the place, jittery skipping low notes that he envisions being played on one of those old stood up double bass things, and led by a guitar that sounds like it's being played by three people at once, firing off notes like a wood chipper. Ross has heard of jazz music of course, but until that moment he's never actually heard it.

Gregor looks over at him, grinning and playing air drums along with the frantic beat as he crouches there at the ancient hi-fi. Ross snorts laughter. He can't help it. Gregor rolls the volume back a bit, just enough to make normal conversation possible, and stands up. "Like it?"

Ross can't really tell. Scratchy and raw-sounding, as if recorded with very basic equipment, it's hard to make sense of, but there's something about it that's making his heart beat a little faster, and he finds one of his feet has found the beat and is tapping along. He nods. "I think so," he says, and laughs again, though he's not really sure why.

Gregor comes over to him, and this time Ross feels no instinctive urge to back away or ball up his fists.

"I'm glad you're here, Ross," he says. He nods over at the stereo, the records, the bass and amplifier. "They're yours now. Call it a housewarming present. Let me know if you want me to show you a thing or two on the bass, alright? What little I know anyway. Same goes for fighting. We all need to do it at some point. Might as well be good at it, right?"

Ross nods back. "Okay. Thanks."

Gregor smiles and offers his hand. Ross shakes it, and thinks that maybe, just maybe, this cunt'll turn out to be alright after all.

"Nice to meet you," Gregor says. "I'll let you unpack while I get the tea on."

"Alright," Ross says. "By the way, who is that?" he nods towards the speakers, still pumping furious jazz into his new bedroom. "It sounds... old. Old, but good."

"It *is* old," Gregor says, pausing in the bedroom doorway. "Was recorded back in the thirties. It's by a guy called John 'Six Finger' Asher."

Fourteen years later, and Ross is standing in the lounge of Easy Rollin Manor, blood smeared on his face and hands, holding an old faded record sleeve and staring down at it as if mesmerised.

He has only the vaguest memories of being in the studio. He remembers being here in the lounge, talking to Luce after her session, then heading down to confront Bale, and then... he can't quite recall. He knows that despite his intentions, he'd put down the bass tracks for the album, but the memory of doing it are hazy at best, as if it'd happened to someone else and he'd just heard about it, because the next thing he'd known, he was waking up on the floor of the studio, blood on his face and terror in his bones.

Now, having chased Ross up the stairs from the studio, Aldo's slumped on the big L-shaped couch behind him, gasping for breath like he's been playing Tig with Usain Bolt. "Dude... what are you... wha you doin?" he wheezes.

Ross doesn't, or more accurately, *can't* reply. Because on the record sleeve in his hands is that same sullen looking, slick-haired dude in the black suit, standing on that lonely dusty road. The memory from that first day in Gregor Picken's house is coming back to him like a baseball bat to the skull. One of those eerie, long forgotten recollections that randomly resurface, unexpected after years buried in the folds of the brain.

But how could he have forgotten *this*?

His hands are shaking, making it hard to read the artist biography on the reverse of the album cover, but out of nowhere, he remembers almost word for word the story of Six Finger Asher, who'd got his nickname on account of the speed and skill of his playing.

Born and raised in the east end of London, Asher had been tipped to be one of the great jazz guitarists of the age, right up there with Django Reinhardt. Never had a music lesson. Poor as dirt, but a natural talent. He made a name for himself as a teenager, playing in London jazz clubs around Soho. Then, in the late thirties, shortly after recording his one and only record with a small independent label and doing a single tour of the States, he'd vanished. Just like that. No body had ever been found. No suicide note ever recovered. He'd simply disappeared. His brief moment in the spotlight hadn't been long enough for people to remember him, and eclipsed by other musicians who'd found a higher level of stardom in the same period, Six Finger Asher had faded from the pages of music history, leaving him barely even a footnote in the annals of jazz.

The album in Ross's hands, which Gregor Picken had also owned a copy of, is a 1972 reissue of Six Finger Asher's only release, an eponymous album which the credits state was originally recorded by Hipcat Music in 1938, the same year he disappeared.

With trembling fingers, Ross turns the album cover over again, looking at the photograph of the forgotten guitarist on the front. Young, lean and mean. The bored, slightly frosty expression. The dark, piercing eyes. Ross flips the album cover over once more to read the back. Feeling like he's in dire danger of losing his shit, he scans the epitaph at the bottom of Asher's biography.

John 'Six Finger' Asher
1911 - ?

Ross remembers Gappa Bale, talking to them on that first morning here.

John is a consummate professional. Strong as an ox despite his age, and he has been in my employ for many years. Is there a problem?

Oh, you're fuckin right there's a problem, Ross thinks.

"Ross," someone says, and he flinches as someone touches his shoulder. He turns to see Luce standing there. "What is it?" She looks a lot like Ross feels, which is to say, freaked the fuck out.

He shows her the album cover. "It's him, Luce," he says, his voice remarkably even. "It's *John*. The fuckin driver."

Luce frowns down at the record, taking it from Ross and studying it for a long moment before turning it over. He watches as she reads the text on the back of the sleeve, unable to speak as his mind does some unsettling mental arithmetic and makes several very scary suggestions.

"No," Luce whispers, visibly blanching as what she's just read sinks in. "No, that's just not possible. No fuckin way..."

Meanwhile, a nasty little slideshow of memories is parading through Ross's head, making him think of a New Orleans marching band, playing horribly out of tune. John - who was old, yeah, but sure as shit not a hundred and five - standing by the car that first night they'd arrived. The almost imperceptible shake of his head as they'd stepped across the threshold of this place. The look of pity on his face. Then John out back earlier, half naked, mincing fuck out of a deer which he may or may not have killed with his own teeth.

Get away, he'd said.

For a few seconds, Ross can't move. Can't think. Can't breathe. Then, on the couch, Aldo makes a strange groaning-whining noise and Ross turns to see him writhing on the cushions, gripping his head like he's trying to hold his skull together.

Luce stumbles over and shakes him by the shoulder. "Al, come on, get up," she's saying, her voice high and panicky. "We need to get the fuck out of here. Come *on*, Al, get *up!*"

"Once again, Lucia," a soft voice like the purr of a panther says from the doorway behind Ross, "there *is* no leaving here, and I believe Aldo can make up his own mind."

It's like every drop of blood in Ross's veins turns in an instant to cold lead. He manages to turn his head, and sees Bale standing in the doorway leading out to the hall. He's holding Aldo's guitar.

Now, how did that happen? he wonders. *Wasn't Bale down in the studio just a moment ago? And Aldo's guitar was in his room earlier when he was doing his naked orchestral manoeuvres in the dark thing.*

He watches as Bale glides across the room and stands at the couch looking down at Aldo. Bale turns his head and smiles at Luce, who seems to slump inside her skin before backing away from Aldo, as if she'd suddenly discovered a vest of dynamite strapped to his chest. Her eyes, glassy as a chronic hash head, are fixed on Bale, and Ross is put in mind of a mouse hypnotised by the dead black eyes and sinuous weaving of a hungry cobra.

Bale leans forward and places a hand on Aldo's forehead. "It's your time now," he says, and Aldo instantly stops his tortured twisting and groaning. He opens his eyes and smiles up at Bale, a big gormless grin like he's just had a hefty hit of high grade smack. He gets slowly to his feet and follows Bale over to the door leading down to the studio, moving with all the shuffling stupidity of a zombie.

Well fuck that, Ross decides, anger flaring up in him.

He storms across the room, intending to grab Aldo, turn him round and slap the shit out of him if that's what's required to wake him up, and Bale too if he gets in his way. But as he reaches for his friend's shoulder, Bale pivots round, his lips skinned back from his teeth like an attack dog. He pins Ross in that empty basilisk stare of his, and it seems the room suddenly grows darker, the shadows in the corners deeper. It stops Ross cold.

Bale holds him there a long moment - with nothing but eyes that frighten Ross more than any blade carrying bam he's ever met - then gives a satisfied smirk and a nod, turns and disappears down the stairs with Aldo in tow.

The door slams closed behind them, all by itself.

4

The hard, flat *bang* of the door to the studio slamming shut snaps Luce out of her trance. She blinks and the world comes back into focus. Ross is standing motionless by the door, staring at it as if *he's* hypnotised.

She runs round the couch and attacks the door, hauling at the handle, but it won't open. She starts slapping and kicking at it, calling out for Aldo. Then Ross is there, pulling her to the side then bodily throwing himself at the barrier, attempting to break it down with his shoulder and a series of brutal kicks. He doesn't even make a dent. The door doesn't so much as tremble in its frame.

"It's no good," Ross gasps stepping back, his hands fisted at his temples. "I can't open it." Then he launches himself at the door again, roaring in frustration and hammering at the wood with his fists and feet. He stops his useless bludgeoning and steps back again, breathing hard through clenched teeth and looking wildly around the room as if searching for something to use as a battering ram.

Luce can only stand there watching, feeling completely helpless, her mind whirling with insane thoughts.

Right, get a grip, girl. You need to get help. You need to get out of here and go and get help.

Except Aldo's down there. They can't leave him.

"Stay here," she says to Ross. "Keep trying." Then she runs from the lounge, down the corridor to her room and barges in, slapping the light on and grabbing her mobile from her jacket. She holds the power button down and tries to quell her rising dread as she waits for the phone to start. She wants to scream at the device's cheery series of beeps and melodies and animations as it boots up. Finally her home screen appears with its rows of app icons. At the top, as she'd known it would, the status bar shows no network signal. The time display shows four minutes after ten in the morning, though from the dark pressing against the window outside, that can't be right.

Then she has a hard time fighting down panic as the time display flickers and changes, now saying it's seven minutes till three in the morning, then twenty-eight minutes till four in the afternoon.

Fuck what time it is, she concludes, stubbornly clamping down on the spiralling fear that's winding up from her guts to her throat, threatening to choke her. *I need a signal.*

Keeping her mind carefully focussed on the task at hand, she goes to her chest of drawers and pulls out her Glasgow Uni hoodie, throws her short leather jacket on and leaves the room again, running back down the corridor and turning right at the main entrance to the building. She throws open the big storm doors, stumbles down the stairs into the courtyard, out into the night, the wind and pelting snow. She ignores the cold and looks at her mobile again.

Still no signal.

"*Fuck!*" she yells into the blizzard, resisting the urge to hurl the useless mobile to the ground and stomp on it. "*Fuuuuuuuuck!*"

You need to get further away.

Luce looks at the Balemobile for a moment, but quickly abandons any idea of attempting to steal the car. All she knows about auto theft comes from the movies, and something tells her that even if she *did* know how to hotwire a motor, the Balemobile would still refuse to budge. She also has the oddest idea that the car would bite her if she so much as touched the door handle.

She looks along the single track road on her left which leads into the woods. It's all but disappeared under several inches of snow, and the howling blizzard speckling the deep darkness like TV static means she can't see more than few metres beyond the lamp-lit courtyard. It'd be madness to try and walk out of here in these conditions, with no real idea of where she's going and no weatherproof clothing. But what else can she do?

Doing her absolute very best to not think about what she's doing, Luce starts walking, leaving the lights of the courtyard behind her and following the rapidly vanishing track, holding her phone up in front of her face, praying with every step to see just a single bar of signal appear on the screen. No bar appears, and in about ten seconds she's in almost complete darkness, the snow up to her knees, her feet already numb and the freezing wind shrieking in the trees, tearing at her with icy claws.

She grits her teeth and walks on, battling forward through the deepening snow, the meagre light from the courtyard behind her fading.

About a minute later, she's completely disorientated, with no idea if she's still even on the track. All around is perfect blackness, the only light coming from the screen of her phone which still refuses to give her any signal. Shaking in the weather's onslaught, her legs tiring, her hands, ears and face feeling like they've been shot full of novocaine, panic beginning to well up in her again, Luce takes another three steps, and something reaches out of the black and scratches at her face.

She screams and staggers back, lifting her hands to ward off her unseen attacker and falling back in the snow. Terrified by what she might see, but unable to bear the all-encompassing darkness, she turns the phone screen outward, and sees the low branches of the fir tree she's just brushed up against. She lets out a shaky laugh, but the relief that she's been assailed by nothing more malevolent than some pine needles quickly fades as Luce realises she's wandered off the road.

Now shaking fit to loosen her molars, she manages to control her unfeeling hand long enough to wipe snowflakes from the mobile's screen and press another icon, activating the flashlight app and shining the stronger light around her. It reveals nothing but more trees all around her, deep snow drifts piling up against the trunks, and deeper pockets of darkness between them. Despair rises in her throat like gorge as she accepts the futility of trying to make it back to civilisation, or even within mobile range of civilisation. She's on foot. In the middle of a night-time blizzard. Freezing already, and with no idea of where she is or even what direction she's facing.

The gnawing cold a physical presence that seems to crush her and push her to the ground, Luce reviews her options. She realises she has only one, and turns back the way she came, shining the mobile's torch on the ground, following her own footprints and praying now not for a bar of mobile signal, but that the battery will last long enough to light her way back to Easy Rollin Manor.

And so she moves, fighting through the ever deepening snow with shrieking blackness all around, conjuring images of unseen beasts howling between the trees. She staggers on, sternly telling herself that *no*, there absolutely *isn't* anything moving in the lightless void around her, and of course it's just her imagination making her think she can hear insane cackling laughter and sinister whisperings out there in the black. She insists that the shifting, indistinct shapes in the gloom are real nowhere but in her own mind, created by stress and exposure. She focusses all her will into taking another step, and then another, trying to shut out everything from her mind but following the pale patch of light her mobile casts on the ground, but noticing with rising alarm that already her outbound footprints are being erased by the blizzard. And with every second, the cold, a deathly bonesaw chill unlike anything she's ever experienced, seeps into her joints, slowing her movements, and every breath is harder than the last, bringing a little screamy gasp of effort from her throat. The light from her phone is fading, and as it does, the vague movements at the edge of her vision, sensed more than seen, seem to draw closer. And she's becoming terrifyingly sure that it's *not* just her imagination making those guttural chuckles and whispers on the wind.

They're closer. More insistent.

A definite rustle of branches somewhere in the darkness to her left makes Luce gasp in fright and swing her phone in that direction, the light enough to show the movement of a low pine bough, swaying as if disturbed.

A low throaty hiss behind her, and Luce pivots, her heart leaping to the back of her mouth, the phone's light just for a terrifying instant giving a half-seen glimpse of a hunched shadow sliding back into the deeper darkness between the trees.

Her bravery finally collapsing, Luce turns and tries to run, but her legs are weak as corn stalks, the cold having burned the feeling and all of the strength from them. She stumbles and falls to her hands and knees, unable to get up again, making breathless sobs in her throat and feeling the last of the warmth in her blood leeching out into the ground beneath her. Somewhere close behind her, something moves in the forest, something that sniggers and rasps.

But then, through the trees ahead, Luce sees a pale greyish light, and with a low, desperate scream of effort, she regains her feet and somehow finds the strength to stumble on.

The pale light brightens as she struggles closer, until she can make out the silhouette of the building, the courtyard and the shape of the Balemobile washed in the white light of the bollard lamps. Paying no mind to the fact that she seems to be coming at the building from the opposite side from which she left it, Luce stumbles out of the treeline, staggers over an uneven stretch of rocky moorland and into the courtyard, reeling across it and practically falling through the storm doors. She collapses on the thick red carpet of the hallway and manages to kick the door closed behind her, still convinced something;s followed her from the woods.

"Jesus. What the fuck happened to you?"

Luce manages to unfreeze her neck joints enough to look up. Ross is standing there, looking down at her, a thoroughly baffled look on his face.

"Holy sh-sh-sh-sh-it that's fu-uh-uh-uh-uhkin c-c-c-old out there," she sort of says.

"Where the hell you *been*?" Ross says, bending and helping her up, brushing snow from her hair and jacket and practically carrying her into the library where, prince among men that he is, he's already got a roaring fire going. Even now, as inviting as the fire is, Luce's not so cold that she doesn't feel an extra little shiver as she looks at the couch in front of it, remembering what she and Gappa Bale did there.

"I w-w-went... went outside to s-see... see if I could get a... a s-s-signal." She's just about managed to stop her jaw from clacking like novelty wind up gnashers, and kneels down in front of the fireplace, reaching her hands for the warmth of the flames.

"Take your clothes off," Ross instructs her. "They're taking more heat out you than they're keeping in. I'll get you some more."

As Ross leaves the library, Luce removes her cold, damp-heavy and thoroughly miserable outer garments. He's back a few moments later with fresh clothes and the duvet from her room. "Christ, did you try and walk to Inverness?" he asks, wrapping the heavy blanket around her.

"I thought about it," Luce says, her eyes closed, feeling the warm, almost painful tingle of the cold being chased from her flesh. "But I didn't get far. Don't think I made it more than hundred metres before I had to come back. It's fucked, Ross. We're not leaving here any time soon. It's pitch black, you can't see the road. I lost the trail in about ten seconds, wandered into the woods. Got groped by a Christmas tree." She barks laughter that's absolutely devoid of humour.

"What are you talking about?" Ross asks.

"A tree branch scratched my face. Just about shat myself."

"No, what do you mean you only made it a hundred metres?"

"Have you seen it out there?" Luce asks, opening her eyes and turning to him. "Feel free to have a go if you think you can make it further."

"No, I don't mean that," Ross says, frowning and shaking his head. "I mean if you only made it a hundred metres and then came back, where the fuck've you *been*?"

"What are *you* talking about?"

"Luce, you've been gone for hours."

Despite the warmth of the fire, Luce feels one last icy scuttle across her scalp. She looks at him. Shakes her head. "Erm... no I've not. I couldn't have been out there for, I don't know, ten minutes, tops."

Ross shakes his head right back at her. "Erm... *naw*. You've been gone for ages. I was out looking for you. A few times."

"Ross, I swear I was only out there for a few minutes," she insists. "No way was it..."

"Luce, listen to me. I've been out to the treeline all around this place trying to find you. I was out there for at least half an hour myself just now, wandering about, shouting for you. I was freaking out. I thought you'd... Christ I don't know what I thought. I only got back a minute or two before you did just now. That's why I got the fire going."

For the first time, Luce notices Ross's jacket slung on a coatstand by the fireplace. There's melting snow dripping off it.

Ross holds her eyes for a moment. Then shakes his head and looks into the fire instead. "There's... something out there," he says quietly. "You heard them?"

"I heard them."

Ross just nods. Says nothing. He doesn't want to talk about it, which is just fine by Luce. She doesn't even want to think about what she may or may not have heard and seen. Turning the disturbing thought and all it's scary arms and legs aside for the moment, she turns her thoughts to their absent frontman.

"What about Al?"

"Down in the studio, far as I know. The door still won't open."

"Ross, what are we going to do?" Luce asks, staring into the fire, lost and scared.

"You're going to come downstairs and listen to your new album," someone whispers behind them.

5

Aldo bursts out laughing at the shape of Ross and Luce, sprawled on the floor, goggling up at him with blank terror on their faces. The two of them had just about fell into the fireplace with the fright he just gave them.

He's just finished his session, come upstairs and heard them talking in the library. He thought it'd be funny to sneak up behind them and give them a right good scare. The thick carpet and soundproofed walls here make it easy to sneak up on people.

And it is. Funny as fuck. Aldo's doubled over, fuckin howling, but Luce – who for some reason's dressed only in her bra and knickers and a duvet - is raging, her expression in the space of about a second going from panic to relief and then fury.

"You fuckin *arsehole!*" she yells, and throws one of her shoes at him.

Ross is the first to collect himself. He gets up, at least having the grace to look slightly sheepish about the girly wee scream he'd let out just now, then comes over and puts a hand on Aldo's shoulder.

"You okay, mate?" he asks, looking at Aldo very closely.

"Cool n' the gang, mate. You both need to come downstairs. You need to hear it." He shakes his head in wonder, then suddenly grabs Ross's head in both hands and plants a big smacker of a kiss on his mate's scalp. He hugs him, and Ross hugs him back, and Aldo's got a lump in his throat. He looks over at Luce, who's now dressed herself, and reaches a hand out. "C'mere, you," he says.

Exchanging a worried look with Ross, Luce comes over and takes his hand. Annoyingly, she doesn't look too happy, but she will. Once she hears it.

"Guys," Aldo says, "it's… it's fuckin tremendous. It's *perfect*. You need to come down to the studio and hear this thing. It's going to be huge. I know it."

Ross gives him a sad look. He doesn't say anything for a moment. As if he's deciding something with himself. "You're finished? Already?"

Aldo gives him a wink. "Done and dusted, amigo."

"You've recorded all the guitar parts? Lead and rhythm? And all the vocals? Since you went downstairs with Gappa earlier?"

"Yep. Got everything on the first take."

"And it's all mixed and mastered?"

Aldo just nods, smiling, but Ross glances over at Luce and they share a wee anxious moment, silently discussing something Aldo's clearly not included in.

Luce lets go of Aldo's hand and backs away from him, shaking her head. "No. No, you can't have, Al," she says. "You just *can't*."

Aldo sighs. "What are you talking about?"

"Recording all the guitars and the vocals for a whole album, then mixing and mastering it would take the better part of a day. At least. You know that, right?"

"Aye? And?" Again, a look passes between Ross and Luce, who's still shaking her head. "Someone want to tell me what the fuck's going on with you two?" Aldo asks, not unkindly.

"Sorry, Al," Ross says, shaking his head. "I've no doubts in my mind that the album's good. Scary good, I imagine. But it's time to go."

"Aw for fuck sake, Roscoe," Aldo groans. "Not you as well?"

"Fraid so, mate," Ross says. "Things are just getting way too weird around here. Surely you can see that? We really need to go."

He wants to scream and maybe throw some shit around, but Aldo keeps his face impassive while he grinds his teeth and takes a series of deep, calming breaths. Why can't they see it? There'd been weirdness aplenty in all their lives recently. The *magic*. And, far as he can tell, the weirdness is working out just fine so far. Long may it continue.

But why is he even having this conversation? Ross and Luce need to come downstairs and hear the album *right now*.

"Alright, fine," Aldo says. "Things have been fucked up. Mental. Totally nuts. Ten flavours of crazy. But we're not going anywhere tonight, are we?"

Luce just shakes her head and turns away. Aldo looks at Ross. "Am I right?"

Ross goes and stands at the window. Outside, the snow's coming down hard, with no sign of stopping. "Aye," Ross admits as he stares out at the blizzard. "You're right."

"Well, cool," Aldo says, as if stating an obvious fact. "We can leave tomorrow. We'll walk out at dawn if you want. It doesn't matter. The album's done. So, let's just all chill out, go down to the studio and listen..."

"I'm not going anywhere near *him*," Luce states, evidently still pissed at Gappa about their fight, or whatever the hell it was.

"Cool yer jets, missy," Aldo soothes her. "Gappa's in his office downstairs. He knows things have got a bit tense..."

"Tense?" Ross says, raising his eyebrows.

"...and he said we should listen to it by ourselves the first time. Start to finish, no interruptions. Just us. Come on down, guys. Please?"

There follows a long and uneasy silence, but Aldo notices that neither of them immediately say no.

Luce keeps schtum, but there's a gradual softening in her frosty expression. Despite all her complaining, she *knows* what this means to Aldo, and despite all his complaining about *her* complaining, Aldo loves her for it. And she wants to hear it, too, make no mistake. Of course she does. And so does Ross. You can see it in his eyes.

Aldo knows he's got them, and he smiles. "Mon the Alibi," he says softly, then turns around and walks out of the room.

He's not gone more than five steps when Ross and Luce catch up to him and follow him into the lounge and down the stairs.

In the control room, Gappa's left the console set up, ready to play.

Aldo takes the big office chair in front of the desk, unable to stop smiling as Ross and Luce take their own seats. "All comfy?" he asks.

"Play it, man," Ross says in a low voice, and there's that tightening of the jaw he does when he's wound up. "Just fuckin play it."

Aldo plays it, and the first song explodes from the speakers, filling the room like a shrapnel grenade going off.

Track one. *Conquistador.* No slow build up. No fannying about. It comes in full tilt on a driving, anthemic chorus; the vocals, bass, drums and guitar already roaring with the album's first breath. It's an epic sound. Monumental. It's everything good that he's ever heard.

Aldo looks over at Luce, who's sitting there with her eyes closed. She's expressionless, but her left foot's tapping on the floor, keeping time. He can see the fine hairs on her arms bristling, the skin beneath bumpy with gooseflesh, and he knows she's feeling the music create the same exquisite tingle along the nerves that he is.

He turns to Ross and sees his friend looking back at him. There's a dazed look in his eyes, and a wee half smile tugging at the corners of his lips as he nods along. He leans back in his chair, closing his eyes and immersing himself in the album like he's slipping into a very warm, very noisy bath.

No, not slipping into a bath. This is more like falling into white water rapids and being swept downriver, bouncing off rocks, breaking bones and fighting to breathe.

Public Alibi listen to their debut album together for the first time, and Aldo Evans finds bliss. The sound is perfect. The levels, balance, panning and EQ of the instruments flawless, as if Bale's already spent a week mixing and mastering. Huge and stomping, then quiet and heartfelt, then funky as all ever loving fuck. It's soulful and hateful and tender and sleazy as a brothel in Hell. It's everything he's ever wanted but never had. As before, but to the nth degree, Aldo feels detached from himself, floating among the notes.

Time passes. How long is the least of his concerns. A joyous noise such as this is *outside* of time. All he knows is that it's going to be colossal when it gets out.

They're going to be colossal.

Sometime unknown time later, the album, *Cuttin Heads*, ends with the deranged symphonic bedlam of the final track, *Down Down Down*. Like the death throes of a malevolent giant. A destructive and brutal climax, a towering jagged wall of distortion and screeching violins that sounds like the end of the universe, punctuated with reverb-soaked multi-layered tracks of Aldo shrieking like a man being flayed alive.

When it finally fades out, Aldo opens his eyes again. There are tears on his cheeks. He feels wrung out. Knackered, but deeply satisfied, as one does in the sweaty afterglow of a particularly epic shag. Ross is hunched over in his seat, head in hands. He slowly looks up at Aldo. Joyously traumatised is probably the best way to describe how his bass player looks at that moment.

Luce also has tears on her face. She blinks a few times, rubs her eyes and lets out a long uneven sigh. "Holy shit," she says, looking down at the floor, her hands visibly shaking on the armrests of the chair. She makes a sound that's half a laugh, half a sob.

"I know," Aldo says, reaching over and taking her trembling hands in his own.

"Dude," Ross says, shaking his head in wonder. "That's fuckin... *fuck!*"

"Aye," Aldo agrees. "Thank you, guys," he says sincerely, looking from Ross to Luce and back again. "Thank you. So, so much." He's having trouble getting the words out, and feels his eyes stinging with tears again. And what of it? He remembers hearing that Thom Yorke broke down sobbing in the studio right after Radiohead recorded the classic *Fake Plastic Trees*.

They have a group hug then, the three of them standing arm-in-arm, laughing and sobbing, their souls scorched raw by what they've created. And it's good. There's just them and this amazing thing they've done. Aldo's thinking how together they are here in the control room.

How much simpler it all is. No arguing or freaking out. Just them and the music. For the first time in what seems like ages, the three of them are on the same page. And of course, there's everything that's yet to come. The Glasgow Green gig. The album launch. A tour, probably. Riches and fame and good times untold.

"I assume you are pleased with it?" a much-loved voice says.

Aldo turns and sees Gappa Bale in the doorway. He tries to speak. Tries to say thank you, thank you for everything, for bringing us here and giving us the freedom to do this perfect thing, but the force of his own emotion cracks his voice. Before he can try again, Gappa holds up a hand, halting his words.

"We must talk," he says. "I have something to tell you, Aldo."

Aldo suddenly realises he's not smiling. Gone is his trademark enigmatic half-grin, that subtle tilt of the lips that makes you think he's on the ball, everything's cool and he's about a million steps ahead of every bugger.

Before he can say anything, Ross goes, "Tell us about John."

Gappa favours him with a bored, *not-this-shit-again* look.

"Tell us about why time doesn't work right here," Ross goes on. "Tell us about..." Ross's words falter and trail off into a half-hearted mumble as Gappa's look goes from bored to a withering glare. Then he turns back to Aldo.

"There has been an incident," he says. "At your ex-girlfriend Ashley's house. A break in. She was attacked. Beaten and raped. Then murdered."

Aldo frowns at him, not understanding. The information seems like a random series of violent words that don't make any sense.

"Your son was also attacked," Gappa informs him. "Dylan is in intensive care at Yorkhill Children's Hospital. He is on life support. I am told that they do not expect him to wake."

For a moment, there's nothing. As if his ears were reluctant to transmit this information to Aldo's brain. But then Gappa's words replay in his mind, and he hears the voice of a little boy screaming in a dark forest, and goes cold all over as a sudden fear - a plunging emptiness in his guts - hollows him out. He physically feels the euphoria of only moments before leaving him like air released from a balloon, a horrible sensation of rapid deflation. He can almost hear the prolonged farting noise of happiness exiting his mind, body and soul, leaving him reeling and empty.

Aldo wheezes and gags like he's just took a hard kick in the stomach, which is exactly what it feels like. He's aware of hands on his shoulders. Ross? Luce? He can't tell. He can't see. Not here and now anyway. All Aldo can see is Dylan on the day he left to come here, standing in Ashley's doorway in his Fireman Sam jacket and Angry Birds hat, looking so small and vulnerable that it broke Aldo's heart to walk away from him.

I am told that they do not expect him to wake.

And Ashley, standing there in the same doorway, saying she was happy for him, but giving him dog's abuse all the same. How she looked especially fine when she was pissed off and her colour was up and those green eyes were flashing...

Beaten and raped. Murdered.

Aldo staggers out of the control room, his brain temporarily short-circuited, no destination in mind, just needing to move, his body acting instinctively as his sucker-punched mind tries hopelessly to comprehend what he's just been told. A stream of words continue to cascade through his head, chaotic bursts of half-garbled, gibbering nonsense.

...Dylan break in raped not expected Ashley to murdered intensive care beaten an incident attacked Ashley's house your son Dylan not expected to wake...

He finds himself in the live room, hands fisted in his long greasy hair, turning in a circle, looking frantically around the room as if trying to find answers amid the amps, mics, monitors and scattered pieces of trashed drum kit.

"I need to... need to..."

He can't think. His head's a waltzer car spun by an overenthusiastic gypsy with mad light in his eyes and a leering devil's grin.

Then Luce comes over and hugs him. Ross is standing behind him, a hand on his shoulder. He could so easily break right now. His friends' wordless gestures of solidarity and compassion almost bring Aldo to his knees, blubbering like a wean with a skint knee.

"I need... I need to get back," he manages, doing his utmost to keep his shit together, breaking away and heading for the studio door, where Gappa's leaning in the doorway, blocking the exit, the fingers of his right hand drumming idly on the doorframe. That little smile's back again.

"Of course," Gappa says, though Aldo notices he doesn't move out of the way. "John will drive you home. All of you. We have what we need here."

"I thought the roads were impassable," Ross points out, coming over and standing by Aldo's side. Luce moves in behind the two of them.

"The conditions outside have improved considerably while you have been down here," Gappa says, those long fingers *tap-tap-tapping* on the doorframe. "Such changeable weather this country has."

"Right. Let's go," Aldo says, starting forward again.

"But before you go," Bale says, still not budging, "we must discuss your show at Glasgow Green."

Luce gapes at him. "For fuck sake, Gappa" she says. "Now's really not the time."

"Oh, I think you will find that it is, Lucia," Bale replies, his fingers continuing to drum on the doorframe. "I think you will find that it is *just* the time."

He's still not moved out of the doorway. Music guru extraordinaire and answerer of prayers, Gappa Bale may be, but right now, Aldo's ready to unceremoniously shove him out the way if he doesn't shift his arse from the exit. He needs to get home. He needs to be with Dylan.

...not expected to wake...

Aldo starts forward again, but then that ever-loving smile on Bale's face broadens, and then takes a very nasty turn, becoming a grin, then a leer, and Aldo's determined momentum slows and stops because...

... oh... oh fuck... his hand...

Up on the doorframe at the level of his head, Bale's long, graceful, pianist's fingers have stopped tapping. They're... *changing*.

There's a series of small popping-grinding-squealing sounds as Gappa's fingers start to twist, elongating, snapping newly formed joints. The pale skin of his hand stretching, darkening to a wrinkled mottled grey. His still lengthening fingers stretch and scuttle across the doorframe onto the wall, like the legs of some huge spider. Long ragged nails gouge scars in the plaster. And although he'd previously decided he wasn't that fazed by a little weirdness, Aldo feels a hot trickle of pish running down the inside of his jeans.

"I must insist that you tarry a while," Gappa Bale says, his voice like fingerbones falling on a butcher's block. "I have *so* much to tell you."

Bridge

First of all, I'd like to thank Satan...

Anthony Kiedis, Red Hot Chili Peppers
MTV awards 1992

1

For several seconds, Ross can't move, speak, or even breathe. The impossible sight of the rearrangement of Bale's hand seizes him, crushes him, and won't let go. Earlier, he'd been ashamed of the paralyzing fear the man generated in him, but there's no shame now. *Hell no.* He decides nearly browning his breeks is well within the bounds of acceptability under the circumstances. Because this isn't just being scared. This is bone-deep *terror*, something primal inscribed on his very DNA. The instinctive awareness of being in the presence of something inhuman, predatory, and old beyond time. Hate, malice and hunger given physical form. Ross remembers a low lit room in the Inverclyde Royal ICU. Sitting beside Duncy Brown's bed as the old soldier had gasped his last. The look on his face as he'd told Ross about something he'd seen in the war, in the horrors of the concentration camp.

That fuckin evil bastard...Mertz, the... rapportfuhrer... block nine... those poor... weans... set the dugs on them... in the pits...made us watch... oh Christ... saw him... in the moonlight one night...His moonshadow, son... wisnae a man.

Ross starts backing away from Bale, still standing there, blocking the doorway, looking at them with a sharkish grin, the hooked nails of those long spindly fingers still *tap-tap-tapping* on the wall. Beside him, Aldo's making a low moaning noise in the back of his throat, shaking his head as they retreat from the thing in the doorway. Ross has to drag Luce along with them, because she's just standing there, with just *nothing* on her face. It's not a good look, and Ross remembers that Luce had it off with Bale. Recognising that she's deeply in shock, he takes her by the arm and pulls her backward. She doesn't resist.

Bale takes a slow step towards them, raking his claws off the doorframe as he comes, showering the hardwood floor behind him with splinters and plaster dust. He makes a quick flicking gesture with his big spidery hand, and *poof!* Just like that, it's just a regular old, normal-sized, thumb and five fingers hand again. Pale skin, flawless manicure. Ross is trying not to think about how the grotesque appendage of a second ago is presumably only the proverbial tip of an extremely creepy iceberg. Just a passing glance of whatever monstrosity hides beneath Bale's perfect exterior.

Gappa, or whatever the fuck he is, continues walking toward them. The band retreat before him.

Then Ross has a sudden, seemingly random recollection of being in the living room of his flat, getting ready to leave for the 13th Note gig, the memory so clear he can smell the sweet heady scent of his home-grown, heavy in the air. *Countdown* had been on the telly. The crucial conundrum had come up, just as he was heading out the door. EARFUSION, the letters had spelled out. Which come to think of it now, wasn't right. The conundrum was always a straight anagram, and cool as it may sound, EARFUSION was no word Ross had ever heard of. He'd got the solution right away, regardless. NEFARIOUS. And though it hadn't happened like this, in his head he hears Susie Dent's soft, sexily posh accent, as she reads the definition from the Oxford English dictionary.

Nefarious, meaning to be wicked. Devilish. Evil.

Bale comes closer. The three of them continue to back off, but now there's nowhere to go. They're almost at the back wall, and the exit's on the opposite side of the room. Ross, guiding Luce by the arm and Aldo by the back of his t-shirt, pulls them to the right, and they start slowly side-stepping along the right hand wall, back toward the control room and the exit. Bale just stands there smiling in amusement and watches them, turning to track their movement, and worryingly, making no attempt to stop their painfully obvious escape attempt.

"As I was saying," he says, his voice again the enticing tones of a snake oil salesman, "we must discuss your upcoming launch event at Glasgow Green." When no one says anything, he shrugs and goes on. "It has sold out. As a matter of fact, it has been sold out for some time. I released a few short cuts of our rehearsal sessions. The response in the press and through the various social media channels has been... extraordinary."

Ross would burst out laughing if he wasn't so scared. "This is fucked," he says, with only a slight tremble in his voice. "You're... I don't know what the fuck you are, but you think we give a shit about a gig right now?"

Bale *does* burst out laughing. A deeply unpleasant sound. He laughs with two voices. "You think I care what you give a shit about? Need I remind you, Ross? You signed a legally binding contract."

"What you gonnae do? Sue us?" Ross retorts, still edging along the wall with his bandmates. Another few steps. He glances quickly back over his shoulder. The exit's behind them, the door lying lying open, no more than fifteen feet away.

"Oh, I think I can do worse than that, Ross," Bale replies in bored voice. "I think you know I can do *far* worse than that."

"Go!" Ross shouts, turning and pushing Aldo and Luce ahead of him, then running with them for the door.

Of course the door swings closed, all by itself, and slams shut with enough authority to crack the doorframe. Aldo, unfamiliar with the way doors could be stubborn, uncooperative things around here, immediately starts yanking desperately at the handle. It doesn't open, and Ross knows that it won't open until Gappa Bale's damn well good and ready. Watching his frontman, Ross's heart breaks a little at the sight of Aldo going spare at the door, punching and kicking at it and sobbing, tears on his face. He can't conceive of how messed up Al's head must be right now. How much pain he must be in. Ashley dead. Wee Dylan on life support. And as he stands there watching his friend's desperate and completely futile attempt to leave the studio, Ross's jaw does that tightening thing.

With their only exit blocked, he turns back toward Bale, anger like a small, but white hot ember in his chest. The rage flares brighter, and just like that, he doesn't care who or what Bale is. Doesn't give a single floppy fuck what horror might be lurking behind that knowing smile. The anger builds, the ember becoming a flame heating his blood and tensing his muscles, burning away his reason, displacing his fear with the need for violence.

His hands curl into fists by his side and he takes a step forward.

"Whit the fuck *you* gonnae dae? Eh, Roadkill?" Bale sneers.

Ross's burgeoning flame of anger goes out like it's been pished on. That genetic terror swells up in his bones again, and he doesn't want to take another single solitary step in Bale's direction. No danger. Because that *wasn't* Gappa Bale speaking just then, not their smooth talking musical mentor with his perfect diction and strangely exotic accent. Right down to the hard Glasgow bur and the use of that cruel, long ago nickname, that'd been Jimmy Weir's voice.

"Eh, ya wee fuckin spunkrag? You gonnae hit me in the throat wi a fuckin book?" Bale/Weir says, taking a step forwards himself.

Ross retreats. It's not just the voice and the things he's saying. It's Jimmy Weir, the psycho from Eastburn, right down to the cruel pleasure in his eyes, the way he's standing there with his chin thrust forward and his arms out to the side in a clear *come ahead* invitation.

"Did yer maw never tell ye no tae make decisions when yer oot yer nut on the drink and pills?" Bale/Weir presses, pointing at Ross. "Aw naw, that's right. She was fuckin deid." He throws back his head and laughs that horrible two-throated laugh again. A thick gurgling chuckle counterpointed with a high chittering giggle. "Did ye know yer folks were fucked oot their heids on smack that day they crashed their motor? Wis yer maw behind the wheel, fuckin noddin aff and doin ninety up the M8 wi yer dad sittin beside her, shootin up in the passenger seat."

Ross continues to back away, until he's pressed up against the immovable studio door.

"Ya worthless wee *cunt*," Bale/Weir croons, his widening grin flashing a mouth full of rotten razor blade teeth. "Yer *nothing*. A wee fuckin no-mark wank that thinks he's a hardman. Only reason you didnae end up in the abortion bucket wis because yer junkie hoor of a maw wanted the cooncil flat you'd get her."

Ross, his very soul shrivelling inside him, is unable to move as Bale reaches out and takes a hold of his chin. His fingers feel like maggots, and he can't help the pathetic shuddering moan that escapes his lips.

Then, as if by the flick of a switch, Bale's voice changes again, going from the neddish, nasal taunting of Jimmy Weir to something even worse. Something soft and breathy, almost feminine. A voice carried on stinking onion-scented breath, a voice from a darkened bedroom with draughty windows and clown patterned wallpaper. "Oh, what's the matter, my little man?" he says, the hand cupping his chin slowly tracking down Ross's throat and across his chest to his belly. "Are you upset? How about one of our special handshakes, *mmmmm?* It'll make you feel *so good*."

Bale's hand inches lower, and he leans in so close Ross, his mind reeling on the edge of insanity, believes he's going to kiss him, which he knows will drive him over the edge and into a bottomless pit of madness. But just as his mind comes close to shattering like a bricked window, Bale steps back, shaking his head and chuckling to himself. Ross slides down the wall, taking great ragged gasps of air, covering his face with his hands and waiting for the feeling of his brain unspooling to cease.

"Three," Bale says, a bit randomly, but speaking in his normal voice again. Then he points at each of them in turn. "One. Two. Three."

For a weird moment, Ross expects a crash of thunder and lightning, and for Bale to throw back his head and go *ah-ah-ah-ah-ah!* like The Count from *Sesame Street*. Ross feels the sudden urge to snort out a big dumb donkey bray of laughter at the poorly timed notion, and realises the urge to give in to giggles right now is a sure sign he's dangerously close to losing his shit. But he has to keep it tight right now. Fight the fear down, even though if feels the size of a mountain, pressing down on his chest and mind. He has to *think*. He doesn't know where Bale's going with his one-two-three counting thing, but he's certain it's nowhere pleasant.

"Many of the finest minds on Earth posit that mathematics is a universal law," Bale informs them. "They insist that one plus one equals two is as much an inarguable fact here as it is in the unknowable reaches of the void. While not completely true, there is merit in this idea. Numbers are important. The number *three* in particular, yes?" Bale smiles at them, raising his eyebrows as if waiting for them to catch up, but no one speaks.

"It is everywhere," he continues. "In cultures, modern and ancient. The basis of a myriad of theories, myths, stories and architecture. It is in the stars. It is in the worship of your gods. The Christian Trinity. The Wiccan Law of Three. The three Gunas of Hinduism and the three sons of Cronos. As they say, it is the *magic* number." Again, he points them out in turn. "One. Two. Three. It has *power*. Mathematical and otherwise. Can anyone tell me the *third* power of three?"

In Ross's head - which is doing its best to find a happy place - Rachel Riley, looking particularly fine in a classy yet saucily cut red dress, is doing the numbers game on *Countdown*. The selected numbers are three threes, and Rachel presses the big button on the board to start the random number generator, which stops on...

Rachel, can it be done?

Yes, Ross, Rachel says, pure grace and intelligence personified as she smilingly demonstrates the solution. *If you say, three times three is nine, and then multiply that by the other three for...*

"How old are you?" Bale asks. He flicks his eyes over them in turn. Then says, "No, really. How old are you? Ross?"

"Twenty-seven," Ross says, though his voice breaks a little on the last syllable.

"And you, my sweet Lucia?"

Luce just stares back at him, visibly trembling. "Twenty-seven," she eventually says.

"Yes, you are. And of course Aldo. My troubled troubadour. You are...?"

"*Fuck you*," Aldo says through clenched teeth. "You know."

"Yes, I do. Twenty and seven. The third power of three. All three of you." Bale says nothing more for a second. Just stands there in the middle of the live room, with his eyebrows still raised expectantly, waiting for someone to figure something out.

And Ross knows what he's talking about. They *all* know what he's talking about. Of course they do. It was something they joked about. Something they raised a glass to. A lot of musicians did.

The Twenty-Seven Club.

Finally arriving at the inevitable bad place that this conversation was always heading, Ross's mind starts churning out a familiar roll call of musicians who never saw thirty. Or even twenty-eight.

Jimi Hendrix. Jim Morrison. Janis Joplin. Brian Jones. Kurt Cobain. Amy Winehouse. Dave Alexander. Kristen Pfaff.

Oh, and add John 'Six Finger' Asher to that list. John Asher, who signed with Easy Rolling Records way back in the day. Except it turns out he didn't *die at twenty-seven.*

"You have heard the expression, to bare one's soul," Bale says, turning away and stepping casually over to Aldo's Marshall stack. He softly runs his fingers across the knobs and switches. "It is often used when speaking of musicians. Poets. Painters. Writers. There are millions in this world who call themselves *artists*, though the vast majority lack any genuine talent." He turns back to face them again. "But sometimes, not often, true lights are born. Those who *shine*. The ones with genuine mojo, and that mojo is a powerful force. In such individuals, the light of their soul is never stronger than in their twenty-seventh year. Three by three by three."

He steps away from Aldo's set up and wanders over to Luce's destroyed kit, looking down thoughtfully at the scattered drums, most of them with burst skins. "It can be a destructive power, this magic," he continues, nudging a toppled cymbal stand with the toe of his highly-shined shoe. "And it comes at a price. For as you know, there is no light without darkness. Those gifted shining few carry darkness all their lives, and it shapes them. Moulds them. Affects the world around them. Manifesting as bad luck. Broken homes. Death. Many struggle, and find oblivion in narcotics and alcohol. Every *true* artist has their own personal demons. And mystery often surrounds their passing."

Bale looks at them again and smiles a little wider. He starts walking over, and Ross, who's been listening to all this with a growing dread fascination, has to force himself not to cower away as he approaches.

"Just one true light bearer is rare," Bale says, stopping before them. "*Three* such individuals together, and all at the peak of their powers at the same time... *well*. When you truly let go while playing, baring your souls to the world, it is a beacon to those that take an interest in such things."

"And that's where you come in, right?" a quiet voice says behind Ross. He turns and sees Aldo, sitting on the floor, his back against the door. He's looking up at Bale, and never has a man looked so gutted.

"Exactly," Bale says.

Another little mental commercial break, and Ross is watching himself on a tv screen, standing in a circular book-lined room, completely out his tits on bevvy and whatever powder and pills had been necked that night, laughing and barely able to stand straight as he signs a document filled with text he's too wrecked to read, and then pricking his thumb with a needle, pushing a bloody fingerprint onto the fine white paper.

Robert Johnson. He was in the Twenty-Seven Club as well.

On the wide screen HD picture in his head, the one displaying him signing his contract with Easy Rollin Records, the section of bookcase behind Bale's desk changes to the *Countdown* letter board, and the tiles are spinning again, so fast they're just nine...

...*which is three times three by the way*...

...blue and white blurs. They stop, displaying a nine letter name this time.

GAPPABALE

And then the name's gone, the letters are changing again, preparing another conundrum. Because that's what this cunt is. A conundrum. Blind to all else but this mental little daydream, Ross's heart hammers in his throat as he hears the *Countdown* theme playing in his head, that instantly recognizable thirty-second jingle, except now it's being played on what sounds like an old, hard used guitar with blood rusty strings.

The letter tiles flip faster and faster, spinning and spinning and spinning…

As the tiles stop and the solution hits Ross like a knife in the neck, he's yanked out of *Countdown* dreamland. He's back in the room. The live room, with Gappa Bale in front of him. He's nodding slowly, smiling his pointy toothed smile and looking right at him.

The bastard knows. He knows that *Ross* knows, and a truth that's been shuffling around in the shadows at the edge of his subconscious, to insane to be seriously considered, steps fully-formed into the light.

"Papa Legba," Ross says, and realises *hellbound* is also a nine letter word.

2

Papa Legba.

Luce knows the name. Seven years ago, in her second year at Glasgow Uni, she'd found it in a book on American folklore while researching an assignment she had to hand in for an elective anthropology course she'd taken. She'd been writing an essay on Haitian Voudou, which she remembers had annoyed her hardcore catholic mother no end, a reaction Luce had fully intended at the time. Witchcraft she'd called it, and hadn't appreciated her daughter's retort about the Vatican's three-hundred-year witch extermination campaign and the tens of thousands of innocents who'd been flayed, racked, whipped, beheaded, burned and dismembered in the name of the Father the Son and the Holy Ghost, often for nothing more than being born with a birthmark.

The spirit Legba originally came from Haitian Voudou, which had its roots in West Africa and had been brought over to the Caribbean via the slave trade. Legba was said to be a silver-tongued intermediary between the gods and humans; a *loa* who stood at the crossroads between worlds. In the Voudou offshoot Hoodoo, the folk magic of the Mississippi Delta, he was known as *Papa* Legba, an evil spirit who could be found hanging around lonely crossroads at midnight, and who could grant wishes. For a price, of course.

Any musician worth their salt knew the tale of Robert Johnson, the legendary bluesman who in return for fame, fortune and unearthly musical skill, was said to have sold his soul down at the crossroads, only to die at the age of twenty-seven, shot, stabbed, poisoned with strychnine, or crawling around on all fours foaming at the mouth and barking like a dog, depending on which version you believed.

And now, as Luce tries to assimilate this information, starting to understand what they've done, and doing her best to not crawl into a corner and start blubbering, Aldo lurches up from the floor.

"Fuck off!" he says emphatically, taking a step towards the thing formerly known as Bale and levelling a finger at it. "No, no, no. Fuck *right* off!"

"Please, Aldo," Legba says. "Do not pretend you did not know, or at the very least suspect."

"Know? How could I could have known... *this*?"

"Every detail of our agreement is in your contract."

"We were fuckin wrecked when we signed the contracts!" Ross protests loudly. "You can't *do* that."

"Oh, you would be astonished at the things I can do, Ross." Legba shrugs lazily. "The contracts have now been in your possession for quite some time, freely available for your perusal. Have you not read the terms of our agreement, as I recall urging you to?"

No one answers, and despite the circumstances, Luce feels like she's back in school, getting a telling off from a disappointed teacher for not doing her homework. Apart from on that first day at the breakfast table when she'd glanced at the back page and saw her signature and bloody fingerprint, she's not so much as glanced at the contract. At first it was simply because she'd been so involved with the album, fully immersed in rehearsing and writing. She hadn't been thinking of the paperwork behind it all. And over the past few days, her mind's been otherwise occupied. Luce shudders and has a sudden urge to throw up, her mind on a very slippery slope as she remembers again that night in the library. The things they'd done. What he'd made *her* do. And she'd acquiesced. Willingly. Wantonly. She'd debased herself.

Legba lets out a weary sigh and gives another shake of the head. "Then allow me to give you the abridged version. The essence of our agreement is that you have signed with Easy Rollin Records. For your signature, you have each been paid a generous monetary advance. You have been given time in a studio in which to write and record one album which will be released and promoted by Easy Rollin Records, and you are to play a showcase performance at Glasgow Green two days from now.

"In return for all this," Legba leans forward slightly, "I get *you*. All that you are. All you've ever been. All that you ever *will* be, as long as you live, and everything thereafter. *Mine.*"

After a long silence, Ross, always one to cut to the chase, just asks him straight. "So what? Are you the Devil then?"

Legba just rolls his eyes in an *oh for fuck's sake* manner, as if hearing a question he's been asked a thousand times before. "No, Ross, I am not the Devil," he says patiently. "Neither am I Santa Clause or Superman, and I most certainly am not the Easter Bunny. I am not fiction. I am *fact*. I am *history*."

Luce stands there hearing this, understanding it, and more afraid than she'd ever been in her life. The bleak chill of horror slithering thought her flesh and bones tightens its coils, winding up her spine and flicking at her mind with a black forked tongue. Her chest hurts, and she realises she's stopped breathing.

But then, all her disgust, fear and anger coalesces into a bitter toxic lump, which explodes like water poured on a chip pan fire, and she finds herself flying at the bastard, her mind going *what the fuck are you doing?* while her heart and her hands are screaming *kill!*

All Legba needs to do is turn those eyes on her.

She stops a few feet short of him, frozen in mid-step as if she were playing musical statues at a birthday party. Luce's almost brought to her knees as a horrible invasive cold, like a shot of poisoned novocaine, floods the inside of her skull.

"I know you want me, Lucia," Legba says, "but please. Sit down and be quiet. Do not make me cockslap you in the face in front of your friends. *Sit. Down.*"

Although she can't move, though it feels like a skeletal hand with too many fingers is poking and rummaging around in the folds of her brain, sapping her will, trying to push down on her spine and make her sit, Luce holds fast to her rage. "*No*," she grunts, forcing the word out between clenched jaws.

"*Yes*," Legba counters.

The bony hand in Luce's brain becomes a fist, and she cries out as a shock of blinding pain slams through her head, forcing her to her knees. She topples to the side, wracked in agony, and watches helplessly as Legba then turns those terrible bottomless eyes on her bandmates.

There's a sudden heavy pressure in the air, then a terrifying sensation of falling, as if the floor beneath her's disappeared. Aldo and Ross pile to the deck as if tripped by an invisible prankster, ending up on the floor next to her.

The three of them lie there, grunting and writhing and whimpering. Legba keeps them like that for a few more moments, standing over them, looking down with a wry little smile. Then the nauseating paralysis, the feeling of plummeting through space, and the pain slowly fade, and Luce finds herself able to move again. She doesn't move much, though. It seems risky.

"Now," Legba says, brushing a non-existent piece of fluff from his jacket sleeve. "If I can have your attention for just a moment longer, you will soon be free to be on your way." He pauses to make sure they're listening. As if they had a choice.

"The Glasgow Green show. Two days from now. It is going to be spectacular. Fifty thousand souls. Full media coverage. Magazines, papers, radio and television. This event will be the making of you. This is when you introduce yourself to the world. However, I sense that you have some misgivings about our arrangement. Despite what you may think, I do not wish to see my artists overly downhearted. It is not good for business, and never let it be said that I am unreasonable."

He squats down so that he's at eye level with them. "The terms of our pact are unbreakable, but that is not to say that they cannot be bent. I own your souls, that light that makes you so special, in this life and afterwards, but you still have free will. You have a choice."

"What choice?" Luce manages.

Legba gives her a sly grin, and even now, she feels herself drawn to him, and shudders with self loathing. "You are familiar with the term 'it is better to burn out than to fade away'?" he asks.

"Neil Young. *Hey Hey, My My, Into the Black*," Ross says dully as he struggles to his feet. "Cobain wrote it in his suicide note. And it was in the film *Highlander*." Even now, at this most insane of moments, he's unable to resist a bit of trivia. Or more likely, he's just clinging to something familiar in an effort to stop himself sliding into drooling, rubber room resident madness.

"Very good, Ross," Legba says. "That is the choice I give you. Option A; you can make legends of yourselves. Play Glasgow Green and launch the album. Cement your place in music history. Do this, and Public Alibi will *never* be forgotten, I promise you."

Luce really doesn't like the way he verbally italicises the word *never*. "What do you mean?"

"I mean, Lucia, that the Glasgow Green event will be so memorable, so extraordinary, that it will be forever burned into the minds of those who bear witness to it, and every time your music is heard thereafter, down through the years and decades and centuries until the end of all things, people will remember Public Alibi, and what they did."

"Did?" Aldo croaks, his voice a cracked, empty sound.

Legba looks at him like he's impossibly dense. "Why, *suicide*, Aldo," he says, as if stating the painfully obvious, then he smiles at Ross and Luce in turn. "All three of you."

He pauses a moment to let that take root, grinning at them, and Luce closes her eyes. "You want us to kill ourselves. On stage." she says.

"Precisely."

"But... *why?*"

"As I said," Legba says patiently, "the light - the spiritual energy, if you will - that burns in the three of you is never stronger, never more potent, than in your twenty-seventh year. The energy released when such a spirit passes from this world is very powerful, but *three* such deaths, wrought by the bearers' own hands simultaneously, and witnessed by an adoring multitude who worship them... *Well.* Your burnout and the resultant reaction will be... spiritually spectacular, and will echo through time immemorial."

Luce can just imagine. It makes an insane kind of sense. Like Legba said, the group's ritual suicide, committed on stage in front of fifty thousand people, would be remembered whenever a Public Alibi track was heard ever after. And she can imagine how a creature like Legba would relish, would feed off, the horror and panic such a spectacle would cause among the multitude who witnessed it.

"Or," Legba says, "you can choose Option B. You can choose *not* to play Glasgow Green. You can choose to leave your album buried here, never to see the light of day. You will be forgotten. Your music will never be heard again, and that one show at the Barrowlands will quickly fade from the public's fickle mind. You can walk away from all of this. You can fade away. But you will still be mine, and for the rest of your days, I will be on your shoulder. I will be in your head and in your heart. You will grow old. *Very* old, and your minds and your lights will fade beneath my shadow, until you are nothing but husks. Cursed, empty and alone. Then, when there is nothing left, not even your last breath or a single stuttering heartbeat, you will die, and your souls, your lights, will *still* be mine." He rests his eyes on Aldo then. "And so will Dylan."

Aldo, who's been sitting there with his head in his hands, staring at the floor, looks up sharply at the mention of Dylan's name. "What?"

Legba gives him a look like a gloating card sharp who knows he's just won the last hand in a high stakes poker game. "Your son is vulnerable right now. So defenseless. Floating in the darkness between worlds, between life and death."

Aldo's mouth moves, but no words come out at first. "You... what have you done?"

"I have done nothing," Legba replies, mock offended. "*You* have. *You* gave yourself to me willingly. *You* gave me your vow. *You* gave me your blood. Dylan is of your blood, is he not? Ergo, *you* gave me Dylan."

Aldo scrambles to his feet in a panic, and Luce stands up with him, a hand on his arm, a new and bitter flavour of dread filling her mouth. "No, no I didn't," Aldo babbles, shaking his head, his eyes frantic. "You... you can't..."

"Oh, but yes you did, and yes I *can*," Legba says, and laughs in Aldo's face. He leans closer. "He has your light. He *shines*, Aldo. He shines so bright in the blackness. So young. So innocent and unspoiled. So easy to *take*."

"No, no, no, no... please," Aldo begs, tears now tracking down his ashen face. "Please don't..."

"Do not *make* me," Legba snarls, taking a step forward so he's only inches away from Aldo, who cringes away from him like a beaten dog. "Let me make it crystal clear for you," Legba states, his tone black ice and his eyes blazing as something inhuman shimmers behind his features. "The three of you will play a show at Glasgow Green two days from now, and for your encore, you will cut your own throats, live on stage. Do this, and your side of the bargain is fulfilled. I take your souls, Dylan will be left alone, and your album will be released, a testament to your legend. You will forever be known as rulers of the Twenty-Seven Club."

He leans in even closer, and gently lays a hand against the side of Aldo's face. "Refuse," he says, "and I take Dylan from where he floats in limbo. And understand this. I will make your remaining time in this world a lesson in suffering that you cannot *begin* to imagine."

The door to the studio swings opens behind them.

"You have two days to decide," Legba says. "Now go."

3

Aldo doesn't need to be told twice. The moment the word 'go' falls from Legba's lips, he runs for the open door with Ross and Luce close behind him, terror putting wings on their feet. Then they're up the stairs, through the lounge, into the corridor and out the main door as if fleeing a burning building. They run out into the courtyard, and come to a sudden halt.

Aldo looks around in bewilderment, his heart hammering and not understanding what he's seeing, because the snowy midnight landscape of what must've been only a couple of hours ago, is gone. All around are heather-shrouded hills spotted with mountain blooms, and thick verdant forest beneath a clear blue sky and a midday sun that warms Aldo's terror-chilled skin. There's not so much as a puddle of slush to be seen anywhere, as if the fierce blizzard and impassable foot of snow that had stranded them here just last night had never been.

John 'Six Finger' Asher, who disappeared in 1938, aged twenty-seven, right when he was on the cusp of fame, is standing there beside the Balemobile in the courtyard, waiting for them. He has their jackets draped over one arm, their bags at his feet (though not their instrument cases Aldo notices), and his usual blank expression on his face. "I am to drive you home," he informs them robotically.

Biting down a scream at seeing the living evidence of their situation, Aldo slowly walks over to the old man standing by the car. He walks slowly because his legs feel like they could give out at any given second and he has to concentrate on each step. The *crunch-crunch-crunch* of his feet on the white courtyard pebbles sounds like the breaking of tiny bones.

John wordlessly hands Aldo his jacket, and he shrugs into it, never taking his eyes from the old driver's expressionless wizened face. His eyes aren't just haunted. They're completely empty. Aldo had once seen a series of wartime photographs taken of Auschwitz inmates, and the expression on the faces of the skeletally emaciated men, women and children - an utter lack of hope, devoid of any last shred of spirit – is very similar to what he sees when he looks at John Asher. Looking at him, seeing that terrible emptiness in his eyes and the air of defeated hopelessness that hangs off him, is to look into a mirror showing his own future self.

"Is this what happens?" he asks John in a hoarse whisper as Ross and Luce come over and take their jackets and bags. "Is this what happens if we don't do what he wants?"

John, as is his way, says nothing, but there's the slightest tremble in his thin, bloodless lips. "I am to drive you home," he repeats eventually. A rock would speak with more feeling.

"Fuck *that*," Ross says in a strained voice. "A thousand times, fuck that. I'm not… I can't… just… *No!*" He regards John with a mixture of horror and pity for a moment. "You took option B, didn't you, John?" he asks the old man. Unsurprisingly, John says nothing, though Aldo thinks there's a slight twitch in one of his old wrinkled eyelids. Ross then steps forward and offers his hand to the old man. "Whatever happened to you afterwards, John," he says, "I want you to know that that one record of yours changed my life. I just wanted you to know that, and to say thanks."

For a moment, Aldo thinks John will actually shake Ross's hand. The twitching of his eyelids increases for a second, a brief look of something like amazement passes across his face, there and gone again, and his hand starts to come up. But he quickly drops it again and resumes his usual blank expression, regarding Ross with all the expressiveness of a mannequin. Ross sighs, lowers his own hand, then turns and starts striding away along the single track road leading away from the building into the trees. Luce gives Aldo a look of deepest sorrow and then follows him, her head down.

Aldo turns back to the old man, who watches impassively as Ross and Luce make their way along the road on foot, spurning his offer of a ride home. "What can we do, John?" he asks, his voice cracking. "There must be *something*. Please."

John looks at him. "There is... nothing," he whispers, his dry dusty voice like a draught in a long abandoned building, and the desolation in those three words is almost more than Aldo can take. "Do what he says," John says, his old soulless eyes flicking fearfully in the direction of the building behind Aldo. "*End it.*"

Then he leaves Aldo standing there by the car, walks across the courtyard and goes inside the building, pulling the storm shuttered doors closed behind him with a loud thump and rattle.

Aldo's aware of a sudden air of desolation as he looks at the squat single storey structure, and has the queerest certainty that were he to follow John and open those doors, there would be no plush red carpet with pictures of rock stars on the walls. No recessed lighting and glossy wood-panelled ceilings. No. He's knows that if he went back inside, he'd find Easy Rollin Manor a derelict, empty shell, dead and cold, all mouldy water-stained walls, collapsed ceilings, rotted timbers and bare floorboards where only ghosts walk.

Aldo turns and hurries after Ross and Luce, catching up with his rhythm section as they enter the forest. No one says anything. They just walk silently along the dirt track that cuts through the trees, each of them too numb, too deep in shock for conversation.

It's not long until the road bends to the left and slopes downward. Through a gap in the trees ahead, Aldo sees the glimmer of sunlight on water, and they hurry down the hill, coming a few minutes later to the end of the dirt track and stepping out onto a two lane road than runs along the banks of a loch.

"Where the hell are we?" Luce asks in a small, tired voice, looking right and left along the empty road.

"I've got a signal," Ross says, looking at his phone, which he's found in his jacket pocket. "I'll check the GPS." Then he frowns. "Erm, guys? My phone says the date's the fifteenth of May." He looks at Aldo. "That can't be right, can it?"

Aldo frowns. It'd been mid-November when they left home to come here. While jamming, writing and recording the album, the days had blurred one into the next, and the passing of time had seemed unimportant, but at best guess, he'd have estimated they'd been in the studio for a few weeks. A month at most.

"He's right," Luce says quietly, looking down at her own phone which she holds with a shaking hand. "We've been out here for six months. I've got over two hundred missed calls." She looks at Aldo, her face stricken. "How can... how can that *be?*"

Aldo just shakes his head. It's too much right now, has all sorts of implications too confusing and impossible to think about. Besides, in the scope of things, the apparent warping of time in Legba's domain isn't the most pressing issue at that moment. He has to get home. He needs to see Dylan.

...*not expected to wake...*

... *you gave me your blood. You gave me Dylan...*

"Just check the GPS, dude," Aldo says to Ross, fighting the urge to just sit down and start bawling. He watches as his friend taps icons on his phone's touchscreen.

After a moment, Ross's eyes go wide and his mouth drops open, and Aldo and Luce look at him in confusion as Ross suddenly starts pishing himself laughing.

"Of course!" he cries. "Why the fuck not?"

"What?" Luce asks. "What is it?"

"See... see for yourself," Ross manages. He hands Luce the phone and then slumps down on the grassy embankment, rocking back and forth, hands covering his face and laughing like he's just witnessed the greatest practical joke of all time.

Aldo stands next to Luce and looks down at the phone's screen. The GPS marker shows that they're standing on the south bank of

Loch Ness. The nearest named towns are Foyers to the south west, and Inverfarigaig to the north east. But for a moment Aldo can't breathe, and he understands Ross's hysterics as he reads the text on the map showing the closest landmark, which lies just behind the marker on the phone screen showing their current position.

Boleskine House. Formerly owned by Led Zeppelin guitarist Jimmy Page, and before that, by the infamous occultist Aleister Crowley.

"Oh," Aldo says tonelessly, staring down at the screen. "Oh, right. I guess… that makes sense."

Luce just hands the phone back to Ross, who's still sitting there chuckling to himself and pulling fistfuls of grass from the roadside. "There's a bus coming," she mutters, pointing along the road, where a big blue and yellow Citylink coach is winding its way toward them along the lochside.

Aldo steps out on to the road and waves his arms over his head.

The coach takes them south and drops them in Fort William a little over an hour later, where they then head to the railway station and catch the next train to Glasgow.

There's little conversation between them during the five-hour journey. It's all too close. Too fresh. Aldo knows that to discuss their situation out loud would break them. Make it real. As long as no one talks about it, they can, for a while at least, tell themselves it's all just a bad dream. But Aldo knows it's not, and he knows it's a conversation that they'll have to have sooner or later. But not right now. They need time to try and find their feet, to attempt to process what's happened, as frightening and impossible as it is.

And they need to think about what's going to happen next.

On the train, Luce phones her parents and spends the next half an hour speaking in Italian, her voice low and subdued, before eventually ending the call and turning her face to the window, gazing blankly out at the passing world with tears on her cheeks.

Aldo, who also finds several missed calls on his phone, makes a call to the Yorkhill Childrens' Hospital, where they confirm that yes, they do have a Dylan Evans-McColgan in their ICU, and yes, he is on life support following an assault at his home sme months ago, an assault in which Ashley McColgan, his mother, had been murdered. Dylan had been strangled, the doctor says. He's sketchy on any further details, saying only that the police had responded to an emergency call placed by a neighbour after they'd heard screams coming from Ashley's flat. There were frank discussions that had to be held. Forms to fill out. The police were also keen to speak to him, the doctor says, his disapproval at Aldo's lengthy absence evident in his tone.

When he ends the call, Aldo considers phoning the police, but then decides against it. Things are complicated enough, and if he were to make that call, there would be a whole lot of very difficult questions he wouldn't be able to answer without sounding either highly suspicious or outright insane. No, the police could wait. If he spoke to them now, he can easily envision himself in either handcuffs or a straitjacket by the end of the day. His only thought is to go and see Dylan.

Their train pulls into Glasgow Queen Street just after five pm. They disembark and wordlessly walk from the platform to the main concourse. The station's busy with rush hour commuters heading home for the day, and the three of them stand looking around at the bustling tide of humanity sweeping around them. It's unnerving, all these people, all this noise, after being secluded in the isolation Legba's soundproofed highland retreat for so long. It's a riot of noise and colour and movement and people that sets Aldo's teeth on edge, and he feels acutely uncomfortable as he nervously looks this way and that. The amplified voice of the station announcing departures and arrivals, the ceaseless murmur of all the commuters, the squalling of a baby in a pram, even the everyday sight of crowded branches of Costa Coffee, WH Smith and Burger King, it's all unfamiliar and frightening. Threatening somehow. Especially the sight of two police officers wandering around the concourse, and the poster on the wall by the ticket office, advertising Public Alibi's gig at Glasgow Green two days from now. There's a 'Sold Out' banner pasted across it. Just the sight of it causes a cold sweat to form on Aldo's brow.

"I need to go," he says, trying to stop the incessant trembling in his legs. "I need to… need to get up the hospital. See Dylan."

Ross nods. "I'll come with you."

"I need to go and see my folks," Luce says. "They're totally freaking out, wondering where I've been and why I haven't called in six months. I'm sorry, I…"

"It's fine, Luce," Aldo says. "Go. I'll catch up with you later."

Luce doesn't move away. She looks at them both, tears shimmering in her eyes. "What the *fuck*, guys? What the fuck are we going to do?"

"I don't know," Aldo replies, shaking his head. "I just… I don't know."

From the corner of his eye, he sees the two cops ambling in their direction. They don't seem to be coming for them specifically, but their nearness is making him increasingly nervous. "Just go. Call me later. We'll… we'll figure something out."

Luce nods, gives them each a quick, desperate hug, then turns and joins the river of people heading for the exit which leads out to George Square.

Aldo and Ross head for the side exit taking them out onto Dundas Street, then turn left and make their way down the crowded pavement onto West George Street where they get into a black cab at the taxi rank.

"Where to, mate?" The driver, a young Asian guy, asks, glancing at them in his rearview mirror.

"Yorkhill Hospital," Aldo says.

"Nae bother."

The driver pulls away from the curb and joins the one-way traffic, then slams on the anchors and gives a prolonged blast of his horn when a car in the lane beside them strays into theirs, almost hitting them. "Fuckin watch what yer daein ya fuckin fudnugget!" the driver shouts, scowling and making the wanker sign at the offending vehicle. "Christ on a bike," he says, sighing in irritation as they move off again. "You'd think people would be more careful around here after what happened, eh?"

"How? What happened?" Ross asks.

"That mental shit wi the bin lorry running all those poor cunts over at Christmas," the driver says, frowning back at them in his mirror. "Where you been, mate? It was all over the news for months."

"We've been... away," Aldo says evasively, thinking about what else they might've missed in the past six months.

"Fuckin awful, so it was," The driver comments. He glances back at them a few more times as he goes round George Square and then takes St Vincent Street, heading west. "Do I know you boys?" he asks. "You look familiar."

In the back seat, Aldo and Ross exchange a quick, nervous look. "Nah, don't think so, mate," Aldo says.

Then the driver's deep brown eyes widen in recognition. "Fuck! Aye!" he says excitedly. "Yous are in that band! Public Alibi! I was at yer gig at the Barras last year. Fuckin brilliant, by the way."

Aldo closes his eyes and grits his teeth. "Thanks," he murmurs.

"What a show that was yous put on," the driver continues eagerly. "That was some crazy shit that happened to the other band but, eh? That must've freaked yous oot big time. The band yous were supporting gettin their heids cut aff like that? Fuckin mental by the way."

"Aye, just a bit," Ross says, his voice tight, looking across at Aldo.

"I'm comin to see yous at the Green on Friday," the driver informs them. "Cannae wait. Big squad of me n ma mates. So is that where yous have been, then? Away recording yer album? It's been all over the papers and the net. What's it like? Cannae wait to hear it."

Aldo groans and puts his head in his hands. He can't handle this. Not now. He's just about to tell the driver to pull over when Ross comes to his rescue, leaning forward in his seat and addressing the driver.

"Listen pal," he says in a low voice with plenty of ice in it, "don't want to be a dick, but just shut up and drive. Okay?"

"Awright, awright. Chill, big man," the driver says, getting the message loud and clear.

They drive on in uncomfortable silence while Aldo nervously watches the city pass by outside his window. It's a pleasant early summer evening. The cab winds its way out to the west end, through Charing Cross and up towards Glasgow Uni, cutting through the green acres of Kelvingrove Park, the rush hour traffic making the journey almost half an hour's worth of constant starting and stopping, honking horns, oily exhaust fumes, the tortured shrieks of bus air brakes and the mechanical muttering of car engines.

Desperate to get to the hospital and see Dylan, but dreading it at the same time, Aldo grows more jittery by the minute, grinding his teeth almost to nubs and drumming his fingers on his dirty jeans. In the close confines of the back of the taxi, he can smell the stale-sour stench of himself, and wonders how long it's been since he bathed.

By the time the cab finally pulls up outside the kids' hospital, Aldo's sweating profusely and shaking like an alky having a bad case of the DTs.

"Much do we owe you?" Ross asks the driver.

"No charge for celebrities, pal," he replies cheerfully.

"Cheers," Ross says, "and sorry about snapping earlier."

"Nae bother, big man," the driver then turns round in his seat and fixes his eyes on Aldo. He smiles - giving them both a good look at the six inch fangs that cram his mouth.

"Go and see your runt," he growls, his voice a malicious mud and gravel filled sneer, his eyes now dead black orbs flecked with crimson. "Mr Legba will see you on Friday night."

The cabbie-thing laughs, a hideous chittering sound like the scurrying legs of a cockroach swarm, and Aldo and Ross scramble out of the cab like it's about to burst into flames. They back away as the taxi tears away from the pavement, tyres screaming, and watch as it vanishes round the corner.

Aldo's vision greys and blurs, and he stands bent over, head swimming, hands on his knees and taking deep breath while a high tinnitus whine fills his head. He feels Ross's hand on his back.

"You alright?" Ross asks, his voice less than steady.

"Not even close," Aldo mutters. "You?"

"Fucked, mate."

"Aye." He straightens up and looks to the entrance of the hospital. "I don't know if I can go in there, Roscoe. I don't know if I can… see him like that."

"You have to, dude."

"I know. But still."

"Aye. I know. C'mon."

Aldo takes a deep steadying breath which does absolutely nothing to steady him. Then he nods to himself and enters the hospital.

4

They're in Dylan's room in the ICU, sitting by his bedside. The wee man's chest rises and falls with a slow robotic regularity. His face tracing paper pale, his lips bloodless, his eyes just dark slits in bruised purple hollows.

Beside Ross, Aldo's holding Dylan's hand, occasionally reaching out to stroke his hair. Aldo hasn't said a single word since the doctor let them in, and Ross just lets him be. Talking seems wrong right now. Obscene.

The walls are painted with a cheery parade of Disney characters, their smiling faces and the bright colours totally at odds with the grim atmosphere in the room. The brittle, stillness and the nearness of death, so close Ross can quite easily imagine hearing the rapping of skeletal fingers, or maybe a scythe blade, on the window. Dylan's alive. Just. His spirit hovering in the twilight nowhere of a coma. His grip on life fragile. A guttering candle flame in a bare, draughty room.

Severe anoxic brain injury, caused by restriction of the flow of oxygen, Dylan's doctor had told them. Ross - who'd picked up a thing or two about medicine while working at the Inverclyde Royal - knows the term, and knows what it can lead to in the event the patient survives. Long term disability. Permanent brain damage. Reduced physical and cognitive function. Permanent vegetative state.

But those were all medical terms, and they were far beyond that. Ross knows there's a lot more wrong with Dylan than could be found in any med school textbook, and trembles inside as he remembers the hungry anticipation on Legba's face that morning when he'd spoken about the wee man.

So young. So innocent and unspoiled. So easy to take.

An agnostic at best, with no concrete beliefs either way about life after death, Ross McArthur had never really subscribed to a belief in souls or heaven and hell. From his experience, the only good and bad that mattered was in the here and now; what he saw and heard and remembered and lived through every day. There was plenty of heaven and hell right here on Earth as far as he concerned. Anything beyond that, he figured he'd deal with when the time came.

That time had arrived, and as The Monkees said – admittedly in a far cheerier context – now he was a believer. He sure as shit believed in Papa Legba, and he believed now that he did indeed have a soul. It just wasn't his anymore.

They'd been snookered. Punked. Played like chumps. And it was checkmate. Game, set and match to Mr Legba. No matter how he turned it over and over in his mind, coming at the insane problem from every angle he could think of, there was no way out. At the end of the day, it was really quite simple, and if he'd ever had any lingering doubts, the dead black eyes and the mouthful of yellow fangs on the taxi driver earlier had been the clincher.

He wasn't going to end up like John 'Six Finger' Asher; a mindless living corpse existing under Legba's spell, sucked dry of everything he had and everything he was, like some walking spiritual buffet for who knew how long. Fuck that.

He wondered what it would feel like, slitting his own throat in front of fifty-thousand people. And we wondered what would happen afterwards. That was what scared him the most, and he'd been unable to think about anything else all day. Their future had been on his mind while walking away from what'd turned out to be Boleskine House (and wasn't that just the kicker?). On the bus from Loch Ness to Fort William. On the train to Glasgow. In the cab on the way here.

It was a long time to be thinking such fucked up thoughts.

Ross's grim musings are interrupted as the door to Dylan's room opens, and George McColgan, Ashley's dad, Dylan's grandfather, comes in. He doesn't say anything, doesn't even look at Ross and Aldo, just walks over, sits down in a chair on the other side of the bed from them and sits there looking at Dylan with a dull expression.

Ross recalls briefly meeting the guy at Ashley's surprise birthday bash when she and Aldo were still an item. A tall, craggy-faced man in his mid-fifties with a circlet of silvering hair around his bald pate. Ross remembers him being civil enough when Ashley'd introduced them. He knows he'd never liked Aldo, though. When Aldo'd lost his job after Dylan was born, he and Ashley had had to move in with her dad as they couldn't afford their own place anymore. That living arrangement hadn't lasted, and two weeks later, Aldo and Ashley had split up, and Aldo was sleeping on Ross's couch.

George McColgan still doesn't say a word. Just sits there, his bloodshot eyes blank, face haggard, his lips pressed into a tight, bitter line. The very picture of a parent who's lost a child.

Aldo's looking across the bed at George, his lips moving silently, like he's trying and failing to form words. "George," he croaks. "I'm..."

"Where've you been?" George McColgan asks in a low voice.

"I've... been away," Aldo murmurs. "We were recording..."

"We've been trying to get hold of you for six months. Six fuckin *months* Ashley's been dead. Six months Dylan's been lying here like... like *this*." George McColgan's voice cracks. One of his big bony hands wrings the bedrail, whitening his knuckles. A silent sob shakes his shoulders and he lowers his head, wiping a tear away. When he looks back up at Aldo, the look there is pure hate. "And where were you? Eh, Aldo? Where the fuck were *you*?"

"I told you," Aldo says. "We've been..."

"Ashley murdered. Your boy in hospital, and not even a phone call." He shakes his head in disgust. "You just don't give a fuck, do you?"

George is visibly trembling now, the muscles around his mouth twitching with barely suppressed rage, and Ross, who's seen plenty of grieving people lose it during his time working at the Inverclyde Royal, knows the guy's perilously close to flying at Aldo.

"Come on, Mr McColgan," Ross says gently, trying to calm the volatile atmosphere. "Now's not the time, alright?"

George turns to Ross and looks at him like he's just been spoken to by a walking talking turd. "Who the hell are you?"

"I'm Ross. Ross McArthur. A mate of Aldo's. We met a few years ago at Ashley's birthday party. I'm so sorry for your loss. Ashley was..."

"You're mates with this no-mark?" George scoffs. "Have a word with yourself, son. He's a waster, and a piss poor excuse for a father."

"Mr McColgan..."

"No, wait, I *do* remember you," George says, levelling a finger at him. "You're in that band of his as well, aren't you? Jesus Christ, another one. Are you not supposed to grow out of all that kind of pish when you're a teenager? Why don't you get your head out your arse and..."

George McColgan's tirade is abruptly cut off, as Aldo suddenly gets up and rushes round the bed. Ross is too stunned to move for a moment as Aldo launches himself at the older man and cracks him an absolute *peach*, square in the mouth, spilling him from his chair. Aldo then dives on top of him, evidently with the intention of delivering a severe shoeing.

But then Ross is up out of his seat and round the bed, trying to separate the two men now rolling about on the floor, cursing and flailing at each other. Receiving a few misplaced digs himself in the process, Ross manages to get his arms under Aldo's armpits from behind, linking his fingers behind his neck and forcing his mate's arms back. He heaves him up and drags him backwards toward the door, Aldo still shouting and kicking and thrashing.

"*You're a fuckin loser, Evans!*" George McColgan's bawling, pointing at Aldo, his bald head an alarming shade of purple, his shirt torn, blood smeared around his mouth. "*That's all you are, and if that wean dies it's* your *fault! You hear me, ya selfish wee cunt? Your fuckin fault!*"

"*Fuck you ya old bastard!*" Aldo shouts back, twisting in Ross' arms. "*You don't know a thing about this! You don't know the first thing about me! You never fuckin did!*"

Ross is trying to drag him out the door and down the corridor, but Aldo's having none of it. He's going tonto, struggling even harder in Ross' grip, writhing and lurching forward, and despite the fact that Aldo's built like the side of a fiver and doesn't weigh eleven stone soaking wet, Ross, who's a lot stronger, is having trouble keeping hold of him. The hateful ferocity of his normally placid, slight-framed friend is frightening, and Ross feels his grip start to fail as hospital staff start to come out into the corridor, drawn by the foul-mouthed uproar.

Aldo's his mate, and Ross doesn't want to see him getting into bother, so worrying that someone's about to call the cops, he deftly turns his full nelson hold into a figure four sleeper, one hand behind his head, the other arm across his neck. Though it's not exactly health and safety approved, he's used this technique a few times in his job at the Inverclyde Royal and knows what he's doing. Even so, the manic intensity of Aldo's struggles lasts longer than he expects, but eventually the pressure on his carotid arteries slows the flow of blood to his brain, and Aldo finally goes limp and passes out.

Managing an apologetic smile to the medical staff in the corridor, Ross assures them he's got the situation under control and quickly drags the insensate Aldo into a private waiting room, one of the small beige painted ones with a two-piece suite, tea set, soothing paintings on the walls, flowers and a box of tissues. He settles Aldo on the small couch, checks he's breathing okay, then tucks a cushion behind his head. His friend suitably pacified, Ross sticks his head out the door, smiles and again assures the ward staff he's got the unruly visitor calmed down and that there's no need to call the constabulary.

He closes the door and takes a seat in the armchair next to the couch. The door opens again a few minutes later and Dylan's doctor, who'd introduced himself as Harry McBride earlier, looks in. He's a tall, middle-aged man with short, wiry brown hair, a Peppa Pig tie and kind eyes. "Everything okay?" he asks softly, nodding towards the unconscious Aldo.

"Aye," Ross says. "I've managed to chill him out. Sorry about all the noise. Is Dylan's grandad alright?"

"He's fine," McBride says. "Bit of a sore lip is all. He's gone home for now. I asked him to give Dylan's dad some time to deal with what's happened."

"Thanks. And sorry again."

McBride nods and again looks at Aldo, genuine sympathy in his eyes. "I'll give you a few minutes."

"Cheers."

Aldo soon comes around and sits up, wincing and rubbing his neck. He looks over at Ross, a puzzled look on his face.

"Sorry, dude," Ross says. "Had to make you go beddy-byes before someone called the fuzz." Aldo doesn't reply. He just stares across at Ross, as if he's not sure where, or even who he is. "What the fuck happened with you there, man?" Ross asks. "I know there's some heavy weird shit going on, but that... that wasn't you, mate. I've never seen you like that before."

Aldo still doesn't speak, just gives Ross this weird, and decidedly creepy, smile. "You've never seen me, but I see *you*. Ha. I. C. U. That's... funny." He's got this glazed expression, unfocussed, like he's not looking at Ross, but at a spot on the wall behind him. "S'all good, Roscoe my man. It's just the spider and the fly. Aye, s'all right, wee man," he mutters vaguely, his eyes a thousand miles away. "Daddy's bringing it on home..."

Ross slaps him. Not hard, but a fair enough wee dish on the jaw. "You want to stop talking shite, mate?" he suggests, not unkindly. There's a dodgy moment when Ross thinks that Aldo's about to swing at him. His hand rises slightly from his lap, making a fist, but the dark sunken look around his eyes fades just as quickly as it appears, and Aldo just slumps back on the couch. They sit in silence like that for a while, till eventually, Ross realises Aldo's fallen asleep. Fair enough. It's been an absolute cunt of a day. Ross is feeling it himself. All the stress, fear, confusion, and the long road back from Boleskine. He could do with catching some zees himself. Even before the thought is fully formed, he feels his eyes slipping closed, and a moment later, he joins Aldo in sweet dreamless oblivion.

Sometime later, there's a knock on the door and Ross flinches awake. He checks his watch and sees that almost two hours have passed. Mentally thanking Dr McBride, he gets up and opens the door to find Luce standing there. She's drumming her fingers on her legs as she stands there, tapping out a nervous little rhythm. Ross steps out of the private waiting room and softly closes the door behind him.

"How is he?" Luce asks. "How's Dylan?"

"In a coma," Ross replies. "Has been for six months." He pauses a moment, then, after looking around to make sure no one overhears, he tells Luce know about the taxi driver.

"Oh Christ," Luce murmurs when he's finished. She says nothing more for a moment, then lets out a shuddery breath. "And Aldo? How's he?"

Now there's a question. Ross doesn't know how to respond to that. "He's... a bit messed up. Flew at Ashley's dad earlier and I had to drag him away. He was going fuckin spare. Had to put the arms of Morpheus on him before someone called the polis."

He's saved from giving further details of Aldo's mental state when the man himself emerges from the privacy room. Luce immediately goes to him, enfolding him in her arms and hugging him tightly. "He's going to be okay, Al," she says, taking Aldo's face in her hands and forcing him to meet her eyes. "You know that, right? He's going to be fine."

Aldo frees himself from Luce's arms and steps back. "Just fine?" he repeats. "Why do people always say shit like that? Who the fuck knows how he's going to be?"

Luce stares at him for a moment, and Ross can see how strong she's trying to be. "We're here for you, right?" she says. "Anything you need. Anything."

Aldo shakes his head. "You sure about that?" he asks. "Come on, Luce. You *know* what I need. What Dylan needs."

"Let's not talk about this here, eh?" Ross says, nodding toward the private room. They go inside and close the door.

"Alright, let's not bullshit each other," Aldo says, turning to them. "We can't put this off forever. We've got a decision to make."

Ross sighs. "Aye," he says. "Decisions decisions."

"It's fucked up, but that's where we are," Aldo says. He takes a breath, gathering himself. "I don't have a choice. If topping myself on stage is what it takes so Dylan's left alone, then that's what I need to do."

And he will, Ross knows. Fuckin right he will. Say what you like about Aldo Evans, but he loves his boy. He's never going to win Father of the Year, but that doesn't change the fact that when Ross sees him with Dylan, sees how he *is* around the wee man, nothing could be plainer. Maybe he doesn't even know it himself, but even when they're jamming, Aldo doesn't look that happy. That contented. Right now, however, Aldo looks acutely uncomfortable. "I hate to say it, I really do, but..."

"You don't need to, mate," Ross interrupts. Legba wants all three of them dead on the stage. He won't make Aldo ask him. "I'm in. Best option of a shitty situation." He offers Aldo a crooked smile. "Besides, it really is a *peach* of a record. Be a shame if it never got out."

Aldo looks at him with such a torn expression of sorrow and gratitude that Ross has to turn away so Aldo doesn't see his eyes misting up as they do an awkward fistbump. Then there's another extremely uncomfortable silence as they wait for Luce to speak. When she does, what she says is about the last thing Ross expects.

"I told my parents," she says. "I told them everything."

5

As soon as her car pulls up outside Luce's parents' house, they're out the front door, hurrying down the garden path and out onto the pavement, enfolding her in a desperate loving crush of arms amid a lot of weeping and relieved remonstrations.

Luce goes inside with them, the sights and smells of the house she grew up in instantly swelling her chest and tightening her throat with a rush of memory. The Rowan tree in the front garden, the berries of which had made her violently ill when she'd experimentally eaten a few when she was six. The trellis of ivy covering much of the wall around the front door. Inside, the ever-present smell of her mama's tomato sauce, which it seems is in a perpetual state of bulk production for the restaurant.

In the living room, Luce takes her jacket off and slumps down on the old couch, which is just as comfortable as she remembers it, her folks taking seats on either side of her. Then she bursts into tears.

It's not just the culmination of the madness and horror she's endured. It's the old familiarity of her surroundings, the feeling of being in a safe place in the presence of her parents. Like a soldier grievously wounded in battle and screaming for his mother, Luce experiences a strange emotional regression, and here, in the company of the ones she would instinctively turn to for comfort as a child, she bawls like a four-year-old with a skint knee while her parents sit with her, holding her, murmuring soft soothing words.

And it all comes out. She doesn't mean it to, and had told herself repeatedly on the long journey down from the highlands that there was no way on Earth she could tell her folks, especially her mother, the truth about the situation she'd found herself in.

But she does. She tells them all of it. The worst of it. Every inexplicable, terrible detail. She can't help it. The whole story comes pouring out of her in a great cathartic rush of words and tears. Between broken sobs, she tells it all, much of the time with her hands covering her face, unable to look at them. Once or twice, like when she tells them about how she'd slept with Legba, she feels her mother's hand tighten painfully on hers, and she's aware of a certain tension between her parents, but through it all, they never speak a word. Part of Luce finds this strange, but a larger part of her is too concerned with venting to care, and so she plunges on, verbally purging herself.

When she's finally done, when she's confessed all she has to confess and all the words have dried up, she feels about two stone lighter, and thoroughly exhausted. She noisily blows her nose into the latest of a series of tissues her dad's been handing her throughout, then wipes her eyes and forces herself to look at her parents. They still haven't said anything.

"You're both taking this remarkably well," she says warily. Her mama especially. Considering the circumstances, Luce would have expected Defcon 1 levels of religious histrionics from her hardcore Catholic mother. The fact that she's just sitting there holding her hand with this look of profound sadness on her face is almost disappointing. Luce figures that her mama probably just thinks she's gone completely mental, and is so quiet because she's sad about having to institutionalise her only daughter.

Then Itria Figura looks at her husband, gives an almost imperceptible nod, and quietly says. "Show her, Salvo."

Her dad lets out a heavy sigh, then gets to his feet, kisses Luce on the top of the head and leaves the living room. She hears him trudge slowly up the stairs, hears the familiar creak of the seventh step. Just that one little memory from her childhood is almost enough to set her off again, but she's all cried out, and curious as to what her mother wants to show her. "What is it, mamma?" she asks, confused, and not a little uneasy.

Her mum squeezes Luce's hand and says. "Do you remember your nona, Lucia?"

Luce frowns, not understanding. "A little," she says. "Why?"

Her nona Corada, her mother's mother, had lived with them when Luce was very young. She'd died when Luce wasn't much more than four years old, so she only has vague memories of her nona. An old lady with long snowy white hair, olive skin, and an army of silver bangles on each wrist that would jingle musically whenever she moved. Luce can picture a woman who dressed in colourful, flowing clothes, who had watchful eyes and a quiet voice which would rarely be heard, but which Luce remembers soothing her to sleep with lilting Sicilian lullabies when she would wake in the night from bad dreams.

She hears footsteps on the stairs again, the creak of the seventh step, then her papa comes back into the living room. He's carrying a carved wooden box, similar to the one Ross keeps his assorted weed smoking paraphernalia in. Her dad regards the hinged box nervously, as if it contains a nest of venomous spiders, or maybe a small bomb. He places it carefully on the coffee table in front of them and sits down again, taking Luce's other hand.

"What is it?" Luce asks, her uneasiness rising. "What's with the box?"

"Lucia, *silencio*," her mamma says in a tone that brooks no argument. "I have something to tell you. Something important. I will talk. You will listen. Is that understood?"

Chastened by her mama's sharp tone, Luce nods, and Itria Figura takes a moment to gather herself before beginning to speak.

"You know that I am from the town of Maletto, but I was not born there. I was born in the back of a wagon in the mountains in the far north of Italia. My mother's people were Romany travellers, and moved with the seasons."

"Wait, *what*?" Luce exclaims. "Your parents were *gypsies*?"

Itria fixes Luce with the same look that had been a warning of a severe scolding when she was a child. "*I* will talk, *you* will listen," she repeats. "*Capisci?*"

Luce nods, and her mama goes on.

"After I was born, my people travelled south, and came to Sicilia to spend the winter months there. When summer came, the travellers moved on again, but my mother and father stayed behind. My birth and infancy had not been an easy one. The delivery and the long journey south had left my mother, your nona, weakened, so they settled near a place called Gela, in the south of the island, moving into an old farmhouse in the country just outside the town. We kept a few animals. Chickens and a few pigs. My father worked in the fields, picking olives and lemons, and my mother took on work as a seamstress.

"She had another talent, though, and would sometimes make a little extra money as a *'nnimina vintura*, a fortune teller. Such things were very much frowned upon by the church, but word of her talent and accuracy was whispered from ear to ear among those in Gela and the surrounding villages who sought her out. She was not only a palmist, you see, Lucia. Your nona truly had the *sight*. She was able to speak to the dead. She helped many people. Gave them peace. Healed them. The bereaved, the terminally ill, the lost, the lonely and the frightened ones. She had a gift, and it wasn't long before she no longer had to take on seamstress jobs with so many people seeking her out, willing to pay her well for an appointment. I never inherited the sight myself, but as a child, when I was old enough, I acted as her assistant, and she taught me much about the Romany ways. Their culture and history. Their magic."

Luce knows fine well that she's sitting there with her mouth hanging open in stupid astonishment. This was her *mama* talking. Her diehard Catholic mamma who attended Mass three times a week, was never out of reach of a set of rosary beads, had pictures of the Pope, Mary and Jesus above the fireplace, and who read the bible on a continuous loop. Imagining her as a gypsy kid assisting her mystical Romany mother with palm readings and love potions took some doing. She'd have been less surprised if her father had suddenly declared himself Supreme Ruler and President for Life of Outer Mongolia.

"When I was nine years old," Itria goes on, "a woman came to see my mother. This woman had travelled over a hundred miles, all the way from Palermo in the north to see her. Her daughter, little more than a baby, had gone missing, vanished one day while playing in the garden. At that time, there had been several such disappearances in and around the city of Palermo, and the police thought it to be the work of a child murderer. This poor woman came to your nona, distraught, desperate to know what had become of her daughter. It had been over a year since the child had vanished, and the police had nothing. No suspects, no evidence, no witnesses. The mother, to stop herself going mad, had told herself that her child was surely dead, better that than imagining her baby still alive and suffering in the hands of a beast. But telling oneself something and *knowing* are not the same thing, and the woman needed to *know*.

"I remember the night she came to our house. She was a ghost. A broken, pitiful thing, aged beyond her years by worry, by not knowing what had happened to her daughter. She brought with her a lock of her missing child's hair, which she had saved from the baby's first haircut. Also a favourite toy, a rag doll which the child had been playing with in the garden when she disappeared. My mother embraced her and led her into the room where she did her work, then told me to go and do my chores."

Itria Figura pauses and looks down at the floor. Luce can feel the tremors in her hand as it holds her own. Then she looks to her husband. "Salvo. Can you bring us some wine?"

Luce's dad nods and goes into the kitchen, returning with a three glasses and a bottle of red. It was never a good sign when you needed to have a drink to finish a story, Luce thinks, now decidedly nervous about where her mama's tale is going.

Itria raises her glass and takes a long swallow. Luce watches, amazed as her mum half drains the glass. She's never seen her mother drink alcohol in her life. Not so much as a Babycham at Christmas. She picks up her own glass and follows suit, strongly suspecting she'll need it for whatever her mama's about to say.

"I was doing the dishes in the kitchen when I heard the screaming," her mum says after a long silence in which she finishes her glass and has her husband pour another. "Such a sound I had never heard, Lucia. It was the woman who'd come to see my mother, but there were others. The voices of children, several of them, screaming in pain. And the voice of... something else. Then there was a terrible tearing sound from deep in the earth, and the house started shaking as if in an earthquake. I ran to my mother's room and threw open the door, and I saw it. A dark figure, conjured in smoke and shadows, floating above the table where my mother sat. The air in the room was freezing cold, so cold that I could see my breath in front of my eyes, and there was an unholy smell in the air, like spoiled meat and human filth. The woman who'd come to see your nona was cowering on the floor, shrieking and clawing at her face with her nails. My mother saw me in the doorway and screamed at me to get out, but I could not move. The thing in the smoke held me transfixed, and I could feel its eyes on me. I could hear it *whispering*, words I could not understand. Then my mother was slamming the door in my face, and I stood outside, while on the other side of the door I could hear her chanting, reciting words of banishment, while around and beneath me the house continued to tremble and groan as if it were being uprooted."

Itria pauses in her story to take another fortifying mouthful of vino before continuing. Luce sees the way her hand shakes on the glass.

"When it was over," she continues, staring into the past, "the shaking of the house stopped, and the woman's screams had become a pitiful whimpering. My mother opened the door, knelt before me and took my face gently in her hands, which were covered in blood from cuts she had made across her palms as part of her incantation. Her face... it was a picture of purest anguish, Lucia. I had never seen her look so wretched.

"She said nothing at first, only looked at me with tears in her eyes as she drew something on my forehead with a bloody finger. Then she took me in her arms and held me close, so tightly I could barely breathe. She released me and sent me to my room, then closed the door and went to the distraught woman, who was lying curled up on the floor, still sobbing and gibbering like a madwoman.

"In my room, I looked at myself in the mirror and saw the symbol your nona had drawn there in her blood. It was a character I knew. One of many that my mother had taught me. A powerful warding mark, used to protect the bearer from evil. I dared not wipe it off my skin, because I understood why she had put it there, and a great fear came over me as I remembered the voice of the demon. Yes, Lucia. A *demon*. Do not look so surprised. The catholic church has known about the reality of demonic forces on Earth since its inception.

"I had been touched by its presence. And knowing this, terrified for my very soul, I fell upon my bed and I wept. I wept for a long time, and when I was not weeping, I recited every chant and spell used in the warding of evil that I knew.

"My mother came to my room later that afternoon. She sat down on my bed and told me what had happened. She had reached into the spirit world to try and find her client's missing daughter, and she *had* found her, but the child was not alone. The thing that had taken her was there too, along with the souls of the six other children who'd vanished from Palermo that summer, snatched from our world by the dark presence I'd seen in the smoke. By reaching through the veil, my mother had opened a doorway, and the spirit had come through. It had taunted the poor woman, let her hear her child's tortured cries, showed her what it did to her daughter. And when I came into the room, it had marked me.

Never taking her eyes off her mama, Luce drains her own glass, noting how the rim rattles on her front teeth.

"We stayed in my room the rest of that day. My mother had me sit cross-legged on my bed while I whispered prayers and spells of protection and she sprinkled salt and vinegar around the bed. She burned mandrake and benzoin incense, and wove a garland of amaranth for me to wear under my shift against my skin. All the while, for hours, she never stopped casting warding spells, murmuring protective incantations, placing charms and amulets on the doorhandles and windowsill, flicking the sign of the Evil Eye at the window and door to my room. Eventually, when she could do no more, she lay down with me on my bed, took me in her arms, and sang to me until I fell asleep.

"Late that night, I was woken by a knock at our door. My mother took me by the hand and led me out of the room. It was Enzo Salerno, a friend of my father who worked with him in the olive groves. His face was streaked with sweat and ash, and he reeked of smoke. He told us a fire had broken out in the olive grove where he and my father had been working that day, trapping several men in the grove and burning them alive. My father among them."

Luce sits there on the couch listening to her mum's story. As a child, she'd asked her mum about her grandfather on the maternal side once, curious about her roots, but she'd only said that he'd died in an accident long ago. Itria Figura had never explained the full circumstances. Come to think of it, Luce now realises, her mother had always been closed mouth about her childhood in Sicily, giving only vague answers, making it out to be very boring, and changing the subject whenever Luce asked. Now she understands why her mama had always been so evasive.

"After my papa's funeral," Itria goes on, "your nona and I packed up and moved away. In the three days days after my father's death, the grass and trees around our property had withered and died. The well where we drew water was fouled, and our pigs and chickens we found dead in their pens. Our home had been cursed. Soiled by the demon.

My mother scattered herbs, spoke words of consecration and marked the walls of the house and the ground outside with her blood. Heartbroken by the loss of her husband, and fearful of the thing that had marked me, she vowed to never again reach into the spirit world, and she made me vow the same, which I did without question. After seeing and feeling the touch of the entity in my mother's parlour, I wanted nothing to do with magic or wards or charms.

"We set the farmhouse to flame, with all her things inside. All her herbs and crystals, amulets and charms. Everything that had a connection to that part of her life.

"We left, and moved north to the village of Maletto on the slopes of Etna. My mother found work in a textile factory close to Catania. She began visiting the church, and had me baptised by a local priest, Padre Silvano. Though he was not an *esorcista*, he knew of evil, and he listened to my mother's story. Silvano wanted to baptise my mother as well, but she refused. Though she no longer practiced her arts, she still had her beliefs, and she knew she could never truly believe in the doctrine of Rome. The priest kept me close to him, watching over me, letting me help around his little church, which was built on the slopes of the volcano. A church that had been destroyed five times over the centuries, and rebuilt each time. Padre Silvano used to joke and say it was the ultimate expression of faith.

"I spent two hours there every day after school. Cleaning, stacking bibles, changing candles and scraping away hardened wax from the old ones. And every day, I studied the bible with Padre Silvano.

"So, as I told you, I grew up in Maletto," Itria says. "We lived there quietly for the next fifteen years, until I met your father. Then we were married, and we came here."

Itria picks up the almost empty bottle of Vino d'Avola and offers it. Luce readily accepts.

"A few years later," Itria says, "after we had moved here, my mother turned up on our doorstep, having travelled from Sicily without telling me she was coming." She pauses and fixes Luce with a meaningful look. "The day she arrived was the same day I found out that I was pregnant with you, Lucia.

"She never said it out loud, but she *knew*. She knew even before I did. She said it was just blind luck, that she meant to surprise me, and that she was just glad she could be here to do her duty as a grandmother. I knew her, though. There was no coincidence in her turning up at our house when she did, and no coincidence that the plants and herbs she began bringing into the house were ones used in the old ways of her people. The blackberry plants in your father's greenhouse. The pots of basil that filled our kitchen window and which she said were only for cooking. The rowan tree she planted in the front garden, and the trellis of ivy around our front door. More than once I overheard her whispering the old words when she thought I wasn't listening, and in the mornings, there was always the faint smell of incense, as if she'd been burning it in the night while your father and I were asleep.

"She admitted it on the day you were born. It was the caul, Lucia. You came into this world with part of the birth sac covering your face. In the old ways, this is a powerful omen, a sure sign of the child's connection to the other side. Seeing this, your nona gave up trying to hide what she'd been doing. She told me she'd dreamt that I would have a child, a daughter, and that the child was special. Fearing that we were in danger, she'd broken her vow to never again practice the old ways and had come to me, to protect us, and make sure the house was safe.

"When we brought you home from the hospital, your nona Corada barely left your side. For the first six weeks after your birth, she would sleep a few hours during the day and then stay awake all night, sitting by your crib at the side of my bed, watching over us both. She placed things made of iron around the house, hung horseshoes above every door, kept an open pair of scissors next to your crib. I told her she did not have to do this, that she was being foolish with her old superstitions, but she was not to be argued with. And secretly, although much of what she was doing was against the teachings of Rome, which I'd come to know and revere, I was glad she was there, and I made a show of tolerating her beliefs."

Itria Figura leans forward and takes the small wooden box from the coffee table. She opens it, releasing the smell of dried herbs, She withdraws a folded piece of tissue paper held closed with a frayed powder blue silk ribbon. Untying the ribbon, she carefully unfolds the tissue to reveal what's enclosed.

A daisy chain necklace, like a child would make. Dry and brittle.

"She made this for you, Lucia," her mum says, looking down at the little garland of dried flowers. It looks so fragile that it seems it would come apart and fragment into dust if so much as breathed on too hard. "You wore this every day and night for the first six weeks of your life. Even when we bathed you."

She reaches into the box again and takes out a little blue velvet bag with a drawstring top, opening it and letting the contents fall into her open palm. Several two-inch iron nails.

"She would leave these point-up on the windowsills," she says regarding the nails thoughtfully for a moment before putting them back in the drawstring bag, returning it and the wrapped daisy chain to the box, and closing the lid again. Placing the carved wooden box back on the coffee table, she turns to Luce once more.

"When nothing happened in those first six weeks, your nona relaxed, but not all the way. After you were baptised, she eased up a lot more. She removed the nails, the horseshoes and the open scissors, and stopped murmuring spells and burning incense around the house. She went back to sleeping at night, but would always stay in the same room as you during the day, never letting you out of her sight. She loved you so, Lucia. She loved you so *much*."

Her mother pauses, and wipes away the single tear that runs down her cheek.

"When she died in the hospital four years later, her last words to me were that I had to keep you away from anything to do with the old ways, to always raise you catholic. She believed my faith had kept me safe, and it would do the same for you. She believed that the thing from Sicily had not followed us here, but she always knew you were special. *This child shines* she said when you were born. That is why she gave you the name *Lucia*. Neither your father or I argued. It was right. The name suited you."

Luce feels those icy fingers that have been running all over her body pick up the pace a little, and she shivers. Legba had said something about the special ones. The ones who shined.

"And so I raised you in the church," Itria goes on, squeezing Luce's hand. "I gave my *life* to the church, praying that my faith would keep you safe, and I thought I had succeeded, until..."

"Karen," Luce says, her voice a dry whisper. "Until Karen died."

"Yes. When your friend passed away, and you stopped attending Mass, stopped going to confession, I did not know what to do. I feared for you, Lucia. You are my daughter and I love you more than anything in this world. All I could do was try to make you come back to your faith, but you were so *wilful*, so stubborn. When you began playing music, it was all you were interested in. It was the only thing that gave you peace, but I knew, even then I knew, that turning your back on your faith was dangerous for you, and I knew that music would take you away from me. That is why I have never approved. But seeing how happy it made you, how it brought you back to life after your friend died... The first time I saw you play, I saw how you lit up. Though it frightened me, I could not take that light away from you. It is who you *are*, Lucia. I also knew that if I tried to forbid you from your music, I would only push you further away. Do you understand?"

Luce nods, tears spilling onto her own cheeks, and embraces her mama, suddenly regretting every unworthy thought she'd ever had towards her.

"I'm lost, mama," Luce whispers into her ear as they cling to each other. "I can feel it already. Like there's a little less of me inside. And the time we've been away. Six months, mama. *How can it be six months?* Six months and my hair hasn't even grown. I haven't had a period. Is this how it is now for me? For us? Like John? I'm sorry, mama. I'm so so *sorry*."

"*Calma, mi amore*," her mother replies softly, stroking Luce's hair.

"But what can I do?" Luce sobs, looking for answers in her mother's eyes. "Aldo and Ross, they're my friends, and now Dylan... mama, he's only *five*. If you know about this kind of thing, all the things nona taught you, isn't there something we can do?"

Luce's heart sinks as her mum solemnly shakes her head. "There is no walking away from a thing such as this, Lucia," she says softly. She leans forward and places a hand on Luce's knee. "The demon demands souls, and it must have them. But where there is darkness, there is light. Remember that. Even now. That light is your strength. Just as the darkness is his, and the evil spirit is powerful." Itria Figura's hand tightens on Luce' knee, hard enough to make her wince. "But so are you, Lucia. That is why he wants you. Because you *shine*."

During the telling of her mum's story, Luce, Aldo and Ross move back into Dylan's room. The wee man lies there, ash pale and looking so small and vulnerable that Luce wants to cry. The sight of him hurts her in a way none of the other recent horrors in her life have.

When she's finished telling them everything her mama had related to her, when she's told them there are things they could do to protect themselves, she produces a handwritten list her mother had given her, which Ross is looking over.

"Amaranth, salt, hawthorn, rowan, hazel..." he reads wearily. "Totems, amulets... fuckin eye of newt and toe of frog..."

"Where can we get that kind of stuff?" Aldo asks quietly. He hasn't moved in the last hour. He's just been sitting there, listening to Luce talk, never taking his eyes off Dylan, holding his hand.

"I searched online earlier," Luce says. "There's a wiccan shop out in the east end. Should be open in the morning."

"There's a couple of things on here we could get right now," Ross points out, though still with a trace of scepticism. "Salt, vinegar, basil... Could get them in a twenty-four hour Tesco..."

Luce's phone rings. An unknown number. She flicks the green icon to accept the call. "Hello?"

"Put me on speakerphone," Legba says, his voice like a worm crawling into Luce's ear. The fear hits her like a hard bodyshot. She finds herself unable to breathe for a moment. "It's him," she tells the others when she can speak. Aldo and Ross tense, and Luce sees how her hand shakes as she presses the speakerphone icon.

"Are you serious?" Legba asks from her mobile, voice thick with scorn. "Do you really believe you can get out of this with some Tesco Value groceries?" He laughs that horrible two-throated laugh.

At Dylan's bed, Aldo closes his eyes. Ross looks like he wants to snatch the phone from Luce's hand and smash it off the wall. Luce herself stares at the mobile in her hand, as if expecting it to sprout fangs, and possibly a barbed stinger. Legba's derisive laughter comes through her mobile with terrible crystal clarity. He could be standing in the same room with them. And Luce's not so sure that he isn't.

"You humans," Legba sighs. "You are hilarious. What exactly do you hope to achieve? Do you truly believe you can beat me with some potted plants and seasoning? Even for your species that is naïve." He laughs again, clearly immensely pleased with himself. Luce would swear blind that the phone in her hand has suddenly become ice cold, and feels like it's... pulsing.

"Have you made your decision?" Legba asks, the laughter in his voice abruptly gone.

"We're still kicking it around," Luce says.

"Ah, Lucia. How enchanting it is to hear your sweet voice. How does the day find you, my little honeycunt? And your blessed mother. Is the little gypsy whore still pretending to be a devoted catholic?"

Luce closes her eyes and grits her teeth, telling herself not to react. He's taunting her. Trying to get a rise out of her. Though her mind's screaming *what does he know about my mum how can he know anything about her* Luce bites down on her lip almost hard enough to draw blood. She will not answer. She may well scream if she opens her tightly clamped jaws.

"By the by," Lega goes on, sounding bored now. "It would be advisable to avoid too much close contact with people from this point onwards. Especially family members. Loved ones. Your *blood*, you understand? Your company would... not be beneficial to their luck. Or their wellbeing. I think you know that by now, do you not, Aldo?"

Aldo still doesn't open his eyes, but Luce can see his hands, white-knuckled as he grips the safety rail of Dyaln's hospital bed in his fists.

"How do we know you're not bluffing with all this bullshit?" Luce hears herself say, surprised at the calmness in her voice. She's terrified inside, but there's some part of her, the part that seems to be in control of her mouth, that's had enough of this arsehole's pish. "And is this how you do business? Threatening pensioners and babies?"

Legba finds this hilarious, and cackles at length in a voice that makes Luce think of a murder of crows, cawing above a bloodstained field of corpses. "Are you actually trying to *shame* me, Lucia?" he asks. "I must say, I admire your moxie. But the morals of humans mean nothing to me. They are in fact a completely alien concept. I may as well ask you to imagine a colour that does not exist. In any case, I have never lied to you. To any of you. The speaking of untruths is a solely human trait. Think what you will of my methods, but it is not in my nature to lie."

"That's a lot of shite right there," Ross protests. "This is a scam. The whole thing. You fucked us."

"You fucked yourself, Ross," Legba replies. "Everything I have ever told you is true. I promised you a handsomely paid support slot at the Barrowlands, which I delivered. I promised you a recording contract and a generous monetary advance, which I delivered. I promised you a studio and the production of an album, which I have delivered. I promised you a headlining showcase event and the launch of said album, which I *will* deliver."

"Not if we don't play the show," Luce says. "You've got nothing without us."

He laughs again. "Lucia, I already *have* you, do you not know that by now? And if you do not step out in front of that crowd tomorrow night, I will have this boy as well."

Before Luce can draw another breath, it feels like the window's just been opened in a space station. Every last molecule of air is abruptly sucked from the room, and as Luce's lungs are abruptly denied oxygen, her moxie evaporates in huge surge of blind panic. The lights in the room flicker and go dim, pitching them into a murky half-light. New shadows seem to creep up in the corners, slithering along the walls and ceiling, spreading out from beneath Dylan's bed like a pool of spreading black blood. There's an awful groaning, grinding noise, whether it's in her head or in the floor or the walls, Luce can't tell, and it feels like she's in a plane torn open and depressurized at fifty-thousand feet, plummeting toward a cold night-time ocean. She can see the unfettered fear in Aldo and Ross as they too suddenly find themselves suffocating in the darkened vacuum the room's become. Aldo's face is going purple already, his eyes saucer wide and rolling in their sockets, and Ross is on his knees, clawing at his neck as if trying to tear open an airhole.

Then the air comes rushing mercifully back into the room, and the three of them are gasping and gulping. Black dots swim in front of Luce's eyes as she tries to calm herself, to stop her heart from trying to fracture her breastbone with its panicked thumping. She collapses back into her plastic seat.

Then Dylan starts to move.

His limbs jerk spasmodically on the bed, twitching and jumping as if attached to a car battery. He sits up. Bolt upright, bending from the waist in a horribly fast sit-up. His eyelids flutter open, revealing the whites of his rolled back eyes. The facial muscles around his mouth twitch and twist into a rictus grin, all drawn back, writhing lips and jutting jaw. A dry dusty voice - never the voice of a five-year-old - croaks from behind his bared teeth.

"*Al-i-bi,*" Dylan grates. "*A-li-bi. A-li-bi.*"

Luce has to clamp her hands to her ears, because it's too much, the sight and sound of Dylan being used like this. Across the bed from her, Aldo, his features wrenched in utter horror, reaches for his son, but one of Dylan's skinny little arms flails out like a whip and catches him across the mouth, knocking him backwards.

"*A-li-bi. A-li-bi,*" Dylan chants.

Luce jams her fingers into her ears, but she can still hear it. That terrible grinding voice, older than the Earth, than the universe, gnawing at her brain. She wants to get up and run but can't move. Aldo's standing there by the bedside, gripping the safety rail like it's all that's keeping him tethered to sanity, blood dripping from his burst lip, vivid crimson against the shock white of his skin as he looks at his son helplessly.

"*You fuckin cunt!*" Aldo rages helplessly, looking around the room. "Get away from him!"

"Stop it," Luce whispers. "Please. He's just a baby."

"*A-li-bi. A-li-bi,*" Dylan chants.

"Stop," Luce sobs. "Please, just stop. He didn't do anything. I believe you."

"*Yessssss,*" Legba hisses through the phone. "You do believe me. And you believe that I could snap this runt's neck and take his soul right now if I wanted."

The temperature in the room suddenly seems to drop another several degrees, and Dylan's head starts to turn. Slowly, slowly, so he's staring at Luce with his sightless white eyes. Then his head *keeps* turning, and keeps going, as far as it can go. Then further.

"*No!*" Aldo screams, reaching for him. Dylan's arm hand flies up again, impossibly fast, his little hand clamping around Aldo's throat.

"*A-li-bi. A-li-bi,*" Dylan chants, his voice becoming higher with every impossible inch his head turns, becoming a strangled, distorted squeal. His head rotates a little more, his chin now almost behind his shoulder, the skin of his neck hideously twisted. He's still grinning. Luce thinks she hears bones and tendons creak and crackle.

"*We'll do it we'll do the fuckin show,*" Aldo babbles in desperation, his own voice distorted by his son's hand. "*Please please leave him alone don't hurt him.*"

"Are you going to stop fucking around and start doing as you are told?" Legba demands, the mocking civility gone. The awful groaning from the walls, floor and ceiling increases, as if the room itself were closing around them with crushing intent.

Aldo gasps. "Yes, fuck yes, just leave him. Please, don't hurt him."

"All of you," Legba snarls. "*Say it.*"

"Yes," Luce says.

"Yes," Ross says.

"Excellent," Legba says, and a second later, Dylan's neck untwists and he looks forward again. His eyelids slide closed as if pushed down by gentle fingertips, his features go slack, and he collapses back onto the bed.

"I will see you at the show, then," he says, his voice once again a velvety croon. "You go on at nine pm. There will be a marked private entrance on the east side of Glasgow Green. On Templeton Street, close to the People's Palace. Your instruments will be waiting for you."

Luce's phone goes dead. The lights flicker back to full strength, and the creeping shadows on the walls and ceiling vanish as if they never were. The door to the room opens, and a nurse pokes her head in. "Everything okay in here?" she asks. "I saw the lights flickering out in the hall."

Luce looks at Aldo and Ross, and her heart sinks lower than she would have thought possible at the defeated expressions they wear. She feels it too. Knows it. They're fucked. How can they hope to fight something that can do... *that?*

"Is everything okay?" the nurse asks again.

"Aye," Aldo says hoarsely, wiping blood from his mouth with one hand as he takes Dylan's with the other. "Everything's just peachy."

6

It's been twenty minutes since Legba did what he did to Dylan. Now the wee man's just lying there, for all the world just looking like he's having a deep and peaceful sleep. Trying to not think of what's just happened, and how close Dylan had come to dying right there in front of him, Aldo immerses himself in the sight of the wee man. Studying every curve, slope, fold and plane of his amazing little face and burning it into his memory. The way his dark blonde hair falls over his perfect, smooth forehead. His eyelashes, and the tiny scar above his left eye where he banged his face on the coffee table when he was two. Aldo'd been in a near panic to see him bawling indignantly, all tears and snotters and a thin trickle of blood running down his cheek. He'd been fumbling for his phone to call an ambulance, but Ashley had told him to stop being such a blouse, calmly picked Dylan up and cuddled him, getting blood on her old Megadeth t-shirt in the process, then taken him into the kitchen to apply a bag of frozen peas and a plaster. Dylan was back in the living room five minutes later, happily babbling his usual semi-coherent toddler speak while he stumbled around the room, bouncing off furniture and giggling as if nothing had happened.

Luce and Ross stay until the nurse pokes her head in the door again and politely ejects them at the end of visiting hours. She says Aldo can stay if he wants to. He says he will. She smiles and says she'll arrange to have a fold up bed brought in.

Ross and Luce stand up to go.

"Guess I'll see you guys tomorrow," Aldo says, standing up as well.

"Aye. Guess so," Ross says, looking down at Dylan. Then he meets Aldo's eyes and gives a grim smile. "We rocked the shit out a few places, didn't we?"

"That we did, mate," Aldo replies, trying not to cry. They clasp forearms and then exchange an acceptably brief man-hug, complete with back punches.

"Right," Ross says, shrugging his jacket on. "I'm going home to get good and stoned, crack open a bottle of red and stick some tunes on. I think a bit of Bob Marley's in order."

"Good call," Aldo agrees.

"I'm going to my folks' place," Luce says. "You're welcome to come and crash there if you want, Ross. If you don't want to be alone."

"Cheers m'dear, but I'm fine. Want to have a little me time."

"Sure." Luce turns to Aldo and hugs him. When she looks at him there are tears in her eyes, and in his. "I'll pick you up about six, alright?"

Aldo can't find his voice, so he just nods, feeling like someone's twisting a knife in his heart. Luce nods and hugs him again, then they leave, and Aldo's left alone with Dylan.

He sits in the chair again, takes the wee man's hand. He's exhausted. He can't remember the last time he slept, or ate, or had a shower. He's just hollow, and wonders if this what it feels like to have your soul slowly taken from you. Gradually leeched away, little by little for years, or whatever the fuck passed for time in Legbaland, hollowed out and constantly afraid.

Fuck that. Fuck that directly in the ear. Both ears.

Tomorrow night, we rock the Green.

And with the thought, which has a ring of finality to it, Aldo's eyes are closed before he realises it, and he's out for the count seconds later, sleep taking him like a black hole.

In his dream, he walks across a burned, featureless desert of broken valleys, low rocky hills and the charred skeletons of trees.

There's a guitar on his back, and a lonely crossroads behind him, the two intersecting paths rutted trails that run to the infinite horizon. The red sky above is ripped with a cataclysmic lightning storm, electric blue bolts ceaselessly scoring the heavens above with bullwhips of jagged energy. The titanic rolling bang and crash of the storm, like God performing a drum solo, is a devastating fusillade that tears the air; a terrible sound like the end of all things. And under it, burned and twisted corpses, human and animal in things in between, lie by the scorched roadside, while unseen beasts prowl and screech in the shadows among the rocky wasteland and gullies.

Aldo walks across this bleak and barren no man's land, afraid of the hunched things that skulk in the murk, stalking him. He's following a sound in the far distance ahead, a soft and mysterious beckoning, which in that dreamlike way, he can hear despite the bedlam of the storm above. Like some gently played instrument, just on the edge of his hearing. And a light. Every now and then on the cracked horizon; a brief flash and sparkle. And so he walks on, a guitar that feels like it's made of freshly butchered body parts on his back, and those half-seen things in the shadows by the roadside, tracking him every step of the way.

He wakes hours later, curled up in a foldable cot bed, fully clothed and partially covered by a child size *Paw Patrol* blanket. He doesn't remember getting into the small bed, but feels marginally fresher for it.

He sits up, looking at the cartoon duvet. Marshall and Rubble's cheerful puppy grins, their irrepressibly upbeat demeanour and cute fireman and construction worker outfits do little to lighten Aldo's mood. Dylan loves *Paw Patrol*, but it does Aldo's head in. *Ben and Holly* is far better. Nanny Plumb in particular cracks him up.

He swings his legs off the cot bed and looks out the window. The sun's up, revealing the west end of Glasgow in a soft early morning half-light. His mobile tells him it's just after 9am. There's a knock on the door. It opens and another nurse comes in with a tray on which sits a plate of scrambled eggs and toast. A pretty girl with coffee skin, dark almond eyes and raven black hair pulled back in a business like ponytail. Naya on her name badge. She smiles over at Aldo. "Did you get some sleep?"

"Aye, thanks," Aldo replies, trying to rub some feeling into his still half-asleep face. "Thanks for letting me stay over. Really appreciate it."

"No bother," the nurse, Naya, says. She puts the eggs and toast on the wheeled bed table. "Thought you might like some breakfast." Aldo's stomach turns as he looks at the plate. He's not in the slightest bit hungry, though he can't remember the last time he ate.

Naya goes round Dylan's bed, checking tubes and instruments and drips. "You should go home and get some real rest," she says kindly. "Eat something, and may I suggest, take a shower?"

Aldo managed an abashed smile. She's got a point. He can smell himself. He's absolutely barking.

"We'll call you if there's any change," Naya says. "I promise."

"Aye," Aldo says, standing up.

"By the way," Naya says smiling shyly. "I'm really looking forward to your show tonight."

"What?"

"The Green. Tonight. I got the night off for it." She takes a step closer, her smile broadening. "I saw you at the Barras last year. You were amazing. Just... so... oh my *God!* Awesome. Where have you *been*?"

That's a damn good question, Aldo thinks.

"Just... away. Recording our album."

"Yeah, I heard the little leaked parts on Facebook. Really can't wait for tonight."

Aldo's not sure what to say to that. How do you speak to someone who's unwittingly excited about watching you commit bloody ritual suicide later that evening?

"I'll erm... dedicate a song to you," Aldo hears himself say, and has to choke back a burst of insane laughter.

"Oh my *God!*" Naya says, practically jumping up and down on the spot, clasping her hands. "That would be so amazeballs!"

"Erm, aye. Well, I'll see you there. Can you give me a minute with the wee man?"

"Of course, of course," Naya says. "Sorry, I got a bit starstruck. We don't get many rock stars in here." She smiles again, giving Aldo a sly, sultry look he can only describe as an unabashed eyefuck, and then leaves, gently closing the door behind her.

Aldo stands by Dylan's bedside, just looking down at him. He stays that way for a few minutes, motionless. The only movement about him are the tears tracking down his cheeks. He's saying goodbye, because he knows this is the last time he'll see his son.

After a while, he leans down and kisses Dylan on the forehead.

"Be good, wee man," he whispers. "Daddy loves you."

Heartbroken, walking out of that hospital room is the hardest thing Aldo's ever done. He doesn't know how me makes it outside, but there he finds himself, in the forecourt outside the hospital hailing a taxi. A black cab pulls up in front of him and he forces himself inside, all the time wanting only to go back upstairs and just look at Dylan one more time, but he says, "Inverclyde, mate. East Crawford Street."

The driver – who Aldo is glad to find displays no fangs or black and red eyes - makes a few attempts at conversation during the half hour trip down the M8, but gives up when his cheery patter's met with stony silence. In truth, Aldo barely hears him. All the way out of the city and down the motorway, he stares blankly out the window, marvelling with bleak fascination at how the people out there on the street and in the passing cars can just get on with their life, blindly unaware of the terrifying truth. The reality of what else inhabits their world, and how easily all that peaceful, bovine ignorance and normality could be stripped away, with just one drunken decision.

It's been growing in him, the incremental *leeching* feeling of being slowly emptied. Like a water tank with a slow leak, a hairline crack from which his soul drips, drop by drop by drop, ever so slowly. It's only noticeable if he focusses his attention and concentrates, but it's there, no doubt. Colours seem a little duller. Sounds a little fainter. His every thought and movement requires that little bit more effort. Even his emotions seem diluted. And beneath it all, there's that constant undercurrent of fear, a subtle tickle of impending dread.

He has the cab stop at a cash machine not far from his flat, and Aldo ponders how ironic it is that the simple act of withdrawing £200 and knowing he can easily afford it, makes him feel physically sick. Changed days indeed. When the taxi drops him outside the scabby tenement he calls home, though the fare is only a little over sixty quid, Aldo gives the driver a hundred, and then all two hundred, and is out the cab and halfway up the path leading to the broken secure entry door to his block while the driver is still gaping unbelievably at the generous wad of notes.

In the flat, Aldo just stands in his living room, looking about at his worldly goods. *What a shithole,* he thinks, surprised by the realisation that he's actually missed the place. Aye, it's a shithole, but it's *his* shithole, and it's honest.

He takes off his jacket and throws it in its accustomed place on the back of the rickety wooden chair in the corner, purchased for a fiver from a used furniture shop. Then he slumps down on the ratty, groaning sofa bed, which always threatens to collapse every time he sits on it. He checks the time on his mobile. 11am. He has to be on stage at the Green in ten hours. How to kill the time?

Phone loved ones? He has none to speak of. With Ashley dead and Dylan… wherever he is, Aldo has no one close other than Ross and Luce. He'd never been close with either of his parents, and had left home at just sixteen. His folks had already been separated a year, his mum making a run south for the border with her new boyfriend, vanishing somewhere in Manchester and remaining incommunicado ever since. His dad had been practically a stranger for Aldo's entire life. He'd worked as a ship's engineer on oil tankers, and spent most of his time on foreign seas through Aldo's childhood. Even on the infrequent occasions he was home he'd been a thousand miles away, rarely speaking, spending most of his time between bookies and bars. Aldo had heard that he'd died some years ago, hollowed out by lung cancer. It was no big loss.

So with no nearest and dearest to call, he considers a suicide note, but this begs the question of who the fuck would read it? He supposes that the band's new legions of fans might be morbidly interested in it, especially following what was going to happen tonight. He finds he doesn't care, though, and again, the thought strikes him as bitterly funny. Not so long ago, he'd liked the romantic rock n' roll fantasy of live fast, die young and leave a good looking corpse and a poignant suicide letter behind. Now, the thought is as depressing as it is terrifying, and just about the last thing he cares about is leaving some parting words for the band's fans to ponder and weep over. He still finds it hard enough to accept that they even *have* that many fans. If he hadn't seen the posters, the newspapers and the stuff on social media - at last check, the band's Facebook page was approaching three million followers - he would have laughed in the face of anyone who told him how big they apparently were.

So, no suicide note. A letter to Dylan, though. Something he can read when he's older. Something that attempts to explain why Aldo's done what he's going to do, and without sounding like a prize headcase. No easy feat. And on that gloomy note, Aldo realises there's something else he needs to do for Dylan first, and with a distinct lack of enthusiasm, he scrolls through the contacts on his phone until he finds the entry for George McColgan.

Ashley's dad answers after a couple of rings. "Hello?"

"George. It's Aldo."

There's a few seconds of silence in which Aldo fancies he can hear George McColgan grinding his teeth and drawing a deep breath to vent his normal tirade of abuse. He dives in before his nemesis can get started.

"Listen, George. I know you hate me, and to be honest I'm no great fan of yours, but this isn't about me and you. I've got a few things I want to say, so before you start hurling abuse at me, just let me say what I want to say, okay?"

Again, stony brooding silence, which Aldo chooses to take as compliance. He takes a deep breath, and says it. "I want you to take custody of Dylan."

George McColgan still says nothing for a moment, then, "You're unbelievable, Evans, you know that? You leave your boy lying in a coma while you're away playing at being a pop star, and now you want to abandon him altogether? You're a..."

"It's not like that," Aldo interrupts, keeping his voice calm and even. "I didn't know about what happened to Dylan and Ashley until yesterday. I don't know if you believe that, but it's the truth. And I'm not abandoning him. This is... just in case something happens to me."

"What in the name of God are you talking about? Have you been smoking that wacky backy?"

"Not recently, no. I've..." Aldo thinks furiously, groping for inspiration, then he just decides to tell the truth, or something like it. "I've had a death threat, George. Someone wants me dead. I think it's the same person who attacked Ashley and Dylan. They've told me I'm going to die on stage tonight at Glasgow Green. And not just me. The whole band."

"Fuck off," George says sceptically.

"Look, George, it doesn't matter if you believe me or not. I just need to know you'll look after the wee man in case anything happens, alright?"

Another few seconds of silence while George considers this. "Have you told the police?" he asks.

"Aye," Aldo replies, the lie coming easily. "They've taken a statement."

"So you think the bastard that killed Ashley is... what? Some demented fan of yours?" There's an audible wobble to his voice, and Aldo realises the man on the other end of the phone's fighting back tears. And just like that, guilt at the memory of attacking George in the hospital last night sticks in Aldo's throat as he remembers that the man's lost his daughter. Thinking of Dylan lying in that hospital bed, at the mercy of Legba, thinking of what he's prepared to do to protect him, the thought of *losing* him… That scares Aldo more than anything he's experienced so far. He can't imagine anything worse. And that's exactly what's happened to George McColgan. He's lost his child.

"I'm sorry, George," Aldo says. "I'm so sorry. About last night. About… everything."

"I *told* her," George almost sobs. "I told her you'd never do her any good. And now… now my wee girl's dead. Did they tell you what the bastard did to her? They fucking butchered her. *They cut her head off, Aldo.*" For a moment, he can't continue, and Aldo, who's gone cold all over, listens to the sound of George McColgan's heart tearing apart on the other end of the line.

"And my grandson, lying there…" George continues when he's able to compose himself, the hate in his voice sharp enough to make Aldo flinch. "And all because of you and your fuckin *band*." He spits the word out like the taste of vomit. "You never gave a shit about anything else, did you? Eh? *Did you?*"

The guilt clogging his craw noticeably thickens as Aldo admits to himself that George - who's openly weeping again - has a point. His view that he never gave a shit about anything else was off; he loved Dylan and he'd loved Ashley, but Aldo Evans's first passion had, and always would be, the music.

And with that realisation comes a memory four years old, of walking out the door of the house he'd shared with Ashley and Dylan, leaving for a gig at some anonymous pub in Dundee, his guitar on his back and Ashley behind him, screaming at him, calling him a selfish prick. She's thin, haggard with post-natal depression, her hair lank, face drawn and baggy-eyed from months without proper sleep. She's holding Dylan, just a baby at the time, howling and red-faced with colic and new teeth. Aldo remembers all he wanted to do was get the fuck out of the house, away from the noise and the tears and the suffocating pressure that made him feel like he was in an iron box that was getting smaller and smaller. Just get out and go far away so he could play music for uninterested strangers. He'd walked down the path, got into Luce's Tardis, and they'd driven away. He hadn't looked back.

"You're right," Aldo says now. "I was a selfish prick. Ashley deserved better than me. So did Dylan. I loved them, George, and I still do, but the band came first. The band, the *music*, always came first. That's what makes me. That's me being *me*. I think… I think me being dead's the best thing for everyone."

"Jesus Christ," George whispers. "Do you hear yourself? What the hell kind of person *are* you?"

"I don't know. Right now, I really have no idea. I'm just trying to make it right. Promise me, George. Promise me you'll take custody of Dylan."

"You're fucking warped, Evans," George says. He sighs heavily, and Aldo can just picture him shaking his head. "Of course I'll look after him. I was going to apply for custody anyway. I know he's your boy, and I don't doubt you love him in your own way, but you… you're just not a father. You don't have what it takes. I just want what's best for Dylan."

Aldo closes his eyes and swallows hard around the shame and failure in his throat. "So do I," he whispers. "That's why I called. Thank you, George. I'm sorry."

He hangs up, and sits staring into space for several seconds. Then he screams and launches his phone across the room, rattling it against the wall. He slumps back on the lumpy thin sofa bed, and the hateful, hurtful, unfair world and everything in it just dissolves. He gives himself to the crushing despair, feeling utterly wretched, and he sobs and howls like a madman on his cheap couch, arms round his knees as he rocks back and forth, insensible.

Perhaps it's a survival mechanism, but at some point, at his lowest point, when he's scratched self-hating abrasions on his face and arms, when his sobs have turned to spiralling cackles of broken laughter and Aldo can actually feel his mind teetering on the brink, just a gentle nudge away from falling into an abyss of drooling, permanent madness, he simply passes out.

In the fever dream that follows, he finds himself again walking through that strange, charred country. A burnt, featureless land of scattered corpses and stunted bare trees that stretches to the horizon in every direction. Above, a blood red sky, tossed with roiling clouds constantly shifts and twists, forming giant leering faces like the hungry features of malevolent gods. Lightning rips the troubled heavens and thunder pounds the land below like all the guns of the world fired at once. A hot, gritty gale, stinking of the dead, blows in Aldo's face as he struggles ever on, the diseased wind shrieking and rattling in the cindered tree branches like the voices of hellbound souls. Those half-glimpsed figures, mutated and predatory, stalk him just out of sight, staying in the shadows by the broken dusty roadside, whispering and grunting in some ugly, guttural language.

But there again on the horizon, that one beguiling point of light, a lighthouse in a nightmare ocean, beckons him on.

It's all there is to do, so Aldo walks on into the storm, guitar on his back, eyes half-closed against the burning wind and hellhounds on his trail.

Then the burnt dreamscape fades away, everything goes black, with only the sound of the thunder remaining, now striking up a familiar rhythm.

Bang, bang, bang-bang-bang

It's something from a song. A riff?

Bang, bang, bang-bang-bang

The black fades to grey, then blurry broken colours. And Aldo wonders, has he lost his mind? Can he see, or is he blind?

Bang, bang, bang-bang-bang

He wakes up in his living room, standing in the middle of the floor.

The bedsit's been trashed. Every object in the room smashed and scattered.

There's someone knocking at the front door. For a bad moment, Aldo has the utter conviction that the creeping, whispering things from his dream have followed him into the waking world, and are pounding on his door with hungry intent. But then he recognises the rhythm.

Thump, thump, thump-thump-thump.
The first five notes of the main riff in *Iron Man*. Ross's knock.
Ross is at the door.

Aldo looks around the room, which has been well and truly fucked up. Like Taz from Loony Tunes had come through with a chainsaw. Tv screen smashed, coffee table overturned and the legs snapped off, the sofa bed lying half open, the upholstery and cushions slashed, their foamy white innards scattered about. His old, slower-than-a-week-in-the-jail laptop's on the floor, screen only attached to the keyboard by a few wires. The smashed screen bleeds black liquid crystal blood, and the keys lie on the stained tacky carpet like broken teeth. His old stereo's had a sound doing, the CD tray snapped off, the control panels cracked and missing buttons as if set about with a hammer. The speakers are slashed. And his CDs. All his tunes. Lying on the floor, in a broken plastic heap, every disc systematically taken from its case, snapped, and apparently trampled underfoot going by the zig zag pattern of the soles of Aldo's trainers. The mirror on the wall. The one framed by a carved wooden musical notes, which Ashley had bought in a street market in Glasgow during the love-crazy intensity of the first year of their relationship. That mirror, one of a very few material things that Aldo truly cares about, is cracked in the middle from a single violent blow, the kaleidoscopic shards stained with dried spit and blood. Aldo looks down at his right hand, sees the knuckles and backs of his fingers smeared a muddy red and crusty with coagulated blood, sees the long, mirrored shard embedded in the flesh between the knuckles of his index and middle finger. His first thought is, *Good, it's not my fret hand.* He plucks the two-inch sliver of glass out of his hand and doesn't feel a thing. The wound doesn't bleed much, though Aldo's pretty sure it should.

The kitchen area's in no better state. Every cupboard door stands open, what little food, crockery and other kitchenware Aldo possesses heaved out and flung about. Not a single saucer, plate, glass or mug remains unsmashed. Even the mismatched cutlery's been taken from the drawer and bent out of shape.

Again, the opening notes of *Iron Man* at the door.

Thump, thump, thump-thump-thump.

Aldo wades through the detritus on his carpet into the hall and opens the door.

"Evening," Ross says formally, one eyebrow raised in suspicion. "You're looking a bit... weird, mate."

"Aye. Just smashed up the bedsit."

"Is that right?" Ross says, looking over Aldo shoulder at the destruction. He shrugs. "Fair dos. Why the fuck not, right? You ready to go?"

Ross looks and sounds remarkably calm considering the circumstances. Then Aldo realises that he's feeling pretty relaxed himself. A sort of novocaine numbness. A strange sense of unfeeling acceptance. He's not scared. He's not happy. He's not sad, or angry or worried or... anything really. He just *is*.

"Aye, I'm ready," he says. He goes back into the living room, searching amongst the destruction for his jacket, which he eventually finds half kicked under the sofa bed. His phone lies on the floor over by the destroyed TV, the screen and casing cracked, but surprisingly still functioning. More out of habit than anything else, he automatically pats himself down, doing the crucial - but under the circumstances, rather pointless - pocket check before leaving. Wallet. Keys. Phone. Cash. Geetar picks.

He takes one last look around the bedsit, wondering vaguely about the fact that he feels absolutely nothing. No regret, no nostalgia. He turns and walks for the door where Ross is waiting, but pauses.

He's forgotten something. What it is, he doesn't know, but it pulls at his mind like a hooked fish. Insistent and panicky. It's important, whatever it is. He frowns and goes back into the wrecked main room, looking about the carnage for... something. Nothing seems to grab his attention. He doesn't even know what he's looking for.

Ross comes in behind him. "What's up? Lost something?"

"Aye, I think. Fuck, I've no idea," Aldo replies. "There's *something* though…"

"Is it because you don't have your guitar?" Ross asks. "Mind *he* says all our gear's waiting for us at the gig."

"My what?" Aldo says, turning to him.

"Your guitar. You know, that weird looking bit of wood with the strings? Makes noises?"

Something slides into place in Aldo's mind with an imagined *click*, and he leaves the main room, steps back into the hall and opens the door to the small storage cupboard. He pushes aside the hoover, an old rucksack, a pair of wellies and other assorted household junk, and uncovers a grungy old guitar case, dusty, bedecked with peeling band stickers, the cheap faux leather scuffed and worn away in several places.

"No way," Ross says behind him. "Oscar? Not seen that bad boy in years."

Aldo takes the case out the cupboard and lays it on the hall floor. Kneeling over it, he unsnaps the rusty hinges, the lid creaking open like a mummy's sarcophagus. And there he is. Oscar. A beat to shit Oscar Schmidt acoustic, bought second-hand in a Glasgow pawnshop with paper round money when he was thirteen. Aldo's first guitar. He remembers endless hours secluded in his bedroom, buried in tablature books and playing along to CDs, the music and his own concentration an anathema to the bitter silences and/or screaming matches of his parents downstairs.

It had been a hard apprenticeship, with hard-won calluses on his fingertips the evidence of his efforts. Learning how to tune the thing, then finding the notes, the basslines and the chords. Then getting through the hellish, maddening phase of learning how to change from one chord to another, all the while resisting the urge to smash the guitar off the wall in frustration. Getting a handle on scales and arpeggios. Fingerpicking. Slide playing. Open tunings, palm muting, bends and pinch harmonics.

Oscar had been a cruel master, all about blisters and cramps, infuriating and unforgiving, but insistent, and eternally patient. And gradually, that old beat to shit acoustic had begun to sing, and it had taken Aldo by his cramped, calloused hand and shown him a way out of the unhappy directionless wilderness where he'd found himself in his early teens. Oscar had guided him to his mojo. Eventually, Aldo had got a better guitar. His first electric. He hasn't played Oscar in years.

"I need to take it," he says, closing the lid and picking the case up.

"Couple of wee acoustic numbers?" Ross says, nodding thoughtfully. "Alright."

They leave the bedsit, Aldo locking the door behind him, then dropping his keys back through the letterbox. Luce's waiting in the Tardis outside, her wee motor, their trusty steed on so many road trips to gigs, parked at the pavement. Engine running, window down, Morcheeba playing on the car stereo. *The Big Calm* album, which strikes Aldo as fitting considering the unexpected sense of relaxed indifference about tonight that he feels. Luce has the same look about her. She's not smiling, but she doesn't look scared either. Just an air of neutral serenity about her.

"Alright," Aldo greets her as he climbs into the back seat of the car.

"Hey. Is that Oscar?"

"Aye."

"Cool."

"How you doing?"

Luce shrugs. "Fine actually. It's like, it doesn't matter anymore. Like it was always going to pan out this way."

"There's only so much crazy that people can take," Ross says as he climbs into the passenger seat. "After a while, folk just get so filled up with fear that you just can't fit any more in, and you just accept it. It's a survival mechanism."

Aldo considers this, and thinks Ross has probably nailed it. "Your parents okay?" he asks Luce.

"They're weird," she says, frowning. "It's like mum just won't accept I'm not coming home tonight. She didn't leave my side all last night and today, her or my dad. They didn't stop me leaving, though. Mum just kept saying she had faith." She sighs. "This is so fucked up," she says as she pulls away from the pavement.

No one speaks as they drive out of town, heading east. As the Tardis makes its final voyage along the M8 with the Clyde on the left, the early evening sun sparkles diamonds on the river. The sky's a deep unbroken blue to the point of violet as it darkens at the edge of the atmosphere. They come off the motorway and enter the city half an hour later, and Aldo once again starts to feel a little nibble of nerves. The Tardis makes its way down past the Necropolis, Glasgow's City of the Dead, and Aldo imagines himself becoming a permanent resident in the near future, his bones in the company of uncounted thousands of others beneath the forest of black headstones. The image is compounded as right next to the cemetery, they pass a billboard advertising tonight's gig. Lurid, horror movie lettering plastered twenty-foot-tall in blood red Times New Roman font against a black background.

Public Alibi – Cuttin Heads Launch.
Live at Glasgow Green.
Sold Out.

They go out by the Barras, and Aldo watches that famous, beloved marquee go sliding by the car window for the last time. He's had many of the best times of his life in that place, especially the last time, when he'd been on the stage.

As they get closer to the Green, he starts to see groups of people heading to the gig. Many of them wearing black t-shirts with the band's name printed in blood red, same as the posters.

"I never thought the band would break up like this," Ross says, looking out at their fans.

They're in sight of the Green now, driving along the edge of the Green on Templeton Street. Up ahead, Aldo sees a couple of Legba's black clad heavies milling about in front of an opening in a newly erected wooden wall ten feet high.

As a cold sweat starts to form om his brow, Aldo's phone rings and he takes the battered mobile from his jacket pocket. The screen's smashed, but he can still read the display. A withheld number. Frowning, he takes the call.

"Hello?"

"Mr Evans? It's Harry Kellman. Your son's doctor?"

Aldo's heart drops into his guts and feels like it could carry on all the way down to his ankles. "Is he okay?" he says, his voice not quite steady. "Is Dylan alright?" He closes his eyes, certain that Kellman's going to tell him that Dylan's gone.

For several agonising moments, the doctor says nothing, but then, "He's... awake."

Aldo's heart just stops dead this time. "What do you... mean?" he asks, stupidly.

"Dylan's awake, Mr Evans. He wants to say hello to you."

For a horrible few moments, he's convinced this is Legba's latest headfuck, that he's going to be hear that horrible two-throated laughter, but then...

"Hi, daddy," Dylan says, his voice the sweetest sound Aldo's ever heard. The megaton weight of worry sliding off him is more than he can take, and he can't reply right away, the sudden avalanche of relief choking him. His face twists as the tears come, and then he's shaking, biting his jacket sleeve to stifle his sobs.

Thank you thank you thank you thank you...

Who he's thanking, he has no idea. He's aware Luce and Ross are turned round in the front seats, gaping at him losing his emotional shit in the back seat, but he doesn't care. He manages to compose himself, clears his throat, wipes his eyes and sniffs. "Hey, wee man," he manages. "I've missed you."

"Daddy, I had a great big big enormous *monster* sleep!"

"I know, wee man. You must've been super tired. Lazy sausage."

Dylan giggles, and Aldo's heart just about tears in two at the sound. "And I had lots and lots of dreams, Daddy."

"Did you? Were they nice dreams? What happened?"

Dylan hesitates a little before replying. "Daddy, where's Mummy? I had a bad dream about her. The spider got her."

Aldo's not got the heart to tell him, and somehow manages to keep his voice from breaking. "She's sleeping, pal. Mummy was super tired as well. Don't worry. Grampa George is coming to get you. Tell me about your dreams."

Eager to tell his dad about his adventures, he launches in with his usual verbal enthusiasm. "It was so crazy, Daddy! It was snowing and we were playing in the snow and I was throwing snowballs at you, and then we played hide and seek but I got lost in the woods and I was trying to find you and I was scared because the *spider* was in the woods, and it found me before you did and it *got* me."

"Oh no," Aldo says, the cold sweat on his brow going icy.

"Yeah! And then I was somewhere far away, Daddy because the spider stole me and took me away somewhere I couldn't see anything because it was very very dark, and there were bad ghosties and they kept trying to get me and eat me up but the spider wouldn't let them because it wanted to keep me for himself."

"It's okay, wee man. It's over now."

"I was there for *ages* and I was very scared but then it was okay because the lady came."

That little plot twist throws Aldo for a moment. "The lady?"

"Yeah she was awesome, Daddy! The lady with the silver rings on her arms came in and she was pretty like auntie Luce and she made the dark go away because she was on *fire* like Human Torch in Fantastic Four!"

"Wow," Aldo says, simultaneously horrified, baffled and completely engrossed.

"Yeah it was *sooooo* cool because the lady said magic words and then held my hand then we were flying way way way up the sky and into space and then I woke up and now I'm in the hostipal." Dylan's excited retelling of his comatose escapades comes to this somewhat abrupt end with the mispronounced word which he always had trouble with, and he falls silent, waiting for Aldo's verdict.

"Well, wee man," he says, "sounds like you had a big adventure. Do you feel okay?"

"Yeah I'm okay, Daddy. Are you coming to get me? I don't want to stay in hostipal anymore. I want to go home."

"I know, wee man. Grampa George is coming to get you right now. I promise."

"I don't *want* Grampa George," Dylan insists. "I want *you*, Daddy."

"I know, pal. I want you too. But there's something I need to do, okay? It's to keep you safe. To make sure the spider stays away."

"No, Daddy! You have to stay away from the spider! He'll eat you up! Please come and get me. Don't go away again."

Aldo squeezes his eyes closed. Every atom in his body wants to get out of the car and start sprinting in the direction of Yorkhill Children's Hostipal.

But he can't do that. Because he's made a deal.

His soul, or Dylan's.

But then again, if Dylan's story means what Aldo thinks it does, it might mean that Legba isn't quite the bulletproof ticket he makes himself out to be.

"Be good, wee man," he says to Dylan. "Be brave. Be… yourself. I love you. Let me speak to the doctor again, okay wee man?"

He's crying a little, and Aldo feels himself about to go again as well.

"Okay," Dylan eventually says, though with massive reluctance. "But *please* come, Daddy."

Dylan gives the phone back to Dr Kellman, who tells Aldo they've called George, and that he's on his way to the hospital. Aldo thanks him, and hangs up.

Then, he looks up at Ross and Luce who are looking back at him expectantly from the front of the car, and fires them.

Solo

In that year, there was an intense visitation of energy. I left school and went down to the beach to live. Slept on a roof. I met the spirit of music. An appearance of the Devil on a Venice canal. Running. I saw Satan.

Jim Morrison

1

Ross's thoughts are ricocheting around inside his skull like a spilled box of rubber balls, trying to figure out what's being said on the phone between Aldo and Dylan. The wee man's apparently woke up. Except that wasn't supposed to happen, was it?

Aldo stays on the phone for a minute longer, his face going through any number of emotions, from amazement to confusion to outright grief. When he hangs up, he sits holding the phone in his lap, staring at it as if trying to figure out some vexing puzzle, and pointedly ignoring Ross and Luce's questioning looks. Then he looks up at them and says, "Dylan's awake."

"That's brilliant, mate," Ross says, meaning it, "but... how? What was that about a lady?"

Aldo tells them.

"Holy shit," Luce whispers. Ross can see the hairs on her forearms standing to attention, and feels the ones on the back of his neck doing the same.

"He says she was pretty," Aldo says. "Like you, Luce. And she said magic words and set him free."

Magic words, Ross thinks, a very strange, but insanely logical idea forming in his mind. Eye of newt and toe of frog indeed.

It's as he's furiously chewing this over that Aldo throws another curveball. "I'm going solo," he says.

There's a few seconds of complete silence in the car, then, "You're going what now?" Ross asks, waiting for the punchline.

"You're fired. Both of you."

"But..." Luce begins, shaking her head and frowning, clearly baffled, "but you can't *do* that."

"I can, and I am. I put this band together. I'm the founding member, main songwriter and the leader. It's my decision."

And it is. It's what they agreed on five years ago when they formed the band. All decisions about the doings and direction of Public Alibi should be, and usually were, unanimous, but on any occasion where they couldn't agree and a choice had to be made, as the founding member, it fell to Aldo to make the call.

Then Ross understands, or thinks he does. "Look, Al," he says, "I know what you're trying to do, and I appreciate it, but he wants all three of us. That's the deal."

"*Fuck* the deal," Aldo replies firmly, "and fuck Legba. If Dylan got out from... wherever he was, then maybe the prick's not as untouchable as he makes out. You said it yourself. He's a scam artist."

"Well then maybe none us have to do this," Ross reasons. "If he's not untouchable, if we *don't* all have to slit our own throats in front of fifty-thousand punters, let's get the fuck out of here and figure out what to do. The three of us."

"I can't," Aldo says. "Dylan's *my* blood, not yours. I'm the link. Legba got to him twice already, and he won't stay away from him as long as I'm around. That I can't take a risk on. But he's fallible. Dylan getting away proves that. I get it now." He pauses a moment. "You guys don't need to be here. I do."

"No," Luce says firmly. "You're not doing this by yourself."

"Agreed," Ross says. "Fuck that."

Aldo gives him a crooked smile. "Roscoe, I love you like a brother, but I'm pulling rank. You're out the band. You too, Luce. End of."

Then, as a good band leader should when there's a difficult call to make, he tells them how it's going to be.

Ross never talked about his time as a ward of the state, not even to Aldo or Luce, and had only once spoken about his real parents. That had been on the day of Gregor Picken's funeral, eight years ago when he nineteen. It was also the last time he'd wept.

On that long ago cold autumn day, Aldo had found him, drunk, angry, and utterly heartbroken, beating his fists bloody on the roughcast wall out the back of the local pub where Gregor's wake was being held. It'd taken all Aldo's strength to restrain him, and Ross had broken down, slumping to the ground and sobbing like a child. Then it had all come pouring out in a great cathartic rush. He'd babbled and raved, not about the death of Gregor, who he figured had save his life, but about the car crash on the M8 that had killed his natural parents. Why had he lived? Pulled from the wreck unscathed, still in his baby seat, while his parents had been reduced to bloody pulp shot through with slivers of shattered bone and twisted metal.

Aldo had simply sat there on the ground with him and held him, not saying anything, not trying to provide answers to impossible questions. He'd cried with him. Already good mates, their friendship had changed that grey afternoon as they sat there together in the dirt behind an Inverclyde pub, the October drizzle soaking them, and their bond had taken on a new, deeper level, sealed in tears, blood, torn skin and broken knuckles.

Ross hadn't wept once since that day nearly a decade before, but his eyes are stinging now as he turns in the passenger seat as they drive away from the Green, watching through the rear window of the Tardis as Aldo, that old battered guitar case on the pavement beside him, raises a hand in farewell. Then the car turns a corner, and Aldo's gone.

Ross turns back and stares straight ahead through the windscreen, wiping his eyes and trying to find his equilibrium after what's just happened.

"Fuck," he says under his breath.

"Aye," Luce says quietly, tears in her eyes as well as she drives away from the Green. She reaches over and gives his hand a squeeze. "So. North?"

Ross takes a deep, steadying breath. "North."

They drive away from the east end, back out through the city centre and up through the west end onto Great Western Road, merging onto the A82. Back along the Clyde they go, this time on the northern bank heading west. Once again, they turn north, highland bound.

Just outside Dumbarton, they make a stop at a big retail park on the edge of the town. After visits to a few warehouse sized stores, they load their purchases into the car, fill the tank at the Asda petrol station - where Ross also fills one of five twenty-litre jerry cans bought from the retail park's branch of Halfords - and then continue north.

It's a long drive, and they've got to do it fast. The navigation app on Ross's phone informs him that the road from Glasgow to Loch Ness takes three hours and twenty-five minutes in normal traffic. They're hoping to do it in three flat, and praying for a lack of roadworks and traffic.

"You think this is going to work?" Luce asks later, somewhere past Crianlarich. It's the first either of them have spoken since leaving the retail park an hour ago.

"Who the hell knows," Ross replies, staring out the window at the passing landscape that's getting more rugged with every northward mile. "But what have we got to lose? Other than our souls, I mean."

The last signpost said it was fifty-one miles to Fort William, the next town of any note, and outside the car it's all hills and wide valleys with mountains on the horizon, the slopes and open moorland dotted with forest and lochs. The road winds gradually up and up, getting in amongst the big hills now, where the highlands start getting serious. Up ahead, Ross can see the steep slopes of the Glencoe range looming in the distance, blocking much of the horizon. The haunting enormity and emptiness up here never fails to give Ross a pleasant chill, and he's glad to find that it still does. Because that means he's feeling things again.

After the incident in Dylan's room at the hospital the night before, he'd been in a daze, all hopes of resistance crushed by Legba's manifestation and the sight of the wee man's neck being twisted like that.

Cold acceptance of their fate had set in, and he'd been like a ghost after Luce dropped him off, barely aware of his own surroundings as he's stumbled from her car up to his block and then up the darkened stairwell to his flat seven floors above.

Once in the door, he'd seen his reflection in the mirror in his hallway, and wasn't all that surprised to notice that he could partially see through it. Like he was some half-arsed vampire. Without really thinking about what he was doing, he'd leant forward and breathed on the glass. No condensation.

And he'd felt nothing. Even this disturbing revelation had produced little more than a vague *shit happens* response.

By one in the morning, though he was exhausted in all possible ways, the sandman had refused to put in an appearance. After an hour lying in bed scrutinising the insides of eyelids and thinking very dark thoughts, Ross had got up again, made some coffee, rolled a generously packed joint, and sat smoking on his couch with the lights off, headphones on and tunes playing. All his favourites. Sabbath of course. A bit of Jimi, Zep, Nirvana, Maiden, the Pistols, Pixies and Kyuss. Ray Charles, The Prodigy, Beta Band and Smashing Pumpkins. He played it loud. Really loud, and concentrated on the music, tried to study the bass notes and rhythms and let it wash him away. Just so he wouldn't have to think about what was going to happen tomorrow. But it was all just noise. The music that had built him, that had rescued him and never failed to thrill, got nothing from him that night. He wasn't even getting much of a stone from the weed.

Poor show.

He woke up with the dawn, headphones askew over his face, feeling that same hollow nothingness, and spent the morning and afternoon deep cleaning his flat. When it was hoovered, dusted, mopped, polished and squeegeed to a state of cleanliness that would meet the approval of a NASA lab technician, Ross boxed up all his books, CD's, DVDs, Blu Rays, Xbox games and console and clothes, took a big black marker and wrote on the boxes the name of a local charity shop run by a cancer hospice. The same hospice where Gregor had spent his last few days as the cancer took the last few bites out of him. Later, when Luce came to pick him up for the gig, he got out the car at a post box and mailed a cheque for twenty-seven thousand pounds addressed and made payable to the same hospice. His advance from Easy Rollin Records, which he still hadn't touched. He hoped it would do some good.

Giving away all his money and possessions should have given him some sort of emotional response, but there was just nothing. No sadness, no nostalgia. He was empty. When they picked up Aldo and made their way into Glasgow, he'd recognised that same listless, weary acceptance in his bandmates, and knew they too were resigned to their fate, going into their last few hours, and caring not a jot.

Then, outside the Green, Aldo'd got that phone call, and everything changed.

Like shrugging off a sodden duffle coat, the heavy *fuck-this-for-a-game-of-soldiers* defeatism had slid from Ross's shoulders the moment Aldo announced he was going solo and told them what they had to do next.

Now, as Ross stands in the forecourt of the tiny one-pump petrol station in Glencoe village, filling another jerry can with unleaded, with a plan in the hand and nothing to lose, his senses and thoughts seem ramped up after being smothered. He feels slapped awake, energised, almost giddy, and, he's sure as fuck feeling a lot more purposeful.

2

Considering she'd only slept two hours last night, and has been driving for almost the last three, Luce's remarkably alert as the Tardis enters the densely forested hills rising up from the southern banks of Loch Ness.

It's not long till the car crests a slope that opens up into high open moorland, and the woods on the left thin and open up, revealing the valley and loch below. It's postcard stuff. Ness's dark waters cut away through the hills to the north east like a great black glacier-carved slash in the earth. Luce's been up this way a few times, and still can't resist taking her eyes off the road a little too often for safety, more than a little awed by the view, but mainly of course, checking the murky surface of the loch for any sign of you-know-who. She can't help it. It's the kid in her. Plus, her new respect for the reality of the supernatural has opened up a whole family-sized bag of bonkers possibilities about the reality of other supposedly impossible things. Considering what's been going on in her life recently, if Nessie had broken the loch's surface at that moment and started synchronised swimming with Bigfoot while Elvis waterskied around them while being towed by a flying saucer, Luce reckons she'd just *about* bat an eyelid.

She reckons Ross was right about only being able to handle so much insanity. At some point, you either caved in, or just got on with it. She's not caved in. She's cool. The horrors of the past few days are still fresh in her mind, but she no longer feels like hiding in a cupboard. And a lot of that's to do with her mum.

They'd talked a lot last night. More than they had in years. For hours, well into the early hours of the morning. Her mum had talked like someone forced to keep a secret for too long, telling Luce all she remembered from her childhood apprenticeship in the ways of gypsy magic. She'd gone into particular details about the subjects of demons and deals, and salt and fire. Itria Figura had kept herself together remarkably well throughout, better than Luce was at that point. She'd been caved in *then*, but her mum had spoken with a quiet, firm authority, forcing her to listen, even giving her a pad and pen to take notes, when all Luce wanted to do was crawl under her covers and cry herself to sleep.

So her mum talked and Luce listened and wrote, and though she was calm, Luce could hear the underlying tension in her mama's voice. The fear. In a strange contrast, all the while she'd talked of the uses of various spells, herbs and potions, Itria Figura had constantly fingered and footered with her trusty rosary beads, nervously *click-click-clicking* them while she talked at length about another belief system entirely.

Luce's thinking about all that as the car continues through the hills above the loch. They pass another road sign. Foyers, six miles. The digital clock on the dashboard shows eight forty-five.

Luce's also thinking about what Dylan said. About the lady who spoke magic words and set him free. That family-sized bag of bonkers again. Growing up, her mum had often commented on how Luce had the look of her Nona Corada, dead now for many a year. Nona Corada, who'd put iron nails, business end up, on the windowsills of the house and a daisy chain necklace around Luce's neck when she was a baby. Luce has those nails in the little drawstring bag in her pocket, and that same daisy chain around her neck under her shirt. Her mum had made her take them. Luce hadn't believed they'd do any good. Not after Legba laughing at them discussing the use of oregano. Not after what he'd done to Dylan.

Now though, she's not so sure, and she's feeling a little differently about the nails in her pocket and the daisies round her neck. Not to mention the Asda carrier bags in the back seat filled with bottles of table salt, or the other carrier bag containing the emergency flares they'd bought in an outdoor gear store in Fort William, and certainly not to mention the car's full tank of gas and the fact the boot was further loaded with several twenty-litre jerry cans of fuel which Ross had filled at various petrol stations on the way here.

Yes, Luce felt surprisingly okay about the fact that her beloved Tardis was now essentially a salty, motorised Molotov cocktail. She felt just fine about it, and had done since that conversation with Aldo in the car outside Glasgow Green a few hours ago. When he'd fired them.

Go north, he'd said, *and burn that fuckin studio to the ground.*

Luce wonders what's happening with Aldo right now, back in Glasgow, and a knot of sadness tightens beneath her breastbone as she thinks of what *he's* planning. Perhaps the weirdest aspect of this entire clusterfuck is that despite everything, she actually feels pretty disappointed that she's *not* playing in front of fifty-thousand people on Glasgow Green tonight, even though she knows fine well that that gig would have ended with her being forced to open her own throat and hose the front row with her blood. She supposes that the fact she feels this way - plus the fact that despite not having eaten anything in, what, two days? she doesn't feel hungry – is further proof, as if any were needed, of the change in her, and of Legba's ownership over her.

And let's not forget the fact that you haven't had your period in... how long's it been now?

Luce shuts that shit straight down, and thinks about fire instead.

"Ross," she says as the car rounds a bend to the left and starts downhill toward the lochside and the village of Foyers. "Stick *Ride the Lightning* on, would you?"

"Now that's a fine idea," Ross agrees, finding the CD in the centre console between the front seats and slipping the disc into the stereo. A moment later, gentle classical guitar music fills the car, the peaceful, shimmering twelve string intro lasting for all of forty-two seconds, before it's rudely destroyed by the manic speed metal riffing of the album's opening track *Fight Fire With Fire*. Then the drums kick in. Lars Ulrich giving it laldy. The speed and aggression of vintage Metallica instantly sets Luce's blood a-pumping and her skin a-tingle. Glancing across, she sees Ross is wearing a dark grin, bobbing his head as he taps his thigh in time. She can feel the contained tension in him, like an overwound bass string that's about to snap and take some cunt's eye out.

Foyers isn't much more than a campsite, a few cottages, and a small post office and general store by the lochside, and they're through it in moments. They almost miss the turnoff for Boleskine House a mile or so past the village. It's not much more than a dirt road on the right, leading into thick woods.

Beside her, going into stealth mode, Ross reaches forward and turns the stereo off, cutting off Kirk Hammett in mid facemelter. From the storage pocket on the passenger door, he takes something else they bought in B&Q earlier. The hand axe. Luce watches as he takes the leather sheath off and examines the gleaming brushed steel of the business end, running his thumb along the curved blade and nodding approvingly. "Aye, that'll do it," he says.

"Can you use that?" Luce asks.

"How hard can it be?" Ross asks. "Chop chop chop, right?"

"I mean *could* you use that? On a person?"

Ross mulls this over for a second. "On a person, no. But if there's anyone hanging around up at the studio, I'm not so sure they're human."

"Good point."

Luce takes a deep steadying breath as the Tardis continues along the single track road, heading for Boleskine House.

3

On the pavement outside the Green, Aldo watches his now former rhythm section drive away up the road. When the car turns left at the corner and is out of sight, he stands there for a moment longer, feeling more alone than he ever has in his life.

He wipes his eyes then takes his mobile out his pocket to send a text to George and let him know the wee man's okay and to go and pick him up. He does it quickly, getting it over with and keying send before he can second guess himself. Knowing that he's never going to see his son again is too much to take, so he slams a door on it every time the thought intrudes.

Text sent, Aldo then brings up the Facebook app. The Public Alibi page now has a little under two million followers. He taps the status bar and his thumbs go to work.

To all those attending the show at Glasgow Green this evening, it is the band's responsibility to inform you all that a terror threat has been issued targeting the event. The concert has NOT been cancelled, but for safety's sake, we urge you to consider not attending the event. Furthermore, in the wake of personal death threats to the band, it is with regret that we announce that drummer Luce Figura and bassist Ross McArthur have officially left Public Alibi with immediate effect, and will not be performing tonight. Due to contractual obligations with the band's record company - and as big 'fuck you' to terror in general - the show WILL however go ahead, and will be a solo acoustic performance by singer and guitarist Alan Evans. Love, P.A.

Seconds after he posts it, the feed goes mental, and Aldo's mobile starts beeping and vibrating like a motherfucker as the notifications pour in. Shocked, angry, weeping emojis, shares and comments of outrage, defiance, sadness, and more than a few plainly racist posts. A second later, Aldo's phone rings again, but he doesn't answer it. He drops it on the pavement and stomps on it a few times before kicking the pieces down a drain cover. It's a very liberating feeling.

Aldo picks up the old guitar case by his side and walks towards the artist's entrance. As he gets closer to the gate, he recognises one of Legba's hulking roadies standing guard. Black denims, black t-shirt, shaven-headed, damn near seven-foot-tall and built like a grizzly on steroids. He'd been there that night in the 13th Note. The particularly big, mean looking bastard that Aldo remembers thinking probably breakfasted on post boxes. As he walks up the gate, the giant looks at him uncertainly, a confused frown creasing furrows in his sloping brow. The small, apish eyes below the ridge of his forehead glare out at Aldo suspiciously. The guy couldn't look more like a gorilla in a t-shirt if he tried. Aldo wonders where Lega gets his staff from, and realises that there's no shortage of desperate people in the world. People who for whatever reason, might sign a contract of employment with a smooth talking, sharp suited man who promises a stack of cash and to make all their problems go away.

"You're alone," the bruiser states stupidly, as if struggling to comprehend the concept. He has an oddly high-pitched voice. "Why are you alone? There's supposed to be three of you. Not one."

"Change of plan," Aldo says casually, moving to walk past him into the Green.

The roadie has other ideas, and plants a dinner plate sized hand on Aldo's chest. "Three. Not one," he repeats in that weird piping tone, shaking his head and frowning.

Aldo looks down at the massive hand. The big fucker could most likely crush every rib in his body simply by flexing those huge bratwurst fingers.

"Take your hand off me," Aldo says calmly, looking up into the roadie's big thick-as-mince, broken-nosed, heavy-jawed coupon. He grins back down at Aldo, revealing a mouthful of crooked yellow teeth, and he can see the joy of impending violence written large on his face as if it were scrawled in day-glow orange marker. The hand on Aldo's chest tightens into a fist, gripping the front of his jacket, and just as he's preparing himself to be turned into paste, Aldo spots Legba behind the roadie, striding towards them along the path leading into the Green. He doesn't look best pleased.

Legba reaches them just as the behemoth in black's drawing back a fist like a cannonball. Legba, who's not much more than half the guy's size, grabs the roadie's hand from behind, pulls, twists, and in an eyeblink, the shaved ape's lying in the grass ten feet away, writhing and making a disturbing keening sound like the whine of a dying dog, his hideously broken arm flopping around at all sorts of horrible angles, and the splintered, jagged end of his collar bone poking out from a rip in his t-shirt.

Then the breath explodes out of Aldo as something hits him in the chest really, *really* hard, and he thinks maybe he's been shot as he reels backwards and falls arse over tit onto the pavement. He lies there, looking up at the sky, trying to remember how to breathe, when a highly polished, expensive looking leather boot descends from above, plants itself firmly on his forehead and begins to press down.

"What the fuck do you think you're playing at, you worthless little cunt?" Legba seethes down at him. Aldo can't really see him that well, with his bootheel obscuring his vision and everything. "Do you really think just because your runt got away from me I can't get him again if I want to?"

Legba presses down harder, and Aldo gasps for breath as the pain comes and the pressure on his skull increases.

"Did you really think kicking the other two out the band *changes* anything?" Legba rages. "I will fucking have them anyway, and there is no human definition for much I will make all three of you suffer. I will keep you and your friends alive and screaming until you are the last cunts alive on Earth, and this sewer of a planet is engulfed by your *fucking sun.*"

He presses down harder, an irresistible, horribly mechanical power like an industrial press, and Aldo's vision washes red as wholesale agony crashes through him and he hears something creaking in the back of his head, and all he can think of is that scene in *Game of Thrones* when the Mountain crushed that dude's skull with his bare hands. He feels a scream rushing up his throat, but refuses to give voice to it.

"When are you going to fucking *learn?*" Legba snarls, his voice taking on a gritted, sludgy quality. "You stupid, ignorant *insect*. You are mine. You are *all mine.*"

Just as Aldo expects his skull to cave in and send his brains *slorping* onto the footpath, Legba lifts his foot off his forehead and the terrible crushing pressure's gone. He presses his hands to his head like he has to hold his skull together, manages to crawl away a few feet onto the grass, then rolls over and throws up. He spits bile and blood, then manages to make it to his knees, facing away from Legba.

"You're right," he says shakily. "We're yours." Then he takes a deep breath and manages to get his feet under him. He turns to face the thing looking back at him, and just for a second, the air seems to tremble, and Aldo gets a quick glimpse of what's beneath the smooth exterior. Though Ross had said that thing about getting to a point where you simply couldn't be any more scared, Aldo can't bear to look at what he sees, and turns his eyes away quick smart.

"But the band's mine," he says, picking up the old guitar case with Oscar inside. "I put it together. There wouldn't *be* a band without me. I'm the catalyst. Right? Ross and Luce could do anything else they wanted, but I told you before, this is all I have. If I'm not doing this, I'm dead anyway." He forces himself to look at Legba, and though something fundamental deep down inside him dies at what he sees behind the well-groomed, sharp-suited, perfectly manicured disguise, he doesn't look away. "So fuck you."

For a moment, Aldo thinks Legba's going to just kill him where he stands, but just like that, he's Iceman again, cooler than the Fonz at the North Pole. He gives one of those little knowing grins and a rueful shake of the head.

"Fucking humans," he says. "Alright, have it your way. Play your little acoustic set, but remember, you die on stage tonight." He takes a step closer. "Or I will be paying another visit to your boy. And I will rip out his spine and suck his soul from his brain stem while I make you watch."

"Aye, you're a real hardman, eh?" Aldo says, the fear ebbing a little as anger lights like a match inside him. "Threatening five year olds? You're a fuckin lowlife scam artist and nothing else. Now take me to my dressing room so I can tune up. Ya prick."

Legba's recovered cool slips again, and Aldo has a moment of satisfaction, knowing he's got to him.

Then Legba punches him in the face, and everything's just *gone*.

4

It's gloomy inside the tunnel of trees as the Tardis makes its way up the bumpy dirt track. The upper branches of the forest form a thick canopy overhead, interlocking above the road, blocking much of the sunlight, and the trees seem closer to the side of the road than Ross remembers.

Looking out the side window, he can't see far into the woods. Just a metre from the roadside it's a dense, lightless jungle of tightly packed tree trunks and brambles. On the way, they'd debated leaving the car by the lochside and cutting through the forest on foot in an attempt at a sneakier approach. They were, after all, intending to burn a building down. It made sense, but Luce was reluctant, and to be honest so was Ross. He remembers that last night in Boleskine, when he'd gone out into the trees looking for Luce. About two seconds was all it'd taken to convince him that trying to locate his erstwhile drummer in that pitch black wilderness in the middle of a midnight blizzard was futile at best. Plus, he'd had the distinct conviction he wasn't alone out there, and he'd hightailed it back to the studio, pretty damn sure that there was something tracking him all the way.

There's no snow now, though. As they emerge from the forest it's still a fine summer's evening. The land opens up onto the large sunlit clearing, the wooded hill rising up on their left and their destination down the gently sloping trail ahead and to the right. The car rolls to a stop and they look down the single track road toward Boleskine House, AKA Easy Rollin Manor.

It looks deserted. No car in the small courtyard, the windows they can see shuttered. The air of desertion's almost palpable, and not just around the old single-storey U shaped coach house. Ross winds down his window, and immediately notices the unnatural silence. The stillness. There's not a bird in the sky or chirping in the trees. Not a whisper of sound. Nothing moves. Not so much as a blade of tall grass rippled in a breeze. They could be looking at a life sized photograph of some quaint highland retreat for all the life this place seems to have, and Ross has a creepy feeling that may not be too far from the truth of the matter in some weird way. He glances at his watch, and isn't surprised to see it's stopped. There's a tangible *deadness* in this place, a deadness that kills even time.

"So," Luce says, turning to him. "Want to go over the plan?"

Ross shrugs. "We go down, lay a big circle of salt around the place, then break in, head down to the studio, throw a lot of petrol around, trail some gas up the stairs and douse every room on the ground floor. Then we go outside, take the shutters off the windows at each side of the building with the crowbar and hatchet, smash the glass and chuck the flares in. Then we run like fuck."

"Crude, but effective," Luce says. "At least, I hope so."

"Damn skippy. Plus, with the amount of vinyl in the lounge, the place should burn like Satan's arsehole."

Luce nods, puts the car in gear and they start down the hill.

When they're still about fifty metres from the building, the big storm door opens and a familiar figure steps out into the courtyard. John 'Six Fingers' Asher, dressed in his usual sombre black suit stands there staring up at them, motionless.

"Shit," Luce mutters as she brings the car to a halt halfway down the gentle slope. "Plan B?"

Plan B wasn't really much of a plan at all. It basically boiled down to *If anyone tries to get in the way of Plan A, knock fuck out of them and carry on.*

"Aye," Ross says, thinking about John out the back that day, half naked and covered in the blood of a freshly killed and mangled deer. A deer which he may or may not have killed with his bare hands and which he may or may not have been chowing down on.

"So, do you think *he's* human?" Luce asks, looking pointedly at the hand axe in Ross's lap.

Ross sighs. "Aye, he's human. What's left of one anyway."

"How do you know?"

"I don't," Ross says. "Who the fuck knows what that guy's been through over the last ninety years or whatever. What he's turned into. But he was still just like us back in his day." He nods down at the old man in the black suit, standing sentinel, waiting for them. "That's us if we don't do something about it."

He's got no wish to take an axe to John, but at the same time, isn't there just that wee bit of him that's buzzing inside at the thought of an impending pavement dance? All his life, all those fights. He'd never started them, or wanted them, but he'd damn well finished most of them, and Ross knows fine well that that part of him always had, and always would, enjoy a good square go. And maybe that's part of how the Devil gets in, he thinks. That wee glint of darkness. The propensity for inflicting damage on another human being, and not absolutely hating it.

"Let's get this done," he says.

They drive the rest of the way down the track to John, still standing in the courtyard, patient and still as a well-dressed statue, and stop at the edge of the courtyard. Ross gets out, the wood axe in his hand, then unhurriedly goes to the boot and takes out one of the twenty-litre jerry cans of petrol. He's joined in front of the Tardis by Luce. She's got another can, and the crowbar. He considers chivalrously insisting she stay in the car and head for the hills if this goes bad, but he knows Luce better than that. She'd be liable to lamp him.

"Alright, John?" Ross greets the old man.

John, true to form, doesn't reply. Just stands there, regarding Ross with those old faded eyes of his. His heavily wrinkled face devoid of...

everything really, and Ross is sickened for him. This was just a guy who had genuine musical talent, the man Ross had first heard in his bedroom in Gregor Picken's house when he was an angry teenager. That old vinyl record on the monster hi-fi system. Six Finger Asher giving it plenty, laying down tunes that got under his skin, into his bones and brain, and saw Ross picking up that old busty bass in the corner a few days later. So Ross is gutted for John, looking at him now. The man's an empty vessel.

"We're going to burn this place down," Ross informs him.

"I can't let you do that," John informs him right back, his quiet voice not much more than a papery rasp.

"We're going to try and break this deal," Luce chips in. "We're going to…"

"It. Won't. Work," John says, speaking with slow, haunted authority. For a moment, the empty mask of his face cracks a little. His pale lips tremble, the eyes flick left and right, as if he's afraid someone's listening. "You *can't*," he whispers. "Don't you understand that? You're *his* now."

"Help us, John," Ross says. "Help *yourself*."

John regards Ross sadly and shakes his head. "You don't understand, son," he says wearily. "None of you *ever* understand."

Ross really doesn't like the implication of that. No time to ponder on exactly what John means by it, though. He's clearly not for letting them torch the place. Problem is, that's exactly what they have to do.

"We're going in there now, John," he says softly, putting the jerry can aside. "Move aside."

"He knows you're here," John says. "You're to wait for him."

Ross smiles, because there it is. That anticipation of impending violence that gets him on his toes and gets his blood pumping. As bad as he feels for the old man, Boleskine has to burn, and John's in his way. "Sorry, man," he says. "No can do."

He takes a step forward, watching John's hands closely, but he's still caught completely by surprise by the old man's left fist, which fires out like a piston, catching Ross dead centre in the solar plexus. He flies back several feet back, skids across the ground and winds up on his back on the driveway, breathless with hot pain shooting through his windpipe and organs, unable to move. Through eyes squinted in agony, he sees Luce run forward and take a wild swing at John's head with the crowbar, but he catches it in hand and tears it from her, then deals her a rap on the side of the head for her cheek. Luce yelps and goes down like a sack of spuds, lying motionless on the courtyard pebbles.

John tosses the crowbar away then stoops to pick her up, and Luce suddenly rolls onto her back and jabs a fist at his face, a thoroughly decent dig, right in the eye. John recoils and lets out a horrible, inhuman shriek, his hand going to his eye. He continues to scream in that unearthly tone as he backs away and pulls one of the nails Luce'd brought along from his eyeball. It comes out with a wet gloopy sound and a squirt of black fluid which splashes the pristine white pebbles of the driveway. Then John throws the nail on the ground, a noise coming from his throat somewhere between the snarl of a wolf and the clattering hiss of a rattlesnake. He advances on Luce, who's getting to her feet, her hands curled into fists and another couple of nails protruding from between her knuckles. As he reaches for her, Luce takes another swing at him, but John simply bats her arm aside and delivers a short jab to her stomach, folding her like a sandwich and putting her on the ground again where she lies gagging, fighting for air. John bends and lifts her up by the back of her jacket, jabs another hard punch into her temple, and Luce goes down for good this time, out cold.

At the sight of a friend taking a doing, his anger swells, and Ross swallows through the crippling pain in his torso and forces a breath into his lungs. Then he's setting his feet and bringing the axe up in his right hand.

"I don't want to hurt you," John says, taking a step towards him, but Ross can see from the shape of his shoulders that the old dude's lining up another punch. He *just* manages to duck aside as John's fist flicks out like a whip, chinbound. Seeing an opening, Ross springs forward, driving his shoulder into John's chest and forcing him backward a few steps, trying to knock him off balance and trip him, but he's fuckin solid under that suit. Then Ross feels hands on his hips, and abruptly he's just flying through the air. The world spins and he lands on his face, those crunchy driveway pebbles giving his kisser a harsh and painful exfoliation, driving his front teeth into his lips. Spitting grit and blood, he gets his arms under him, still holding the axe, and pushes himself onto his hands and knees. Black trouser clad legs come from the left as John approaches, perhaps to volley him right in the neck, and sure enough, John draws back a well-polished shoe for the intended punt. Ross drops and rolls, then lashes out with the axe. The blade goes into the inside of John's left knee, digging firm and deep. Ross feels the satisfying impact as the sharpened metal chops into John's leg, and that shady part of him that loves this is gritting its teeth and smiling, punching the air in exultation and going *fuckin yaaaaaasssss!*

John grunts and staggers back, the hatchet coming out of his knee with a damp grinding sound, the wound and the axe head dripping not with blood, but with that same black viscous fluid. John stands still for a moment, staring down at his leg, then he raises his eyes to Ross again, and that sad old wrinkled face shimmers and fades into a rotting nightmare.

Ross manages to get to his feet and scramble away as John comes at him again, his face dissolving into a horrific Halloween mask. Near skeletal, wispy white hair awry, the eyes black darkling stones in sunken pits, the flaking skin all stretched yellow parchment, a partially decomposed nose with the nasal cavity showing. John's black, hungry mouth yawns wide, all mottled brown gums, a restless worm-like tongue and crooked, rot-pointed teeth.

A bony hand slashes out with viperish speed and tears the axe from Ross's grip as he's still trying to get to grips with the sight of the suited cadaver, and then John's other hand is fastened round his throat. Ross hadn't even seen his arm move.

"*He wants you to wait,*" John croaks, his voice a death rattle, rancid breath like three day old roadkill in Ross's face.

Forced backwards, tripping over his own feet and his windpipe constricted to a pinhole by the hideously powerful grip, the lack of oxygen to his brain saps the strength from Ross's muscles with horrible quickness, and all he can do is flail ineffectually as Zombie John forces him toward the big storm door, stooping to grab the back of Luce's jacket on the way and dragging her along with them.

Then they're inside, along the familiar burnt orange corridor with the rock n roll prints and into the lounge with the big L shaped couch and all the vinyl, Ross still fighting with every drop of his rapidly diminishing strength, but it's laughably futile. His vision's going grey and red at the edges, and there's a high whining sound in his ears. In desperation, he puts the last reserves of himself into a punch into John's armpit, going for that little cluster of brachial plexus nerves hidden in in the oxter, and he lands a good hit, jabbing in and hitting the spot with straight fingers, but he'd be as well swinging at a punchbag for all the good it does. John doesn't even flinch.

And why would he? Ross considers. *Zombies don't have functioning nerves.*

Consciousness fading, he's vaguely aware of John kicking open the door leading down to the studio, and then the terrible choking pressure's gone from his throat as the walking corpse releases him. Ross barely has time to draw a breath before John plants the sole of his shoe in his gut and sends him toppling down the stairs, tossing Luce after him like a bag of dirty laundry. The world again cartwheels as the bare wooden staircase rises up out of the dark to give him a sound pummelling on the way down to the basement.

When everything stops spinning and the battering of his ribcage, head and limbs stops, Ross finds himself lying in a painful heap at the bottom of the stairs, struggling to catch his breath, wondering how many bones he's just broken, and Luce lying half on top of him, still sparkled.

John comes down the stairs, a mouldering corpse remarkably limber for someone who looks like they'd been in the grave for fifty years and who'd just minutes ago taken a hatchet to the knee. Ross tries to get up, but his bones hurt too much, and he can't get out from under Luce. Zombie John steps over them and unlocks the door to the studio, then turns back and does Ross a turn by pulling Luce off him, though even this causes a bright stab of pain in his side.

Two fractured ribs minimum, he reckons.

Then John drags the two of them into the studio, the movement causing the pain in Ross's ribs to climb several notches up the volume dial all at once, and he tries not to scream, but can't help it. He can't scream for longer than a second though, because there's not enough air inside him, and there's a hot jaggy *burbling* way down there in the roots of his chest. A certain warm wetness and the taste of copper in his throat.

Make that two fractured ribs and a punctured lung.

There were times when Ross wished he hadn't spent all that time with Gregor Picken's bookcases reading close combat manuals, studying pressure points, nerve clusters and the finer points of bodily trauma.

Now they're in the studio. It doesn't look like it's been touched since they left. Luce's kit's still lying in bits on the floor. John dumps them there among the debris of the drums, then goes back over and closes the door. And there he stands, like an undead bouncer, hands clasped before him in front of the door, his face slowly reverting back to that of an elderly gentleman as opposed to something out of *The Walking Dead.*

Ross bites down on another scream as he rolls over and crawls a few agonising feet to Luce, who's lying face down, blood sheeting the right side of her head from a gash to the temple, the surrounding area nastily swollen and discoloured. Ross drags himself a few inches till he's close enough to check her over. She's breathing. Pulse is steady, but she's out for the count. And no wonder. A blow to the temple's a pretty good way of knocking someone the fuck out, and could easily kill you.

And lying there on the floor, looking at Luce, Ross McArthur's jaw does that tightening thing again. He does another internal damage report. His ribs are in a world of pain, but his legs are okay. He can stand.

The fuck you looking at, Roadkill, ya wee spunkrag?

There's a good bit of blood in Ross's mouth, and in his throat. He spits it out and slowly pushes himself to his feet, the pain in his side like something chewing its way out.

John looks over at him. "Don't," he says softly. Almost apologetically. "Just stay down and wait for him. He won't be long."

"And what... what happens then? Eh, John?" Ross says, wheezing and just about standing upright, holding his side.

"Whatever he wants," John says, staring into space. "What he wants is what happens."

"Aye, well, as Mr Jagger said," Ross pauses for breath and spits more blood. "You can't always get what you want."

He starts walking slowly and carefully over to the bass stack. The guitar stand next to it cradles a 1968 Fender Precision Bass which Ross had used for a couple of tracks on the album. It's from Legba's instrument collection upstairs in the library. Ross wonders just how many other bands and musicians might have signed with Easy Rollin Records over those years.

He reaches for the Precision. Olympic White finish, with more than a few dings about the bodywork, it's an absolute peach, and he remembers how good and right the P-Bass had felt and sounded when he'd been jamming. It was heavenly to play and hear, a dream just to have in his hands. But as he lifts it from the stand, he finds that having a four-kilogram bass guitar in your hands is no dream when you've got a few broken ribs. It hurts like a bastard. Ross splutters painful red flecked laughter at the thought, but it turns into a cry of pain as he changes his grip on the instrument and hefts it like a battle axe. In this context, ie. violence, the Precision bass was about as far from a precision instrument as you could get. In fact, it makes a cunt of a weapon, heavy and asymmetrical, unwieldy as fuck, and suitable only as a clumsy, though potentially devastating, club.

It'll have to do.

Ross stands there blinking the dizziness away, swaying on his feet and coughing a little more blood, then he starts lurching across the room in John's direction.

John gives him a look of condescending pity. "Please," he says. "Don't be stupid. Just don't. You can't leave."

"We'll see about that, cuntychops," Ross counters, and swings.

Something tears inside him, and he screams blood, shrieking like a woman giving birth to a cactus, but it's a *good* swing.

John ducks out of the arc of the bass, of course he does. Ross, who knows a thing or two about the noble art of the pavement dance, thought he might do that, which is why he lets go of the bass and aims a low kick at John's knee as he tries to sidestep away. The same knee Ross had chopped earlier. As John ducks under the bass, his weight's on that knee, and Ross's foot stomping the inside of that joint redirects that weight where it's not supposed to go. John goes down, his leg horribly buckled, bending in a way that no leg should bend, and Ross's own knee comes up to greet the old boy's chin as he falls, catching him flush on the mandible bone.

Fuckin *biff!*

John's head snaps back and he slumps to the floor, senseless.

Ross, hunched over and groaning like a zombie himself, holds his ribs and spits some more blood as he staggers over to where Luce's still lying on the floor.

"Luce," he mumbles, his head swimming and his entire torso on fire. "C'mon, mate. Need to get up."

Luce doesn't move.

"Luce c'mon. We need to go."

Big bony hands falls on his shoulders.

Ah, fuck...

Then he's flying backwards and slammed onto the floor amid the wreckage of the drum kit, the impact igniting pain like a grenade in his core. Agony simply devours him and he almost passes out. Almost, but not quite, and he's still awake when John straddles his chest and starts going to town on Ross's coupon.

He only feels the first two or three punches, which land with devastating power. Right cheek, left eye, nose. He feels the cartilage crunch under John's knuckles. Then everything gets a bit warm and fuzzy and distant. John's hateful, withered ghoul's face starts to dim as he continues landing haymakers, and though he feels the fists mushing his face to paste and knows they hurt, they're far away, and getting further, and Ross thinks maybe he's going to die right there, because the monstrous face above those relentlessly pounding fists is nothing human, and there's no stopping it because the hunger and the need to destroy and kill is plain to see.

Punched to death, he thinks as the hits keep on coming, and Ross's mind starts to fracture and distort as his eyes go dark and all he can hear is the low crunching *thud-thud-thud* of John's big bony hands breaking his face apart.

Then, as he's on the very lip of a big black nothingness that Ross thinks looks disturbingly cozy, the punches stop.

Something wet and cold splashes on Ross's face, and the heavy weight that's been sitting on his chest falls away. Wheeze-gurgling breath though a mouth of blood and broken teeth, Ross forces his already swelling eyes to open, and there she is.

Luce, standing over John, who's lying on the floor, a broken drumstick impaling him through the nape of the neck, the splintered end poking out of his throat, and a puddle of that nasty black shit rapidly spreading around his head like an oil spill.

5

Aldo wakes up alone with a sore jaw, lying on his back on a bare wooden floor.

He opens his eyes and immediately squints them closed against the glare of bright lights above. He groans and sits up, rubbing at his chin where Lega'd biffed him. The bastard had some fast hands.

Looking around, he figures he's backstage, dumped on the floor behind what seems a big stage curtain, lying on a wide, raised platform among a stack of heavy duty amp and cabinet transport cases. The backstage area's crowded with mic stands, mixing desks, lighting rigs, effects units and a thousand trailing cables making a snakepit of the floor. No one around, though. Not a soul to be seen. Not a single roadie or sound tech in sight.

On the other side of the curtain, Aldo can hear the stage speakers playing background music. *Lonely Boy* by the Black Keys. And he can hear the low, massed murmur of a large crowd, meaning there were potentially some fifty thousand punters waiting for him on the other side of that screen. He hopes it'll be less. Hopefully the Facebook post about a terror threat's been enough to keep a few folks at home.

Aldo opens the beat up guitar case lying next to him and finds Oscar safe and sound inside. He takes the old acoustic out and just sits where he is with the guitar in his lap, in no particular hurry to get up. His fingers settle into place on the strings, remembering the action and spacing of them, the familiar feel of the instrument in his arms and against his chest like the hug of an old friend you've not seen in a long time. The fingers on his left hand find the E minor chord, Aldo's favourite chord, and the thumb and fingers of his right start slowly brushing over the strings, gently fingerpicking out a sombre classical arpeggio. Surprisingly, or then again, maybe not so surprisingly, Oscar's perfectly in tune, and sounds pretty damn good for having been entombed in a cupboard for the past several years. The strings are dull and half rusted, the fretboard needs a serious clean, but there's certain no-nonsense authority to the tone. In the old guitar's dusty voice is the sound of many years strumming, roads travelled and gigs played. If Johnny Cash were a guitar, he'd sound like this.

He remembers playing Oscar the day his parents finally broke up. Sitting in his bedroom, thrashing out chords good and loud, trying to drown the hateful miserable cunts downstairs screaming abuse at each other in the living room, the sound of his mum stomping upstairs, sobbing and still hurling verbal poison at his dad as she packs a suitcase. The slam of the front door when she leaves and the sound of her car booting it up their street, never to be seen again. Oscar had sung loud and proud and turned it all into background noise. Mostly.

He remembers playing Oscar during his first gig with his first band not long after. Raging Beavers. Him and two schoolmates, Boaby Hamilton on bass and Craig McMenemie on drums. None of them yet seventeen, none of them very good, illegally playing a three song set of covers in a Sunday jam session held in a local bearpit of a pub. The punters had liked their clumsy but heartfelt attempts, and Aldo remembers the owner shaking his hand and saying he'd loved their cover of *Folsom Prison Blues*. He'd rewarded them with twenty bucks of credit behind the bar. It'd been the highpoint of Aldo's life to that point.

He remembers playing Oscar sitting by the side of Dylan's cot, softly fingerpicking *Blackbird* and singing the old Beatles tune in a hushed lullaby. It'd always been good for getting the wee man to nod off on those nights he decided to scream the house down for a couple of hours. He remembers how proud he'd been in the wee man's taste, despite being near delirious with sleep deprivation.

And he remembers playing Oscar in the days after he and Ashley broke up. Sleeping on Ross's couch, his head and heart in bad way. No job, no money, practically homeless. It'd been a bleak time, and a time when he'd written what he considered to be some of his best songs. Songs about love, joy, heartbreak, chance and hate. None of them were on the new album, though. *Cuttin Heads* was all new, Legba era material.

Behind the screen, the music piped through the stage speakers fades out and the noise of the crowd swells in anticipation. There's a heavy clunk somewhere overhead as the stage lights go down, and the sound of the multitude outside spikes into a roar. An impatient, rhythmic clapping begins, and then the chanting.

A-LI-BI

A-LI-BI

A-LI-BI

Appearing as suddenly and silently as a plume of smoke, Legba's suddenly there, standing over him. He smiles down at Aldo. "It's time," he says.

Aldo gets to his feet, and without a word, Legba hands him a box-cutter. The thick metal handle of the Staley blade with the retractable razor blade's cold and heavy in his hand. He looks at it for a moment, bouncing it in his palm, then slips it into his back pocket.

"Now go out there and put on a show," Legba orders him. "And by the end of it, your corpse had better be on that stage."

Behind the screen, the roar of the crowd intensifies, impatiently demanding action.

"Thanks for the opportunity," Aldo says, and gives Legba a wink as he turns and walks out onto the stage at Glasgow Green.

He emerges from behind the screen and the sound of the crowd hits him. Despite everything, a deep thrill of pure exhilaration courses through Aldo as the stage lights flare above him. He can't help the smile on his face. Can't help holding Oscar up in the air, saluting the wildly cheering mass of people below him, the front row crushed against the crowd barrier with their arms outstretched and adulation on their faces. He can't help the feeling of pride and accomplishment as he sits on the stool placed centre stage set up with two mics – one for him, and one for Oscar - and looks out over his army of fans.

I did it. I actually did it.

Aldo knows how rare a thing it is, to actually live your dream. To find yourself in exactly the place you imagined and wished you could be. He knows that the vast majority of people live their lives without ever having made it to that place. But he's made it. Mission fuckin accomplished. Learn to play, form a band, write good music, get a record deal, get famous, play big gigs. It's all he's ever wanted since the first time he picked up a guitar.

Funny how things turn out.

"Good evening, Glasgow," Aldo says into the mic.

The crowd goes nuts.

"Before we get this show on the road," he says, "I'd just like to say, I'm sorry my friends couldn't be here tonight." He pauses while the crowd's tone changes. Whistles and boos, cries of *why?* and *fuck them!* and *Al-li-b! A-li-bi!*

"I know a lot of you've heard a few bits and pieces of what we've been doing in the studio for the last six months." Again he pauses while the crowd's tone shifts again, bursting into rapturous cheering and applause again. A chant of *Down Down Down, Down Down Down* builds. Someone in the front screams *Let's cut some fuckin heads!*

"But right now I want to play a song I wrote a long time ago. A song I wrote on this very guitar. And I want to dedicate this song, and this whole set, to the best people I've ever known. This is for Ross McArthur and Luce Figura, the best fuckin rhythm section in the business. This song's called *Mend the Black*."

The crowd, who Aldo realises must know the song from the Alibi's self released demo on iTunes, respond with another massed cheer of approval, and Aldo starts playing.

The crowd level drops to a near hush as Aldo plucks out the opening notes of the waltz timed intro lick. Oscar's never been so loud or sounded better. The condenser mic in front of the old acoustic's soundhole carrying the notes to ring true and clear and massive from the enormous stage speakers. A shiver of purest pleasure trickles along Aldo's spine and limbs as the crowd cheer again, then start clapping in time to the intro. When he starts singing, they sing along, and Aldo's heart nearly breaks with happiness.

> "I never knew just how to see you,
> And I never cared what you had to say.
> You never saw what anyone wanted,
> And you never cared because that was your way.
> Walk around selling your secrets my lover,
> Those things you can't keep in that old rusty brain,
> I paid well to watch you undress on a table,
> And sang you a song while walking away."

The crowd lifts its voice for the chorus, they roar it out with their hands in the air, and Aldo's never heard such a glorious sound. It's the biggest campfire singalong ever.

> "Time is slipping away.
> It's easy, so easy to say,
> That blood is thicker than all,
> The tears, bitter tears that could fall."

The next half hour or so passes in a blur as Aldo goes through their old set. The songs from the self-titled album they'd paid £150 to record and then put up online, where it had sunk without a trace.

Tonight, here on the Green, they all sound right, good, raw and honest. It'd always been a mission statement of the band. Create music that still sounded good when stripped to the bare bones. *Dog Days, Neverhad, Blowhole, Dreaming Of, Devil May Care, Stone Me.* The songs they used to play. Before Legba. Before Easy Rollin Records.

And he sits there on his stool on that massive empty stage, alone, strumming out the Alibi's early back catalogue with the whole of Glasgow Green in the palm of his hand. He realises that it wasn't the fame or the massive crowd or the record deal or the money that mattered. It never was. In truth, the trappings were fine and definitely desired, but when you got right down to it, all Aldo Evans had ever *really* wanted was to write a few songs that people would *get*. That people would remember. That people would love. With fifty thousand people in front of the stage singing along, he realises that he never needed Legba for that, because these were songs that written when no one knew who Public Alibi were.

He looks over to the side of the stage, and there he is. Legba stands in the wings glaring out at Aldo, his dark, movie star handsome face a picture of absolute fury.

There are tears on Aldo's cheeks as he lets the last fingerpicked notes of *Classical Vapour Blues* ring and fade out. He wipes an arm across his eyes and applauds the crowd.

"You guys are fuckin awesome," he says into the mic, and has to pause for almost a full minute while the crowd respond with yet another roar of adoration.

"You may have heard there was a terror threat before this gig," he says, raising his voice. "But you know what? *Fuck* terror!"

The crowd goes mental at that one.

"We're here because we love music, and love beats the fuck out of terror any day of the week!"

Bedlam behind the barrier. A girl in the front row's got her top off, holding her arms out to him beseechingly, screaming *Love me, Aldo! Love meeeeeee!*

"Now I want to introduce you to someone," Aldo says. "It's been a mental six months for us, and none of it would have happened without this guy. Glasgow Green, please put your hands together and welcome to the stage our manager and producer, *Papa Legba!*"

Aldo throws his arm theatrically to the side of the stage, delighting in the look of complete confusion on Legba's face.

"You guys don't know it," Aldo says into the mic, pointing stage left, "but this man is a fuckin *demon*. That's right, a *demon* on the fiddle. And I know you folks out there want to hear some of the new material."

Aldo waits again as a huge roar, the biggest yet, erupts from the throats of the crowd, and he fixes his eyes on Legba's.

Because this is what you want, isn't it? It's all well and good getting me to kill myself in front of all these people. I'm sure you'll get a right kick out of that. But you want them to hear the new tunes, don't you? Because they're your tunes really, aren't they?

At the side of the stage, Legba continues glaring out at him, and Aldo can feel something vile poking at his thoughts, seeking entry. But though Legba keeps on knocking, trying to take control, he can't come in. It's the rush of being on stage, playing to an audience who love it, singing his songs and feeling the punters' reaction, that feeling of power, of having that outpouring of energy in the palm of your hand. It shields Aldo's head from Legba's influence, which he can feel like rats' teeth on his skull.

You want me to play your tunes? he thinks, meeting Legba's glare. *Come out and play them with me then, and I'll end it right here with you beside me, close enough to smell my blood on the stage. That's what you want, right?*

"Looks like Mr Legba's got a bit of stage fright, ladies and gentlemen," Aldo says into the mic.

The crowd respond by chanting *Legba, Legba, Legba, Legba,* unwittingly, actually summoning a demon. Aldo laughs and shakes his head.

Ah, good times!

"Come on out here," Aldo says, grinning, now beckoning Legba on to the stage. "Or maybe you've not got the chops for it."

At the side of the stage, Legba's face goes very still.

Aldo waggles his eyebrows at him, then plays the opening notes of *Duelling Banjos.* A direct challenge.

That's right, ya prick, he thinks at him. *You want to cut heads? Let's fuckin dance.*

That does it. At stage left, Legba holds a hand out to the side, and that old violin materialises out of thin air. He grips it like a weapon and storms out onto the stage, a man on a mission, completely ignoring the massive cheering crowd who again erupt at his appearance. He stalks across the stage in Aldo's direction, already playing the opening riff of *Down Down Down* on the fiddle, to yet more mass delirium from the crowd, going nuts as they hear the sawing signature notes of the new album's apocalyptic closing track.

Four bars in, Aldo comes in with the chords, swaggering across the stage to meet Legba, looking him in the eye, still grinning, and buzzing with light inside. As they come together, the two of them, man and monster, they both stop on a dime, in perfect unison. A silent four count, and Legba goes into the intro solo, turning his back on Aldo to face the crowd as he *really* begins to work the fiddle. There's another surge in volume from the mass as Legba hits them with the manic flurry of notes, his long fingers skittering around on the instrument's neck with spiderish speed.

That's when behind him, Aldo lifts Oscar from around his neck, takes a big backswing, and cracks Legba across the back of the skull.

The old acoustic breaks apart in a spray of splintered wood and trailing strings, and Legba's fiddling facemelter comes to an abrupt end with an awkward, screech that sounds like a tortured cat.

Then everything slows down.

Everything changes.

Aldo watches as Legba falls to the stage floor in super slow motion, fragments of the acoustic spinning gracefully through the air around his head like matchsticks in zero gravity.

Aldo looks out from the stage, and Glasgow Green and the some fifty thousand strong attendance, have vanished.

A familiar dark rocky landscape now stretches to the horizon in all directions. The dying light. The gritted gale. The cataclysmic storm above, flensing the thick hot air with lightning. The vast desert plains of sick red nothingness and hungry black shadows.

And there's hundreds of *them*. Aldo shields his eyes and squints through the stinging wind. Where a huge crowd of happy concert goers had stood just a moment ago, there's now a seething mass of dark, reaching figures, indistinct in the perpetual twilight of this plane. Inhuman forms, hooked and crooked, snake-like and stingered. A palpable sense of menace and need emanates from the closing shadows which advance on him slowly, patiently. A thousand variations of the grotesque and horrific and predatory, they close and surround him, and in their guttural whispers and snarls, Aldo hears every evil thought he's ever had. Every selfish impulse and unkind thought. Every moment of jealousy and greed. Every tiny little hatred.

He looks down again, and Legba's only just hitting the ground, still in super slow-mo. Bits of Oscar are still falling lazily through the air.

Lightning rips the sky apart a hundred metres away, and Aldo rocks back on his heels as the concussion wave hits him in a blinding flare of sound and light. In the strobe effect, he sees the things in the wasteland in front of the stage rushing closer.

The twelve remaining inches or so of Oscar's broken neck is still in Aldo's left hand, the strings still attached to the tuning keys. As Legba, still moving in super slow-mo, is getting to his hands and knees, Aldo - who finds he can still move at his normal speed - brings his arm round in an arc and whips the loose strings around the demon's neck like a cat o' nine tails, then deftly catches the strings as they come looping round Legba's throat. He adjusts his grip, and twists the makeshift garrotte with his left hand at the back of Legba's neck, tightening the six stringed steel noose. Then he reaches into his back pocket with his right hand and takes out the boxcutter, exposing the razor blade with a push of his thumb.

Aldo looks up at the roiling black clouds above, and barely feels a thing as he draws the boxcutter across his own throat. Blood immediately fills his vision, washing the storm above in opaque crimson as it hoses from his neck and arcs up into the wind and across his eyes.

The beasts in the shadows rush in to take him, and Aldo smiles and gurgles laughter that tastes like burning metal. He holds the boxcutter aloft to the storm as if in salute.

As if in invitation.

The lightning accepts.

6

The black stuff that comes out of John's mouth as he lies on the studio floor pools slowly, expanding around the old man's head in an oily halo. There's a moment of complete stillness as Luce looks down at the body, the broken drumstick still clutched in her fist like a stake, half its length coated in black gritty gore.

When the black blood starts to move and writhe as if with sentient life, and small, questing tentacles form out of the murky sludge, Luce backs away towards the door, crouching to help Ross to his feet as she goes. He's in a bad way, and can barely make it to his feet, his face a misshapen bloody mess.

"Come on, let's get the fuck out of here," Luce urges, looking anxiously over at the squirming pool of ooze beside John's corpse, which is becoming more agitated by the second. As she watches, a many-jointed insectile limb, six inches long and barbed at the end, rears up out of the liquid muck. Something starts to follow the finger-thick appendage out of the puddle, and Luce has the impression of some arachnid horror about to pull itself up out of the floor.

"C'mon, Ross, we need to *move*,"

"Don worry bout me," Ross slurs, holding his side. He gets his legs under him and manages to lurch to the studio door ahead of Luce, who's looking back in dread fascination at the thing being birthed into the room.

They stumble out the studio and Luce slams the door behind them. On the stairs up to the lounge, Ross does his best to make it under his own steam, but has to lean on Luce for the last few steps. Through the lounge, into the corridor, they make it outside into the courtyard, where Ross planks his arse on the pebbled ground. "Have to... burn it down," he wheezes, his words distorted by his split and swollen lips. He leans over and spits a broken tooth in a thick bloody glob. "Ahh..." he mutters, red drool swinging from his burst lips. "Fuck."

"You're in no state to be burning anything down," Luce tells him, already picking up a can of petrol and walking back towards the front door. "Leave this to me."

The fear's gnawing at her bones as she goes back inside, but she refuses to let it in, forcing her mind blank but for one word, which she repeats like a mantra.

Fire.

Back through the corridor, into the lounge and down the stairs again, struggling under the weight of the jerry can, she pauses to take a deep breath, then kicks open the door to the studio.

At the far end of the room, there's nothing left of John but a few charred bones. And still pulling itself from the stinking tar on the floor, is the black thing. An absolute aberration of nature, like some half-melted mix of squid and scorpion the size of a calf, all writhing tentacles, questing insectile legs and stingers. It hisses and screeches in a repugnant alien voice that wounds Luce's ears as she enters, and she can't help falling back in pure fright at the sight of the thing. Every nerve screams *flee*, but she bites her lip and clamps down on the flight reflex. The studio has to burn.

Gritting her teeth and trying to stiffen knees which feel like unset jelly, she uncorks the jerry can and advances, sloshing unleaded petrol around the room. Still partially fused the floor, the creature howls and screeches at her, but Luce stays out of range of its slashing limbs and gives it a good dousing. Then she steps away from it and goes into the control booth, splashing gas on the control boards, the computer, the effects racks and speakers and mixers and monitors. She goes back into the live room and soaks the trashed drum kit and Aldo and Ross's amp setups while the thing coming out of the floor continues to emit those ear shredding screams, thrashing its barbed limbs around. It's getting bigger, still emerging from the ground, as if it's just the head of some unholy behemoth buried in the bedrock of the hills beneath the house, clawing its way up from the underworld. The idea probably isn't too far from the truth, Luce reckons.

She backs out of the live room, throwing the remaining petrol on the walls and floor as she goes, then tossing the empty jerry can back inside before slamming the door closed.

One down.

On her way back outside for more petrol, she finds Ross stumbling along the corridor, holding his side, his eyes no more than swollen purpling slits and his mashed nose pointing due east, but carrying a jerry can. Luce tells him to go and sit down before he falls down, but Ross tells her to shush, and before she can say anything else, he staggers away down the corridor toward his and Aldo's rooms, splashing the walls with petrol as he goes.

Deciding not to waste time arguing with her stubborn bassist, Luce goes into the lounge. At the door to the stairs down to the studio, she hears a loud banging and grinding in the shadows below, as if something were tearing through the foundations, then an inhuman shriek comes echoing up the stone walls of the dim lit staircase. Luce empties the petrol can down the stairs from where she is, sloshing it as far down as she can, then throws the empty can in and slams the door.

Three more times she fetches a jerry can from the Tardis before going back inside and decorating the interior of Bolskine House in unleaded fuel. When she and Ross have depleted the petrol, Luce grabs the plastic bottles of table salt they'd bought on the way here and goes round the building, trailing salt on the ground, softly murmuring the strange words her mama had spent hours drilling into her last night. Words in no language Luce had ever heard, which she'd thought she'd never be able to remember, but finds that she can. Words of protection and banishment and warding.

Despite his injuries, Ross refuses to rest as he follows her, systematically smashing each window with the hand axe and then throwing a lit emergency flare inside. By the time they've completed a circuit of Boleskine, the fire inside is going strong.

When it's done, they retreat to the Tardis and Luce drives the little car back up the trail to the edge of the forest. There they get out and stand on the hillside, watching Easy Rollin Manor burn below them.

The humble U-shaped building is completely ablaze, billowing black smoke like a burning tyre yard, fifty foot flames reaching up into the air. Even up here on the hill, the heat from the blaze is drying Luce's eyeballs. Somewhere behind the hot crackling roar of the flames, she fancies she can hear another sound. Something screaming. Something not of this world.

"You think we did it?" Ross asks beside her, still spitting bloody phlegm. "Don't feel... any different."

"Me neither," Luce answers, staring down the hill at the fire, her fingers doing that nervous *tap-tap-tap* rhythm on her thighs. She'd hoped to feel some sense of release, of freedom, indicating that burning the studio had worked and they'd broken the deal.

But there's nothing.

You have to destroy it all, her mama'd said. *Everything that you received as your end of the pact.*

Luce wonders about how many digital copies of the album there already were floating around in cyberspace, ethereal and formless, downloaded and shared and copied by anyone with internet access, impossible to ever completely destroy. Maybe there was no way out of it, and burning the studio and chanting and throwing some salt around didn't mean a fucking thing.

As for Aldo's plan, that'd been even more out there. It hadn't really been a plan at all, really. Sitting in the back of the Micra outside of Glasgow Green, he'd been rambling a bit, not really making sense. He'd said something about the conversion of energy. About how music was just the conversion of air pressure to audible sound energy, and how electricity magnified and amplified that energy. And how *that* energy created a response in people. About how love and anger and happiness and fear were all other forms of energy, chemical reactions in people's brains, which could be triggered by music.

Aldo'd said he was going to try and kill Legba.

It was something else her mother had told her. That destroying the entity holding claim on your soul was the only certain way of freeing yourself from any deal. After witnessing the power Legba possessed, though, they hadn't really considered destroying him as a viable solution.

And it's as she's thinking this that she feels it. A sudden sensation like some cool wave of air passing through her very core.

For a moment, Luce can't breathe, and thinks she can hear music. Soft fingerpicked notes plucked on an acoustic guitar, and there's this quiet rushing sound in her ears like the roar of a distant waterfall, or maybe a crowd, heard from far away. Emotions well up in her from nowhere, and tears roll down her cheeks as a great swell of bittersweet peace fills her heart, a feeling of release tinged with sadness. Beside her, Ross gasps and trembles, and she knows that he feels it too.

Then it's gone. And as Luce shudders and collapses on the grass, she *does* feel different. Different, clean, and completely exhausted, like she's just taken off a thousand-pound backpack she's been carrying around for a long time.

Ross sinks to the ground beside her and keels over in the heather. "Oh," he gasps. "Ohhhh *fuck.*"

"Aldo," Luce whispers, lying on her back and staring up into the infinite blue of the sky above as she reaches for Ross's hand. She feels his fingers entwining with her own as tears blur her vision. "It was Aldo," she says. "He did it."

Fade Out

There aint no Devil, only God when he's drunk.

Tom Waits

Cuttin' Heads

Public Alibi: Band of Ghosts
By Dan Sayers

Rolling Stone Magazine cover story
July 2017

It's almost a year to the day since Glasgow Green.

Almost a year to the day since I, and fifty-thousand others in the crowd that balmy Scottish summer night, witnessed something special. Something strange and wonderful. Something inexplicable, and terrifying.

What exactly happened on the stage that night, to this day no one knows for sure. The official version of events blamed a simple lightning strike, and to those who were there, myself included, that certainly appeared to be what happened.

Except that's not quite right.

Of the many mysteries surrounding the launch of Public Alibi's debut album, *Cuttin Heads,* perhaps the most compelling, and most debated, of them concerns what exactly took place on stage between Aldo Evans and the man he introduced as their manager and producer, Papa Legba.

At the time, from within the press section in front of the stage, I personally took what happened to be a great bit of musical theatre, something in the vein of Alice Cooper's guillotine or The Doors' mini stage play performance of *The Unknown Soldier.* Frontman Evans - who had given a startling solo acoustic performance that remains as memorable and astonishing as it was haunting – calling out his manager and challenging him to a guitar battle, a practice known in the lore of the blues as 'cutting heads', before smashing his acoustic over the other man's head and throttling him with the strings. It certainly looked convincing. A little skit about sticking it to the Man. A theatrical piece of commentary on the battle between artistry and business in the music industry.

The crowd loved it. They loved it right up to the point that Aldo Evans cut his own throat with a Stanley knife, and was then struck by lightning.

Some still argue that even this was part of some elaborate sketch. Fake blood, trapdoors and pyrotechnics. An overblown, fake rock star death. The whole concert a elaborate one-time rock opera.

But the fact remains that the police later confirmed that two sets of remains *were* recovered from the stage afterwards. It was leaked by sources within Police Scotland that the bodies had been so badly burned and fused that even dental identification had been impossible, but with fifty thousand people who witnessed the spectacular demise of Aldo Evans and his manager, identifying the remains seemed somewhat pointless.

In any case, the coroner's verdict was death by massive electrocution; that the combination of a lightning strike combined with a freak electrical on stage fault had effectively carbonised both victims instantly.

The fact remains that there was a funeral held for Aldo Evans in the Inverclyde Crematorium soon after, attended by thousands, though notably not by his former bandmates, who in a further twist, had sensationally quit the band on the day of the Glasgow Green show in the face of a terror threat.

There are countless theories about the meteoric rise and fall of Public Alibi. Some say they were just a band that put on one great show at the Barras and decided they couldn't handle the fame.

Others have... stranger ideas. Because of the questions. So many questions. And so much death.

Remember May, for example. All three band members; Julia Stone, Marcus Tatum and Jim McElland, found beheaded in a hotel lift the same night their support band Public Alibi comprehensively blew them off the stage and made their explosive entrance to the music scene. Ashley McColgan, Aldo Evans's ex-girlfriend and mother to his son, Dylan. Found brutally murdered in her home, also beheaded, and their five-year-old child left in a coma for six months. And of course,

Aldo Evans himself, killed on stage, along with the man he said had made it all possible. A man he called Papa Legba.

And that's where the conspiracy theories get *really* weird.

The more rationally minded maintain that the introduction of someone named after a Haitian voodoo spirit with links to blues folklore and Faustian deals a-la Robert Johnson, is proof that the band's entire career was a purposefully written fiction.

Other fans, however, and I admit to counting myself among their number, point out that you can check public records and Google all you want, but no one has ever been able to find any trace of a record company named Easy Rollin Records, the label who organised and promoted the Glasgow Green show, and who were supposedly releasing *Cuttin Heads*. They were also the label which released those now legendary videos that appeared on YouTube; the promotional audio clips from the album, three nine second snippets of songs from a record which sadly never saw the light of day. One could also point out that after the Glasgow Green show, those YouTube videos, and the channel which posted them, ceased to exist. Much like Public Alibi themselves.

Aldo Evans apparently died on stage, and drummer Luce Figura and bassist Ross McArthur have never been seen or heard from again. Several journalists, myself included, have tried and failed to track down the elusive rhythm section, but to no avail. Their colleagues at their former workplaces know nothing of their whereabouts after they quit their jobs, and Luce Figura's parents to this day maintain a complete media blackout, point blank refusing to speak to anyone from the media about their daughter. Likewise, George McColgan, grandfather to Evans's son Dylan, stubbornly refutes any requests for interviews.

The Public Alibi Facebook page is still in existence, and today has upwards of eleven million followers. The band's rough and ready self-released demo *Mend the Black* is still available online as a digital download, and is still selling. Also available on the Internet - if you know where to look - are those three samples from the unreleased *Cuttin Heads*. To this day, those three nine second snippets of music remain startling, strange, darkly hypnotic and brilliant; a poignant and agonisingly brief taste of what could have been, had the album ever seen the light of day. That digital imprint in the online ether - plus the multitude of fan websites, tribute bands and legally questionable merchandise available online - are all that remain of Public Alibi. With the continued debate about who they were and what happened to them, it is a remarkable legacy for a band whose time in the limelight was so brief.

A cosmic fluke, or the result of something altogether darker and stranger? The extraordinary story of the unknown Scottish rock band who were the biggest and least seen band in the world for six months, has passed into the realms of music folklore. Shrouded in music, mystery and murder, the fable of Public Alibi will be puzzled and debated over in practice rooms, internet forums and around musicians' campfires for generations to come.

A band that came and went with the quickness, brilliance and violence of a bolt of lightning.

A band of ghosts.

11th April, 2018
Inverkip

Dedication

This one goes out to all the guy and girls I've jammed, travelled, rocked, rolled, pogoed and played with over the last 25 years or so.

Much love, noise and respect to Fraser Hamilton, Aldo McMenemy, Bobby White, Craig 'Deep Throat' Hamilton, Iain Vize, Barry Carter, Jon Hammerman, Jane MacLean, Barry MacIlhinney, David Conn, the guys in Fourplay (Meribel season 1999-2000), Graeme Miller-Service, Lesley McLaren, Rab Evans, Tommy Barnes, Joe Duffy, David Scally, Pat Gillen, Helmut Watterott, Marco Piva, the James Watt College HND Music Performance class of 2010, the University of Glasgow MA Music class of 2014, Jules Estrella, Mark Tait, John McLelland and Les Smith.

To those who have, do, and are about to rock, I salute you.

Dave

Printed in Great Britain
by Amazon